FEATHERS OF GOLD

DRAGONS AND SKYLINES

ROWAN SILVER

ALSO BY ROWAN SILVER

Dragons and Skylines

Feathers of Gold

Eyes of Silver

Scales of Pearl

Cover by Kay Erin "Fleeks" Drzewiecki

ISBN: 9798846724051 (Paperback)

First Edition: September 2022

www.rowansilver.com

To those authors who inspired me. This book would never have existed without them.

PART ONE
DISAPPEARANCE

CHAPTER

ONE

It was a rainy day in Los Angeles when a dragon stumbled down a sidewalk. It attempted to place a paw — no, a foot — down while trying to walk, only to accidentally trip over it, falling flat on its underbelly. A tail whipped out of the haphazardly-placed outfit it had found for the occasion, now soaked with water and covered with oil and grime. A moment later, and the tail was gone.

It laid there for a moment, the water cold and wet on its bare skin, its face lowered in the puddle. A crack of thunder came from above. Since it didn't rain often, the dragon wondered if the rain had been meant to welcome it to the human city, or if it was more of a warning, a demand that the dragon return to its true form and leave the human settlement forever. The dragon wanted the latter right now, as it tried to use a tail it didn't have to get back up to its feet. The maneuver didn't work, however, and the dragon clutched at a strange stone around its neck, attempting to wrap its fingers around it. It took a few attempts before it managed to grab the stone, not used to the odd proportions of the claw-less hand.

A car drove past, not paying a second glance to the human body in the puddle. Water splashed over in an arc, tumbling down and drenching the dragon's clothes even further. It thought about taking them off, but even more, it thought about taking the shiftstone around its neck off, returning to its true form, and giving up on this misplaced quest.

A voice, muffled by the rain, shouted from across the empty road. The dragon raised its head, feathers ruffling beneath its clothes before being sucked back into skin.

"Are you all right, er . . .?" a human asked, coming up to the side of the dragon. But something he saw didn't sit right with him, and he took a step back before rushing off in the rain, covering his sopping hair with an umbrella.

The dragon cocked its head, twisting it in an unnatural way for humans. It placed a finger to where it thought its snout would be before pushing the finger back, sharp fangs growing out from its lips. A rumble of irritation came up from its throat, a few feathers fluttering in the wind as they pierced its skin, a cloud of smoke that looked like it might have just been mist rising up into the rain. It concentrated and the fangs shrunk and dulled, turning back into normal human teeth.

It placed out two hands, dipping them into the puddle as it fiddled with its elbows, trying to get them upright. It succeeded after a couple tries, and was back on all fours. It then attempted to walk along the sidewalk before it pulled its legs beneath it and rose back on two legs, each step forward a struggle. It tried to stretch its wings out for balance, a small rip sounding from the overcoat on its back as the shiftstone flickered, but nothing else beyond that.

A reflection of the dragon glinted up at it; a human-ish face stared back, and it moved as the dragon rotated its head. The skin seemed to be almost melting away, odd features the dragon couldn't distinguish between changing over the course of a few seconds. A nose moved in and out, and as the dragon stared at it, a few golden feathers appeared at the side of its cheekbone, protruding from its skin as the shiftstone lapsed. It turned its head, and the feathers changed in the lamplight above it, the colors of the rainbow shining through. It squinted before placing a finger on its cheek, pushing a feather back into the flabby skin.

It was a few more difficult paces down the sidewalk before the dragon reached its destination. Two storefronts with faded signs above their entrances clutched each other close, a small gap between them poking out to the dragon like the reek of blood from an injured deer. Apartments for humans rested above the top of the door, easily passed over if one didn't know exactly what they were looking for. Normally, the dragon would have smelled the magic on it, along with the prey-scent of the small mammals inhabiting the city, but right now its nose was lacking. The stench of sewage and diesel rising up through the rain was all it registered. Given the nauseating odors, perhaps it was best that the dragon's sense of smell was muted.

It looked down at its feet again, itching to release them from the shoes it had found in its mother's hoard. Talons tried to work their way out through the front, creating small rips in the fabric. It twisted a leg with the greatest of caution, attempting not to fall when it turned to the left until it faced the door. The symbol of a key had been carved into the door in front of it, while small branches had been cut into the frame.

No, not branches, the dragon realized. Runes like small, angular pitchforks drawn on top of each other, the branches turning and touching each other at the center of the beam above the door.

The dragon tilted its head forward, almost falling as it put it to the doorframe. Its face distorted as it sniffed the wood, trying to tell where the magic was from. Similar scents lined the magic of the runes themselves. Written by a family? It couldn't tell anything more with the shiftstone keeping it from smelling anything useful.

The dragon stretched out a hand to the doorknob, shuddering as it attempted to wrap the fingers around it. It clasped the other hand on top and turned them, the door opening as the dragon leaned and stumbled into the room beyond. Rain pounded on its legs as it tripped again, falling face-first onto a doormat. When it lifted its head, the word 'Welcome!' stared back in English. At least it knew how to read a couple human languages. Not all dragons bothered to learn, but it enjoyed human books.

The door had opened into a chamber far larger than the exterior would have indicated, though the dragon had seen similar sorts of magic before. These days, most dragons had been forced to do something similar to have any semblance of the territory they naturally desired. As the dragon turned its head from left to right, the room sloped from a height that towered above even the tallest of dragons down to the size of a mouse. Tables and seats of different sizes were scattered around the inside, the largest on the left and the smallest on the right, though it looked like some had been dragged around, chairs fitted to tables far taller or shorter than them.

The backs and surfaces of many of the furnishings were well-worn with claw marks or scorches, a couple that the dragon recognized as being its own species' talon-work.

The few occupants were just as diverse as the furniture's scars.

A miniscule humanoid with fragile butterfly wings on her backside sat at a similarly-sized table, drinking from a mug as large as her head. Three black wolves with wet fur huddled together on a rug, before one of them stood up on his hindlegs, his fur shrinking and turning into hair as he walked over to another resident, a shapeless figure shrouded in a trenchcoat.

The dragon had thought there'd be more visitors. It sniffed, but its human nose was only able to sense a gentle lavender aroma with a touch of wet dog. Were there just not many here at this hour? Or were the magical creatures of LA rarer than it had thought? Though the wood was new, room seemed sad and desperate, like it longed for days of old.

A small paper hanging on the wall caught the dragon's attention. It read the title at the top: 'Accommodation Requests.' There were a couple written in the lines beneath the paper in different scripts, not all of which the dragon knew how to read. One for an extremely long chair, another for a water-filled tank. The dragon sniffed it, trying to figure out when the one at the bottom had been written. It wasn't much use.

The dragon turned back, wondering if this was the right place. It didn't seem like it would be useful. The back of the room had a few doors, including a large one made of glass. It opened out into a huge courtyard, rain pattering down into green ferns and trees. Even the gray sky was visible, and the dragon felt its wings flutter at the thought.

More than fluttering, it soon realized — with a tear, the dragon's back ripped open the overcoat. It felt feathers burst out as the wings tried to work their way into a human skeleton, the bones and joints unable to find a position. The dragon turned with an anguished growl, one of the wings whacking a chair and knocking it to the ground with a clatter. It winced, clawing at its face, red lines drawn down the skin from human nails as it attempted to get back the shiftstone under control.

When it did, the wings had shrunk into its back, leaving gaping gaps in the clothing extending from its shoulders to hips, a few residents staring.

"Dragon," one of the werewolves muttered, though the dragon couldn't tell from the tone whether it was in surprise, disdain, or another emotion.

One of the doors from the back opened up, and a human stepped out from it. She glared at the staring creatures, and with a wave of her hand they went back to their previous business. She stepped over to the dragon with an exhausted smile, making her way around it and peering out into the rain before shutting the door closed.

"Sorry about that." The human winced, shaking her head with a sigh. Her short-cropped, black hair dripped water to the floor. Brown cloth that looked somewhere between a dress and a robe wrapped around her body, numerous pockets and folds hiding charms and plants nestled within it. A black tattoo of runes wrapped around the girl's neckline, a few more written across her fingers.

The dragon squinted and gave her a sniff, curious if she actually was human, or something else.

"You won't be able to tell much with the shiftstone on," the girl replied unflinchingly, like this was a routine she was used to by now. "I'm human, but I'm a witch. Well, technically a witch-in-training; I've been working and learning here since I graduated. I'm nineteen and female, if you don't know much about human age and gender yet.

The last thing I ate was waffles for breakfast with strawberries and maple syrup, and I recently used sandalwood incense. Oh, and my name is Ashley, though you couldn't have smelled that." She laughed. "At least, I don't think so."

The dragon flicked its tongue, satisfied at the answer. It looked around the room again as another rumble made its way through its throat.

Ashley put a hand to her ear.

The dragon tried again. Unused to human vocal cords, a coarse and gravelly voice left its throat, still barely audible.

"I'm sorry, I can't tell what you're saying," Ashley responded. "Would you like to sit down? Coffee? Tea? Blood? Another drink? No need to pay."

"Trrrrre," the dragon rasped, trying to say the word. It tried to flick its tail in annoyance at being unable to make the sound, forgetting that it didn't have one.

Ashley gestured a hand out, pointing to a human-sized chair at a human-sized table. "Is there all right? I'll be back in a moment."

While Ashley ran off to make the tea, the dragon stumbled forward, swaying back and forth while it tried to retain its balance. Just as it was about to fall, it stuck its arms out, catching itself on the back of the chair. A few more motions and it managed to sit down, lifting its arms and legs to try and figure out a comfortable position. It let out a distressed whine when it leaned back, slipping down until it was on its backside, its belly up and exposed. With another movement, it put its knees under its chest and its hands and elbows up on the table.

A tail snuck out from its waistline, draping over the back of the chair, rainbow feathers swishing from side to side before the dragon realized it and the tail retreated into its body. It squirmed a bit more, trying to make its position in the chair and somewhat on the table more comfortable, giving up on getting any sense of stability as Ashley came back with a bowl of tea.

"Be careful," Ashley warned as she set the bowl down. "I made it lukewarm so you don't accidentally burn yourself, but it might be hard to pick up."

The dragon dipped its head down into the bowl, attempting to lap up the liquid with its snout. It growled when its tongue didn't reach it, before sticking its face into the bowl with a splash.

Ashley didn't laugh or judge. "Put your hands — your claws — around the bottom," she suggested. "Move it upwards until your lips are on the edge, and tilt it back slowly so you don't accidentally choke on it. I could get you a cup, but I thought this would be easier."

The dragon tried again, this time more successful. Its nails dug into the bowl's side as it slowly poured the tea back, dribbling down its neck and onto its clothes. Once it was done, it lowered the bowl.

"So, what's your name?" Ashley asked with a smile.

The dragon growled something back, feathers forming on its throat. Its ears twitched, and it tried to growl it again, not liking how its voice was saying its own name.

"No worries," Ashley said. "Take as much time as you need. Is this your first time using a shiftstone?"

The dragon waited a bit before responding, trying to make the words come out right. "Ertssss nattt. Fiffff. Wurrrstt."

Ashley nodded. "Your form isn't settled. Once it becomes more fixed, speaking will be easier, among other things. If you want help with that, I'd be glad to."

Ashley stepped over to the long bar in the back of the room, and ducked down beneath it before resurfacing with a gray laptop. The dragon watched curiously as the human girl opened it up, searching for something. When she was finally happy, she stepped back over to the dragon, moving away the bowl of tea to make room for the laptop.

The dragon stared at the screen, filled with rows and columns of human faces staring back with dead eyes. It cocked its head, wondering what the purpose of this was.

"Choose one that you like, and concentrate on it," Ashley explained. "Try to envision your own body and face as that picture. Keep it in your mind."

The dragon stared at the faces, but they all looked the same. So, instead, it randomly pointed a quivering finger at one of the faces toward the top and attempted to do what Ashley had told it to. Its face stopped changing, and a young woman with tan skin and black hair stared at Ashley, a human tongue flicking from her mouth.

Ashley clicked the image on the laptop to make it larger. "Good choice. Glad you didn't choose anyone famous. What was your name again? Try now; speaking should be easier."

The dragon tried to say it again, golden feathers spreading out from her neck as she made the sound of a hard consonant followed by a stretched-out trill.

Ashley repeated it back the best that she could, attempting to imitate the dragon's growl.

The dragon grimaced, a few teeth showing.

"I'm sorry," Ashley apologized, "human throats can't say that. I don't know what you'd prefer, but I know some of the other visitors here take their names and say make them as close as they can in a human voice. I think yours would be Grith."

The dragon thought for a moment before clicking her tongue in agreement. Grith. It was familiar enough, but her neck wouldn't try and transform when she said it. "Grrrrith. Isss fine."

She cocked her head, the voice far more human, smooth and high-pitched. Her ears didn't recognize it as her own. She didn't like it.

"May I touch your shiftstone?" Ashley asked.

Grith dipped her head forward, attempting to crane it so that the stone around it dangled down.

Her neck wasn't long enough for such a maneuver, so she ended up trying to tilt it to the side, practically laying between the chair and the table as she did so. Ashley carefully lifted up the shiftstone and touched a finger to it. Light formed at her fingertip, and she traced it around the stone, writing out Grith, the words staying lit up. When she was done, the words faded into the stone, and the dragon lifted her head back up.

A few feathers popped out from Grith's skin every now and then, but it seemed less than before. Grith touched her fingers to them, wincing at the odd sensation. It felt like she was giving up on herself. Was this the only way she could coexist with humans in the mundane world? She looked over to Ashley, who seemed to have a saddened expression on her face, like she was wondering the same thing.

"Thaankh yuuu," the dragon half-heartedly said, barely able to make out her own English through the gravelly accent she spoke in. Grith was already wanting to get the shiftstone back off again. Just staring at her hands made her nauseous. So, she closed her eyelids, the feel of eyelashes strange against her skin. She opened her mouth, closing it again as the odd dull teeth mashed against her tongue, before reopening it, attempting to speak. The words came out slow and drawn. "Wrhaahht issss . . . wrhat iss diss strructurr?"

"You don't know?" Ashley asked. "Guess we're not so famous among dragons as we thought."

"My kusssin," Grith said, her ears twitching at her own words. She knew English well, but not in this voice. She kept staring at her hands, not making eye contact as she spoke to Ashley.

A low growl came from Grith's mouth, golden feathers running up and along her throat.

Ashley reacted, her arms tensing back as she almost fell back in her chair, eyes wide.

Grith squinted, trying to sniff to figure out what the human girl was feeling as she twitched. It didn't work, and her fingernails scraped the surface of the table as she attempted to figure out what had gone wrong in inter-species communication. Thinking through some common human emotions and reactions to them she'd read about, she settled on fear. Apparently, the sound that Grith had made had disturbed Ashley. Grith, however, wasn't surprised; humans were prey animals, it was only natural that dragons frightened them.

"Sorry." Ashley exhaled with a chuckle, relaxing. "Just surprised. You don't need to try again though, I can already guess who you're talking about. Pret, right?"

"Prrrret," Grith replied. She was beginning to figure out how to use this odd voice. "Hisss name. He told me to viss-sit. You know him?"

"Know?" Ashley laughed. "He's an old family friend; we go way back. He's never mentioned me? I'm insulted. But, yeah, he comes all the time. The feathery fucker said something all cryptic about a 'visitor' last time he came by, so I'm guessing he meant you."

Grith clicked her tongue in affirmation. "Dat sssounds much like him. He told me to visssit in quite the crrryptic manner as well. Sssaid that it would 'help,' but nothing more." Tapping her fingers, Grith whispered a few more 'r's and 's's for practice, trying to make them sound a bit more similar to Ashley's.

"Lovable weirdo." Ashley grinned. "Well, since he didn't explain it to you, this is the Key. It's a social area and a safe-house for magical creatures in LA; a safe place where you all can be themselves and don't have to hide. Speaking of that, you don't need a shiftstone as long as you're inside, so if you want to take it off, you can."

Grith snorted at the suggestion. She certainly wanted to, but she resisted the temptation. "If I take it off now, I am unsure that I will be able to regain this form quickly."

Ashley nodded. "Totally fine; your comfort is priority here. If you need help changing, just ask. So, what brings you here? Is this your first time in LA?"

Grith paused, her mouth opening and closing as she tried to think of the words. She flicked her tongue across her teeth. "It is not. I was in the human city a couple times when I was a hatchling, but I was never good at the shift-stone. I am only here because my parents left and as of yet have not returned."

Grith's body curled up a little, tucking her head down to her chest. Her eyes got a little bit wet as she thought about her parents. She wasn't quite sure why, but grieving them felt even worse as a human, and it was pretty bad as a dragon already. It was difficult to push the pain and fear of never seeing them again away.

"All that I have left of them is our territory and their hoards," Grith continued, "and in order to keep that hidden, I need more *rhas*." She felt feathers on her neck. Apparently she'd said something that her human voice didn't like.

"Rhas," Ashley mused, attempting her best to imitate the gravelly rumble ending with a hiss that Grith had made. "I've heard that word before from Pret. It's the dragon word for magical essence, right?"

Grith cocked her head, unsure that magical essence was the correct translation. "The Southern word. I do not know for the other dragon languages. Shimmer is the correct English. My territory needs more shimmer. Our territory. Pret said that I should do services for humans in exchange for shimmer. He believes that all dragons should have experiences with humans. I believe that his brain is full of dung."

Ashley paused, scratching the side of her head. "Oh, rhas means money, not essence!"

Grith blinked. "I do not understand the difference, but you are correct."

"So, you're looking for a job? I can help with that! We're not hiring here at the moment, but there's a similar safe-house in Anaheim that is, and I know a place which could use flying for delivery, if you're up to that, and—"

"No," the dragon interrupted. She twisted her head from left to right, her shoulders whipping to the sides as she attempted to do the correct gesture. "I already have a job. Vertex Technologies hired me."

A frown formed on Ashley's face. "Vertex? Are you sure? They're not . . . friendly to the less human, from what I've heard of them here. A bunch of stuck-up wizards. They don't have a good reputation here. I've even heard rumors that they perform unethical testing on some of the more animalistic magical creatures. There's no proof, but I wouldn't put it past those assholes."

"I am certain, I think," Grith responded, trying to swish her tail. "It is not like I have much choice. They pay well in shimmer, and it's enough for the maintenance of my family's territory. I've read a lot about them in my mother's books, and thus I am interested in investigating the nature of magic there, which is what I was hired to do. The one who replied to my application said that he was very excited to have me there. Regardless, I am willing to do most everything in order to save my home." She paused, tapping her fingernails on the wood and flicking her tongue. "I believe that I have to go there soon today, but since Pret suggested that I stop by here first, I stopped by. It was very helpful, however, I should get to the work buildings."

Ashley grimaced. "Well, if you encounter any trouble, tell me. I'll brew up a storm." She grinned at the dragon. "Literally. And even if you don't, come back here when you have the chance! New company is always welcome."

Grith blinked. "Thank you," she replied. She looked down at the table again and stretched her arms out until her elbows were locked, trying to move a leg off the chair. It fell below it, and Grith let out a small yelp as she rolled off the chair, landing on her back on the floor.

The dragon put her limbs over her belly, trying to protect it.

Ashley looked over Grith, concerned, before extending a hand out. "Do you need help?"

"I would appreciate it." Grith sighed, an irritated rumble in her throat. She swatted one of her own hands at Ashley's, slapping it. With a growl, she tried again to grab it, her fingers still missing.

Ashley grabbed Grith's wrist, tensing up when feathers appeared on Grith's hands. For a moment, sharp talons prodded into the human's arm. With a smile, Ashley pulled the dragon up, quickly letting go. Small drops of blood fell where Grith's talons had pierced her.

"I'm sorry," Grith said, her face stiff as she tried to tuck her tail under her legs without luck.

Ashley shook her head and pulled a small cloth from her robes that smelled of something floral. Grith stared intently as Ashley brushed it across the small wounds. When she'd taken it away, they were gone. "It's nothing. See? You're not the first one; getting a few scratches is just part of the job."

Grith tried to force her face into a grin, though with her peeling back her gums it was more like an awkward grimace. "I am going now."

Grith slowly turned her body around, walking shaky on two legs toward the door.

"Good luck!" Ashley shouted as Grith fumbled around, trying to open it up into the rain.

Grith hoped she wouldn't need it.

CHAPTER

TWO

The Vertex Technologies campus was the exact opposite of the Key. It filled a block of LA with stone benches and small stores, all surrounding the centerpiece of the campus: a huge square building that looked to Grith like one of the uncomfortable, angular benches had been tilted sideways and dropped on the ground. Though the skyscraper was kept lower than the other nearby ones, the dragon still had to crane her head up to see its peak, trying to stretch out her tail to balance herself while she leaned back.

With a yelp, Grith stumbled, whimpering as she fell backward into a puddle. She looked up, but even in the rain, the huge building was a glistening, polished white, looming down over her. The campus itself was pristine and orderly, fallen leaves swept away almost as soon as they touched the ground, muddy tracks on the pearly path leading to the entrance mopped away. One of the janitors kindly offered a hand out to Grith, momentarily stepping away from her endless work of cleaning in the rain.

"Thank you, but I should do get up on my own," Grith

replied, recalling what had happened with Ashley. She didn't want to hurt someone else. So, she rolled around through the puddle until she was on her belly, before getting on all fours and crawling a couple paces. Finally, she got back to her feet, ready to continue her bipedal stride.

The eyes on Grith made her nervous. The campus was nestled in the very heart of the human city, well within the eyes of everyone around it. The windows were tinted at least, but how did they keep mundanes from becoming suspicious? Powerful magic, Grith supposed. It seemed like Vertex could afford it.

She stumbled along the path to the entrance of the great building. The tinted doors slid open, and a few human men in suits came out chatting to each other as they walked past Grith, black umbrellas over their heads. One of them snickered at Grith's wet, muddy, and torn clothing, but they didn't accost her.

Grith walked toward the doors only for another two human men to block her path, staring down at her from above. Each looked as well-kept as the small group that had passed her previously, but far less chatty. A small overhang kept them dry as more water ran down Grith's skin, her ripped clothes soaked and covered in mud.

"Ma'am, this building is for employees only," one of the guards said. "Do you have a pass?"

Grith raised her head again, careful to do it slowly so not to fall back once more. She met the eyes of the human who talked to her, flicking her tongue.

The second guard suddenly stumbled back as he noticed Grith's neck. "Shiftstone!" he exclaimed, seeing it dangle, casting a dim glow on the falling raindrops. His hand went to his pocket as if to grab at a weapon. "What are you?"

"I am a dragon." Grith blinked, sniffing them. Oddly, the guards only seemed to become more nervous at her explanation. She put her fingers around the scruff of her coat, and dipped her head down until her teeth bit a small piece of soaked paper. She held it out until one of the guards took it, reaching toward her, careful not to keep his fingers close to her mouth for long. "I was accepted for a job here."

That also didn't seem to decrease the humans' anxiety. One of them pulled open the dripping letter, trying to read the smudged ink. He looked to the other. "I'll go talk to the Executive and figure out what's going on."

"I got accepted for a job," Grith repeated, unsure why they hadn't understood her first explanation. It seemed clear enough.

The guard holding her letter rushed back inside, leaving her and the other guard alone. Rain dripped down on Grith's head, her hair as soaked as her clothes. The remaining human stared, unwilling to take his eyes off Grith for even a moment.

Grith, unsure what else she was supposed to do, took that as a cue to stare back. Her head cocked to the side, and a few golden feathers sprouted from around her eyes, the pupils shrinking into tight slits.

The human shuddered.

After a while of standing out in the rain, the other guard returned, another human behind him.

Grith squinted. He looked much the same as the two guards, a pale-skinned male in a suit, the main difference she noticed with her eyes being that this one had no fur on his head and was more aged. He wore a suit just like the other two, though this one seemed just a little bit different, with a pointed cape-like blazer stretched over it, held around his neck with a golden clasp. She sniffed him, a sudden tingle of surprise causing goosebumps on her legs, a few feathers standing out straight. He covered himself with the smell of magic and fine metals, a perfume that even Grith's human nose could scent.

The human that had been watching Grith bowed when he walked through the doors.

With his head down, the guard glared at Grith, expecting her to do the same.

"It's fine," the magic-smelling human said with a smile. "She's new here. She hasn't learned the rules around here yet. You all don't need to worry about her presence; I'm the one who accepted her, and she'll be my personal responsibility."

His hand stretched out toward Grith.

She didn't make a motion back, just staring at the piece of meat. A golden signet ring wrapped around one of his fingers, a small bindrune on the surface, an hourglass with a tilted spoke at each end, as if the lids had been opened and all the sand was pouring out. She gave it a sniff.

"Shake it," he said, his tone that of a suggestion with a hint of an order behind it.

Grith turned back down to the hand, slowly placing a few of her own fingers around the tips of his in a careful clasp. She steadied her breath as a few scales and feathers showed up on her fingers, but claws didn't appear.

If the man was disappointed by Grith's handshake, he didn't show it. He pulled his hand backwards and gestured Grith into the building.

Grith stepped in after him, the sliding doors closing behind her. She squinted as blinding white lights hit her eyes, and it took a moment for her to be able to adjust to the glow that filled the inside of Vertex Technologies. She'd walked into a huge atrium, towering up half a dozen stories if not to the top of the tower, though Grith didn't bend her head back to try and check. She cringed, trying to keep the light from her eyes, the unnatural color of them painful.

The interior of the building was just as white as the exterior: the floor, the walls, and even the glass-exterior elevators the same uniform color. Not a hint of litter or disorder was visible. If anyone cleaned it, Grith couldn't tell, and it was likely they weren't allowed to clutter it up for long. She took a sniff, trying to figure out more about the surroundings, but wasn't able to get much but the scent of filtered air.

Another group of humans had seated themselves around the centerpiece of the atrium, a huge, white, angular column, rising up and branching out at the top like a flimsy brutalist imitation of a tree. Its 'leaves' were nothing but rectangular prisms that stuck out from more prisms, somehow managing to appear both randomly placed but ordered in their arrangement. The humans beneath it got no shade from the bright lights, a small group that Grith was unable to distinguish from the two outside, except that one had blonde hair instead of brown.

"How do you like it?" the leader human who'd led Grith in asked. "It's pretty impressive, isn't it?"

"The lights hurt my eyes," Grith responded truthfully. "The tree does not look like a tree. Your humans are—" She noticed a frown form on the human's face, and recalled that meant something displeased him, like when she bared her fangs. "Are you unhappy? Are those not your humans, furless human?"

The human's frown disappeared as quickly as it came, and he let out a chuckle. "Oh, I suppose that they are. I'm the head honcho around here, and most employees follow my orders to a tee, like the ones who bowed to me out front. They respect me that way, like how you would respect a king."

"Dragons do not have kings, and there are not enough of us to need them," Grith replied. She pondered something. "Though, the word is native to the Southern vocabulary, so maybe we did at one point."

"Fascinating," the furless human replied, not a smidgen of interest in his voice. "Do dragons have the concept of respecting authority? Because that's what's done here. It means that so long as you are in this building, each of my commands will be followed, along with the commands of your superiors just overhead. Do you understand that?"

Grith mechanically tilted her head up and down, and placed a hand above her head. "Over my head. I understand it."

"Not ove—" he tried to say before sighing. "Yes. Also, I'm not 'the furless human,' I'm the Executive, but you can refer to me as Paul. It's considered rude to point out someone's baldness."

Grith thought that was odd. Then again, dragons rarely had fur — no, hair — on their heads. Either they had fur all over, or fur nowhere, like Grith. She supposed it would be rude to point out if a Northern dragon had lost all their fur. Had something happened to the furless man's — to Paul's head-fur-hair? She wondered if he'd lost it in a magical experiment.

"That reminds me," Paul continued, "*your* name. It took a few translation books to figure out what the one you signed your application with was, and it's somewhat . . . unpronounceable with human tongues. We couldn't figure out how to put it in our systems, either."

"Grith," the dragon replied, rolling the r in the back of

her human throat. "I think that it is a good approximation. G-R-I-T-H."

Paul didn't seem more assured by this. He raised an eyebrow. "Are you sure? We can't change it later. Wouldn't you like something more normal, say, Gilly? I think Gilly sounds good for you."

"Grith," she replied again.

Paul sighed, and scanned Grith up and down. The water dripping from her clothes had managed to drip into a puddle on the floor beneath her, her boots covered in mud. "If you're *absolutely* certain."

Grith cocked her head to the side. She was certain.

"All right then," Paul continued. "Now, I'll give you a pass, since it's your first day, but you should know that clothing isn't really workplace-appropriate attire. You can't wear something with so many tears and rips, and it's not the eighties anymore!" He laughed at this. "A dress would be more flattering. Also, please hide your shiftstone."

Grith opened her mouth, planning to explain how these clothes had been her mother's human clothes, before holding her tongue. Did that count as orders? What human rags she wore seemed too unimportant, but she was supposed to follow them.

"Now that we've got that out of the way, are you ready for a short tour?" Paul asked with a grin. "Vertex Technologies has a lot to offer its employees, and I'm sure you'll be impressed. I'll take you to the lab, but I need to show you to the most important spot first — the coffee bar!"

Grith followed Paul across the atrium, looking left and right as more humans crossed it. She was getting a number of odd glances. Paul was probably right that it was her odd choice of clothing. In that case, she should try and get one of the suits that everyone else here seemed to have.

Paul led her to a smaller area, opened up to the atrium but still tucked away beneath the floor above it. She recognized the general plan from the Key; the coffee bar was shaped like a bar, with a human behind it creating drinks, while more humans sat around the exterior.

Paul stepped over to the human behind the counter, who already had two drinks prepared.

Grith accepted one from Paul, surprised at the warmth of the flimsy paper cup on her fingertips. This wasn't the first time she'd had coffee. Her mother had been a fan of it, and had made the occasional trip into the human city to get it, along with other human goods she deemed 'useful,' though Grith wasn't quite sure it had helped much. Rather than the tiny cup, she'd used a ridiculously-sized (even by dragon standards) ceramic bowl that she'd heat up with her own flame whenever it had gotten cold. The practice had occasionally led to frantic shouting while Grith was trying to sleep on her hoard, and eventually convinced Grith's father to place a human good *he* deemed useful in Grith's mother's library: a fire extinguisher.

Grith slowly raised the cup, trying to drink it in the same fashion that she'd drank the tea by the Key. After taking a small sip, her eyes went wide, and she spat it out onto the floor.

"Er, you all right?" the human behind the counter asked. "Is something wrong with it?"

Grith stuck out her tongue and held it between her fingers, trying to brush off the heat. "It is very hot," she answered. She'd known that before she'd sipped it, but normally it wouldn't have been a problem. "It hurts on a human tongue."

She tilted the cup upward, looking into it. The dark-brown liquid swirled around. A long forked tongue suddenly flicked out from her mouth, into the coffee, before retreating. That had worked! She did it again, intentionally overcoming the shiftstone as she decided on lapping up the coffee.

Paul stared at her, somewhat squicked at the display. "We don't drink like that here," he said, pulling the cup out from her hands. Her tongue flicked out, brushing against his signet ring. She didn't taste any magic in it except for the shimmer innate in the gold. That was surprising; she'd thought that an important wizard would have worn a magic ring. "Come on. Back to the atrium."

Grith followed, giving a small look to the coffee on the counter, but turning away from it. She thought that she was getting the hang of walking bipedally. It was odd without a tail to balance her out, but if she leaned forward and put her hands to her chest, it made it somewhat easier.

"The atrium is a sort of break room, though we have a few smaller ones," Paul explained, gesturing to the group of humans sitting beneath the white imitation of a tree. "It's not very busy at the moment, but we generally allow our employees to take breaks whenever they need to. Not that they usually need to. Everyone here is a very hard worker, but even the best of us deserves a place to sit down and chat. It helps with productivity."

"It is big," Grith replied, putting her arms out to her side, this time using them to keep herself upright. She spotted two humans traveling up an elevator to one of the floors above open to the atrium. "Big enough that I could fly in here."

Grith shook her back from side to side, the coat shuffling. Before she realized it, she was opening her wings, the coat ripping even more as golden feathers snuck out under it, stretching it taut. Two hooked talons reached out from under its shoulders, poking through the fabric.

"Stop," Paul ordered. With a snap of his fingers, the lights in the atrium seemed to grow brighter, and Grith put a hand to her head, clutching it as she tried to cover her eyes. The wings shrunk. "You're making a scene."

When she turned, she saw that Paul was right. Everyone in the atrium had turned to stare at her.

Paul furrowed his brow, thick lines running across his forehead.

Grith wasn't sure what was wrong. Wasn't this place supposed to research magic? Why was everyone so surprised?

"If you have to stretch your wings, make sure to do it in private," Paul said, snapping again, the lights fading with it. "Most of our employees are wizards, and aren't used to that sort of . . . odd display. I can't have it disrupting the workplace."

"Does that mean that they are all human?" Grith asked. If she remembered correctly from her studies of human magic, wizard almost always meant a human who did magic with created devices or spoken and written words powered by their internal life forces, whereas witches used magic found in nature, from magical plants to the phases of the moon. Mage could refer to either, and wasn't specifically human — like Grith's own mother. Grith had thought that most of the employees she'd seen so far were human, but it was more difficult to tell without her nose. Was she the only one wearing a shiftstone here?

"Well, technically, yes," Paul answered, tapping his fingers on his hand. "Wizards are, of course, human. But we don't think of it like that. Here, human refers to the mundane species, those without magic. It's rude to lump us with them."

"Like calling you bald human," Grith responded. She had a lot to learn about human rudeness.

"Yes." Paul sighed, scratching his head. "We do have a few animals, monsters, or other sorts of magical creatures around here that you might end up meeting, but I believe you're the first dragon to ever apply."

"Oh," Grith replied, trying to droop her ears in disappointment. She was really the only dragon? She supposed that she shouldn't have been surprised — dragons tended to keep to themselves, and Grith already knew most of them in the local area. As far as she knew, Pret and Nritza, a storm mage, were the only dragon mages nearby. At least since her parents had disappeared. After that, the family had exiled Arit, and Pret's parents left overseas to one of the western continents.

"Don't worry," Paul said as he turned toward the elevators. He pressed the button upward and gave Grith a smile.

She didn't particularly see the point in waiting for the elevator; it would've been quicker for her to just fly up to wherever they were going.

"I'm sure you'll be able to find friends here. Chris is going to be your lab manager and your coworker, and I think the two of you should get along well. He's used to being around magical creatures, I believe his family has a menagerie of servants."

The elevator arrived, and the doors opened up, the two stepping through. Paul pressed another button, and Grith put her hands on the wall to steady herself as it lurched, turning to the glass window. It rose higher and higher into the building, the atrium shrinking beneath her as they traveled alongside the fake tree.

"I've been trying to recruit a dragon for quite some time," Paul continued. "Do you know much about the source of magic?"

"My mother researched it some," Grith responded, distracted by the ground falling away beneath her. She concentrated on her hands, trying hard to make sure that wings didn't appear and instinctively flapped at it. "She believed that it came from somewhere outside this world."

"A very plausible explanation, and the one I personally subscribe to. However, a lot of wizards believe that the source of this world's magic originally came from dragons. I think it's one of a few potential sources, but the idea has some merit," Paul explained, tapping his fingers on the side of the elevator, focused on Grith's backside. "Just in the last few years, we've found a lot of evidence that magical creatures come from ordinary animals that spend too much time around dragon lairs, even deserted ones. We have a fish that woke up a mermaid. Oftentimes, dragon gold or dragon body parts are needed in a ritual to make a human into a wizard, their magical abilities proportional to the importance or amount of the body parts." He laughed. "You don't have to worry though, we don't need dragon body parts. We don't particularly want more wizard lineages, and uplifting humans isn't a goal here."

"I think that taking dragon body parts from living is also banned by the Council," Grith remarked, keeping her mouth still so as not to twist it into an instinctive bare. "There is no such thing as dragon gold, either. It is just gold, and sleeping on it or other shimmers, like some gemstones and metals, replenishes our shimmer. What you call magical essence. Gold is not very pure as well; we prefer platinum or rhodium."

"Hm." Paul frowned. "Are you sure? We see so much

dragon gold in the old lairs we've uncovered. Don't you think it's shinier and tastier than the other ones?"

Grith was about to try and explain how they don't, and that it's that gold and silver are valued and mined a lot by humans, and not as rare, and also that dragons rarely eat metals unless they need shimmer urgently, when the elevator suddenly came to a stop. The doors opened.

"Your lab is just down this hallway," Paul said, stepping out from the elevator and adjusting the collar on his cape. "This way."

Grith followed him into a hallway pointed away from the atrium, the same blaring white color as the rest of the building. She couldn't say she appreciated the decor, or lack thereof. It was nothing like the small castle her parents had built as their home, with infinite variations in every stone, beautiful, flowering vines curled around the windows. Vertex Technologies seemed stark and bland. Still, one of her mother's favorite sayings was never to judge a book by its cover. If the human employees were able to tolerate and even enjoy this workplace and its strange hostilities, Grith should be able to.

A door opened up into a decently-sized room. Grith wasn't sure what its purpose was — a number of large tables with empty spaces beneath them were arranged in rows from one side to the other, all clear and neatly washed. A row of old computers rested at the back, with a white chair in front of each one. The only other sort of decor in the blank room were two foot-high stacks of spiral notebooks with neatly sorted pens next to them, and a human standing by the stack, humming as he flipped through one.

He turned as soon as the door open, and bowed his head so far forward Grith thought he'd fall like she would have. A few locks of well-groomed, blond hair fell with it, almost touching the floor. "SIR!" he shouted, his voice rattling through the room.

"You may rise," Paul said, gesturing the young man up. "Chris, this is Gil-Grith, your new assistant. Grith, this is Chris, your lab manager. The dragon one I told you about."

Chris took a few steps forward and stretched out a hand to Grith, his head bobbing up and down as he examined her. "How do you do, ma'am?"

Grith looked at the hand. "It would be best if I did not shake it. I might grow talons."

Unfazed, Chris nodded, pulling his hand back to his side.

"Well, I'll leave you two to it." Paul sighed, giving Grith a quick look she couldn't quite tell the meaning of. "I have important business to attend to. If you need me, I'll be in my top floor office. Otherwise, Chris will show you the ropes."

Paul walked out from the lab, the end of his cape-like blazer swishing from side to side like a tail.

She had the sudden urge to give him an annoyed nip on its tip, but held back.

"Paul told me a bit about you and your research already," Chris continued. "He's not impressed by much, but I am. I'm excited to work with a dragoness!"

Grith let out a puff of smoke, feeling a few feathers appear on her neck. Dragons only used the Southern translation of dragoness when talking to a female superior or during courtship. And at least from what Paul had said, it seemed like he was superior to her here. She supposed he wouldn't have known that.

"So, where are you from?" Chris asked, turning to the

stack of notebooks, running his fingers along the spirals until he found the one he was looking for.

"I am local," Grith responded. "I live northeast of the human city, but I have not been in it. Why are you asking this question?"

"Oh, just curious," Chris said, jiggling out the notebook he was looking for, until it came free. He scanned through the pages. "I can show you around VT, that's Vertex Technologies, and the magical parts of the city sometime. The motto here is work hard, play hard, and I can help with both."

"Okay," Grith responded. Right now, she mostly just wanted to fly home, but learning more about LA might be useful. She knew about the Key, and this place, but little else. "I was told that I was accepted for a magic-related research position, but I am not exactly sure what that is supposed to mean."

"I've got that covered," Chris replied, turning the notebook around to reveal a variety of pages with equations and drawings on them.

Grith squinted, trying to figure out what it said from afar.

Chris turned it back. "You'll be working with me on the project I've been assigned. Understanding the inner workings of teleportation magic. You've played with using some human books on physics to explain parts of it, right?"

Grith tilted her head to the other side, and tried to tap her toes on the ground, squirming uncomfortably in her wet boots. "Geometrodynamical manipulation is what my family specializes in. My grandfather created the techniques required for making bubble realms and territory. My mother progressed his research by combining it with mundane physics. I have followed her."

"Great!" Chris replied inattentively, waving the book around. He gestured Grith forward, who, at this point, was thoroughly tired of it.

She followed him into another room from the first lab, this one smaller. Her eyes caught on two metal rings dangled by wires from the ceiling, swaying back and forth even without any wind, each about large enough for a human hand to be pushed into. Tiny runes wrapped around along each of the rings, and Grith walked up to one, trying to read them.

"Er, you probably shouldn't." Chris winced, stepping between Grith and the ring. "I'll be operating it myself. Your form isn't really stable, and this equipment is really expensive. I don't want a wing knocking it over, since the expenses come from my funding. At least for now, I'll have you just record our observations."

"It would be much easier if I was in dragon form, instead of a body I do not know how to use," Grith suggested, trying to peer around Chris to get another look at the rings. She sniffed, though couldn't figure out what the metal coating was.

"You probably shouldn't," Chris replied nervously, holding the notebook and a pen to Grith.

She attempted to flick her tail in irritation as she reluctantly took it, though the gesture didn't show. She carefully set herself down to the side of the machine, laying down on her stomach as she tried to scrunch her legs up against her side, getting a few weird glances from Chris. It took a few attempts before she managed to find a position that wasn't totally uncomfortable, and she opened up the notebook to the first blank page.

Neatly-written designs for the two rings were on the few pages before. Grith scanned through them, wondering why no one had reported the purity of the metal plating. She tapped her muddy boots against the wall as she saw the weight of the plating, and did the quick calculation necessary.

"The plating is poor quality," she remarked. "Why don't you use something better?"

"It's just standard issue." Chris sighed. "Right now, what we're going to be testing is these ring teleporters. Vertex designed. I'm trying to figure out whether there's any shifts in the color of a light shone too close to the edge."

"Yes, there certainly will be," Grith grumbled. "Your plating is worse quality than—" Feathers coated her throat and smoke rose from her mouth as she growled a phrase that was better left untranslated.

"Well, that's what we're measuring," Chris said. "Something easy for the first day, right?" He placed a finger on the edge of one ring and said a word in a human language that Grith didn't recognize as he circled it. The runes around it glowed a bright blue, and black mist appeared in the center. He stepped to the other one, repeating the movement, and the same thing happened. The mist disappeared a moment later. Inside each teleportation ring the space inside the other suddenly became visible.

Chris tilted the second one around until it faced the ground, the backsides of each ring also visible in the other as Grith caught a glimpse of them. She patiently fiddled with the pen as he set up a few other machines less interesting to Grith: some sort of device that shone a red beam of light into the ring, and another device that would measure the color of the light that came out.

Grith squinted at the pen. It seemed more difficult to use than just dipping a sharp talon into specially made ink. She fit it between her palms and attempted to write like that. The pen twisted out from between them after she squeezed too hard, and rolled across the floor. She rumbled in irritation as she crawled after it, getting uncertain glances from Chris as she neared a bit too close to the equipment.

After retrieving the pen and crawling back to the notebook, she bit the pen, attempting to write by moving her neck. It didn't work much better.

"You ready?" Chris asked.

Grith spat out the pen. "I am prepared." She tilted her head and tried again, wrapping a fist around it. It took her two lines to write anything and everything was practically illegible, but this seemed to be the best so far. How had Chris written so small?

Chris performed the experiment as Grith tried to write down the observations. Every time he flashed the light in different positions, he called out a series of numbers that the dragon diligently wrote down, still struggling to move her hand slowly enough. She gritted her teeth as her hand slipped, and she accidentally drew a line through the observations. Well, it wasn't like it made her handwriting any less legible.

Chris switched to a different color of light. Green. The most exciting thing to happen in this room as of yet.

Grith wanted to gnaw off her own tail out of boredom. Lacking that, she decided to gnaw on the pen's end instead. Hopefully, this got easier, and more interesting. "What is the purpose of this?" Grith asked.

"Um, the color deviations." Chris frowned. "I thought I already told you."

Grith rumbled. "No, the larger meaning of this. Why are we taking this data? Teleportation circles serve a similar use and take up much less shimmer than portals."

"Oh," Chris said, tapping his foot. "Um, I don't really know. I've never thought about it before. Portals have been the primary VT focus for a while now, though I don't actually know why since there isn't much commercial demand. I'm just a junior researcher and do whatever they assign me to. I'm on this because wave magic is my speciality. Electromagnetic waves are my specialty. Light."

"Yes, I know what electromagnetic waves are." Grith's mouth twisted. "It would be helpful to know what the broader thing we are working on is. I could help. Why have you not asked?"

"Eh, they wouldn't tell me anyways." Chris shrugged. "Corporate secrets or something, so their technology doesn't get stolen by rivals. I wouldn't worry about it. Don't rock the boat, you know?"

"Boat?" Grith asked. "There is not enough rain that we would need one."

"It means don't ask too many questions." Chris rolled his eyes. "C'mon, let's get back to work."

Grith fitted the pen back in her fist. Given what she'd heard about VT testing on magical creatures, she didn't like not knowing what exactly she was working on. At least portal technology was something that involved testing on living beings.

It felt like hours before Chris finally said something other than numbers. "All right! I think we've gathered enough. Can I see the data?"

Grith turned the notebook toward him.

He stared at it for a few moments, blinking. "Next time, do you think you can write it in English?"

"I did," Grith remarked. She chomped down on the end of the pen, causing the plastic to crack.

Chris tensed, putting his arms up over his head to

shield himself. He lowered them after seeing that the pen hadn't broken.

"Well, we can figure out how to input the data later." Chris smiled, dragging his finger around the rings in the opposite direction to close them. "How about we go on break now? Coffee your thing?"

Grith flicked out a forked tongue at him, a toothy grin coming over her as he flinched. Carefully, she got to her knees, and then her feet.

"Something feels wrong," Grith said as she staggered back. She stared at Chris, suddenly seeing two of him, and four of the teleportation rings. An odd feeling welled up in her throat, and she put a hand on it, clutching at it, trying to grab her shiftstone. Her eyes opened wide in alarm as she tried to balance herself by extending her wings and tail, which weren't there, which only caused her to stagger around more, getting dizzier. Something definitely felt wrong. "Are there any bushes nearby?"

"Bushes?" Chris asked, confused. "Not nearby. I think there's one or two outside of the campus. Are you okay?"

"No," Grith answered, swaying back and forth, trying to grab ahold of the wall. "I hope that no one minds if I use the corner."

Chris's eyes widened "Wait—" he exclaimed, a bit too late.

A second later Grith had vomited against the corner of the lab, yellow bile dripping from the corners of her mouth, and turning the wall into a shade that she thought somehow managed to be more pleasing than the white. She managed to smell this.

"Oh, oh dear." Chris winced. "Stay here, I'll go call someone."

"That's all right. I think I feel better," Grith said. She

propped herself back all the way upright and tried to turn, her body distending as she didn't time the turn right, unable to move her upper body in the correct unison with the lower. With a trip, she slipped onto the floor and retched again, glad that she hadn't had anything to eat in this body as of yet. A puddle of bile formed around her mouth. Standing was difficult.

"Do you think you're sick?" Chris asked. He walked back. "Wait, what illnesses do dragons get? Should I get a doctor?"

"I do not believe that I am ill," Grith replied, spitting out another glob of bile onto the floor. "It is just the shiftstone. I feel better now and have had enough of a break. I would like to return to work now."

CHAPTER

THREE

After Chris had called in the woman who'd tried to help Grith up outside to clean up the mess on the floor, the rest of the day went as boringly smooth as possible. Grith's bile had thoroughly soaked the observations, along with the rest of the notebook. Fortunately, Chris knew a simple un-soaking spell, and had used that quite successfully, though it hadn't managed to get the smell out. Grith's observations were too illegible for either of them to read, so they'd needed to repeat the experiment anyways. Chris had decided on getting her a cheap typewriter to type on instead for fear that she might break the laptops.

The next time Grith got up, when the workday was over, she stood up slowly, in stages. She kept her balance, making sure she was absolutely stable before taking a step forward.

"Hey, do you wanna see some of the cool stuff we've got at VT?" Chris asked as he held open the door for her.

She carefully walked through, staring down at her feet the entire time. "Is it the coffee bar?"

Chris laughed, and shook his head as he ran to the next door to open that. "No, better than that. Some of the magic here, in the storeroom a few doors over. We've got larger teleportation rings than the ones we worked with, and even a spatial manipulator. It's one of the things unique to this facility. It's kinda fun to play with, and I've got special permission. There's a neat game where you use it to help roll a ball around a maze"

"I am good," Grith replied, letting out an exasperated huff. "I already have one." Had Chris not listened to a word she'd said about her family? Maybe human wizards didn't need to use that sort of magic as often as dragons did. VT didn't seem to use it at all in order to hide this building; it was right and out in the open, where everyone could see. Dragons *had* to use spatial manipulation in order to create spaces of territory where they could survive without mundanes seeing them. It wasn't a game for them.

"Wait, really?" Chris asked. "They're pretty expensive, and rare. How did you manage to get your hands on it?"

"My mother created it," Grith replied, stepping out into the hallway. The lights were brighter than those in the lab, and she carefully put a hand above her eyes, squinting.

"I didn't know dragons could make them."

"She was — she is — a mage," Grith explained. She lifted up her arms, using them to balance as she turned toward the elevator, walking toward it.

Chris nimbly followed behind the dragon, curiously getting a glimpse of her face. "So, that means you're half-human?"

"*What?*" Grith's eyes opened wide at the slightly horrifying thought. She tried to figure out what Chris was implying. Half-humans were not something to be trifled with.

"You do understand that dragons can practice magic too, correct?" She was starting to doubt the competence of her coworker.

"Huh," Chris replied, considering that. "I honestly just thought you flew around breathing fire and eating princesses."

"Not generally," Grith snarled, turning her head toward him. Chris let out a small yelp of surprise, backing up against the wall. "Human-eating is discouraged by the draconic leadership. The practice has mostly stopped since it led to humans hunting dragons in return."

Chris gulped as he heard the word mostly.

Grith's voice changed to a guttural growl. Feathers had grown out from along her neck, and her face had become less human-like, her eyes slitted, her mouth shifting into a snout covered in golden feathers. She bared sharp, white fangs as long as each of Chris's fingers only a few inches from his nose, about ready to bite it off. Smoke wafted up in his face, his eyes stinging and tearing up.

Grith flicked out her tongue, unsure what exactly had caused the human wizard's sudden odd reaction. The waft of fear-scent hit her, far more than she could have sensed with her human nose. She took a step back, trying to surpress the draconic features on her face, her golden feathers shrinking away as her snout flattened.

"I am sorry for that," Grith said quietly, giving Chris another sniff. She couldn't smell the fear-scent anymore, but wasn't sure if that was because it was gone, or because her nose had become human again. "I did not mean to scare you."

"I was just surprised." Chris chuckled, heart racing as he leaned against the wall. "Plus, if you ate me, I think the

Council would go after you. Eating humans is a crime for magical creatures. So, you wouldn't, right?"

"Does that include wizards in the crime?" Grith asked, curious.

Chris gave her a weird look as he stepped over to the elevator, pressing the down button on it. "I don't think that's a problem. Wizards don't usually eat humans. And if a wizard kills a human through mundane methods, that's a problem for the mundane government, not the Council."

Grith had meant if wizards counted as humans for the purpose of eating them, purely for curiosity's sake, of course. Did that mean that wizards tasted different than mundane humans? Perhaps the additional magic made them taste more metallic, like shimmer.

Her train of thought was interrupted when the elevator doors opened and she turned her focus on making her way inside. She looked out through the glass, the odd tree as ugly as it had been at the beginning of the day.

"So, do you actually fly?" Chris asked as the elevator moved. "How does that work?"

"Flapping," Grith responded. She stretched out a wing to show him as she felt the elevator drop, mildly surprised that it appeared, part of a feathered wing poking through the rip in her coat. Chris's eyes opened wide in amazement as the light cast on the golden feathers made them almost glow, each feather a slightly different color under the different reflection of the elevator lights. He raised a hand, like he was going to touch one, before thinking better of it and pulling the hand back.

"I usually have to use some sort of invisibility magic when I fly," Grith continued, pulling the wing back as it disappeared into her back. "Both flight and firebreath use up a small amount of what is called natural shimmer. Er, innate magic in your terminology. Unlike most types of magic, it is not something we have to learn; it is instinct. Too much flying depletes it, but it gets regained by sleeping on precious metals or gems. Or eating them if a lot of shimmer is needed quickly, but they regain the magic normally, and it is a waste of a hoard."

"You have a hoard?" Chris asked, even more interested. "Can I see?"

Grith immediately bared her teeth, narrowing her gaze. "Of course not. Why are you asking so many questions?"

"I'm not trying to offend you!" Chris said, raising his hands. "I just wanted to get to know you better. Hoard private. I get it. I wouldn't give you my bank account number."

Grith kept her eyes locked on him for a while when the elevator hit the ground, the doors opening. She lowered her lips back over her teeth. Maybe he was just curious, but Grith had heard enough stories from other dragons about human thieves to be suspicious. Inviting a human into your home was inviting trouble.

Chris walked out from the elevator, Grith following. "So, if you're not interested in looking around VT, could I show you around the local area? The campus is more than just this building, and there are more magical parts of LA than you'd think, if you know where to look."

Grith tilted her head back and forth as she debated the idea. She didn't want to spend any longer inside this building if she had to, and most of her was ready to just collapse on her hoard for the night and finally get the shift-stone off. Still, seeing the city interested her. The city had been a short flight away from her for her entire life, yet she'd barely gotten a glimpse beyond its lights. She decided not to pass up the opportunity. "I am interested."

Chris beamed, and gestured toward the exit of the building. "Great! I've got just the place in mind."

The fresh air finally touched Grith's nose, and she took in a huge breath of it, just standing outside for a moment. The morning's rain had turned to a light drizzle, and Grith lifted her face up to the sky, this time able to keep herself from falling on her back. Water fell on her skin, dripping down her cheeks and across a few golden feathers that had appeared. Even corralled in by looming skyscrapers and the gray sky above freed her from the claustrophobic blinding lights of Vertex Technologies. She stretched out her arms, feeling drops splatter on her hands, the strangely strong sensation odd but amusing.

After a few moments she turned away, and followed after Chris. She was grateful that the two didn't have to walk far. Just a small path away from the central building, still in sight, was a shorter one with plenty of apartments on top of a row of stores. The noise of a car zooming along a four-laned street caught Grith's attention, and she watched as the machine barreled through puddles. On the other side, a small half-dozen of human adolescents walked down a sidewalk, chatting with each other.

Grith walked into one of the buildings with Chris and quickly learned from the smell of alcohol that it was a small cozy bar. A number of human men in suits like the ones from VT were sitting around the crowded building in groups around tables or at barstools themselves. A few played games with cards, while others just laughed and drank, their voices echoing loudly.

"Coming here after work to unwind is pretty popular," Chris explained, "especially for those who live in the apartments above, like me. Just in case you ever wanna come over."

"That would be rude of me," Grith replied, scanning around the room. "I would not want to intrude on your territory." A few of the wizards had noticed her odd gait and clothes, and she spotted one leering. She touched her neck, wondering if they'd noticed her shiftstone.

Chris pointed Grith over to the bar, where a tired-looking man stood behind it, filling a mug with beer before handing it to one of the humans at the counter. After exchanging a few words, he stepped back over to the two of them, giving Grith a concerned look. "Oh, Chris." The bartender sighed, putting his hand on his head in exhaustion. "What did you drag in this time?"

"Hah hah," Chris replied, rolling his eyes. "A dragon, actually. Her name's Grith; she's my coworker."

The chatting humans at the bar became markedly quieter when they overheard that, and their occasional looks at Grith turned to avoiding making eye contact with her at all costs. She noticed one draw a protection rune on the back of his hand.

The bartender gave Grith another glance, and shook his head back and forth disparagingly. "You're going to end up dead one of these days, you know that? What do you want?"

"Just a beer for me," Chris explained, looking back at Grith. "Can I buy you a drink?"

"She probably has plenty of gold if she's a dragon," the bartender remarked.

Chris glared at him. "That's not the point."

"He is right," Grith said, watching a few more of the wizards at the barstools inch away from her. "But I do not want to eat here."

Grith turned herself around, and without another word, stepped out of the loud and crowded bar into the rain. She stared at the street again as water fell on her hair. A human mother was rolling a stroller across the sidewalk now, holding an umbrella up over her hatchling.

She heard Chris's footsteps as he walked up next to her, the two of them against the side of the curb. A car drove past, and water splashed up into the air.

Chris jumped back with a noise that Grith thought was surprise, but the dragon didn't budge, even as her clothes got re-soaked.

"Sorry about that," Chris said, careful this time to keep a few paces away from the curb. "That was rude of him."

"I preferred the Key," Grith remarked, dipping her boot into the gutter, water pouring in through the holes her talons had made.

"The Key?" Chris asked, a hint of disdain in his voice as he recognized the name. "It's got worse problems. They just let anyone in, even if they're a dangerous unhinged monster. Some of their patrons even eat people! You could get hurt. You should stay here, the VT campus is far safer and has a more upscale company."

Grith craned her head around the best she could and flicked out her tongue, this time human as she stared Chris down. "Am I a dangerous unhinged monster?"

"Of course not!" Chris answered, too quick for him to have actually had time to think about the question. "Look, I know there's been some . . . weirdness around your first day at VT, but you seem like a nice girl, not a monster. It'll get better."

"Hm," Grith said, turning back to the street as another car drove past, this time on the other side of the road.

Would it really get better? Or would she just get more used to it? "I can smell magic here."

"Oh, that's what you were doing," Chris replied. "Yeah, this is the edge of campus. We have some very powerful charms that don't let humans in, dissuade them from coming near, and hide any odd occurrences on the inside. There's more, but even I'm not sure of them all, and illusion magic falls under my expertise. Don't tell anybody, but I've actually been attempting to reverse engineer some of them.

So, the campus uses illusions, not bubble realms, Grith considered. She supposed that it made sense. Unlike dragon territories, the campus wasn't that large, so it didn't make sense to have it be in an entirely separate space than the rest of the world. Was the mundane city better than the magical? She was curious. Maybe she could get a job there instead.

Grith took a step forward, Chris's eyes opening wide as she splashed into the gutter.

"Wait!" he called out as she began to cross the road, stepping across wet asphalt.

She turned to the left, two yellow lights blinding her, a rumble shaking through the road.

She felt her hand grabbed and pulled back as a car barrelled down the street, a loud honk sounding as it swerved around her. Her body hit the pavement as she fell onto the sidewalk, looking up at Chris in surprise.

Chris let out a cry of pain as blood dripped from the hand that he'd grabbed Grith with, sharp talons digging into it. She let go after she realized what had happened, shaking her hand. The claws shrunk into fingers, and feathers on her wrist disappeared. Red splotches stained the white pavement, and three gashes had formed on Chris's arm.

"I hurt you," Grith observed. "I am sorry. I was not expecting to be touched. I think that the wound is small enough that I could heal it if it was licked." She opened her mouth, and a long forked tongue unrolled from it. The smell of blood made her nose perk up.

Chris took a wary step back. He winced and shook his head. "N-no thank you." He used his other hand to rummage through a pouch in the interior of his suit, before pulling out a cloth that was far larger than the pouch itself. Carefully, he wound up his hand, red blood soaking through the first layer or two.

Grith tossed him a confused look. Well, it was his choice if he didn't want her help. Was she supposed to be grateful? It had been his job to show her the ropes after all, and warning her about the cars fit well within that description. "Do they not stop for you if you try and walk past them?"

"The cars?" Chris asked. "Um, no. They don't. You need to be careful around them in case I'm not here to save your life next time! Make sure to look both ways before crossing the street."

"That is rude of them," Grith replied. "It would be far easier for me to just fly over."

Chris's pained expression turned to a mortified stare. "No! You can't! The humans would see!"

"I know that," Grith responded. She *had* just mentioned that she was standing at the edge of the illusion field, hadn't she? "I will not do it. That does not mean that I do not want to. I think that I am going to look outside the campus."

Completely unfazed, Grith stood up, accepting Chris's advice and looking both ways for cars before stepping onto the road. She made her way across.

Chris bit his fingernails before following, forgetting to

check both ways himself. "You can't cross here." He gulped. "You're J-walking. It's illegal."

"I normally walk on all fours," Grith explained as she reached the middle of the road. "Additionally, jays generally do not walk, they fly."

"No, it's J-walking because you have to cross at the corners of the street, and that's more of a straight line, and if you're in the middle it's like you made a J with — oh, nevermind!"

Grith stepped up on the other side of the curb, looking up and down the sidewalk. A similar row of buildings were situated on this side, too, also with apartments above stores. But this was far different. Here, they were on the other side of the illusion magic, no longer on VT campus. This was mundane territory.

She walked down the sidewalk, curious to check out the city. A few humans walked in and out of the stores holding umbrellas above their heads, but this day was quiet. She suddenly saw a hand reach up to her shoulder, noticing that Chris was considering grabbing it, before deciding better.

"I don't think this is a good idea," Chris murmured, fidgeting with his hands. "What if they realize—"

"That I am a dragon?" Grith asked, cocking her head. She pressed a finger to the shiftstone. "I think that I can hold my form in the shiftstone now, so long as I am not startled, or do it intentionally." She grinned to let Chris get a glimpse of a couple fangs. "Do not worry. I will not be out here for long. I have to go this way to return to my home anyways. I cannot take my shiftstone off at VT, correct? I will use the place that I landed. I promise that I will not eat any humans."

Chris shivered at the way she said that last sentence,

without a hint of humor in it. "Sait, you haven't actually . . ."

"Eaten a human?" Grith finished, already guessing the question. "Only once, and it was a hiker that was already dead. I was curious. Why do you appear ill? Paul told me that wizards do not consider themselves human."

Chris looked away, putting a hand to his mouth.

Grith was afraid that he might spill up his stomach contents like she had, attempting to put that image out of his head.

"It's . . . whatever, I guess. I had a vampire ex who'd killed a human once with blood-drinking, but it's kind of different than straight-up eating. Not as hot, haha. You shouldn't be going into human — mundane places much anyways," he warned her, trying to change the subject. "And not just because of the shiftstone, though that risk makes things worse. Even wizards avoid going into human places more than we have to, for things like groceries or dentist's appointments. We're not supposed to interact much, or get attached."

Grith ignored him.

"We live in a different world than the humans," Chris tried to argue. "We're different from them. We need to be kept separate, or things get messy."

Grith wondered who he was repeating that from. "But I am curious."

"There's nothing the humans have that wizards don't!" Chris said, almost frantic, trying to keep his voice from becoming too raised and risk someone hearing him who wasn't supposed to.

Grith turned toward the glass windows of a storefront. A few pieces of human clothing were situated on odd, plastic human figures without faces. She decided they looked more funny than creepy. "This is a clothing store, correct? Paul told me that I must obtain something more workplace appropriate. Will you purchase me something instead of that drink? I do not have human money with me, only 'dragon' gold. Since you are showing me the ropes, you can take it out of your workplace funding."

Chris clutched his head and let out a loud sigh. "Fine, just, let's make it quick."

Grith turned to him and attempted to imitate one of his smiles before walking inside. A woman at a counter gave her a friendly wave as the dragon walked between rows of tops, putting out a finger in order to feel the material, soft and smooth. The interior lighting here was far more conducive to her eyes than the one in Vertex Technologies, although Chris seemed to have gotten a splitting headache already.

Eventually, she arrived in the corner of the stores, where they kept a large assortment of longer articles of clothing that would hang on a human's shoulders and around their waists, with the bottom of the same piece reaching down to the floor. She read a nearby sign. 'Dresses.' That was what Paul had suggested, wasn't it? In that case, she would get one.

She held a few up, feeling the fabrics. "I do not like human clothing," she remarked to Chris. "It is tight and uncomfortable on my feathers."

"There's more loose clothing, if you want." Chris sighed. "You can try it on before purchasing."

"That is a good idea," Grith responded. She shuffled her feet from side to side as she walked down the aisle, until she came to a row of dresses with the bottom large and poofy. She lifted up a golden one with little sparkly gemstone-imitations providing rainbow highlights. "I like this one."

Chris frowned. "It's a bit odd-shaped and a little glittery. Gives off princess vibes. Ironic."

"My legs will be free, and I could even hide a tail under here!" Grith exclaimed, excited. "The color is accurate." Grith placed it down and took off her coat, and then began to take off the torn top she'd gotten from her mother.

Chris's eyes opened wide as he watched Grith start to strip, just gawking and staring before he saw the layer of golden down feathers coating her underbelly. "Wait!" he shouted, reaching forward to try and pull her top back down, before thinking better of touching her. "Put it down!"

Grith gave him a confused look, before remembering that humans didn't have feathers there, and dropped the top.

Chris frantically turned his head left and right. "What if someone noticed that?" he scolded her. "What if we got exposed? Oh God, would I be punished the same as you?"

The woman behind the counter's eyes were focused on Grith.

Chris shuddered. "Maybe we can still salvage this," he whispered. "The penalties for killing a human magically are less severe than beheading. I really don't think I can do that, but you . . . maybe you could eat her or something?"

Grith cocked her head. She wasn't supposed to do that, and humans oddly did not strike her as prey so much when she was in a human body herself.

"I love your cami!" the woman called out to Grith. "Are the feathers real, or not?"

"Of course they are real," Grith answered.

"Amazing! And that color, too?" the woman replied. "Beautiful. Where did you get it?"

"Custom-made! It's one-of-a-kind," Chris said before Grith could answer.

The woman looked a bit disappointed, and Chris turned back to Grith, wiping a bead of sweat from his brow as he lowered his voice.

"That was a close call. Feathers or not, you can't take off your shirt in public! You're supposed to do it in a changing room, and it's not right for a girl to do that!"

"To take off my clothing?" Grith asked. "Why? I am more comfortable without it. What about when it gets hot? It seems odd to keep it on when you do not need a fur coat."

"You just can't!" Chris groaned. "Seeing a woman's belly, and especially her chest is, um, it's sexual."

"That is very silly!" Grith laughed. "Sexual organs aren't up there; they are mostly in the same place as in dragons, correct? It is not sexual unless my tail is raised." She peered behind her, checking for a tail. How did humans communicate their receptiveness without tails or noses that could detect the scent of heat or arousal?

"Human women do it differently," Chris tried to explain, blushing. "Just trust me on this. And you can't have feathers under your shirt either. I'll admit that it's a little sexy, but it's not proper."

"The human woman at the counter thought that they were pretty," Grith retorted. "Is she not a human?"

"It has to be skin, not feathers," Chris said, shaking his head. "There's a lot about being human I need to teach you."

"I am a dragon, not a human." Grith tapped her fingers on the dress. If Vertex Technologies didn't require her to use a shiftstone while she was there, this would have been far easier for the both of them. Maybe she could try and talk to Paul about it again.

Chris sighed, clutching his head. "I know. I know. Let's just hurry. I need to get home before you give me a worse headache. And don't reveal yourself again. In either way."

"I promise," Grith replied, trying to nod the best she could. "I shall make sure that I am hidden from the humans, plucked skin and all!"

CHAPTER

FOUR

A fter Grith had bought the dress, she and Chris parted ways for the day. Grith couldn't say that she particularly liked him, nor any of the other wizards she'd met at Vertex Technologies. Hopefully, however, things would get easier as she spent more time there. That's what Chris had said, wasn't it? She'd get used to being around humans and attempting to act like one. They were adjusting to her, and she was adjusting to them, though it mostly felt like the latter.

The rain formed a gentle drizzle as the sun dipped below the horizon. Streetlights cast a glow on the hazy fog, and after a bit of wandering, Grith found the streets that she'd come down in the morning before visiting the Key. She'd always been a quick learner, and walking was far easier now than before. Her gait was slow and rigid and she didn't trust herself to attempt to run, but she wasn't tripping. At least not in boots — in the store, she'd seen a few thin shoes with long props toward the back, and didn't trust herself to manage to walk quadrupedally in them, much less bipedally.

She walked by two young humans passed out against each other on the side of the road, holding each other in an embrace. She gave them a small look, taking the risk of turning her head while walking. Why was it so bad that the magical and human worlds remained separate, like Chris had said? Why did the Council have such severe rules on exposure and accidental mingling? At least for her, it would be far easier if she could be in her own body while out in the city, even if the inside of the stores would be cramped. Surely humans would just get used to having dragons and other magical creatures around. Though, the wizards' reaction to her had made her slightly skeptical.

Access to magic would have certainly improved many mundane humans' lives. While there were limits to what one could do with it, and overuse would slowly deplete the Terran aura and shimmer, there were so many things it would be useful for, far more than Grith could even think of. Wizards had shown that magic could improve mundane medical technology a hundred-fold, but because of the Council's rules, it was kept only to them. Dragons rarely had access to modern medicine, and mundane humans were limited from magic. It seemed like the rules just hurt everyone.

Why couldn't the two worlds exist in unison? It wasn't as if dragons couldn't keep themselves from killing humans. Cases of that had been rare for the last one-hundred and fifty years, since the Revival of Dragon Magic (or the Final War, as wizards called it). Half a lifetime. Was it the other way around, that humans couldn't keep themselves from killing or enslaving anything different than them? Some of her father's family had claimed that before. Was that why she had to wear the shiftstone, to keep the wizards from giving into their base human desires and attacking her or anything different than them? Were humans unable to let anything that seemed too dangerous to them exist? Grith didn't believe that. Ashley hadn't seemed that way, and the Key seemed like living proof of that. Unless, of course, she was wrong about it and Chris was right in thinking it was dangerous.

Grith reminded herself that she was new to both the magical and mundane human worlds. She'd only ever lived with dragons up until now; almost all her interactions with humans had been through books. The problem was probably more complicated than it seemed at first glance. The Council surely had their reasons, and Chris probably knew more about them than she did.

Grith made a turn to the right and into a dark, unlit alleyway, a few paces from side-to-side, just large enough for a dragon to land in. The tingle of magic rested on the tip on her tongue. She didn't know who'd enchanted this place, but her cousin had told her it was the best place to land in, as no mundanes would disturb her. Perhaps Pret had made it himself, since he needed a place to land if he wanted to frequent the Key. The shades darkened and covered the windows on either side, and after walking into the center, the street was hard to see, covered in a black mist.

Just to be safe, Grith decided to use an invisibility spell before taking off the shiftstone. Without wings to cast it, she instead extended her arms, a crackle of power running between her middle fingers. She didn't like using magic while wearing the shiftstone. Something felt wrong, like she was blind to the world, as if she was attempting to play with the forces underlying the world without feeling them.

Humans didn't have the same shimmer stores that dragons did. Instead, they used magic that they termed aura, a magical force that flowed through all things. When dragons used shimmer, it was like exercising, using up internal stores of energy from food. With aura, each use of magic expended one's lifeforce. It slowly regenerated from the planet's weak ambient aura over time, similar to how sleeping on a hoard gave a dragon shimmer, but it took a toll on the body. Dragons could use their aura in time of need, but they generally didn't prefer to.

Still, as human or dragon, Grith knew the motions of the spell she needed to cast. She growled a few words as she focused her attention to her fingertips, moving her mind through the familiar patterns.

The invisibility spell was one of the ones created by her grandfather and his mother during the Revival of Dragon Magic two-hundred years earlier. By now, it was one of the most wide-spread spells among dragons, as important to their survival as the territory creation spell but far easier to cast. It was simple and direct — all it did was allow light to travel unimpeded through one's body, except for the eyes, which glowed the color of the user's shimmer. It wouldn't let one walk through a human city unsmelled and unheard, but it was mostly used for flying.

Two golden circles of light appeared around Grith's body, runes rotating within them, the same color streaming out from her eyes. Feathers lined her throat when she spoke the final word of the spell. The golden circles disappeared along with the rest of her but her eyes, casting a golden glow like two lamps in the fog.

Even with how ripped they were already, Grith removed the rest of her human clothes to spare them. She placed them in the large stretchy bag where she'd already put the dress, along with spare gold coins and a few more assorted items. Once she was certain no one on the street was watching, she placed her hands to the shiftstone, and dragged the chain on it around her hair. It came off of her with a few sparks, and the glow faded.

The invisibility spell lapsed as Grith's body transformed, the twin circles appearing once more. Her back painfully expanded, bones popping as they grew. Wings that had been trying to break free the entire day finally tore through her skin, stretching to join the magic circle around her arms, as wide as the dark alleyway she was hidden in. As she moved them to take her arms' place, golden feathers fluttered in the air, the longest the length of a human forearm. The colors of the rainbow glinted across them in the magic light, changing their hues as they moved. More feathers of the same colors broke through her skin, soft down covering her belly, while a crest of them stretched out on the back of her neck as it elongated. A slender snout forming on her snake-like head, her eyes moving to the side.

The dragon placed her arms on the ground as her legs changed, scaled talons forming from her toes as their locations changed, heels stretching upward. Her arms changed their positions and lengths as they grew, and she was once again on four paws. She lashed her tail through the air like a whip, feathers glittering as it whacked the side of the alley, hitting a loose brick.

Smoke poured from Grith's nostrils, releasing a tension within her like a cloud that had spilt its tears. Fire in her belly began to spread throughout her, feathers raising and lowering as they felt it beneath her skin, and some of it came loose, a small, orange flame rising into the sky before it went out in the night.

Intense scents that had been previously hidden from her suddenly hit her nose. Both good and bad ones flooded into her, making the dragon dizzy. Disgusting odors of asphalt and sewage were all around her, smog and smoke covering the air, drying concrete and the tingle of electricity. Still, the air contained not just the creations of humans, but life as well. Grass sneaking up from cracks in the sidewalks, pollen itching her snout. Rats and pigeons, dogs and cats.

Yet, more than anything, the odd smell of humans was all around her. Animalistic but unnatural, covered with clothes and chemicals, too clean for an animal. Unlike the rest of the small animals nearby, humans were the only ones large enough to hunt, and their smells carried that information to Grith. Most animals had a prey-scent about them that caused a dragon's hunting instincts to come to the forefront in their mind, and humans were no exception.

The change in her mind and senses caused Grith to falter for a moment, and her brain turned toward seeking prey, muscles tensing in preparation to pounce. She went still as the stone around her as the sound of a car rushed past the alleyway, her golden eyes piercing the fog. Though scents of fumes and gasoline covered the car, human smells also masked it. Grith flicked her tongue against her sharp fangs, the scent of nearby prey tantalizing. The sight of it fleeing her almost caused her to chase after it and attempt to hunt it down.

A rumble rose through the dragon's throat as she resisted the urge, coming back to her senses. There was food back at her home, and attempting to hunt humans in the middle of a human city was an idea so ridiculously stupid it was far more befitting of a hot-blooded young drake attempting to impress a potential mate. She would crash herself into a marketplace window and gorge herself on frozen meals from there before she tried that.

The whole affair bothered her, feathers ruffled. She'd only used the shiftstone in isolation before and for shorter periods of time; taking it off here was a far different experience. All the things she'd been missing as a human had flooded her, her enhanced senses, the feeling of shimmer in her body, the hunting instincts of an apex predator. She would have to be more prepared for it the next time she took her shiftstone off, and was glad that she'd been alone when it happened. She'd be quite embarrassed if another dragon had seen her chasing after a car, and if she accidentally harmed a human, things would be far worse.

Grith raised and lowered her legs, checking that they still worked, and gave a terse flap of her wings. Winds spiraled around her through the alleyway, the gusts on her talons. Her head craned back around her as she whipped her tail again, watching it like she was checking that it was still there and wouldn't disappear once more.

With a sway to the side, she pushed into the brick wall, folding in her left wing as she rubbed her side up and down. The rough stone scratched beneath her feathers in a soothing way she wasn't sure she'd ever forget. Tucking in her wings, she rolled onto her back, belly in the air, tail twisting back and forth as she let the bricks scratch that, too. She forgot what she was supposed to be doing for a few moments, finally free as her talons scraped on the cold stone, her hips splashing in the water as she eagerly let it coat her feathers, lost in her sensations finally being right.

Grith recalled that her invisibility was no longer working with having to change the way she used magic, and flexed her wings again, the golden circles flickering before they went out. A moment later and she'd disappeared into the brick wall, and only the two glowing orbs of her eyes remained visible. She suspected it would be far easier to get away with hunting humans here if she was invisible. Completely hypothetically, of course. She'd have to be quite a bit hungrier than she was now and have far fewer meal options available, to resort to that. It was very illegal, and would break a number of truces!

Grith rolled back to her paws, stomping up and down in the puddles once more as she shook the water droplets from her wings, then looked to the sky, the gray clouds calling her. She snuck her neck beneath the stretchy bag that held her clothes, and carefully pulled a wing and a foreleg beneath it. Her talons clutched around the sides of the wall, digging into claw-holds that someone before her had made, and she leapt to a ledge, a loose brick falling down into the alleyway. She leapt again, almost slipping from the wetness of the stone before she made it up to the top of the alley, still enclosed in the magical black mist that hid it.

Her wings beat, stormy winds whirling through the alleyway as her feathers fluttered. She twisted her body as she felt lift and dove down into the alley, the air catching under her wings as she fell, just wide enough to hold her safely between the sides as she passed by a boarded-up window. With a flap and a crane of her neck upward, she rose, sailing out of the misty alleyway and above the empty street.

Her flight instincts took over as the air ruffled her crest, and she rode the wind, carrying her up as the city beneath her shrunk, millions of lights glowing under her eyes. She swooped down and around as skyscrapers reached toward her, moving toward them. After the time she'd been forced to spend in a human body, she decided she deserved a little fun. Banking to the left, she made a wide circle around one, staring at a few lights in the windows. Humans late at night were still inside, doing something she couldn't tell. One looked towards her, perhaps noticing the two lights in the sky.

With a turn and a change in her wings' angle, she soared upward. The skyscrapers disappeared beneath her, a gentle patter of droplets falling on her oiled feathers. Her tail whipped to the side to make her way northeast, the lines of human roads spiraling out under her like a great spiderweb she'd been caught in the center of; the glow of the lights abruptly cutting off as the mountains provided a natural border to the lands. How had just a slope so easily conquered the humans that had built the expansive, eternal city?

A plane soared down from the clouds above her, more lights glimmering, this time overhead. Her feathers fluttered as the mountains loomed closer. She knew this area well, even outside of her home hidden in its midst. A familiar barren rock between two peaks, a forest just beyond that. Grith dove down, wind blasting past her golden eyes. With a flap of her wings she let out a roar, a great sound of defiance blasting through the treetops, branches bowing beneath her claim. If any humans had heard her call, they would do well to know that this was her territory. Though she was still hidden, here at least she was free.

The smell of magic rippled through her feathers, tingling from her crest to her tail tip. A small motion of her wing spurs caused the gate to open, a golden flash appearing in the sky that could have just been another plane. A moment later, and Grith was gone from the world, entering another.

She soared through pink mists, curling around her feathers as they invited her home. The magic seemed almost alive, glad for a dragon's presence, giving off a delighted hum to the few who could hear it. The mists parted to reveal a forest beneath them rising around the slopes of a gentle peak. Grith was finally home.

The smell and look of the woods was much the same as the forests northeast of the human city, though perhaps a little lush, a little *more*. Just the presence of a dragon invigorated the land around them, filling it with a desire to grow. Like Paul had claimed, a dragon and their hoard brought a little more magic to the world around them; it was unfortunate for everyone that the presence of humans and rules against interacting forced them all to remain hidden away in pocket dimensions.

Grith's grandfather had created her bubble realm, a miniature microcosm of the surrounding land. Hers was around a dozen square miles of mostly forested land populated with the natural flora and fauna that covered the area. The pink-colored mist surrounding the edges of the land would take Grith back to the mundane realm, special enchantments allowing for the movements of certain species of animals through it but keeping humans away so long as the magic was done right.

The sky here mostly carried the same weather as the world outside, though Grith knew the spells needed to change it if the bubble realm was covered in smoke or she was just tired of the scorching sun and wanted to feel rain on her neck. Right now, the same drizzle had formed over it, gray clouds hiding the stars that night. The bubble realm had provided Grith's family hunting grounds and a safe den, and her parents had chosen the location to tether it well.

Similar magics had allowed dragons to survive since the Revival, giving them the swaths of land to roam and hunt in that they needed. Inside bubble realms they were hidden, though Grith had heard stories of the magic occasionally lapsing and a human accidentally stumbling inside. Whether they got out or not depended on how generous or hungry the dragon was feeling and if they knew how to use the standard-issue memory spells created by the Council. The system worked, but it had its flaws. Dragons were forced to live confined within them, unable to roam the world. Naturally, dragons would have larger territories that bordered on each other, and would know their neighbors. Complex relationships would be formed, and two dragons could just as easily fight tooth and claw or mate, or sometimes alternate between the two depending on the season. With bubble realms, the less socially inclined Southern species was even more isolated than normal, making finding partners almost impossible and forcing breeding regimens in order to keep the population stable. Northern family packs no longer interacted with each other and exchanged mates like they should have, causing incestuous pairings within packs.

For Grith, the most important flaw in the system was that bubble realms required a lot of shimmer to keep them from collapsing. Southern hatchlings were unable to leave the nest and make their own bubble realms. The natural magic source from Terra's aura alone was far too little to keep their homes stable, and precious metals had to be used up unsustainably, usually from ancestral hoards. And the hoard that Grith's parents had left her with was fast-shrinking.

She turned toward the peak where her family had situated their den. Her eyes landed on the small building that superficially resembled a human castle, with vines crawling up the gray stone that formed it, sinking their tendrils down into the ground like the tunnels that crept with them. The tunnels formed a multitude of interlocking cavern-like rooms, thrown around without rhyme nor reason, even if their placements somehow managed to make a sort of instinctive sense to Grith. Pillars rose up around the landing pad like the underside of a dragon's jaw, and Grith had plenty of room to slow herself down, gently coming to rest on the stone.

Her wings folded into her side and she stretched out her head, taking in the scents of her home. The humidity of the rain, the leaves of the forest, the grass surrounding the musky scent of the area. The smell of the deer that lived in the nearby area, never straying too close to the peak, mixed with the rising scent of her hoard's shimmer, all beneath the great *rhas* that permeated the bubble realm. Even her own sharp scent was enjoyable after being unable to smell it for the day, from the smokiness that trailed her path to the pungency of her expulsions a long distance down from the peak. Actually, no, she didn't think she could enjoy that, even if her snout stopped working for a few decades.

She glanced down over the territory, now hers alone. She wanted to hunt, to stalk a deer and feel its neck snap in its jaws. She wanted to taste its blood on her tongue as she tore out the fresh meat and devoured its innards. But she was tired, and knew that she'd have to return to the human city in the morning. She didn't have time to hunt, not tonight.

Still, a hungry dragon was a dangerous dragon, and if she was going to be spending time among humans, it was probably a good idea for her to eat something, lest she ended up being tempted to eat something that she shouldn't, such as one of the annoying wizards. She stepped through the small archway into the castle and let out a small puff of flame on a torch by the entrance.

A few moments later, and more torches lit up the dark halls, Grith's eyes adjusted to the orange glow. They would last until she either blew out the flames herself, or the shimmer empowering the magic of the home ran out. Hopefully, it would be the former.

The hall became more of a twisting tunnel as she walked down a slope, and Grith followed it into the room she was most interested in. The chill of cold caused her feathers to puff up, and she stared at a great metal door with a huge latch on it. She stepped up to it and wrapped her talons around it, pulling the door open to reveal a freezer large enough for a dragon twice Grith's size to walk into. Frozen dead animals, most of them deer, haphazardly covered the icey floor.

Grith's mother had always been the adaptive type, as evidenced by the numerous human appliances scattered around the castle, magic converted to the needed electrical power. Grith herself wasn't sure how her mother had managed to get herself a dragon-sized walk-in freezer from a mundane human. She supposed most humans loved their shimmer enough that they would make anything for enough gold, even if they didn't have any use for the shimmer past decorating their bodies and washrooms. Still, it might not have been that different with dragons; Grith knew that shimmer-lust instinct was strong enough that even before the Revival, dragons would risk their lives just to get hoards they would do nothing but sleep on.

While her mother was adaptive, her father had always been more resistant to depending on human goods, or even magic itself. Grith supposed it was just how his parents had reared him. Grith's mother had been brought up, along with the rest of her clutch, to succeed Grith's grandfather. The greatest dragon mage in millenia, whose fusion of human wizardry and witchcraft to ancient draconic magic that his mother had discovered had enabled the survival of their species. Grith's father's family had instead always been resistant to changing their old ways, hesitating even to adopt realm bubbles, much less to stoop so low as to using a shiftstone to hide themselves. Grith's home hadn't pleased them the last time they'd visited. Human decadence, she remembered them calling it, among a few worse words.

Grith pulled off a deer haunch before shutting the freezer door behind her. It wasn't far to a small pit she could drag it in. She drew a couple runes with her talon on the side, and they glowed for a moment before Grith emptied her flame into the pit. The fire whirled around inside the basin, the runes controlling it so that it magically passed through the flank, evenly heating it. Smoke rose from her nostrils, and she kept the temperature of her flame consistent, making sure to keep her fire well away from her feathers. The oil on them was fire-resistant, but it was far from fire-proof, as many Southern hatchlings had learned the hard way. Her gaze was drawn to a fire extinguisher on the side of the cavernous room, just in case.

After a few minutes, it was done, somewhere between what humans would call 'rare' and 'raw.' She vastly preferred fresh meat, but this would have to do, at least for tonight. She could hunt at the end of the week, when Vertex Technologies had told her she would not have work duties.

As she ate her meal, tearing strips of flesh from the deer flank, Grith pondered the desires of dragons. Her mother would have never been happy without her research. For her, magic and learning about how the world worked was as much a part of her as her wings or her feathers. All Grith's father believed he needed was good hunting grounds, a safe lair, a mate, and a hatchling to raise. When they'd been hatchlings, Pret had once told Grith that he wanted to make the world a better place, and that his wings wouldn't rest until he'd made a difference, whatever that might be. Grith's other cousin, Arit, had said that all of these goals were dumb; the purpose of life was to enjoy it, no matter who it affected around him. Dragons were made to feast and fly, to fight and fuck. Perhaps it wasn't so surprising the family had banished him.

Grith didn't know what she desired. None of that felt right.

Her mind drifted, like it often did, to her parents. She missed her hatchling years spent with them. As different as they were from each other, she thought they were the best that she could have hoped for. Neither tried to push their ideals on her like their parents had on them. She missed them. Maybe that was what she desired — to have them return to her, or to at least know what had happened to them. They'd vanished years prior to rainforests in the south on a flight related to Grith's mother's research. Grith had no longer been a hatchling at that point, and had thought she'd known how to take care of herself, which she supposed is why they'd chosen to leave. She knew how to hunt, and she knew magic, though now she was doubting that was enough. She had waited for them to return, and she was patient. But they hadn't. She hadn't been quite sure when, but at some point, she'd stopped assuming they would come back, and had started assuming that they were dead. How? She didn't know. Could they have been slayed? Dragon-slaying was rare, almost as rare as dragons eating humans, but it wasn't unheard of. Whether it was for the creation of powerful wizard lineages from dragon hearts, for wealth or honor, or on a moral crusade against 'monsters,' humans killed dragons.

Grith realized she had finished her meal, and had been gnawing on the leg bone for a while. She dropped it. She needed to sleep and rejuvenate her own shimmer. It had been a long day, and she was tired. Still, she had one more thing she needed to do; Pret had asked her to speak to him. Hopefully, he wasn't already dozing off on his hoard. She doubted he would be; he wasn't the type of dragon to give up on her so soon.

With her not-so-full belly of not-so-fresh meat, she cleaned up the area with a high-temperature blast of flame, puffing the ashes into a chute that fed them out into the air and spread them out over the forest. After that, she walked through a few more lonely tunnels, knowing them by heart. The room was a large smoothed slab of crystal on one end, a magical altar covered in runes in the center. She fumbled through her bag with her talons, careful not to tear her dress within it, far less clumsy than she was in a human body. She brought out a golden coin, placed it into the altar, and set it aflame. The gold turned molten and formed a pool in the center.

She let out a low growl, speaking her cousin's name into the altar. It seemed to grab the words from her maw, and the molten gold burst into a green flame. An image of another similar altar formed on the slab, this room sandstone instead of gray, with a yellow archway at the back. Grith squinted and stared at the slab before letting out a roar, with no meaning other than to be loud enough it would be heard.

The snout of another dragon poked into the archway, flapping his wings as he stumbled in. Pret, Grith's cousin through her mother, looked remarkably similar to her; the dragon had almost exactly the same serpentine body shape, and if one could see only in black and white, they'd look practically indistinguishable but for the two small horns poking out from the back of Pret's head on either side of his crest, one of the few visible differences between male and female Southern dragons. Dragons could see colors, however, and while Grith's plumage was the excited shimmering gold of the sun, Pret was the silvery-white of the moon, a quiet and contemplative color that while more uniform was never dull.

Pret trotted over to the altar and sat back on his haunches in front of his own crystal screen, waving a wing hello to Grith and using his teeth to straighten out his tail feathers.

"I didn't wake you, did I?" Grith asked in the Southern language, a small japing trill forming in the back of the throat. The crystal screen communicated her words to Pret almost perfectly, the green flame on the liquid gold rising as it disappeared faster.

Pret jokingly opened his jaws wide as he pretended to yawn, stretching his wings and ruffling to feathers around his eyes. With a toothy grin, he tilted his head to the side and let a forked tongue hang down. "It's funny that you assume I have time to sleep. No, just counting coins." Grith knew that didn't mean he'd actually been counting coins; it was just some droll task that he didn't care for. "You're back later than I thought. Did you run into trouble?"

"More like trouble almost ran into me," she responded. "There is a lot I need to learn about the human city, and I was very close to getting a tough lesson from a car."

Pret flinched, his wings tensing up as they folded tight against his sides. She hoped that he didn't feel guilty — it hadn't been *his* job to safely show her around. Unlike Grith, Pret's parents had exposed him far more to the human world as a hatchling, and he was very familiar with it. He'd tried to get Grith to make human friends over cyberspace, but she'd never been interested.

"Well, I'm glad you're safe," Pret replied. "Although, I dare to wonder what would have happened to the car had your shiftstone lapsed or been broken. How was your first day at Vertex?"

Grith shifted, her tail whipping as she lowered her head. "I'm . . . not sure. My work itself seems interesting, or that it could perhaps become interesting at some point, but the employees are almost all wizards like you warned. I thought that I was going to fit in well — wizards are somewhat magical creatures themselves, after all, and I'm as interested in magic as the rest of them — but they don't seem accustomed to having dragons around."

"Not many magical communities are," Pret responded, tilting his head. "It's unfortunate that most of us prefer to stay among our own kind. But some adapt better than others. Did something in particular happen?"

Grith tilted her head to the left, averting her eyes for a moment. "Not in particular. It was in some ways a lot, and in some ways nothing big. The shiftstone. I didn't realize how hard it would be to control it in public rather than just at home, or attempt to navigate a human body. I should have practiced more; I can't figure out how to make it work right. I tried hard to keep my human form intact, but it keeps lapsing, and everyone seems startled or scared. Apparently I'm disrupting the workplace."

Pret snorted, and Grith could tell from a few wisps of smoke, barely visible on the crystal, that he was angry. Still, his voice didn't show it. "They probably should stop being so easily disrupted, then. I'm sorry that your first day was as bad as it was. Maybe they'll get more used to having you around, and you won't have to use the shiftstone in there as much? There are size limitations, of course, and remaining hidden in mundane areas, but there aren't many other good reasons to keep you wearing it."

"Maybe," Grith said, an unhappy rumble in her throat. At least from her first impression of Paul, it didn't seem like they would be changing their rules anytime soon. Maybe she was just too much of a burden on them.

"Did you end up checking out the Key?" Pret asked as he tilted his head, trying to read Grith's expressions on the crystal screen. "I think they might be helpful in dealing with situations like this."

Grith clicked her tongue affirmatively. "I did. I don't think I could have made it through the day without going there. Ashley was very helpful in stabilizing my form."

Pret's ears tilted in relief, and the sides of his mouth lifted, though not enough to show his fangs. "I'm glad," he replied. "Ashley's father is a human scholar, non-magical himself, but well-acquainted with the magical world. He's an old friend of mine and your mother. The Key is a good place; you should always be safe there no matter what, and if you encounter any trouble in Vertex, the Key can help you."

Grith recalled Chris's words. "My coworker said that it was dangerous, and that they'll let anyone in." She decided not to say the specific phrase Chris had used.

Pret's eyes narrowed, and he let up another puff of smoke. "In that case, he doesn't know much about the place. Likely just repeating whatever his superiors or friends heard about it. I can assure you that not everyone is allowed in, certain Vertex wizards included in that category." He paused for a moment, ruffling his feathers. "Do you know anything about the Fair Folk?"

"The Fair Folk?" Grith cocked her head, wondering why Pret had suddenly switched the subject like that. He was odd like that sometimes, though he normally had a good reason for everything he did. "A little. They've come up in some of the books I've read. Grandfather looked to them when creating some of his magic."

"That's true," Pret clicked, "but there's far more to them than just that. You might consider them living manifestations of the magic in a land and the beings that live there."

"Land? Like a forest?"

"More than just a forest. They can be rivers, mountains, deserts, or even cities. The Fair Folk are called plenty of different names in English, depending on who you talk to — elves, nymphs, kami, nature spirits, and even local gods — but mostly just fae nowadays. LA's actually got one. He's actually a famous actor who seems to bring misfortune to those around him. Wouldn't recommend meeting him; not a nice guy."

"Okay," Grith responded. "Why are you telling me this?" She didn't suspect she'd get a straight answer.

"Oh, no reason," Pret replied, giving her the faintest toothy smirk. "There are a couple of fae who live at the Key. Not local to the area; they were . . . relocated. I thought you might want to meet them."

"Well, thank you for the advice," Grith replied, bowing her head. She had absolutely no idea why Pret wanted her to meet them, but she always took his advice seriously. It hadn't failed her before.

It was difficult to tell the time in the caverns, but Grith knew that it had already been late when she'd gotten home, and that had been some time ago. The flame on the molten gold was already dying out.

"I should probably sleep soon," she said. "The work hours start early."

Pret clicked his tongue. "Just remember that I'm only a short flight away. If you need help, you can visit me anytime you want."

Grith raised her wing to say goodbye, and blew a puff of flame-less air onto the altar. The green fire went out, leaving a much reduced puddle of molten gold, and the image on the crystal faded. She let out a rumble of exhaustion as she turned, walking to her hoard-room.

Coins, metals, and gems covered the rocky floor, and the feel of them soothed her talons as she walked across the unstable surface. The orange torchlight reflected in the shimmer, secondary hues in Grith's feathers changing as she crossed it. In the center of the room it shined off a dragon-sized divot, a comfortable bed lined with fallen feathers. She lowered herself down into it, eagerly resting her head as the magic of the metals lulled her to sleep, the coins rubbing her soft down underbelly. She curled her tail. The day had been exhausting for the young dragon, and she asked the stars that the next one would be less so.

Grith blew out a nearby torch, and the lights in the castle went out, plunging the dragon into darkness. It was only a few moments before she drifted to sleep.

CHAPTER
FIVE

Chris had been at least partially right — using the shiftstone had gotten easier as Grith had gotten more used to wielding a human body. Her second day at Vertex Technologies, she managed to walk from the alleyway to the campus without a single fall, just a slight stumble. She wore the dress she'd bought the previous day, the golden fabric a small reminder of her feathers. Grith's boots stomped through drying puddles of water, and the dragon wiggled her toes in the wetness that crept in from the talon-holes.

Her newfound confidence in bipedal walking carried into the VT campus that day, and she gave a happy trill to the woman cleaning the pathway, who, while confused at the noise, gave her a friendly wave back in response. Even the human employees in the atrium seemed to be more interested in her dress than of the odd stares of fear and anxiety she'd received the day before. One of them even whistled, a sound that Grith didn't know humans could make, nor she was sure the meaning of. She tried to respond in kind, though it ended up coming out as a decidedly non-human warble of dragonsong, the human males taken aback. Oh well.

Still, everyone did seem less nervous around her in general, though she didn't attempt to try the coffee bar again. She wasn't quite sure why. Was it that she'd hidden her shiftstone and was walking less unusually, and they all just thought she was a human now? Or were they starting to become more comfortable with the idea of a dragon at their workplace? She hoped it was the latter.

She'd learned how the elevator had worked, and remembered the floor and location of the lab. When she walked into the blanch white room, Chris was already at one of the computers, typing in numbers from one of the notebooks.

Grith paused, unsure how to greet him. He'd seemed exasperated with her when they'd left previously. Was he still angry? She wasn't sure.

"Good morning," she announced, causing him to sit up, alert. Had he not heard her coming in?

He turned around, wiping his brow before he waved to her. "Morning, Grith! Glad to see you're still here."

Grith wasn't quite sure what that was supposed to mean, but at least he didn't seem angry with her. She was glad to hear that. This was a new day, and hopefully, just the first one had been rough.

"I've just been working on analyzing some of the data we got yesterday," Chris continued. "It's not very nice, and I was estimating some of the largest sources of the error."

"It is probably the quality of the metal plating," Grith answered, not skipping a beat. "I thought about it yesterday. May I taste the plating? I believe I could figure out more."

"Taste it?" Chris frowned, glancing at the door to the

room. "Er, sure, the ring teleporters are still in there. Just don't eat it, okay?"

Grith clicked her tongue. "I will not. I am not feeling shimmer-hungry right now." She walked into the other room, where the two ring teleporters were still hanging from the ceiling. She inched toward them; it seemed like Chris and the rest of Vertex would be very unhappy if she accidentally destroyed one. Once her face was right in front of it, she carefully stuck out her tongue, giving it a lick. As soon as it touched the plating, her tongue changed forms, the curved outside becoming long and forked. She gave it a lick, trying to figure out what exactly was in it.

"It is an osmium-iridium alloy, correct?" Grith asked as she turned back, her tongue retreating into her mouth. "That is not good to begin with, and there are trace amounts of other elements diluting it. Sulfur and carbon are the most prominent by density, though the iron is the one that will affect the magical properties the most. A purer platinum or rhodium would be better if quality and error-reduction is what we are aiming for."

Chris peeked into the room. "Wow. You got all that just from tasting it? It would take forever for me to figure that out. I admit it, we could use a few more dragons around here."

Grith chirred at him, flattered, trying to keep her tail from peeking out and wagging. It didn't work, and the end poked out.

"I might put in a request," Chris continued. "Until then, we need to figure out how much this affected our data.

"We can run another experiment, like the one yesterday," Grith suggested, her tail swishing visibly under her dress, this time in excitement. "Ruby laser, for the base shimmer, but it will need to be infused with more essence."

"We've got one of those," Chris said, bending down to one of the cabinets, rummaging through it until he found the laser, holding it up for Grith to see. He scratched an S-shaped rune on the surface with a fingernail, glowing a bright yellow. "I'll start with one power rune, and we can move up to five?"

Grith happily patted her hands on a desk, like she was stamping her paws. "That will work." Metals and gemstones were at the base of draconic magic, empowering and focusing, and they were just as important in the hybrid form that her grandfather had created.

As Chris set the experiment back up, Grith gathered the typewriter, pointing her two index fingers in preparation for using it. She crouched into a squat as Chris started up the teleportation rings, slowly typing a couple words using just those two fingers, notes about the devices they were using and the purpose of these measurements.

"I believe that it is becoming easier for me to use human fingers," Grith remarked, strutting her index fingers around the typewriter keys.

"That's great! Did you manage to get rid of the feathers on your belly?"

"I did," Grith said. She lifted her dress up above her head to show him. "Now there is only flabby, featherless human skin beneath. It is very gross, like I have been plucked. It is odd that humans lost almost all their fur!"

Chris's face went red, and his eyes went wide before he averted them. "Y-you can't do that!" he stammered, glancing back to Grith, who hadn't bothered to put the dress back down yet.

"Do what?" Grith asked, dropping it as she returned to the typewriter, cocking her head. "You told me that I was not supposed to have feathers. Should I attempt to return them?"

"Not that!" Chris grimaced. "Human women can't show off their chest like that! Your legs, too! You're supposed to have . . . you know . . ."

"And presumably, human men do not need to worry about that?" Grith questioned him. "It would be far less distracting for me if I didn't wear this fabric."

"Well, it would be more distracting for me!" Chris exclaimed, getting a confused look from Grith. "I'd be staring at you the entire day!"

Grith let out an amused garble resembling a laugh. "At my skin? Do humans find skin that interesting? But it covers so much of your bodies! If dragons were turned on just by seeing feathers, no one would ever catch a meal! How did you conquer the planet like *that*?"

"Not *just* skin," Chris responded, taking in a deep breath. "I can't help it, your entire body looks good."

Grith squinted, unsure what Chris was trying to imply. "It is not mine. It was just created by the shiftstone. It does not look good either. The human form is quite ugly."

Chris shook his head. "Maybe. But I think yours is pretty sexy."

Grith felt her fingers clench up as she translated the last word, and finally understood what Chris was trying to communicate and had been trying to communicate the day earlier. She felt her tail wrap over her legs, hiding them with feathers in her discomfort. "No," she growled. "I am not interested in human courtship, and I am especially not interested in yours. My interest in your species is at most academic in nature." She let herself puff smoke and flashed a few fangs, just to make the point clear to him.

"I was just being nice," Chris replied, his face drooping

as he looked away. "Come on. Let's continue the experiment."

The two took their measurements in silence, except for the occasional calling out of a number by Chris, their sentences limited to terse statements. Still, it wasn't long before Grith had tucked the incident away in the back of her mind. She didn't know how humans courted, and maybe she'd accidentally signaled her interest to him at some point. Besides, she didn't particularly care that a human had expressed interest in her human body, no more than she would care if a deer had. Except, this human she was supposed to follow commands from, and deer generally didn't hold that power over her.

Afterward, the two went down to the lunchroom, Chris carefully keeping his distance in the elevator. At least she'd managed to communicate her disinterest to him. Grith herself wasn't particularly interested in attempting to eat in this form, but she knew she'd have to do it at some point — the food she consumed as a dragon didn't end up filling this body, as she'd learned from a gurgling stomach.

The lunchroom itself was a vast chamber of the same blinding white as the rest of Vertex Technologies, with the additional complication of how *busy* it was. A sea of humans seemed to crash from side to side of it, filling numerous tables. Their chattering was as loud as a dragon's roar, though it was instead a constant drone of unintelligible phrases. The smells alone were the strongest she'd been able to sense in this body up to this point, with various pungent foods and human scents confusing her. They were nothing like the smells she was used to as a dragons, and trying to compare the two made her head hurt. She clutched her fingers into her scalp, tearing out strands of hair.

"Are you all right?" Chris asked, unsure what she was doing.

"I am not all right. This place hurts and it makes me feel nauseous."

A hint of alarm came over Chris's face at that last word. "Do you think you're going to throw up? There's a restroom nearby, and I can take you there."

"I do not know." Grith stared at the floor, the distance from her head to it not right, making her even more dizzy. She decided instead to close her eyes for a moment, holding her breath. "I think . . . I think that I am feeling a little bit better. I will attempt to eat now." Grith opened her eyes again and carefully started to walk through the crowd, the puffiness of her gown making it difficult for her to get through. She stumbled around, stretching out her arms as she tried to judge the distances right, the size of her body far too small. Normally, she'd be running into all the humans here had she walked like this, though she supposed that they would have likely given her a wider berth.

Her gaze eventually made it to a buffet station, and she smelled the familiar roasting of meat. Walking around an odd line of humans, she grabbed the rarest piece of food she could find off a small platter, holding it in her hands as it dripped red onto her dress.

Chris apologized to the humans behind her before he caught up and directed her to a table.

Standing at the side of the table, Grith brought the piece of steak up to her mouth. She tore into it with her teeth, attempting to rip off strips like she normally would have.

Chris jumped back as juices splattered, making sure it didn't get on his suit.

Grith caught his eyes as she tilted her head and ripped off a huge chunk, swallowing it down.

He shivered. "That's not how humans eat." He held up a fork and knife, and put a plate and napkin down at the table. "See, you're getting blood on your dress."

Grith looked down. She didn't mind; she thought that the red spots added flavor. "It is not blood," she corrected Chris. "I have tasted fresh blood before and it is not this. This is a juice. Unless humans drink blood like juice?"

"Um, nope." Chris chuckled. "We don't. No blood juice boxes unless you're a vampire. Wait, do dragons drink blood?"

Grith cocked her head, considering the statement. "We do not, unless it is within a fresh kill. Although, my mother occasionally made potions with blood when I was feeling ill." There was a pang of nostalgia at that memory.

Chris gestured again, and Grith slapped the meat down on the plate with a sigh, resting her knees on the chair.

"Instead of using your hands to grab it, you have to use your silverware," he said, handing them over to her. "Cut it into small chunks, with them. You're sitting . . . nevermind, we'll work on that later."

Grith focused her eyes on the steak as she wrapped a fist around the silverware, and stabbed the fork and the knife into the meat. She pulled them apart, attempting to use them like how she'd tear her talons into flesh. It didn't work very well.

"You'll get better." Chris winced. "Just keep practicing. Now, take your fork, that's the one with the prongs, bring a chunk of meat to your mouth, and put it in."

Grith stared at him skeptically, before picking up a small sliver of meat that she'd managed to separate from the rest with the fork. She brought it up to her mouth, before chomping down on the fork and meat alike. "Not silver," she grumbled. "It tastes bad and it hurts when I bite it. Why would I eat it?"

Chris put his hands to his face. "You don't eat the silverware! It's to pick up your food, to keep your hands and face from getting too dirty."

Grith snorted. She thought that was silly, like so much else around here. She wondered if this was just Vertex Technologies, or if all humans behaved like this. Ignoring Chris's complaints, she dug into the steak again with her fingernails, biting into it and swallowing the pieces she tore off down. She decided that human fangs and claws weren't very useful.

She looked up at Chris, who seemed a bit too grossed out at her own eating style to get any food for himself. She tried to bring the steak towards him, wondering if he wanted any. He backed away. His loss. She found it somewhat amusing: though she *certainly* hadn't intended it as such, just a kindly gesture, it could have been interpreted as courtship if she'd shared a meal like that with another dragon.

She finished gobbling up her meal, licking her tongue around her lips to clean it. An uncomfortable feeling in her stomach made her realize she was full. She wouldn't have expected it from such a small meal. She was learning so much about humans.

"Is the break over yet?" Grith asked. Now that she was no longer focused on eating, the turmoil of the lunchroom was getting to her again. Part of her still felt like she should eat more, full as she was. A big meal normally would last a dragon a while, but she'd heard that humans ate three times a day. That seemed very inconvenient. "Are you planning on eating?"

"I'll pass." Chris winced, staring down at the mess around Grith's seat.

She followed his eyes to it. "Oh, I can clean it," she said, taking in a deep breath as smoke rose from her nose.

"NO!" Chris squealed, diving under the table. "Not here!"

Grith chortled, a rumble of laughter scratching her human throat as the smoke faded. "Do not worry! I know very well that much of this room is flammable, you included. I am not even sure I could breathe fire with the shiftstone. How should I clean it?"

Chris stared at her. He grimaced and tried to force a bit of laughter out. "I-it's fine. Someone will do it for us."

Grith wasn't quite sure what that was supposed to mean, or why anyone who wasn't her parents would clean up her mess for her, but her head was starting to hurt. She turned, focusing her eyes on the doorway before standing up and walking toward it, Chris following. It felt like navigating a storm, little but her 'blood-stained' dress keeping the humans from running into her, forcing them to weave around them as she made her way to the exit. She started to feel her vision go blurry, and she squinted, trying to focus.

"Oh, hey, guys," Chris said, and Grith noticed a half-dozen humans that she couldn't distinguish from Chris blocking her path. "Sorry I couldn't make it to the bar last night. We were actually there, but we left a little early. Shopping."

One of the humans chuckled as he gave the stain on her dress a look, not raising his eyes to meet hers.

Grith didn't mind. It startled her when the humans did that, like they were about to attack her.

"Who's the new girl? She yours?"

"Not in the way you'd think!" Chris laughed. "She's a

new employee. I've just been showing her around, explaining how things work here."

"Lucky," another remarked, Grith unsure where exactly the voice was coming from, barely able to make out the words. "She's a real eye-catcher." He laughed, and a hand slapped her butt.

The shiftstone went dark.

A moment later, yells and screams filled the lunchroom, the sound an intense pressure on Grith's ears like the wildest wind. Her wings were spread wide, knocking away any close humans. Before she knew what had happened, she was acting fully by instinct, on all fours, talons clenched into the stone. Her tail whipped as her nostrils opened wide, the scents of everything in the room over-whelming.

What was going on? Why were there odd lights? Where was she and why was she surrounded by a herd of prey? She growled, attempting to reorient herself, but she couldn't figure it out. Everything was confusing, and very little here made sense. But more than anything, she smelt prey. There were animals all around her, just waiting to be hunted. Their fear-scent was intoxicating.

The metallic tang of warm blood caressed her tongue, and she felt flesh in her jaws. Right in front of her was a huge mass of fear-scent mixed with human urine. She dragged her tongue across the flesh, letting the blood dribble down it. It tasted good. She wanted a fresh kill.

Her eyes opened to see a human on the floor beneath her snout, his arm raised. Grith tugged her snout a little to realize that the meat in her maw was attached to the arm, her jaws clenched around a hand. Her fangs pierced the skin, their sharp tips sunken in just enough that blood pooled up from it. If she snapped, it would be hers.

Golden slits stared into the human's eyes. The fear-scent coming off him was so strong she could barely think. He wasn't moving. Why? Prey normally tried to run from her. She remembered that she had his hand caught between her teeth. That and the fear might have done it. She licked it again. Was it right for her to eat the hand? If she ate the rest of him, she thought that would be far more filling.

A blue glow in the air caught her attention, drawing it away from the hand. A human that she thought she recognized had drawn a rune in the air, fingers trembling as he hesitated to cast it. Grith's eyes glowed brighter as she registered what he planned to do, and she heard a faint ticking in her head. She knew a spell that would counter it, one that she'd practiced over and over again until it was as natural as flying. It would take only the smallest bit of thought and effort to cast it. Then, she and the prey in front of her would be alone.

Grith's bewilderment cleared as her eyes glowed, magic permeating her body and mind. She looked down at the human again, wondering why she hadn't eaten him already. There had to have been a good reason, but she wasn't quite sure what. Oh, right. She was in a building full of extremely powerful wizards, and eating humans was illegal. Even if the blood was *very* tasty, and she had been wanting a fresh kill. She could just take the hand, right? He wouldn't mind; he had basically given it to her to begin with. He probably didn't deserve it if he went around whacking dragons' rumps with it. Someone else would eat it if she didn't.

Still, a hand wasn't very much. It wouldn't be worth the trouble. Grith wasn't quite sure why she'd ever thought that would be a good idea in the first place or why she was biting down on the skin. She was in the middle of a work-place and an employee there; that probably wasn't something that would endear everyone else to her. She opened her jaws, and instead let out a furious roar, blood and spittle spraying in his face as she brought her fangs to a few inches away from it. She heard the shatter of glass, the smell of urine in front of her growing stronger.

Then, she stopped and brought her head away, folding her wings back.

The human didn't move, tears running down his face. Grith didn't think she'd made that much smoke. Finally, he let out a cry, and scrambled away, and Grith sat back on her haunches with a snort.

"That was very rude of him," she growled to Chris, her English coming through as barely intelligible rumbles.

Chris didn't respond, trembling in terror at Grith's jaws, now looming over him.

She squinted at the rune he'd drawn in the air, not yet activated, and breathed a puff of air onto it, causing the colors to fade. "I did not eat him. I am certainly not going to eat you," she explained, her snout twitching at the fear-scent. "I ate last night, and I do not eat humans. Or wizards." Although, she'd just come *very* close. He shouldn't have surprised her like that. Surprising a dragon out of a shiftstone was a very stupid thing to do.

By now, the screams had stopped and the entire room was frozen, staring at Grith. She had to duck her head so that the top of it didn't hit the ceiling; even a younger dragon was taller than all of them. She folded her wings in, not quite sure why the humans weren't going back to their business. She *hadn't* eaten him; they didn't all have to smell so scared. They weren't even working, so she couldn't have disrupted the workplace.

The sound of footsteps caught her attention, and another human she thought was familiar walked forward. She recognized him by the golden signet ring and gave him a sniff, only sensing the faintest tingle of fear-scent. "Hello, Paul."

Paul gave her a disapproving glance as he looked into her eyes, not the least bit intimidated by the fangs in front of him. He turned his back on her and waved a hand to the rest of the lunchroom. "Everyone, please! Resume your lunches! There's no problem here, just a minor mishap."

Grith agreed with him, for once. She flicked her tail, happy that someone was on her side and not terrified of her.

Paul sighed. "Grith. Your shiftstone."

Grith blinked. She'd forgotten about that. She flicked her claw against it, and the light came back on. Her wings and tail shrunk into her body, her neck retreating along with her feathers. She ended up on her hands and knees, on top of a thoroughly ripped and flattened dress. Oh well. Human clothing didn't seem to last long.

A feeling of shock instantly came over her, her muscles tensing up and heart racing. She was afraid, but wasn't sure why. Was it because another human had been hurt? Did human emotions pass between each other? It wasn't just fear, but concern for the injured human as well, and even anger at the one who had hurt him. Which was herself. Why did the shiftstone have to make everything so confusing?

Grith rose to her feet, nakedly staring Paul in the eyes.

A few of the human wizards nervously looked at her, though none with any hint of lust in their eyes.

Paul looked down at her feet. "Clothes on."

"Er," Grith replied, stepping off the torn garment and

picking it up. She draped what was left of it over her body. "Is this considered 'on?'"

"No," Paul responded. He raised a finger and drew five runes in the air, whispering a few words as they flew onto the dress. It mended itself, Grith unable to help but growl at the feeling of someone else's magic being used on her.

The dress tightened around her body. Grith turned uncomfortably.

"Thank you," Grith said to him after it was done, getting only a grimace in return.

She tried sniffing him again, but couldn't tell his emotions. Maybe was he happy?

"We need to have a talk," he ordered. "In my office."

Grith didn't think that was a happy thing to say. As she followed him out of the lunchroom, she passed Chris, his eyes still wide open as he stared at her. She cocked her head. "I said that I was not going to eat you. Humans smell odd and do not taste as good as deer."

Paul didn't say a word as Grith stumbled after him toward the elevator, the few people in the atrium going silent and bowing as he passed.

Grith decided that she wouldn't attempt to bow. She tried to smell Paul's mood again, but didn't get anything.

When they entered the elevator, Paul pressed the highest up button and they rose.

Grith stared down at the ground falling under them, resisting the urge to flap her wings. More and more, she was getting the sense that Paul was unhappy with her. The human was absolutely silent, his eyes focused on the concrete tree.

There was a ding, and the elevator doors opened out into the top floor of the building. Grith couldn't help but gape at the room they exited into, and wondered if Paul really was a king. Gold lined the walls of the office, paintings of humans that Grith didn't recognize displayed prominently. Unlike the rest of the building, the white light didn't appear to permeate here, and Grith raised her head into natural sunlight, basking in the calming glow of it. A few feathers on her skin fluttered, before a glare from Paul reminded Grith that she wasn't supposed to do that.

A spectacled human woman sitting at a desk gave the two a nod as she wrote on a piece of parchment with a quill, dipping it in ink. Grith twitched her tail in annoyance. They had ink here, and they had made her use a pen she could barely hold, instead? The two walked past her, and Grith looked up to see an azure glass ceiling, water held above it. She licked her lips as she saw a school of colorful fish swim over her, followed by a strangely human-like creature. A nude merman or mermaid, Grith wasn't sure how to tell the difference, with gnarled, black hair flowing from their head, their fish-like tail pushing water aside. She wondered how they would taste: like a human or like a fish? Maybe the upper half tasted like human, and the lower like fish. What was a merperson doing in a water tank? That seemed illegal. Did *Paul* eat them? That seemed *very* illegal.

"Sit," Paul commanded. He walked behind a huge mahogany desk and rested on a golden chair that seemed more like a throne. Open blinds behind him let the natural light in, and Grith peered through them to see a view of the city. More skyscrapers rose up, and she caught a glimpse of cars on highways in the background. The aquarium was weird, but she understood why Paul had chosen the highest office in the building for his lair.

Grith squatted on the less-impressive wooden chair on the other side of the desk. Though the seat of it was about a foot lower than that of Paul's chair, her position, with her feet on the seat and her hands grabbing Paul's desk, kept her eyes level with his. "Did I do something wrong?"

"Yes," Paul stated, rapping his knuckles on his desk. "You did. You shouldn't have shown your dragon shape. You shouldn't have bit an employee. And you *especially* shouldn't have roared."

"I did not hurt him or anything," Grith protested. She couldn't see what the problem was, she hadn't even bit off his hand. "It was just a couple of fang-marks. Is biting each other not normal for humans? If you would like for me to heal them, I will lick his hand. And the roar was just a warning. Just like what humans do when they get angry when someone does something bad. You . . . yell?"

"Wizard, not human," Paul corrected her. "And it's not the same at all. You threatened him. You scared him."

Grith kept her tail from flicking in irritation. "It is not my fault he was scared of me. He is a wizard, yes? He is not powerless or mundane. He should not have touched my rump. I cannot keep my shiftstone from lapsing if I'm touched, *especially* not in places like that."

Her family had warned her that a lapsed shiftstone could be dangerous, and not just because it exposed her true form. It took a few moments for the shimmer within a dragon's body to spread out after changing back, and those moments affected them immensely. Even non-mage dragons were magical by nature; their bodies and brains required shimmer to function. Fire-breath, flight, and complex thought all needed it.

Dragons who'd been without a hoard for too long were struck with 'shimmer-sickness'; their bodies became weak, their minds addled. First, they stopped being able to fly or breathe fire. Then turned ravenous and desperate, dangerous to all around them. There were stories of them recklessly charging into old human cities searching for any sort of refined metal, even attempting to eat metals such as iron that took more shimmer to consume than they gave. Since both lack of shimmer and of food caused hunger in dragons, shimmer-sick dragons sought out any sort of nutrition in addition to metals; carrion, plants, and dung were some common ones.

As shimmer-sickness progressed, they became unable to speak or think clearly. Oftentimes they would accidentally kill themselves in various ways, such as overeating, consuming something poisonous, or attempting to eat a metal that they were unable to melt down. Sometimes they would attempt to fly but be unable to. Since other dragons contained both meat and shimmer in their bodies, they would even hunt out their own kind. A feeble shimmer-sick dragon couldn't put up a fight against any adult, but there were horror stories about shimmer-sick dragons going after hatchlings, although Grith suspected it was just a way for adolescents to frighten their younger siblings (or cousins in Grith's case).

If a shimmer-sick dragon managed to survive all that, then their fate afterward was worse. Their body would collapse under its own weight, and the dragon would slowly die as their organs failed, their mind reduced to nothing but pure instinct. It wasn't a kind fate, but all dragon mages were more than familiar with it. While flying or breathing fire couldn't do it normally, using powerful magic could cause a dragon's shimmer to deplete all at once. It wouldn't kill them right away, as dragons could survive on the essence given to them by Terra's aura for an amount of time, but many of the symptoms would appear. Grith had learned this the hard way when she'd been a hatchling, which was why she always kept spare shimmer on her, such as the gold coins in her bag.

This was why a lapsed shiftstone was so dangerous. The sudden addition of instincts that the shiftstone had previously suppressed combined with an addled mind could cause a dragon to do things they might have consciously decided not to do, and the overwhelmingness of her surroundings and stronger senses hadn't helped Grith with that.

Grith wanted to explain this to Paul, but she suspected that he wouldn't care.

"I'll have the employee in to talk about unwanted physical contact with other employees, but you got to choose your human form and dress," Paul said, frowning. "Maybe it would have been better if you'd chosen one less conventionally attractive."

"Maybe he should have not given into his sex-drive instinct and touched me," Grith growled, baring her teeth, leaning forward until her torso was over the desk, keeping her eyes locked with Paul's. "*My* instinct was to eat him. I chose not to. Are all humans slaves to their desires?"

"The weaker, more human, of the wizards can be," Paul answered. "Our ability to reduce our instincts and emotions is what separates a great wizard from a lesser wizard, a lesser wizard from a human, and a human from an animal. It's what makes us better than them." He gave the snarling Grith a quizzical look, like he was unsure what category to place her in.

Was that why Paul hadn't had any fear-scent on him? She thought that the whole theory was a load of dung. Her instincts were useful and a part of her. She ignored them when they needed to be ignored, and followed them when they needed to be followed. She wouldn't deny her own nature, as much as Paul seemed to want her to do.

Paul clutched his head, shaking it as he sighed. "All right. I'm just going to give you a warning this time for what happened in the lunchroom. You're new to VT and decent magical society. But I expect you to control yourself in the future, even if someone accidentally bumps you again."

Grith tried to tell him that it wasn't an accident before holding her tongue. She was pretty sure Paul already knew that, and talking back to him would just make things worse. She needed the shimmer from this job, and as emotionless as he was, she wasn't sure how many more chances she'd get from him. Still, if that human was dumb enough to touch her again, she wasn't sure she'd be able to resist snapping off at least a finger or two.

"Thank you for giving me another chance," Grith grumbled.

Paul gestured her up, and she walked away from the office, the merperson staring at her as she waited by the elevator.

She stepped into it when it arrived. One of her fingers hesitated over the button for the ground floor. She just wanted to go home after this, to turn away from the human world forever. But that wasn't an option, and she didn't think Paul would like it if she left work early. Instead, she pressed the button for the floor of her lab.

Chris tensed up as she entered it, already at work.

"He did not fire me, if that is what you were wondering," Grith said.

"I-I'm glad," Chris replied, forcing a smile. He put his hands behind his back, where she couldn't see them, or more likely, couldn't bite at them. Well, she still could, she'd just have to go through the rest of him first.

"I'm sorry about what happened back in the lunchroom. That wasn't right. Touching a girl like that is bestial, not something that anyone in respectable society should do. I wouldn't ever touch you like that without asking you first."

Grith glanced at the small bandages on his hand, covering where she'd scratched him the day before. She wondered if not touching her was out of fear, or out of respect. Well, she was glad for the apology, at least.

"What will happen to the human who touched me?" Grith asked. Paul had said that he would talk to him.

"He's not severely hurt, thank God," Chris replied. "It was just his hand, and even mundane healing could fix that." He paused. "Wait, are you asking if he'll be punished? Probably not. I guess you could go to HR. WR? Are dragons included in human resources? I wouldn't though, it's a long process, and probably not worth the effort for something so small. He's a good person and didn't mean to hurt you. And you didn't mean to hurt him either, right? You were just surprised, like when you scratched me."

Grith couldn't say that she hadn't been tempted. There'd been a bit more than just instinct in her hesitation to drop his hand.

"Plus, if you go to HR, you could get in more trouble yourself," Chris continued, thinking about it. "You threatened violence against him."

"I did not," Grith explained. "I let him go and roared. It was a warning. If I had wanted to do violence against him, I would not have let him go."

Chris didn't seem convinced. "Maybe you didn't mean it that way, but it sounded like a threat. Roaring isn't really workplace appropriate. It doesn't have a place in respectable society."

Grith didn't particularly care about being respectable or workplace appropriate. She let out a mix between a grumble and a sigh. "Fine," she rumbled. "I'll make sure not to roar next time."

CHAPTER
SIX

That evening, Grith dragged her boots as she walked into the Key, head lowered. She wasn't sure if it was in shame, anger, or a bit of both. The rest of the day at VT had gone better than the morning, and they'd finished the calculations, making some progress. Not that the dragon's mind had really been on her work.

The Key itself was somewhat busier than it had been the morning of the day before, filled with a low hum of conversation, and not just human tongues. Still, Grith was hardly paying attention when she stepped into the lavender-scented room. She slumped down onto an empty area, rocking the chair up onto two legs as she laid her face across the table, wondering how far she could go before it fell.

She lifted her head at movement, annoyed that she had to move it instead of just rolling her eyes.

Ashley stood above her.

"Hey, Grith," Ashley said, turning the corners of her lips into a smile.

Grith let out a rumble, a sad attempt at a hello.

"I'm glad you came back," Ashley replied. "Are you all right? How are things?"

Grith puffed smoke, coughing as it reached her eyes and went back up her throat. She let out another grumble. "I do not know. I am happy that I did not get fired." She tilted her head. "Can I get a drink, please? One of the ones with alcohol in it."

"Er, sure," Ashley said. "Just like, anything with alcohol?"

"Anything," Grith rumbled. "I do not care."

"This isn't exactly a legal venue, so I'm not gonna ask for ID." Ashley chuckled. "You're the same age as Pret, right? Mid-thirties? So, what, twenty-three in human years?"

"I suppose."

Ashley went behind the counter and poured the contents of a couple bottles into a hard crystal glass, widened at the top. As Ashley placed the glass down on the table, Grith pressed her face over the opening, the fragrant liquor drowning out anything else her human nose could smell. She pursed her lips and stuck out her tongue, trying to lap it up. When that didn't work, Grith sucked in air and tilted the glass back, pouring the drink down her throat, burning like fire.

Grith held her head back for a while, staring at the crystal glass on her face as she stuck her tongue out again, licking the edges. Feathers poked out from her cheeks and around her eyes, her face covered in their golden color. She looked at the wooden ceiling, her attention drawn to a knot in a beam.

"You can take off your shiftstone if you want," Ashley suggested. "You don't have to wear it as long as you're in here."

Grith thought that she would like that. It would make it all the harder to put it back on when she left for home, but she didn't particularly care. That was a problem for her future self. Perhaps she could just use her invisibility. It was risky, but Grith couldn't care less at the moment.

She moved her hand to her neck, about to take it off before remembering the cup. It wouldn't feel good If it shattered. She slammed it down on the table and reached for the shiftstone again, before letting out another low grumble, her ears trying to droop. "I cannot. My clothes."

"We have rooms in the back if you want to take them off, but nudity is allowed here, human or not," Ashley explained. "If anyone behaves creepy, they won't be around here for long."

Grith was glad for that. Chris had been trying to teach her that humans weren't allowed to be nude, but dragons had no such rules nor shame. Grith thought that it would've been far more odd for a dragon to wear them. Still, she had another, more important reason for not wanting to take off the shiftstone.

"I do not know what will happen if I take it off," Grith whimpered. "I am afraid that I will hurt someone. I will be prepared, but it makes me confused and dangerous. What if I hurt someone?"

"We've got protections," Ashley assured. "If something happens, you'll be forgiven."

Grith moved her eyes back to the glass. What if she attacked Ashley? What if she lost control of herself again? The feeling of how powerless she was to stop herself had been awful. Still, she was out of excuses, and she badly wanted the stars-cursed thing off.

"Then be prepared to forgive me."

None of the other patrons even noticed as Grith

stripped, though Ashley averted her eyes. Finally, Grith stepped back from the table, and removed the shiftstone, changing back into a dragon for the second time that day, this time intentionally. When it was done, she had to bend her head down to keep her head from whacking the ceiling, the area of the Key quite cramped. Smells that she hadn't even smelt before filled her head, types of prey that she hadn't ever before tasted. She didn't act on the urges; the previous time had prepared her for the sudden hunting instinct to make itself reknown.

Grith let out a long breath of relief as her magic fully returned to her. Nothing had happened. She'd gotten through this without hurting anyone. It hadn't been as hard as she'd thought it would, maybe because this time she'd been expecting it.

Now that she had taken the shiftstone off, the other patrons *were* staring.

"Maybe this was a bad idea," Grith rumbled in English, looking down at the shiftstone in her talons, remembering how the wizards had reacted after the lunchroom incident. She started bringing it back towards her snout.

"You don't have to; you're safe here," Ashley reminded, far smaller than Grith remembered her being.

Grith realized that before today, she'd never been up against a live human while not using the shiftstone. With her head far clearer than it was earlier, they seemed so small. Grith could have fit Ashley's entire head in her mouth had she wanted to. Which she gladly didn't.

"Sorry about their stares," Ashley continued, glaring at a few of the other patrons.

They looked away and went back to whatever they'd been doing.

"Most haven't seen a dragon before. They're just a little

curious, but they *shouldn't* be so rude. Come on, lets go to one of the larger booths."

Grith followed Ashley further to the side of the building, where the ceiling became higher and the tables and chairs larger, and moved toward one of the tables. She had little desire to use a chair, so just sat back on her haunches. Grith craned her head down and gave Ashley a sniff, taking in the human's scent, hidden behind by a variety of plants and herbs. It was far harder to distinguish humans than it was dragons, though still easier than by sight. Mostly, they all just smelled like prey. Maybe that was part of the reason why dragons avoided interacting with humans or other magical creatures much.

Ashley didn't seem at all afraid, looking back at Grith's snout while careful not to stare too closely into her eyes. She held out a hand, and Grith poked her nose into the back of it, feathers brushing Ashley's skin. Only the smallest bit of fear-scent rose from it.

Ashley surprised Grith. At VT, the dragon had terrified all of the humans other than Paul. Grith decided he might have been partially right about some wizards not being quite human, albeit in a far different way than dragons were. Ashley instead almost seemed to be admiring her, not in the same lustful way as the human men had stared, or the ravenous curiosity in which Grith admired the spilt guts of prey, but like how one might admire a sunset.

"You are used to seeing dragons?" Grith asked, the words unnaturally rumbling up in her throat. Even if she had learned English without the shiftstone, the vocalizations were still unnatural to her. "You do not seem scared or curious."

"Just Pret," Ashley replied with a smile.

Grith trilled as she lifted her head. "He is very friendly to humans."

"I was wondering why you looked so familiar." Ashley laughed. "I think I met his brother as well, but it was a long time ago, so I don't remember him well. What was his name? Eris?"

"Oh." Grith rumbled. "Arit. He is not very friendly to humans. I have not seen him in a long time as well. "

"Huh." Ashley glanced over at the crystal cup. "Do you want me to get you something more dragon-sized?"

Grith purred affirmatively, getting a quizzical look from Ashley before the dragon bobbed her head up and down.

Ashley went back behind the bar, pouring a few more bottles into a large pottery bowl, shimmering gold running along cracks in its surface. "Want blood? We've got pig, cow, and human, all ethically and legally sourced. Type AB on the last, in case that matters. Not warm or fresh, sorry."

"I will pass," Grith replied, ears drooping. She'd had enough of the taste of blood for today. It seemed like an odd thing to drink as well without being with meat.

Ashley brought the drink over to Grith.

The dragon peered her head over it, giving a sniff, the scent of fragrant alcohol mixing the gold of the bowl. A clear liquid filled the bowl, with a violet liquor spreading through it like. Grith stirred it with a talon, and it turned blue before she gave it a lap with her tongue. It was odd how well the flavors mixed with the metallic taste of the bowl. She decided that she wanted one of these gold-repaired pottery bowls at home.

Unlike the first one, Grith drank it slowly, which was far easier when she was just lapping it up. Yet as much as she enjoyed it, she remained quiet and solemn. She curled her tail around a hindleg, the feathers on the tip brushing the base of the table.

"You look distressed," Ashley said.

Grith ears were still drooped.

Ashley climbed up on an oversized chair at the table, her legs dangling down from it.

"I am unsure," Grith grumbled. "I think that I am."

Ashley grimaced. "What happened? If you don't mind me asking."

Grith lapped up a bit more of the drink before she responded, the surface of the liquid down to half its original height. She let out a puff of smoke as she curled her tail tighter. "I was touched at Vertex Technologies. I got startled, and accidentally transformed and bit the wizard on his hand. Not hard, just barely enough to break his skin. I roared and scared him. Along with everyone else in the room."

Ashley frowned. "When you say touched, do you mean he just accidentally bumped you? Or did he push you?"

"No," Grith replied, with a growl behind her words. "He touched my rear. Do humans do that normally?"

Ashley stood upright, planting her feet on the floor as she clenched her fists. For the first time, Grith witnessed a human get truly angry. "He did *what*?" Ashley almost yelled, the other patrons in the bar turning toward her. "That's awful, even for a Vertex wizard! If anyone does that to you in here, you're *more* than welcome to roar at them as much as you'd like, and I'll turn a blind eye to any biting either. I hope he got in big trouble for that."

"It does not sound like it." Grith huffed. "The bald man, my boss, was more angry at me for the roaring. I disrupted the workplace again."

Ashley rolled up her sleeves, a few runes and sigils

tattooed on them. "Oh, I'll show them some real disruption! I've got half a mind to go over there right now myself!"

"They have a lot of powerful magic in there," Grith remarked, shaking her head before laying her snout back down on the table. "It would be dangerous to try that."

"They're not the only ones with magic," Ashley glowered.

Grith suspected that Ashley would have filled the room with smoke had she been hatched a dragon. "I'll place a curse on them they won't forget!"

Grith tapped a talon on the table. "Please do not do it. If not for your own safety, I could lose my job if you tried."

Ashley paused and calmed down slightly. She sighed as she got back onto the seat. "Yeah, you're right. Hey, I guess you got to taste pig's blood today." She smirked.

Grith forced a toothy smile. She didn't want to tell Ashley, but she didn't feel particularly good about that, either. She'd almost broken one of the most important rules that dragons held — no killing and eating humans. Her parents would have been ashamed of how close she'd been. If she killed him, her family might have exiled her like Arit had been, not that she had much family left. Though she likely wouldn't have survived the encounter regardless. Even if most of the Vertex wizards didn't seem well-prepared for magical combat, particularly against her own specialty, she doubted she could escape so many of them. Paul in particular had an aura of powerful magic around him that set Grith's feathers upright.

"There are better places to work than Vertex," Ashley suggested again, "even if they don't pay as much."

"I do not know. I do not think so," Grith responded, lapping up the rest of her drink. She put her talons around the rim and pushed it out of the way, giving her more room to lay her snout down. "My job there is what I am good at. I need the income from there, in shimmer, to keep my home's magic stable until my parents return. There are no other options for me."

"I understand," Ashley said, dipping a curious finger into the bowl and giving it a lick, her face scrunching at the flavor. "You're not the first magical creature to run into problems working at Vertex. They expect all non-humans there to behave and look as human as the rest of them, and have little tolerance for anything outside of that. You'd think that a magical technology company would be used to the unusual, but no."

Grith flinched as the human touched the gold, having to resist the urge to bare her fangs.

"Pricks. I think that you should be able to be yourself in all magical communities, as much as possible. The Key was formed on that principle, to accommodate everyone. Here, we want everyone to be free and safe, as much as the two can coexist with each other."

Grith grabbed the bowl with her fangs, nibbling on it. "Thank you," she said as she poked her head against it, causing it to tilt upright, and she gathered the last drops with her tongue, running along the gold. "I am glad that I found this place."

She paused as she remembered something Pret had said, lifting her head up as the bowl rocked back and forth. "I almost forgot," the dragon spoke, "that my cousin suggested that I talk to the fae here."

Ashley frowned. "Like, one in particular? Or just any fae? Why?"

Grith tossed her wings in a shrug. Pret could be unreadable and obtuse at times, but if he'd asked this of her, he probably had a good reason for it. She looked around the

Key, not quite sure what a fae looked or smelt like. "He just asked me to talk."

Ashley followed Grith's gaze, the dragon's head swerving left and right above Ashley's own like a feathered wrecking ball. Ashley pointed to someone sitting in the corner towards the other side of the room. "There are a couple that frequent here, though Holz is the only one who's here right now, weirdly enough. I could introduce you, if you'd like?"

"That would be appreciated," Grith responded, stepping away from the table as she made her way across the room, sticking her tail out as she lowered her head so as not to hit the ceiling with it.

At least to Grith, Holz wouldn't have been distinguishable from a human by sight — the fae looked much like a human of indeterminate age, and not just because Grith couldn't tell it. The features on Holz's face seemed to change as Grith tilted her head, from one perspective appearing as a young girl with a chain of flowers around her head, and the other as an elderly woman with wrinkles. Grith wondered if mundane humans, or even magical humans like Ashley, could see the same effect.

But to Grith, the most interesting thing about the fae was her smell. Unlike creatures of flesh and blood, Holz didn't give off any prey-scent, instead reminding Grith of her home and the forest around it, like dew on the leaves. Grith appreciated that; the more time she'd spent in the human world without the shiftstone, the more she realized how uncomfortable it was talking to someone that her nose wanted to classify as food, hungry or not. Instead, talking to Holz seemed like it would be talking to a tree. Far less awkward.

She picked up another scent beyond the foresty one and

alcohol, slightly more surprising. A type of magic not that unlike her own, but innate rather than learned.

The fae didn't look up until Grith was a tail-length away from her, the dragon moving almost silently for such a large creature. When Holz caught the dragon's scent, a smokey and animalistic smell not difficult for even a human nose to sense, her eyes went wide, and she turned to the fangs looming down over her.

With a squeak of alarm, the fae disappeared, vanishing into thin air.

Grith blinked once before she caught the scent again, craning her head as Holz popped back into existence a few feet away.

Grith let out a rumble and lowered her head all the way to the ground, hoping that would be somewhat less intimidating. "You do not have to be afraid. You smell like a tree, not like prey, and it would be illegal for me to eat you."

Holz blinked, staring down at the dragon before sniffing her own arm as if that was news to her. "Sorry," she apologized, shaking her head. "You just startled me, I didn't see you come over." She glanced over at her drink with a half-hearted laugh. "I'm a little out of it."

Grith fluttered her feathers. She'd noticed that. "My cousin said that I should talk to a fae here, so I am doing that."

Holz gave Grith a quizzical look and turned to Ashley, hoping that she would elucidate the matter.

Ashley just shrugged, and the fae sat herself down back on her chair, squinting.

"Is your cousin a dragon?"

Grith flicked her snout up in a nod, and Holz scratched her head, running her fingers through long, brown hair.

"Sorry. I haven't talked to any dragons recently, except for you. Sorry. I've been on edge a little recently."

Grith thought for a moment. So, Pret hadn't been talking to Holz? She'd have to do more work to figure out what he'd meant her to ask. Maybe he'd just wanted her to make another friend? "That is all right. You have less fear-scent around me than most of the humans I have seen today. I am *grrawwwwrrrrrffffff*." It took her a few moments for her to realize that she hadn't said her name in the human pronunciation, not having done that before without the shiftstone. "Grith."

"Holz," the fae responded with a smile, holding her hand out for Grith to shake it.

Grith stared at it, not quite sure what to do. She decided to ignore the hand; she'd already almost bitten one off today.

"Why are you on edge?" Ashley asked with a frown. "Is something wrong?"

Holz nodded as she returned her hand to the drink, clutching the edge of the cup. "Yeah." She gulped. "Normally I meet Alb, twice a week, but this is the third time they've missed it. They're not at home and there's no sign of where they went and what happened to them, and I'm really really worried and I haven't seen them since we met at the observatory. I didn't think we left on bad terms there, but what if they decided that they hated me or I said something wrong and they don't want to be mates anymore but would they really disappear and what if something worse happened like they got eaten or killed or something even worse than that?"

Grith flicked her ears, the whole thing having been a bit too fast for her to process.

"Her friend is missing," Ashley explained. "Albiwegan. I

was wondering why they hadn't been here for a while. The two of them are kinda bound to the grove in the back of the Key, so they can't exactly move away, and have to come back here every so often to replenish their essence. I hope that nothing bad happened; how have you looked?"

"Just a few searching charms." Holz sniffled. "No luck."

"My mom could help," Ashley suggested. "She's pretty good at that kind of thing. Wanna give her a visit?"

"Thank you," Holz said again, wiping her eyes as she followed Ashley toward the back of the Key.

Grith crawled after them, keeping her head low so as not to startle anyone else.

Ashley opened one of the doors into the back, letting Holz through before giving Grith a skeptical glance.

"I can fit," Grith explained, flattening the feathers on her back and pulling her wings in as tight as she could. Much like cats, dragons could fit into surprisingly small locations, though it wouldn't be particularly comfortable.

Ashley shrugged and continued through, leaving Grith to sneak through the doorway, her head out in front as the wood rubbed against her wings. On the inside was a small, wooden hallway with a stairwell off to one side, a stairlift running up it, and a number of doors off to the other. Ashley took Holz to one at the end and knocked on it while Grith shimmied from side to side, half-slithering and half-crawling through the small space. Unlike the other parts of the Key, this seemed to be a more personal area, made for those human-sized. Getting in hadn't been so bad, but getting back out would be somewhat harder.

"Mom!" Ashley called, knocking again. "It's me!"

The door opened, a human woman peering out, with a finger over her lips to shush her daughter. There wasn't much of a family resemblance beyond that — the woman had a paler skin color than Ashley and long, curly, crimson hair, unlike Ashley's straight and short black, and was a good head-height over her daughter. Similar robes to Ashley's covered her, a massive large moonstone dangling from a chain nestled in the folds like a quarter-moon. Still, Grith knew that the two were related from their smell, with their kindred fleshy prey-scent interiors surrounded by the smoke of incense caught in hair and cloth, numerous herbs and the earthy sparkle of magic caught in the waft.

"I see you've brought visitors," Ashley's mother said. Like Grith, the way she formed her words sounded different than the other humans in the area she had met, harsher and rolled, though not draconic. "Hello, Holz. I don't believe we've met yet, dragoness? I'm sorry these hallways are so small."

The way that the witch had used the word pleasantly surprised Grith — the formality matching with the deferentiality that Ashley's mother had given her, unlike the way Chris had used it. She lowered her head respectfully, though there wasn't far for her to lower it in here. "We have not."

"I'm Sorcha," she said with a smile, giving her daughter a pat on her head and ruffling Ashley's hair. Ashley rolled her eyes and pushed it away. "Your Pret's cousin, right? *Grrawwwrrrrrrffffff?*"

Grith's eyes opened, the slits widening at the mention her own name, Even if she'd badly mangled it with a human throat. Still, the human had done surprisingly well; Grith had to wonder if Pret had taught her any Southern. "Grith is acceptable."

Sorcha gave Grith a smile, peeling her lips back in a fashion that seemed almost as draconic as it was human. She brought her hand away from her daughter and gestured at the room. "Well, I'm glad you made it here after all! Please, all of you, come in. What's the problem?"

The room that Sorcha took the three into was a far different atmosphere than any of the others in the Key. Her eyes had to adjust and open to the darkness, the room the color of twilight, the polar opposite to the pale, artificial white of Vertex Technologies. It wasn't the only way that the two differed: instead of the chemical smell of bleach, fallen leaves and a light smoke scented Sorcha's room. As they crumpled under Grith's paws, she realized that it wasn't just a scent: the floor was made of dirt and leaves, with twisted trees and vines forming the walls, reaching up to the sky. The dragon lifted her head at the smell of fresh air: a quarter-moon glinted down from a clear sky filled with speckled stars, magnitudes more than Grith could even see from her home outside the city. She stared at it before Ashley's voice interrupted her stargazing.

"Holz is looking for Alb," Ashley explained to her mother. "They've gone missing. Holz has tried a couple already, but I was hoping you could do a searching spell."

Sorcha gave Ashley a nod. She turned to a small wooden desk on the side of the room — not a desk, Grith quickly realized, but an outcropping of the trees themselves — and opened a bound leather book, skimming through old pages. "It looks like I'll need either something important of theirs, or a body part, like a fingernail clipping. Do you have anything like that? If not, I could try using one of their trees, but that might just point to the grove rather than Albiwegan themselves."

"I've got something," Holz replied, taking the flower chain from her head, the petals changing color as she did so. She tugged at something in it and pulled out a clump of white hair. "Will this work?"

"Perfectly!" Sorcha announced before dipping her head into the hollow of one of the trees. She rummaged, pulling out a couple odd plants and herbs that Grith sniffed in interest, reeling back. Dragons were mostly carnivorous, although Grith had occasionally had the odd cravings for fruit and sugar since wearing the shiftstone, but these reeked far more than they smelt appetizing. She hoped no one would have to eat them.

Sorcha brought out another object, a small, metal bar that Grith quickly smelled was iron. Horz took a visible step back at that, becoming cloaked in what Grith thought was fae fear-scent.

"Apologies, it's needed for the spell," Sorcha said, muddling the herbs together in a small clay bowl filled with water and setting the iron bar in the center. Making sure to keep it away from the fae, Sorcha plucked the white hair from Holz's hand, pulling out a few strands of it and dropping them into the bowl. As soon as they touched the iron, they shriveled and twisted up, the white hair graying and crumpling. "Ashley, can you heat it?"

Ashley nodded and rolled back a sleeve. She then placed a finger to a black rune of two twigs at a right angle on her forearm, the tattoo dragging along beneath her skin until it was on her palm. A bright green light shined from it, and Ashley placed her hand between her mother's. A few moments later, the water boiled.

Grith let out a puff of smoke, masking the pungent odor of the herbs as they wafted toward her.

"It acts as a compass, pointing to wherever your friend is," Sorcha explained, both Grith and Holz moving away as she held the ceramic bowl. The iron bar had rotated in a circle, the fraying hair wrapped around it dissolving. Sorcha dropped another one in. The witch frowned. "That's odd. It should have stopped moving by now."

Holz let out a loud sob, placing her hands on her head. The leaves beneath her feet decayed and crumbled away, and Grith's feathers stuck up as the room's temperature dropped a few degrees.

"They're dead!" Holz cried out, distraught. "Oh, I should have known."

Sorcha gave her an apologetic smile, but shook her head. "Darling, no, not dead. The iron would have rusted, and we would have seen a change in their trees. They're very much alive, just . . . lost."

"Oh," Holz sniffed, wiping the tears from her eyes. "They're alive?" The leaves at the fae's feet seemed to perk up at that, shades of green shifting through their shriveled husks. "Then why doesn't it work?"

Grith stared curiously at the bowl. The spell could figure out if someone was dead or alive? She wondered if it worked on dragons, and regretted not having brought any items of her parents.

"It could be a bubble realm," Ashley suggested, pulling her hand away from the bowl and pinching her nose. "That causes weird behavior, right?"

"That's right." Sorcha nodded, with a hint of pride in her daughter. "However, if that was the case, it would only be swinging in the angle of the area of this world that the bubble realm overlapped with. For example, a friend told me there's a large bubble realm somewhere northeast of LA —" she gave Grith a wink "—and if they were there, the needle would still be pointing north-east, but would just be moving back and forth in an angle, and wouldn't help find their location inside it. The swinging around in all directions could only occur if there was a bubble realm overlapping the Key, and if there was one, Pret or I would have sensed it by now."

"Then what does it mean?" Holz asked hopefully. "Are they somewhere nearby? Are they in the Key still?"

Sorcha shook her head. "I would know if they were here. Unfortunately, I have no idea what this means; nothing like this has happened before. I'm sorry I couldn't have been of more help."

Holz let out a cry of agony, throwing up her hands, her hair turning flame-red, the leaves around her smoking. She shook her head again, clutching her hair and pulling out a few strands of it, sparking like embers as they fell to the ground. Her anger faded to grief, and she buried her face in her hands again, shaking her head.

"It's fine." Holz sighed, her voice glum and cold as snow. "It's not your fault. I'll just go."

The fae turned around, looking up to see that the dragon stuck within the doorway completely blocked it. Holz didn't seem to care, just stepping forward and disappearing before she walked into Grith.

Grith let out a yelp of surprise as she sensed Holz reappear behind her, flicking her tail up, startled. It slammed into the ceiling of the hallway, and there was a crack of wood, Grith wincing as splinters buried beneath her tail feathers.

"Oh dear," Sorcha said, trying to peer around Grith to see the damage. "No matter. The wood likes me, and repairing the ceiling is easy. Holz might be a bit harder to deal with."

SEVEN

After returning to her home, Grith decided to hunt. She knew that it would take up time that she should have been using for sleeping, but she wanted to make sure that what had happened the day before at Vertex wouldn't happen again. Though she thought it would just be a one-time thing — the combination of hunger, the sudden change in her brain and body from the shiftstone's lapse, the overstimulation of her senses, and her anger at the human that had touched her along with the rest of Vertex — it still worried her about what would happen if there was another situation like that again, and everything went wrong. If she ended up eating a human, she'd end up hunted by both the Council overruling all magical affairs, and more frighteningly, the local draconic leadership.

Pret had warned her that the first few days of being around humans would be odd, shiftstone or not. While Grith, of course, knew that humans were as intelligent as dragons, and that it was probably wrong to eat them because of that, she realized that it wasn't something that she'd internalized yet. Even with buildings and language and coffee, part of her still couldn't see humans as anything more than just another prey animal. It was odd talking to someone that she might have instead eaten had she hatched three-hundred years earlier, as odd as it would have been for her to talk to the deer she'd just about finished picking the bones clean. Pret had explained that there was an adjustment period; after enough contact, they viewed them as a fellow dragon-like species rather than potential prey, and talking to them had become as normal as talking to her. Similarly, humans had an adjustment period when talking to dragons for the first time. Ashley had clearly gone through that, while the rest of the VT had not.

Grith regretted not having asked Pret how long that adjustment period was. Still, she thought that after talking with Ashley without the shiftstone, it seemed like she'd made a bit of progress. She thought that she'd have to be very hungry to not recoil in alarm at the thought of hunting her. Paul or Chris . . . a bit less so.

Her mind went back to the missing fae. Sorcha's spell hadn't worked to find them, yet they weren't dead. Did that mean that there was another spell that might work? Grith thought back to the odd hoard of magical and mundane appliances that her mother had left her. She'd inventoried them a while back. Was there anything useful there? She thought that she remembered either a compass or map that had a searching enchantment on it, but that was probably too similar to what Sorcha did, and would cause a similar effect.

As Grith laid down on her pile of coins, digging into her down as the magic in the metals soothed her, she recalled what the witch had said about bubble realms. Based on what Pret had said, Grith's mother probably was the one to create the one around the Key — they were a relatively new form of magic, created only during the Revival and still used mostly by dragons. Her mind drifted, her imagination stimulated by the scent of shimmer around her. What if the fae *was* caught in a bubble realm, one that contained the Key, but that no one had sensed? Usually, one could find bubble realms by touching their edges, and a sensitive nose or the prick of feathers would notice the presence of odd magic in the space they overlapped with.

What if the fae was trapped in a bubble realm so large it covered LA? No, in that case, someone would have noticed when they left the city. How big would it have to be? What if there was a bubble realm that overlapped with the entire world? Would anyone even know, or would they be so used to the magic shedding off it that it would be like trying to see air?

Grith's head perked up, something her mother had once told her unburying itself from her memories. Her feathers stuck up, and a chill ran from her crest to the tip of her tail. She closed her eyes, trying to grasp the memory before it faded.

"When your grandfather created his magic to save dragonkind, he got the idea from an old legend," Grith's mother purred, draping a feathered wing across her daughter.

Grith was once again a hatchling, barely the size of a deer. She tried to peer up on her mother's stone desk, filled edge-to-edge with parchment and ink.

"Dragons once lived in a paradise, a perfect world where we lived free and peacefully, where beautiful mountains pierced the sky, and lush rainforests filled the valleys between them. We played in warm azure oceans, ruffling our feathers as we caught fish the size of lions."

"That doesn't sound like a paradise for the Northern dragons," the young Grith replied, scattering a few papers as she tried to climb on the desk, her claws unable to get a hold in the stone. "Pret told me they like cold waters."

She felt a lick on the back of her crest, and her mother grabbed Grith's scruff in her jaws, pulling her away from the desk and setting her back down on the floor.

"Well, maybe there were also cold waters in paradise?" her mother tsked, giving her another lick on the neck. "This is a Southern legend, my chick, thousands of years old. Though we all lived in paradise, happy and free, one day, the sanctity of paradise was destroyed by the greed of humans; for a hundred years, ash and dust filled the sky. Death crept across the land. The waters were no longer clear, the fish perished, the air poisoned our lungs, and we had to leave paradise."

Grith sneezed out a puff of flame as if to demonstrate, her mother giving a yelp of alarm as she pushed Grith's snout to the side, just in time to avoid getting a piece of fallen parchment set on fire. "Like that?"

Her mother rumbled and grabbed Grith's scruff again, placing her down away from the parchment, and used a talon to hold the hatchling in place. "Maybe. My father wanted to create paradises for dragons, which is why he learned to create the bubble realms. Here, we could live in peace, so long as we had enough of a hoard. But one day, I hope that I can create a bubble realm that sustains itself, one so large that it will form a new paradise for dragons. A huge paradise, for you, Pret, and everyone else."

"For me?" Grith squeaked, pouncing at her mother's

tail, unable to catch a feather as it was flicked away just in time. "Bigger than the forest?"

"Far bigger than the forest," her mother rumbled in laughter. "So big that you could fly for seven nights, and you wouldn't hit the edge."

Grith flapped her wings, barely large enough to keep her aloft, even when shimmer filled. "I don't think I can fly that long."

"Then I'll carry you, my darling chick," her mother replied, picking the hatchling up by the scruff again. She wrapped her wings around the two of them, and for a moment, Grith was lost in her mother's scent once more. "I'll carry you to the edge of the sky."

Grith's eyes fluttered open, her talons clutching around the coins of her hoard, the scent of her mother all but gone. It took her a moment for her to realize that she was shaking. Her quiet home felt far lonelier, like it had when her parents had first left.

Another realization hit her like a bug on her snout. She didn't remember enough of what her mother had written on the papers she'd shown Grith to copy them down, but now she knew what her mother had been talking about. A bubble realm large enough to sustain itself: hatchling Grith hadn't had the knowledge then, but now, older Grith knew exactly how to do those calculations.

With a surge of energy, the young dragon stood up from her hoard, coin falling from its sides in her rush to find someplace to write down before the ideas fled from her head. She slid down into the tunnels of her home, turning corners until she was in the room closest to her own hoard with parchment; fittingly, her mother's library and workstation. Her parents had remodeled it much since the memory, the fire extinguishers an important addition in particular, but it was still recognizable.

Bookshelves covered the walls of the rotunda, filled to the brim with books of varying sizes that seemed to stare down at Grith as she rushed to the stone desk in the center. Even Grith barely knew how to read most of them, written in the other dragon languages or human tongues, many forever lost to time. Grith had inherited much of the hoard from ancestors that Grith didn't even know the names of, passed down from her grandfather and his mother before she passed into the sky or the earth, or wherever dragons went when they died. Grith doubted that they went anywhere, but she still observed the usual Southern burial ritual of burning the deceased along with some of their hoard, so that their soul would rise with the smoke and join the Celestial Dragon as a star.

The clutter on the stone desk had been cleared away — Grith was a methodical dragon and preferred her lair clean — leaving behind a nicely-sorted stack of leather bound tomes on the side, ink-wells covered so as to prevent spills. Most had belonged to Grith's mother and were her claw work, though recently Grith had made her own additions. She heaved the top-most tome onto the desk, opening it to the latest untouched page.

Her head turned to the inkwell, and she spat into it, mixing the liquid with two talons and scraping them against the sides until they were no longer dripping. Then, she placed them on the paper and wrote.

Unlike English, the Southern language was only properly written with two talons, most letters curved and made of two simultaneous strokes. It made for an efficient system, though with the calculations Grith was making, she haphazardly threw Arabic numerals, Greek letters, and

Dragon Pidgin in there, in accordance with the conventions used when collective bodies of magic and science were fused together in the Revival. She furiously wrote in the book, golden eyes leering down as if they were tracking prey, occasionally using a claw to lift the pages to a small reference section she'd written in the appendix.

Half the night was over before she was done, but she finally had the result her mother had wanted. Her ears drooped as she saw the number.

To create a self-sustaining paradise for dragons, a bubble realm that would never collapse, she'd need as much rhodium as Terra's moon, or five times that amount in platinum.

Grith's snout collapsed to the desk. She shouldn't have been so surprised. Her mother would have known how to do the calculations as well. Had it been so easy, at all feasible, she would have done it already. Grith let out a puff of smoke. It would take a lot more than a few hours to fulfill her mother's dream, if it were even possible.

For now, dragons would just have to remain living with humans, and Grith would need to continue working at Vertex Technologies.

Grith snorted as she turned her head over, getting a splotch of ink on her golden crest. Was that why she'd embarked on this foolish endeavor? Did she really hate the place so badly? She supposed that she did. Working there meant that she not only had to subject herself to a strict hierarchy, but it meant complete denial of herself. They'd humiliated her as both a dragon and a human. Part of her wanted to burn down the campus and everyone inside. She was angry, not just at Vertex Technologies, but at the entire world of humans. Her people had to hide, to either lock themselves away in small pockets of nature they couldn't leave without becoming literally invisible, or they had to attempt to become human themselves and ignore their own nature.

Grith realized that was the first time she'd thought of her species as her people. Before, they'd just been dragons; as isolated as she'd been, they'd been her entire world. The rules and politics regarding humans had just been hypotheticals. But now, something changed. She wondered if Pret would be happy: if dragons were a people, then so were humans. Ironically, she realized that she was on the first flap to internalize that dragons were not alone, and that humans were more than just an invasive species of prey.

Grith took a deep breath, the scent of the old pages of the tome in front of her calming. No, not just the pages. She could barely smell it anymore, but it was impossible for her to forget: the scent of her mother still remained. Once again, her mother's wings held her, wrapping around Grith like the shell of her egg. She engrossed herself in the scent, almost desperate to get more than just one whiff. Her ears drooped to the stone desk, and she let out a sniffle and wail.

Her head rested as she kept trying to take in the scent, only getting the occasional touch of the stale smell of her mother. Her mind went back to the lost fae again with a final sniff. Grith wanted to help. She didn't want someone else to lose a loved one to an unknown fate.

As her nostrils flared, her eyes went wide. She understood how she could help.

How had she not thought of it before? Fae didn't have a prey-scent; their smell was unique. A spell might not have been able to find out where Albiwegan was currently, but with Grith's nose, she could easily figure out where they'd been. It had only been a week, hadn't it? It would be more difficult with the rain, but all Grith had to do was catch the fae's scent, and follow it around LA until she found them!

That did raise a problem. Grith couldn't use her nose while she was wearing the shiftstone, and she couldn't exactly wander around LA without it. That would cause quite a shock. Her invisibility wouldn't be enough if she was actually inside the human city instead of just flying over it. She'd need some sort of illusion magic to disguise herself, something that would hide her own scent and size. Something that would be able to hide her if a human ran into her side, that could make her feathers feel like skin.

Grith didn't know magic that could do it, but she could figure that out. She *did* work at a magical technology company, after all.

When Grith rested herself down on her hoard for the second time that night, she was quickly able to get to sleep. Now, she had a plan.

THE NEXT DAY Grith went to Vertex Technologies, she decided to wear her mother's old, torn-up clothes, covered by a shawl. No one bothered her; in fact, they all seemed to be steering well clear from her, avoiding making any sort of eye contact. After the previous day, she doubted they would have bothered her even if she'd decided to wear nothing, like she normally did.

The morning was droll, and Chris started another experiment with the teleportation rings that Grith didn't find particularly interesting. This time, they were attempting to deliver magical power between them, and the two checked both the power loss and fluctuations caused by the rings. Grith's mind, however, was on other things. Particularly, the fae, and how she could find them.

Would she need multiple enchantments on her to disguise herself around the mundane humans? She supposed she might be able to have the shiftstone not transform her snout, keeping that hidden, but with how uncontrollable the shiftstone was, that was more of a last resort than anything. She wasn't even sure that would work.

When a clock on the wall hit noon, Chris stretched his arms and let out a yawn. "Well, I'm going to go get lunch." He glanced over at Grith, still at work at the typewriter, lost in thought as she stared at it without moving her fingers. "Are you planning to go?"

"No," Grith responded. She had other plans. Vertex probably had something that she could use, right? She just had to find it.

"If this is about yesterday, no one is going to try and touch you again after what you did," Chris said. "I think they'll stay away."

Grith wasn't sure if that was supposed to be comforting or not. She twisted her head from left to right in an exaggerated shake. "I am not hungry," she lied. Her meal last night hadn't nourished this body. "Dragons do not have to eat as often as humans. I will continue working."

Chris raised an eyebrow, but shrugged. "Well, all right, but taking breaks is good, and it's easier to find friends down there. Hey, if you want, I can get you something to eat and bring it back here."

Grith peeled back her lips and bared her teeth at Chris with a growl. She'd already told him she wasn't interested.

Chris raised his hands in the air, not finding the expression as intimidating with Grith's human teeth. "All right, all right! It's your choice; I'm just trying to be friendly."

Grith was far more suspicious of his intentions after the previous day. She doubted it was just trying to be friendly.

She only stood up after Chris had left the room. By now, she was pretty sure there wasn't anything in their lab that could help her with what she needed, but she remembered that there was a storeroom down the hall. She walked out into the gleaming white open-space, staring down into the atrium for a moment. Now, humans filled it, employees all chattering with each other as they took their break.

Grith walked down the hallway, scanning left and right for the room she wanted along with anyone planning to try and stop her. She ended up finding both.

A human guard with as much hair on his chin as on his head stood in front of the door, a thick steel slab of metal with the word 'Storeroom' carved into the surface. She placed herself in front of the guard, looking eye-to-eye.

"I need something in here for research," Grith lied. "I work in Chris's lab."

The guard frowned and pulled out a piece of paper from his pocket. He scanned it back and forth. "Your lab has clearance. Can I see your hand for identification?"

Grith lifted her hand up, showing it to the guard. He reached his own out, about to grab it, when Grith pulled it back with a hiss. "You said see. Not touch."

"Er, sorry." The guard winced, not quite sure what the deal was. "I need to touch it to make sure you're part of the lab. Just standard procedure."

Grith paused, before extending her hand out again. She kept it still, trying to focus on something else as she felt his skin against it, holding it tight. Anything, just to distract her. She tried to imagine the clanking of the typewriter keys, filling her head, as feathers appeared on her wrist, moving around her skin.

"All right, you're good," the guard said, and Grith

noticed that one of his fingernails had turned green. He stepped to the side. "Go ahead."

With a relieved puff, Grith opened the steel door and walked into the storeroom. The same metal of the door covered the walls, the room filled with shelves of odd contraptions. Grith could smell the magic in here, practically buzzing through her skin as she stepped through the chamber. How could she figure out where something that would disguise her was?

She decided to start at the end of one shelf, a place as good as any. There were a few more teleportation rings, and she felt a pang of anger as she sniffed them and realized the metal plating was a slightly better quality than the ones in the lab. A ceramic vase was next to those. Would that contain some illusion magic? Grith doubted it.

Her nose landed on the shimmer of the next one: a large, clear diamond. She gave it a look, surprised at the inside. The reflections seemed to distort away from her, angles and light where it shouldn't be, and when she tried to look through it, the diamond appeared to give way to a huge, endless pit inside it. From its make, it seemed like it was something designed to store magical essence, but the inside space was warped to become large enough it could hold a ridiculous amount of it. When full, it could have so much shimmer, Grith wondered if it would even be able to create the self-sustaining paradise her mother had spoken of. The entire thing, however, was empty. The hard part, of course, would be filling it.

She turned away from the diamond. A curiosity, but it wouldn't help her in her quest. Next to it was a silver triangle with runes drawn onto the surface. She read them, trying to figure out what it would do. Transmutation of some sort? Not what she wanted.

A human clearing his throat echoed through the chamber, and Grith let out a loud squeak as she jumped up in alarm, a feathered tail whipping through the air.

Chris was at the entrance to the storeroom, giving her an uncertain look.

"What are you doing back from lunch so soon?" Grith stammered, her tail shrinking back into her.

"You shouldn't be snooping around the ware closet, especially after what happened yesterday," Chris derided, not answering the question. He stepped over to the shelf Grith was up against, frowning at the artifacts she'd been sniffing. "I'm not stupid. I *know* how shiftstones work. If you're in a human body, you'll have a human appetite, not a dragon one. Which frankly, I'm somewhat glad for."

Grith clenched her hands, her nails digging into her palms. She'd been caught. "Are you going to tell on me?"

Chris seemed to ponder that for a moment. "Technically there's no rule against going into the storeroom if you have clearance, which you do, but I think that depends on why you're snooping around. I'll report you if you don't explain yourself, as is expected of respectable Vertex Technology employees. You're not trying to steal anything, are you? I don't think we have a lot of gold in here."

"Not stealing," Grith replied, carefully holding back a growl. She thought for a moment about lying again, and telling Chris that she was looking for better ring teleporters, but lying hadn't worked well the last time. Was there any harm in telling him the truth? "I am looking for a fae that went missing, and I think I can find them if I use my nose. But I cannot do that with the shiftstone, so I need something stronger than my invisibility to disguise me. I was hoping there would be something in here to do that." She fretted a little. How bad a thing was this? She'd already been close to being fired the day before, would this be enough?

"That's it?" Chris asked, like he was expecting something more devious. He frowned, looking around at the shelves. "Oh. Well, you won't find anything useful here. But I think I can help."

"Really?" Grith asked, her eyes widening. Chris was going to help her on this? From her impression, he didn't really seem like the type to help find a missing magical creature. She tried to twitch her ears uncertainly; now, she was slightly suspicious of his intentions.

Chris nodded. "You just need to hide yourself without the shiftstone, right? I actually know a glamor spell that can do that. Er, long story short, but I had a poorly timed date with a werewolf once, and decided to learn it before the next full moon. We'd broken up by then, she was a bit of a lunatic and doing it with a straight-up wolf like she wanted was a bit too much for me, haha, but I think I could do it again. For you. However, it's pretty finicky. It requires the continuous use of magic and takes more power the larger and less human the target is. It also gets disrupted easily; if the target uses anything beyond the smallest iota of magic, it'll stop working. If you're just following someone's scent, it'll be fine, but you can't like, get involved in any magical fights."

Grith shuffled her back happily, perking up. This had worked out well! She wasn't getting fired, *and* she'd found the solution to her problem! "Thank you!" she purred. "How hard is it to learn? Can you teach it to me?"

Chris shook his head. "I could, but I'm not going to. There's no way I'm letting you roam unsupervised around LA as a dragon. I'm willing to cast it for you, but I want to be around you when you're searching. I don't want you to get into trouble by revealing yourself to humans, or *eating* anyone."

"Oh," Grith replied. Her ears would have drooped if they could have. Part of her was angry, but another part of her wondered if Chris was right. She'd been close to hurting the human who'd touched her far worse than just a few fang-pricks. What if something similar happened? "I will not eat anyone, I promise. That only happened because the shiftstone lapsed, and instincts I didn't have before were suddenly there, and other instincts were gone. As long as I am not wearing the shiftstone, you can trust me. I will be safe."

"I'm not budging on this," Chris warned, crossing his arms. "I don't care if you think you're safe. *I* don't think you're safe."

Grith shifted her glance away from him guiltily. Had humans had tails, she would have tucked hers between her legs. "All right," she murmured. "You can join. But you will have to come to the Key after work tonight. Please try not to get eaten by anyone else."

Chris stiffened, and Grith let out a noise between a snort and a giggle. "Fine," Chris nervously agreed. "I'll go to the Key. I'll do it for you."

"Sure," Grith responded, not particularly sure why Chris was trying to put emphasis on that. "Oh, speaking of helping me. You are a very strong and powerful wizard, correct? How would you go about obtaining a moon full of rhodium? I need a lot of shimmer for something."

Chris squinted. "Are you joking? What could anyone use that much magic for?" He laughed. "I think I'd find a planet to chisel the moon out of."

CHAPTER

EIGHT

The two left work a few hours early that day, while the sun was still in the sky. Chris explained that he was high enough up in the Vertex Technology pecking order that he had some freedom over choosing his hours, and since Grith was in his lab, she could join him, though they'd probably want to make it up at a later time. Grith didn't particularly care for the strict hours regardless, and hoped that she'd one day rise up enough in Vertex Technologies to have the same freedom. Even if she wasn't particularly forward to having to work there that long, or even one day more. She never wanted to go back again.

Chris already knowing where the Key was had surprised Grith, and he explained that he'd been there once on a date with a vampire, but hadn't enjoyed the Bloody Mary that he'd tried. He hadn't thought that he'd have been taken so literally and was too afraid to ask what species the blood had come from. Grith wasn't sure why, though — she'd thought most humans ate meat. Maybe Chris didn't? She hadn't seen him eat any at lunch, and had rejected her offer of sharing.

Grith opened the door, far more proficient with the handle than the first time she'd entered, and walked into the Key. It was early enough in the afternoon that there were only a few patrons today, including a brown cat basking in the sun from the interior glass window, and the shapeless patron in the trenchcoat the Grith remembered from the first day. Just like always, Ashley was there, and the witch-in-training gave Grith a huge grin and a wave before it turned to a frown.

"Who's that?" Ashley asked, peering behind the dragon to Chris as he nervously shuffled in. She bit her lip. "He's human."

"Wizard," Chris muttered back, his eyes glancing back and forth between the two patrons, like he was worried one of them would attack him but wasn't quite sure which.

"This is Chris," Grith explained to her, as she stepped over to one of the tables, putting her hands on it as she shifted her weight onto them. "He is one of my coworkers and he is going to help us find Albiwegan! Chris, this is Ashley."

Ashley glared at Chris, narrowing her eyes. "So, he's from Vertex. Is he the one who touched you?"

"What?" Chris exclaimed. "No! That wasn't me. I'm not that sort of guy, Grith knows I would never do anything like that."

Grith tapped her fingers. "I do not know that, but he was not that one. He only touched me once, and it was grabbing my talons so that I didn't hit a car."

Ashley's glare softened. "Oh. Well, that's a good reason for touching you." She frowned. Chris's eyes weren't on her, but at the patron in the trenchcoat. "We don't appreciate staring here. It's impolite."

Chris grimaced, looking a little squicked. "It shouldn't be doing that in public."

Grith turned to a black, shadowy tentacle that had crept out of the trenchcoat, and the patron was using it to scratch the back of their neck. "Neck scratching?"

"Well, the Key isn't public," Ashley replied, crossing her arms. "Arms, tentacles, talons, and wings are all appreciated here. Grith, what good can he do? He doesn't seem particularly helpful."

"He knows a very useful spell!" Grith explained, her excitement returning. "I believe that I am able to sniff out Albiwegan with my nose, but I will need to not have the shiftstone on. Chris has a spell that will make me smell, feel, and look like a human, but I will still be in my own body!"

"Oh. That's a good idea!" Ashley said. She reached into her robe, and pulled out a few strands of white hair. "Holz left these with my mother, so you can use them to find the scent. Holz isn't here today, but I think she mentioned last seeing Alb at an observatory, so if we're going to go searching, we should start there. I'll ask my parents to take over for tonight, just in case we're out late. Good with you?"

"Quite good!" Grith purred, glad that they had a plan. "Do you have the spell ready? Will it take long to cast?"

"It'll just be a few moments," Chris explained. He opened up his blazer, sticking a hand into one of the suit pockets.

Grith peered curiously as pulling out a thick, spiral-bound notebook that seemed far too big to have fit in the little pocket, along with a vial of glittering silver powder.

He flipped through the book, each page filled with his own handwriting and small sketches and drawings, before stopping at the page he wanted to and reading over it.

As Chris prepared to cast the spell, Grith walked over toward the taller-ceiling area of the Key, taking off her clothes and placing them in her bag. She noticed Chris drawn away from his reading to give her a quick look of surprise, before she cupped her hands around the glowing shiftstone, and gently removed it from her neck.

She set her talons onto the floor as freed feathers burst forth from her skin, her body growing to its normal height. Her sense of smell returned, along with the prey-scent of the humans and fear-scent from Chris as her head loomed over him, two golden slitted eyes peering down, large fangs a few feet above his head. His blue eyes were open, drawn away from his reading as his hands shook.

"Silly." Grith purred in laughter, flicking her tail as his fear-scent grew. "I told you already that I am not going to eat you."

Chris frowned, and the dragon sensed a bit of what she thought was anger or embarrassment. "You were prettier as a human," he muttered, looking down at his book again, still giving Grith a nervous glance every few moments.

Grith sat back on her haunches, her head almost bonking the ceiling. She looked at her wing-feathers, preening them. Was there something wrong with them?

"She's plenty pretty as a dragon," Ashley snapped at Chris. "Grith, do we really need to keep him around?"

"I have to be nearby for the spell to work, and it uses my essence supply continuously." Chris sighed, picking up the vial of powder and putting it up to one of his eyes, as his blue iris distorted and became huge in the glass. "Besides, I need to make sure Grith doesn't get in trouble."

"Grith can do that herself," Ashley said, clenching her hands. "And I'll be there if she needs any help."

Chris shrugged and uncorked the vial before standing,

holding the book in one hand as he looked back up at Grith with a gulp. "Grith, bend your head down; I'll need to pour this over you. It's a crushed silver mirror, needed for the spell. It doesn't cause itching in dragons, does it? Apparently it itches like fleas on werewolf fur."

Grith gave the powder a sniff, Chris holding as still as possible as the dragon put her nostrils to it. True to his word, it was silver. "Silver is fine," she spoke, Chris turning his head away as he smelt the mix of smoke and deer in her breath. "I have it in my hoard."

Chris sprinkled the powder on Grith's snout with care, glittering against the golden feathers. He then placed the empty vial away and held out the book to the side, using a finger to draw glowing blue runes in succession in the air.

Chris's magic filled her nostrils, drowning out the other scents, as he slowly spoke, reading in a language that didn't sound quite human. Grith thought it was curious when she recognized a few words of Dragon Pidgin. Was this a derivative of one of the other dragon languages she didn't know? She wondered where he'd found the spell.

Finally, he stopped, and the scent of magic around Grith faded to a soft metallic buzz. She flicked her ears as Chris took a few steps back and closed his book.

"Did it work?" Ashley asked. "She still looks like a dragon to me."

"It only affects mundanes," Chris explained. "You and I can see her as normal. I think it's working, since I'm still using magic, but I'm not sure."

"I could go outside to check," Grith suggested, craning her head over toward the door.

"No!" Chris and Ashley shouted in unison, looking at each other as they did so.

"We can't take that risk," Ashley explained. "A dragon appearing in the middle of LA would *not* be good."

"The Council might have *all* our heads for that." Chris gulped, placing his hands on his hair as if to check that his was still there. "I like mine where it is."

"Just give me a moment," Ashley pleaded. "I'll get my father. He's mundane, but is well-acquainted with the magical world, so it should work on him." She glared at Chris. "*Legally* acquainted."

Grith shrugged her wings and walked over with Ashley as she stepped into the hallway they'd seen before. If she had, too, couldn't she just eat any human that accidentally noticed her? *No,* she remembered quickly, *that's wrong.* Not just because it was illegal by both Council and dragon laws, but because humans were also as intelligent and had emotions as dragons, and killing one would be as immoral as killing another dragon would be. She wasn't quite sure which of those separated humans from other prey, but other prey usually didn't tend to make large structures or speak as much. Except perhaps beavers and parrots, which she *was* allowed to eat. It had been a big topic of debate a few decades ago, but the draconic leadership had decided to only expand their no-hunting list to include humans, elephants, dolphins, and other dragons, though Northern cannibalism of other Northern deceased was still permitted, along with already-dead members of the non-dragon banned species (though most dragons preferred fresh kills).

"DAD!" Ashley called out into the hallway. "Can you come out for a moment?"

One of the doors to the hallway opened, and an elderly human rolled himself out on a chair, adjusting his spectacles and ruffling a hand through straight, graying hair. Even with how old he was, he was more similar to his daughter than Sorcha, his skin darker but a warmer tone. He took a pen out from his mouth, the end chewed and as shriveled as his face.

"Yes, Ashley?" he asked in an accent as think as Grith's and Sorcha's, but different from both; his words were smoother and the tones more varied. He peered back and forth from Ashley to Grith. "Did you want something?"

"Does she look human?" Ashley asked, pointing at Grith.

The man nodded, like this was a question he got asked often. "She does. Is that it?"

"Oh, also I need you or Mom to take care of the Key tonight," Ashley quickly added. "I'm going out with Grith and one of her friends. Thanks! See you!"

"Well, stay safe." The elderly man sighed, rolling himself back into the room.

Ashley shut the door to the hallway. Grith wondered why a scholar of magic would choose to stay mundane instead of trying to cast magic himself. It wouldn't have been that difficult for him to become a wizard, especially if he knew Pret. It would just require a few silver feathers and a couple rituals.

"Well, then we're off!" Ashley shouted, marching toward the exit.

Grith followed behind her, keeping her tail tucked against her side so as not to accidentally whack Chris in the head with it. A gust of warm air hit the dragon's feathers when Ashley opened the door, mixed with the smell of exhaust, humans, and asphalt. Grith had to keep herself from gagging as they swirled around her head, wobbling as she adjusted to the strong scents.

Ashley paused to ask, "You okay?"

"I am okay," she rumbled, pushing herself forward.

Grith peered around at the street. It was busier than it had been on the rainy day she'd first entered the Key, with humans walking back and forth along the sidewalks, cars zooming past her in the afternoon sun. Her talons tensed as a couple looked toward her head poking out from the doorway, but if any of them noticed something odd, they didn't show it.

The dragon tucked her wings tight to her side, and stepped out onto the sidewalk herself, lifting her head to the sun. Her golden feathers glittered as it beat down on them, and she ruffled her crest at the warm feeling, basking in it for a moment with a purr. Chris walked out after her, carefully stepping over her tail to get around. Another car whizzed past, Grith's head tilting toward it with a leer, her heart racing as it moved like sprinting prey.

"Try to stay away from the cars," Ashley warned. "Dragon or not, I doubt it'd be fun to get hit by one."

"Do not fear!" Grith chirped. "They do not smell particularly saliva-inducing. And iron and thus steel contain less magic than it takes to process. It is not one of the eleven shimmer metals. All dragon mages must learn those by heart!"

Her head twisted again, and Grith's tail flicked as another one came past her. She was surprised at how different the experience of actually being in the city was without the shiftstone. Humans didn't seem to have the instinct to fly after cars, instead, the cars more shocked them with the loud noise and movement. For a number of reasons, the least of which being that she knew what cars were and that they weren't something to hunt, she decided not to soar after one. Trying to fly seemed like it would stretch the limits of Chris's glamor. While it wasn't a spell, flying took at least a little bit of magic for dragons, depending on the wind, the dragon's weight, and the strength of their wing muscles, compensating for where mundane physics wasn't enough to lift them. It would be better to avoid much use of natural magic, in case it disrupted Chris's spell.

As Grith's mother was fond of saying, dragons were creatures of flesh and shimmer, two sides of the same coin working in unison. That knowledge had been lost until the Revival, and with it had come the philosophy of using magic to survive in a human world, whether with bubble realms, shiftstones, or invisibility. Meat and coin both fed the body, hunting and magic both fed the soul.

The three walked through the city of LA, and though Grith's talons grew tired, her happiness of at least having talons for the moment drowned out any soreness. She opened her jaws wide in a yawn, stretching out her tail. Grith's feathers fluttered in a gentle wind, and she turned her head. The sun beat down on the left side, blocked out every so often by the taller of the buildings. More cars drove past her, their fumes filling her nose, and crowds of humans began to fill the path.

Grith flinched as one rudely pushed past her, his shoulder pressing against her wing. She was about to bare her teeth at the impoliteness, when another ran into her chest, causing her to leap up onto her hindlegs. She yelped as someone stepped on her tail, growling at the human who did it before he walked on like he hadn't even noticed.

"Grith, are you all right?" Ashley asked, looking up as Grith tried to figure out where to place her forepaw without accidentally stepping on any of the humans. Cautiously, she placed her own hand against the base of Grith's neck, as close to her crest as she could, careful not to touch the dragon's throat or the nearby arteries. "Is this fine?"

Grith flicked her ears, but the touch at her scruff calmed her, the fingers scratching beneath her feathers. She lowered her talons to her side as someone else pushed past her, wondering why the three were stopped in the midst of the crowd.

"It is fine," she murmured. "I am not used to being bumped into by prey. It is like a stampede. However, being touched is far more tolerable without the shiftstone."

"You're not going to . . . " Chris gulped, "you know . . ."

Grith shot him a glare, baring her teeth. "No," she growled. "I am not going to eat any of them."

"Hey, you did call us prey!" Chris chuckled uncomfortably, putting his hands over his shoulders.

Grith cocked her head. "You are prey," she stated. "Humans have prey-scent, and thus, are prey. Pigs are prey to humans, correct? Do you eat every pig you see? Do all humans eat pigs? I do not think so, that is why English has the word vegetarian. Unless they behave as stupidly as your friend and intentionally provoke fight-or-flight instincts, humans are usually safe from dragons, shiftstone or no shiftstone."

"Even vegetarians sometimes cheat on their diets," Chris muttered and flinched as someone shoved one of Grith's legs, trying to push her to the side.

"Are you head injured?" Grith asked, wondering if why that was why Chris still couldn't understand that she wasn't going to eat him or any other humans.

"No." Chris sighed. "The spell takes up more of my magic whenever someone touches you. When someone pushes you, it needs a decent amount to make them somehow believe that they're bumping into a human that's actually a couple feet away from them."

"Oh," Grith responded, feeling a little bit bad now for

referring to humans as prey. She supposed that she could use a different word if it made Chris uncomfortable. "I am sorry. I appreciate the spell a lot."

"It's nothing," Chris responded. "I've still got a lot of magic left. Let's just find this fae as quick as we can."

Ashley took her hand from Grith's neck and gave Chris a glare, although Grith wasn't quite sure of the meaning of it, and continued on her path.

A building to Grith's right stuck out to her as taller than the other ones; the boxy shape reminding her of VT. Her ears drooped as she recalled the incidents and environment, confined and unwelcome, forced to try and hide herself and be someone else. She'd have to go back to that after this, and wasn't looking forward to it. How long would she have to be there? Months? Years? Decades? She wondered if she was just using the search for the fae as a distraction from that. If so, it was a good one; the new experience of being within the human city was keeping her mind away from her job. It surprised her, but even with how overwhelming it was, she was enjoying this.

After they'd pushed through the crowds, the confusing roads became a path up a hillside. Grith was glad to have her talons no longer on the hard concrete and now on the dirt, and the lack of sweat and fatigue on Chris made it seem like he was glad that it was less busy here than and he had to use less magic.

"It's just up there," Ashley explained, pointing to a white building on the top of the hill, with brown domes. "That's probably it."

Grith's ears perked as she saw a human woman walk by with an odd-smelling child, holding the child by his hand as they went down the hillside. The woman didn't even notice the three as they walked up, but the child seemed just as interested in Grith as she seemed in him, staring intently at the dragon, eyes open in wonder. She waved a wing hello to him.

"Dwagon," he said to his mother, pulling on her dress. "Look. Dwagon."

Grith turned to Chris, flicking him on his side with her tail to get his attention. "The spell is still working, yes?"

"I-it should have," Chris said, staring at the kid, his palms sweating, his fear-scent drowning out everything else.

Ashley squinted and let out a laugh. "It's fine," she said, as the mother pulled her child down the path, and his attention turned to something else. "He's probably half-magical. I'd guess an affair with a fae on the other parent's side, and the mom probably doesn't know it or is pretending that he's a fully human child."

"That is impressive," Grith remarked. She hadn't realized that with her nose, though she supposed that she might have known if she knew more of how fae or other magical creatures in the area smelled.

Ashley shrugged. "We see a lot of hybrids at the Key. Give it another decade, and he'll accidentally stumble into some dangerous magical situation and dramatically learn about his heritage. Then he'll end up at the Key, and we'll be there to guide him through it. It happens a lot."

Grith thought that was a little silly, like much of the mundane and magical worlds she'd experienced so far. She stretched out her wings as she trotted up the rest of the path, finally standing in front of the observatory.

"Griffith Observatory," the dragon remarked with a cheery warble. "Without an 'iff,' it is Grith Observatory. Or maybe without a 'ffi.'"

Ashley and Chris had to run to catch up as Grith

squeezed in through the front doors, tucking her wings tight to her sides as she wiggled through. She gave the two humans behind her a look as the lights changed color from the afternoon sun to a dim orange glow inside.

Grith peered around a small rotunda as humans walked around the edge of a circular balcony in the center, and noticed a flash of movement from it. She looked over their heads see a large silver ball on a pendulum, slowly swinging back and forth.

"Is this a clock?" Grith asked Ashley, accidentally flicking her tail into a human, scowling at her before moving on. "My mother had a lot of clocks. We even had a clock room! It is still there, but most of them no longer function."

Ashley looked over the edge and nodded. "I think so," she said as the pendulum moved, the wire getting dangerously close to Grith's snout as it swung. "Remember, we're here to search for Alb, right?"

The dragon cooed in agreement and turned herself around, attempting to weave in and out of the crowd as she put her snout to the ground, golden eyes staring up at the people. She looked over at Ashley, and gave her a nuzzle against her robes, pushing the human back.

"The hair?" Grith asked, realizing that Ashley hadn't understood what the nuzzle had meant.

"Oh! Right." Ashley laughed, opening up a fold in her robes and pulling the white strands out from it. She held her hand out, hot air from the dragon's nostrils covering it as she gave the hair a sniff.

The human girl gave the underside of Grith's jaw a scritch, the dragon letting out a purr, flicking her ears and whacking someone with her tail again.

Chris caught her attention, quite pale. That was right; the dragon had a job to do.

Grith put her nose to the floor again, sniffing it as she walked down one of the hallways, trying to catch any scent of the fae. There was little luck. Even if the observatory wasn't as busy as it was on a weekend, the scent of humans clouded the dragon's nose, all around her. She was about to make a remark to Ashley about prey-scent before thinking better of it.

An interesting glowing panel stole Grith's attention, and she turned to it as she walked. White specks of light shimmered against a striped background of dull yellows, blues, and pinks. She squinted as she focused on one of the slabs of text on it, trying to read what it said, before she inattentively stumbled into someone, both of them letting out yelps.

Grith turned her head as she stepped back, peering down to see that she'd accidentally knocked a human down to the ground on his back. She craned her head to give him a sniff, her sharp fangs inches from his face. He'd had some sort of plant matter for lunch, and was wearing a wool sweater over a silken tie on his upper body.

"Oh, I am sorry," Grith said, remembering her manners. "I did not mean to knock you over." She held out a paw as Chris and Ashley caught up to her.

"It's all right." The human laughed, grabbing a hold of it. A strange expression of utter confusion came over him as his hands wrapped around talons, and for a moment, Grith was worried that the spell wouldn't be enough to hide it, but he just shook his head as he got to his feet. "I guess that's what I get for not looking where I'm walking!"

As he adjusted something in his eye, Grith sniffed him again. She guessed from it that he was male and close to

Chris's age. His skin was a few shades darker than Ashley's, but his hair was as white as snow, which surprised Grith as she'd thought that humans only got white hair when they grew old. It was the same color as the missing fae's, but the smell was different, instead, a chemical that she remembered smelling on the VT campus. Bleach? Her mother had told her that Southern dragons would occasionally dye their crests and wings with stripes or patterns for special events and gatherings, but dragons rarely met anymore with the bubble realm system, and Grith had never seen such a thing in her lifetime. She wondered how she would look with a white crest.

The human blinked, and Grith wondered again what exactly he was seeing.

Chris tensed up in exhaustion, and took a step back from the human. A small nametag on his sweatshirt told her his name: Professor Daniels.

"Hey, do you know much about the exhibit or the observatory?" he asked, brushing off his sweater. "I'm a tour guide here in my spare time, but I'm on break and just wandering at the moment."

Grith studied the bright exhibit again, placing a claw against its surface. "Can you see it from here? The Celestial Dragon?"

"The what?" The professor frowned, shifting the thing in his eye again, as if he wasn't quite sure that what he was seeing was right whenever he looked at Grith.

"Oh, um . . ." Grith looked back to Ashley and Chris, the latter of which anxiously tapped a foot on the ground, eyes wide. "The Milky Way! That is what it is."

"Of course!" the man laughed, like he should have figured that out himself. He scratched his head while looking at Grith. "Unfortunately not. Too much light pollution in LA, sadly. You could drive out to one of the parks; I'd recommend it! I've never heard it called the Celestial Dragon though."

"It is what my species calls it," Grith explained, looking over at the exhibit. She extended her wing, the claw on the tip of it tracing out the Milky Way in an arc. "It looks like a long dragon across the sky, does it not? Well, no legs nor wings."

The professor gave Grith an odd look. "Species?"

"Her family!" Ashley interrupted. "Sorry. She's still learning English. She's visiting from Costa Rica."

"Ah," the professor replied, a hint of skepticism in his tone. "Well, I'm glad you chose to visit our observatory while you were here, your English is very good! I didn't know that about Costa Rica, but the Babylonians had a myth about the Milky Way being the tail of Tiamat, a dragon god, after she was slain. It does look like it could be a dragon."

"That sounds not fun," Grith remarked. "I would prefer not to have my severed tail placed in the sky. Do you know a lot of dragon myths?"

The professor shook his head. "I can't say that I do. I know a lot of star myths, though, and a few of those have dragons. Would you like to hear another?"

Grith purred and flicked her snout. "Yes, please share! One without slaying? I do not like that, but I am interested in learning more about human myths."

"Actually, we're kind of busy and need to go before we run out of time," Chris said, stepping forward.

Ashley nodded.

"Oh, that is true," Grith replied, her ears drooping. They needed to stay focused and search for the fae. "I am sorry for knocking you over again, and I am sorry I do not have time to hear more myths."

"That's all right," the professor said. He pulled something out from his pocket, handing it to Grith. She took it, a small, white card that she carefully held between her talons with the name Dr. Tyler Daniels on it, a university, and a long number Grith wasn't sure the meaning of. "Just give that number a call and ask for Tyler in case you're ever interested in hearing more about star myths. I'll see if I can find any ones with dragons and not slaying in them, alright?"

Grith purred again, and placed the card in the small bag beneath her right wing. "Yes, I will make sure to once we find this fae! I mean human friend. Oh, my name is Grith, like the observatory without an 'iff.'" She went to turn, before perking her ears as she had a thought. "Oh, do you know any planets with moons made out of rhodium?"

The professor stared for a moment, like he was trying to comprehend all of what the dragon just said. "Er, no, I don't think so. I'll look into it?"

Grith flicked her snout before walking off, Ashley and Chris going after her as she once again sniffed around the observatory, trying to catch the scent she was looking for.

Ashley let out a sigh as they walked outside the observatory, walking up a small stairwell up to the roof, Grith having to straddle the side to fit.

"You can't be friendly with humans like that," Chris grumbled. "You could have given us away. In fact, I'm pretty sure you *did* give us away."

"I do not think he suspected anything," Grith replied, fluffing her tail feathers in his face. "Is that not what your spell is for? I thought he was interesting. I want to talk with him again!"

"The spell doesn't work like that, it doesn't change what you say!" Chris scolded. "You can't get close with mundanes. He could find out about you and our world. You should just throw away his card or burn it."

"Hey, back off," Ashley said, turning to Chris with a glare. "It's her choice. It wouldn't be the first time a human and a magical creature went on a date."

"We're not supposed to tell humans," Chris retorted. "Grith, you have to understand how important secrecy is! You're a dragon, you should know this. If humans find out about you, they'll hunt you down until you're *extinct*."

Ashley shook her head. "Chris is wrong. There are strict guidelines and regulations around telling humans about magic, but it's not illegal as long as you follow the appropriate steps. If the Council beheaded every magical creature who brought a human into the fold, well, there'd be a lot less of us than there are. There are plenty of legal hybrids, like me, for a reason."

Grith cocked her head as she stepped onto the observatory roof, golden feathers fluttering in the wind. She felt like she'd missed something important, and it took a few moments for her to realize what it was.

"Was he courting me?" the dragon asked, the idea not having occurred to her before that.

"Maybe?" Ashley responded. "He seemed nice. I like him."

"He didn't seem that nice," Chris muttered.

The trees on the hill in Los Angeles turned to squares of buildings, with the downtown skyscrapers in the distance. The idea of being courted by a prey animal was somewhat ridiculous, but if she tried to think of humans as small dragons, like Pret had suggested, it became somewhat less so.

"Dragons have our own laws beyond the Council ones," Grith replied, placing her snout out into the wind, her front talons wrapping around the balcony edge. "Maybe it is all right for other magical creatures, but dragons making offspring with humans always leads to the most terrible tragedies. Additionally, there are not enough of us left that we can afford to mate outside our species. Dragons may only take other dragons as our mates, and we are required to produce eggs." She looked back toward Chris and Ashley. "Making eggs with humans is as illegal as it is to eat and kill humans. If I meet with the professor again, I will have to be very strict with him that we are not allowed to court or mate."

Grith raised her head, the evening sun beating down on it. Scents wafted across her nose in the breath, and she took them in. Her eyes widened as she recognized one, a staleness that wasn't that of prey, but rather of trees that moved.

"Oh," the dragon announced, spreading her wings. "I believe I have found the fae."

CHAPTER
NINE

Ashley and Chris ran after Grith as she followed the scent, her nose to the ground while she trotted down another trail, following it back into the city. The sun was low in the sky, cars honking loudly. Grith spread her wings wide as the road went downhill, the wind slicing beneath her feathers, before pulling them back in with a yelp as a car drove past her.

Palm trees lined the road as the three crossed over a large intersection, coming to a large pit in the ground, stairs leading down into it. Grith placed a paw on a moving stairway, before deciding that it was probably too small. She looked back at the two humans.

"The scent continues down here, into the caverns," Grith explained. "What is down here?"

"A subway station," Ashley explained, stepping onto the escalator as it moved her down, Grith pacing alongside on the normal stairs, careful not to trip on the tiny steps. "It helps humans move around quickly, like cars, but—"

"Ah, trains!" Grith replied, realizing what Ashley meant. She knew the term from some of the history lessons her family had given her; the bubble realm system had been created around the same time as railroads had spread across America. "Yes. So they probably went on a tunnel train."

Grith squinted as the light changed colors, the walls and floor of the subway station filled with multicolored square tiles arranged in nonsensical patterns that made her head hurt. She shook it, stumbling and sticking out her tail and wings for balance. It was difficult to judge distances in this place, so instead she focused on the scent, following it until she reached a point where the squares abruptly hit a ledge.

"The scent disappears here," Grith observed. She put her talons on the side of the tracks and craned her neck over, flicking her tongue. There was a loud rumble, and something grabbed her tail.

The dragon looked back with a snarl, baring her fangs until she realized Ashley and Chris were both pulling her tail, hands wrapped around it, though they had nowhere near enough strength to move her. She cocked her head and backed up from the edge, as lights appeared in the tunnel. A silver train with red stripes roared down the tracks.

The wind from it made the feathers along Grith's snout flutter as it slowed, coming to a stop once the doors opened up. Humans walked out, pushing past the dragon into the station.

"Jesus Christ!" Chris groaned, letting go of Grith's tail. "Stop almost getting hit by things! I'm surprised you haven't flown into an airplane before."

"I am sorry," Grith apologized, her ears drooping as she tucked her tail beneath her hindlegs.

"Hey, it's all right," Ashley said with a pat on Grith's neck. "You'll learn. Come on, let's get on before it leaves;

I've got a couple extra Metro Passes. You might be able to pick the trail up at one of the stops."

Grith purred and flicked her snout. She stepped onto the train, humans grunting and glaring as she pushed them aside, not quite sure what else to do. Chris and Ashley squeezed against her side, and she covered the two humans with a wing, patting them on their heads with it.

More of the humans in the train murmured and tried to move around, the subway car packed tight with a dragon inside it. Grith bumped her head against the top as Ashley waved a hand to get her attention.

"Can I try and turn you until you're positioned better to smell outside the station?" Ashley asked. "I'll have to touch your wings and legs."

"That is all right," Grith replied, shifting as Ashley grabbed ahold of her limbs. It wasn't as if all the other humans in the subway car weren't already rubbing up against her. She was very glad she hadn't tried doing this with her shiftstone. The dragon flicked her tail as she realized how long it would take to wash out the smell of exhaust and human from her feathers.

"Watch it!" a human shouted as Grith's tail whacked him in the face.

"Sorry," Grith murmured, curling her tail around a hindleg. It would have been nice if they made train cars that were more dragon-sized.

Grith swayed back and forth as the train moved, easily able to keep her balance on four legs. She noticed that Chris slumped against the train doors, and that the human was looking even paler than he normally did.

"Are you all right?" Grith asked, the scent of fatigue and weakness coming off him. Had she been hunting humans, he seemed like the one she would have gone for, exhausted and probably an easy kill. "You smell weak."

Chris grimaced as he pulled himself to his feet, trying to stand tall and strong. The train jostled him, and he ran into the edge of Grith's wing, dangerously close to the sharp claw on its tip. He held, trying not to fall.

"Everyone here touching you takes a lot of magic." Chris winced. "You look like a human to them, so they're all trying to get into the area where your body is since it seems empty. I'll be fine. I just hope we're out of here soon."

Grith purred and gave the top of his head a lick, causing him to tense up and take a wobbly step back. "Do not worry," she said. "Your hair does not taste very edible."

Chris was giving her a stare like he was wondering how he got into this mess when the doors opened, and humans jostled Grith back and forth as she tried to catch a scent of the fae.

"None here," Grith told the two. "Shall we continue on?"

Ashley nodded, and the doors shut once more, the train moving onto the next stop.

"Is she all right?" Grith heard an eldery human with wrinkles whispering to Ashley. "Why is she smelling the floor?"

"Just a cosplay thing," Ashley responded without missing a beat, like she'd used this excuse a hundred times before. "Don't worry about it."

The elderly human looked at Grith and shook her head back and forth, before grabbing onto a metal pole.

It was a few more stops before Grith finally caught the scent of the fae outside the subway, letting out a loud coo as she waved her wing for Ashley and Chris to follow. She pushed through the crowd into a larger station, this one thankfully without the odd, multicolored pattern that the previous one had. With her nose to the ground, she continued along the trail.

This time, it led up and out of the station, and Grith stepped into downtown LA. She lifted her head, where a huge building with glass windows reached toward the sky, glinting orange in the sunset. More buildings far taller than a dragon corralled the streets, squeezing the humans beneath them into rows and columns with narrow sidewalks, chatting and pushing past in the evening. Grith diligently kept her attention on the trail as the loud noises and myriads of smells pushed her back and forth. The human city was chaotic, far more than the forest around her home, and the overwhelmingness of the sensations caused the dragon's wings to clench up.

She held her ears against her side to blot out the noises, hidden in her feathers like how they would have been when flying, as Ashley walked beside her, trying to keep humans on the sidewalk from bumping into her as much as possible. Grith rumbled thankfully as she walked down the road, the smells of human foods wafting across and attempting to draw her attention away from the fae's scent.

Finally, she reached her destination, and the crowds quieted down. In front of her stood a building that, while still large, was dwarfed by the towers surrounding it, nestled in their shadows. An angular tower capped with a pyramid rose up above a multistoried facade, the visage of a sun imprinted on its surface. The dragon read the English by the entrance.

"A library!" Grith announced, raising her paws up and down in a dance-like movement. "I have not seen any human libraries before."

She twisted her tail gleefully as she pranced up the

stairs toward the entrance, squirming through the doorway as she followed the fae's scent, the two humans struggling to keep up. She forgot to glance behind her as she climbed up a staircase, walking out into a huge rotunda. She had to admit that this was a great distraction from her troubles at VT.

"Look at this!" she said to Chris and Ashley as they entered, spreading her wings open as she walked in a circle around the atrium. "It is so big! Far larger than my parents' library! How many books do you think are in here?"

She sprinted into another room leading off from the atrium and down a hall, still following the fae's scent. Grith twisted and twirled into a room full of bookshelves, careful that she didn't knock any of them with her tail, just barely fluffing her tail feathers against the books' spines. Her head perked up, and the dragon let out a small warble of song as she spotted a book on music.

"I think the fae read this one," Grith announced to the humans, carefully pulling it from its shelf. "I smell their scent on it. *Baroque Instruments.* Do you think that is an important clue?"

Chris panted as he caught up. "So, are we just going to follow the scent until we find some idea of what happened?"

"I will bet that there are some interesting books in here," Grith continued, not paying attention to the wizard's whining as she flipped through the pages of the book, making sure not to tear any. "For prey, humans do have a lot of instruments."

Chris glared , and the dragon tapped him on the head with her tail.

"This time it was a joke!" she purred. "It is funny, is it not?"

Ashley laughed and shook her head, before Grith noticed someone out of the corner of her eyes.

A tall woman with brown hair and large round spectacles was standing agape, her stare focused on Grith.

Grith tilted her head. Had she overheard her? That was unfortunate.

The woman's hands clenched up as she turned to Ashley, a scowl forming on her face as she practically fumed. "Pets!" she squealed. "Are not! Allowed! In the library!"

Grith lowered her ears. Chris's spell had disguised Grith as a human, right? Which meant that either something had gone wrong with it, or this woman wasn't fully human herself.

"She's not a pet," Ashley said, narrowing her eyes. "She's *reading*."

Grith placed the book back on the shelf and crawled over to the librarian. She bent down her head and gave the librarian a loud sniff, squealing as she whacked Grith in the snout with her hand. It wasn't strong enough to do anything but annoy the dragon, and she tilted her gaze toward the hand. The distinctive waft of magic came from the human, along with the smell of gold from a ring, the familiar pattern of a sideways hourglass with its ends open emblazoned on its surface.

"Back!" the librarian ordered, taking a step back herself. "Stay back!"

Grith flopped down onto her underbelly, flicking her tail. "I have seen a similar ring before," she remarked, flicking her tongue out to get a taste, not particularly caring as the rude librarian made a face of disgust and wiped the dragon saliva off on her clothes. "Paul was wearing one. What does it mean?"

The librarian frowned, crossing her arms. "Why does a dragon need to know?" She looked over to Chris, letting out a sigh of relief as she saw his suit. She raised the hand, and for a moment, Grith was worried that she'd try and punch her in the snout with it, but instead, she just flashed her ring at Chris. "You. Wizard. What is a *dragon* doing in my library?"

Chris opened his mouth to respond, but Grith moved her head between him and the librarian, giving her a glare. "We are here looking for a fae, and I tracked them in here," she growled.

The librarian tried to move her head to see over Grith, looking for Chris for confirmation.

"She's right," Chris said tersely. "That's all."

"There was one here a week ago, but it's long gone by now," the librarian pouted. "You should leave. I don't want the dragon setting any books on fire."

"I do not burn books!" Grith adamantly huffed, a low rumble in her throat as she kept herself from snorting smoke. "I have not set any books on fire since I was a hatchling, and I do not plan on ever doing it again!

"We'll keep following the scent trail," Ashley stated, sticking her tongue out in defiance. "When we figure out where our friend went, we'll go too. Until then, we're staying. Be my guest if you want to try and kick a dragon, a witch, and a wizard out of a *public* library."

The librarian squinted and adjusted her spectacles, as if she was sizing her up. "Then be *very* careful, young lady!" she squeaked, before eyeing Grith's tail. "Make sure your dragon doesn't cause any trouble."

"I am not her dragon," Grith mumbled, placing her head on the ground. "That would be silly. I could eat her in a few bites."

Chris's eyes opened wide. "Don't!" he pleaded. "We shouldn't mess with her."

Grith was surprised of the bit of fear-scent coming from Chris. Was he afraid of her? She doubted it, it wasn't as if laying on the ground was a particularly threatening position, and he'd been around her for the last few hours without much fear-scent. Did that mean he was afraid of the librarian? She was sitting at the desk, still glowering at the three. The scent of magic around her did seem stronger than the one around Chris.

"Well, that was rude," Ashley muttered.

Chris shook his head. "She was just doing her job to keep the place safe. There was a fire here years ago; I'll bet she was worried about that."

"Still doesn't mean she wasn't rude," Ashley responded.

Grith whimpered, tucking her tail between her legs and lowering her ears. For a moment, she'd forgotten about her treatment at VT, but this had just brought it back. Perhaps she didn't belong with humans. So long as she was with them, they would treat them like a monster, just like Chris had said. Yet, there was no way out, and she had no choice but to work with them.

Grith continued following the trail scent, ignoring the librarian's stares even as they seemed to prick her feathers. She meandered between bookshelves, momentarily stopping at one every once in a while. Even among the books, she wasn't able to get her mind off what the library had said. She just wanted to go home and sulk on her hoard.

"I think that they were just casually browsing," Grith observed. "I do not think they were actually looking for books here."

"You can smell that?" Ashley blinked. "Wow."

Grith shuffled her wings. "I cannot; it is just a guess.

They did not stay in any place just for long, just wandering around. It is like what I have done, when I was browsing my mother's library." Her ears drooped at the mention of her mother. Again, she felt trapped in a world that wasn't hers. If she didn't remain at VT, she would lose the library with the rest of her home. The dragon turned a corner, heading back out through the door they'd come from, returning toward the rotunda. "I suppose that this was just a detour to meet with a librarian with a few ingrown feathers inside her cloaca? At least I got to see some books."

"What?" Chris asked, scratching his head.

Ashley laughed, turning to the wizard as the group walked down a flight of stairs. "A stick up her—"

"Oh," Chris interrupted, his face going red. "Oh."

At the end of the stairwell, Grith turned, her tail whipping against a door in the small hallway. Her eyes tilted up to a sign. "A meeting room?" she asked, stepping into it. "I wonder what they were meeting about. A musical instrument, perhaps?"

"I'm more wondering with whom." Ashley frowned.

Compared to some of the other locales Grith had visited, she didn't find the meeting room particularly interesting, except perhaps in its uninterestingness, which might have been interesting all on its own. She swept her tail across a dusty table in the center, wiggling a chair with her talons. Her snout bumped against the wall opposite to the entrance, and Grith realized that the fae's scent had stopped. She flicked her tongue. There was something else odd in here. "The trail stops, but I can smell magic. However, I cannot tell where it is coming from."

Chris put his hands in his suit-pockets, shrugging. "I guess. I'm not surprised, given that one of the librarians is a wizard, and a GMI one at that."

"Give me a moment," Ashley said, opening her robes and reaching into one of the myriad of pockets sewn onto the interior. When she took it out, Grith tilted her head at a small twig between Ashley's fingers, and scooched to the side as the witch-in-training wandered around the room, holding it out.

Grith's eyes widened as the stick started to glow a dim white, and Ashley waggled her hand around, before getting on her knees. She crept beneath the table, and lying on her back, looked up at the underside.

"Found it!" Ashley shouted. "I guess the best place to hide a rune is by a bunch of old gum, but ew. I think it's a lock of some sort. Wizard, any idea what the key is?"

"Dunno," Chris said, glancing at Grith before turning his gaze back down to the floor.

"Hmm," Ashley mused. "Hey, how about a rune for magic?" She traced a finger out over it in a cup-like shape, a bright green light shining between the white globs of gum.

Grith leapt into the air as she felt movement behind her, turning around and letting out a growl, her fangs bared as smoke rose from her nostrils. It took a couple moments for the dragon to calm. Instead of a threat, she saw that a hole had opened up where the fae's scent had cut off, and a stone staircase clearly not meant for dragons crept down, lit by faint orange torchlight.

"That worked?" Ashley asked. "Seriously? That's like making your computer password 'password.' Chris, you need to teach your wizard friends some magical security."

"It's probably just to keep mundanes out," Chris said, nervously glancing back toward the meeting room entrance. "It wouldn't be hard for an experienced wizard to have busted in if he'd wanted to. It's just a general rule that advances in magical security are countered more easily than they're created, and exchanging them every six months for an even more complicated and expensive spell is a pain in the . . . butt."

Grith put her head back down to the trail and followed it along into the stairwell, squishing her body and keeping her wings low. The torches here were too close for her comfort. Unlike the scaled Western and Eastern dragons, the oil on Grith's feathers made them fire-resistant, but not fire-proof.

She smelled more than just the fae as the stairwell went down for what she thought might have been more than just a few human-sized floors. She picked up the librarian's scent also, the more recent one overpowering Albiwegan's. Grith followed them both until she came to the stairs' end, the dim light growing brighter. The dragon barely noticed that she'd almost knocked over a torch when she lifted her head in amazement.

Ashley let out a yelp when Grith stopped, tripping over the dragon's tail, barely managing to catch her balance by sticking her hands out into the wall. "Grith? What is it?"

"It's beautiful!" Grith purred, flapping her wings in excitement. She stepped out into a huge chamber, like the rotunda above but ten times as huge, stretching her wings out as she basked in the glory of the secret library. Magically-created lights glimmered in through stained-glass windows that led to nowhere, and as Grith looked up, her eyes scanned across a painted mural of humans performing feats of magic, runes forming a circle around the edge. But more than that, there were curved bookshelves that reached above her head, forcing her to stand back on her haunches to see the rest of the room. Three concentric rings wrapped around the rotunda, spaces between them forming a six-spoked wheel.

The dragon let out a trill of excitement; seeing that books filled each shelf to the brim. "Look! There are so many!" she squeaked, rushing up to one of the bookshelves and pulling a book out. "Look at this one! It is an entire volume only on teleportation circles! And the next one is only on teleportation squares! I did not even know there was such a thing as teleportation squares!"

"I'm starting to see why you were interested in Vertex Technologies," Ashley remarked. "You're kinda a nerd."

Grith let out another happy trill as she pulled out a book and flopped onto her back, the down of her belly sticking up in the air as she closed and opened her wings. "This one is on metallurgical calculations! Look! They have a list of metals by shimmer count. I was not aware that human wizards knew about that!"

"Can we focus?" Chris snapped. "I'm still using my magic here, and I really don't think we should be down here."

Grith's ears drooped, her tail and wings flopping to the ground as she looked toward Chris with a soppy expression more befitting of a dog. "Oh. Well, I suppose that makes sense."

The dragon rolled back onto her paws, placing the book back before continuing on the trail. Maybe she'd be able to have more time down here after they found the fae. This was a public library, after all.

"Hm," Grith remarked with a flick of her tail as she stepped into the center of the room. "That is interesting. Albiwegan started to have fear-scent around here." She twisted her head as she turned down another one of the spokes, trotting as Chris and Ashley ran after her. "I think they sped up here. And then . . . gone."

"Gone?" Ashley asked, walking up to where Grith was

standing and peering down at the spot in the ground. "Like, disappeared? Or teleported?"

Grith sniffed again. "Teleported," she decided. "I recognize the scent of the old magic."

"So, they were running," Ashley pieced together, "and ran over here, and then teleported away. What were they running from?"

"From me," a terse voice said from behind them.

The three turned around, Grith almost knocking Ashley over with her tail.

The librarian faced them, her lips pursed in a scowl.

Grith felt an aura of magic surround her, setting the dragon's feathers on end, and the librarian lifted a glowing blue orb in one hand, drawing fire from it with the other.

Grith decided that scales might have been convenient right about now.

CHAPTER
TEN

"Oh dear, we are very, very sorry for coming down here without permission," Grith murmured, her voice a bellow as it echoed through the library. She dipped her head down, looking up at the librarian with pleading eyes. "It was just that it was extremely easy for us to solve your lock and come down here and we figured that you wouldn't mind. We can leave at once, as the scent ended down here!"

The dragon let out a yelp as a glowing blue fireball sailed just above her head, hitting the wall behind her. "Sorry again!" she yelled out as she turned and ran, following behind Chris and Ashley, who'd already gotten a head-start on her. Heart racing, her tail whipped around the corner of a bookshelf, ducking behind it as another fireball blasted out from the hallway, almost singing her tail feathers.

"And she was worried about *Grith* setting fire to things?" Ashley yelled, sprinting down the hallway as the dragon overtook her in a few leaps. "Chris, tell her to stop!"

Chris shook his head with a gulp. "Ohh, we shouldn't have gone in here, we shouldn't have gone in here!"

Grith turned her head back as footsteps pounded through the ground, and she spotted the librarian sprinting after her. Another fireball whooshed over her head, and Grith let out a shriek of agony as it hit one of the bookshelves, the tomes engulfed in blue flames.

"Not the books!" the dragon squealed, trying to flap one of her wings as she passed them and put the flames out. She let out another yelp as a sharp pain tore into her wing, ripping away feathers. Her eyes went wide as she saw that the books engulfed in flames had grown sharp teeth, flinging themselves at Grith.

"That is a relief," Grith puffed, shaking her wing and snarling at one of the books as another blue flame shot over her and more books came to life, snapping as they bobbed up and down in the air after the dragon. She spread her wings wide open, knocking away a few books as her eyes glowed, golden ribbons of light swirling around her feathers, and she drew runes with the claws on their tips to dispel the magic around the books before they could get more injured.

"Wait, stop!" Chris yelled, waving his hands up at Grith to get her attention. "No spells! The glamor will shatter, and I can't cast it again with the magic I have left! I really don't want to collapse here and get eaten by books!"

Grith snorted and pulled her wings back in, the magic glow fading. She whacked one of the books with her tail as it tried to bite it, and hit another with a wing-spur, ripping it through the pages. "Sorry!" she apologized to the book as it limply tried to bite her again. "I did not mean to hurt you!"

Ashley shook her head as the three turned another

corner, sprinting as she struggled to keep up with the dragon.

"How are you more empathic toward books than you are to humans!" Chris cried out, clutching his head as a book flew at him. He drew an S-shaped rune in the air with glowing blue magic right before it could chomp his head off, and an orange blast of fire shot out, only cinders remaining when it had disappeared.

Grith's eyes went wide, mortified. "Humans only last maybe fifty years!" she explained, staring at the ashes of the poor book the cinders had destroyed. "Dragons last three-hundred, but books made of quality parchment can last a thousand!"

"That's not—" Chris stammered.

"IT DOESN'T MATTER!" Ashley yelled. "Grith can't use her magic and probably doesn't want to set this place on fire. My magic really isn't supposed to be used for combat. Chris, you're a wizard, how do we stop her?"

Chris glanced back again as the librarian turned toward them, holding the arm with the orb out. With a frown, he reached into his suit pocket, pulling out a handful of glass stones. "I've got an idea, but I'll need a distraction."

"I can be a very large distraction," Grith pointed out, spreading open her wings as she batted another few tomes away with her tail. "Oh, not the dictionary!"

"I'll help," Ashley said. "Grith, lift me into the air."

The dragon turned around and ran back toward Ashley, the human girl's eyes going wide for a moment as she saw the huge beast charging toward her. Grith leapt into the air, gliding between the bookshelves as more of the books snapped at her tail, and extended her claws down toward Ashley, wrapping her foretalons around Ashley's torso and lifting her up.

As they rose up into the rotunda, Grith moved her talons around the human's weight, leering down at her, trying to be as careful as possible. It was an odd sensation. When she normally carried prey like this, they were already dead or were about to be, and she didn't have to worry too much about accidentally impaling them on her claws. She resisted the sudden urge to bring the human up to her jaws and tear out her throat.

"No hunting," she murmured to herself. Her eyes landed on the librarian shooting a blast of flame up into the air. Grith tucked in her right wing and lifted the other one up, rolling to the side and out of the way. The human lurched in her talons, and looked down to make sure she was still alive.

"I was kinda expecting to be on your back." Ashley grimaced, sticking her left hand into her robe and pulling out an herb with it. She let out a yelp as a book tried to bite her ankles, and flailed out a foot, trying to kick it away.

"How could I hold you if you were on my back?" Grith asked. She gave the book a good thwack with her tail, causing the two to lurch again as she lost her balance mid-flight. More books were flying up after her, sharp teeth chomping as the dragon shifted left and right.

"Right there!" Ashley shouted, pointing toward a spot in the center of the room beneath the leering murals. As Grith tilted to the side, turning, Ashley dragged the black rune on her forearm up to her hand, turning it green. The herb went up in flame, and smoke spread out from it.

"That's a very strong smelling herb," Grith mused, taking it in with a loud purr. She barely noticed as her eyelids began to droop, her wings faltering for a moment as she dropped a few feet.

Ashley screamed, clutching around the dragon's foreleg

with her arms, pounding on Grith's feathers with a fist. "GRITH!"

"Oops." Grith yawned, spreading her wings back out. She looked down at Ashley, shaking her head from side to side. "Do not worry, I will not drop you nor eat you. Neither of those would be good in this situation, would it? Are you normally so pink and fleshy?"

Ashley slapped Grith in the snout. "Stay awake, please!" she pleaded Grith, the dragon purring loudly in response, bringing Ashley's up to her mouth and giving her a wet lick on the back of her neck.

The books chasing them moved slower, their bounces through the air becoming little hops before they drifted down to the ground.

"Seriously? I *know* you're smarter than those books."

"Nothing is smarter than a book," Grith purred, tugging on Ashley's hair with her fangs. "You should take off that hair, it doesn't taste good."

"Grith, look out!" Ashley shouted, whacking the dragon in the nose once more.

Grith opened her eyes wide as the librarian shot another fireball. She shifted to the side, swinging back and forth mid-air like a pendulum. "Mmm. Tick, tock, I am a clock."

"Grith!" Ashley whined, clutching her head. "Please! We're trying to distract the librarian!"

The dragon flicked her snout as she swooped down toward the librarian, letting out a roar that resembled a yawn. "I am a big, scary dragon! I will burn this library to the ground!"

With a sniffle of sorrow, Grith let out a small blast of orange flame at the librarian, coursing through the air before it stopped a few yards short of actually touching any of the bookshelves. She angled her wings back upward, turning back toward the center of the rotunda. "Was I distracting?"

"Very," Ashley groaned. She scanned the ground until she saw Chris, backed up against the wall of the secret library, waving wildly at the two of them before gestured his hands down. "Grith! Land by Chris, over there! Carefully!"

"Yes, mother," Grith murmured, tilting her wings as she weaved back and forth, spiraling down. The smoke let up at the edge of the library, and Grith cocked her head. "Mother?"

"LAND!" Ashley yelled, banging her fist on Grith's foreleg.

Grith dove down toward the ground, flipping her wings back up as she neared Chris, carefully holding Ashley out as the floor zoomed toward the two. A few feet from it, she opened her talons, hoping that she'd judged the speed right and that Ashley didn't break anything. The human landed on all fours, wincing as she hit the ground and rubbing her hurt palms on her robe.

Grith landed as light as a feather, the dragon towering over Chris.

The librarian ran toward her, her blue orb still out.

Grith bared her fangs, smoke coming out from her nostrils as she readied her talons. She suddenly recalled her conversation with Chris, wondering if wizards counted as humans for the purpose of legally eating them. Was there an exception for self-defense?

"Stay back!" Chris yelled, taking a step between the dragon and the librarian.

Grith gave him a small snarl, not particularly apprecia-tive that he'd stepped between her and her prey.

169

A circle of blue light had appeared around the library, arcing between each of the stones that Chris had placed down. "Cover your ears!"

The wizard pulled out a tuning fork, drawing three blue numbers on it with his fingers.

The dragon cocked her head as he flicked it with his fingernail, the silver metal glowing a bright blue.

A moment later, and Grith let out a shriek, drowned out by a piercing, monotone hum ringing across the library. She folded her ears against her head, shaking it in pain as she clutched her talons around them and rolled onto the floor.

The noise didn't stop, and Ashley let out a similar yell, though Grith only knew from the movement of her mouth.

There was a crack and a flash, and a pillar of blue flame rose into the air around the librarian. The librarian's orb flung shards out across the room, a few of them getting caught in Grith's feathers.

Chris lowered the tuning fork and the tone went abruptly silent, replaced by the screams of the librarian as the blue flame crawled up her clothes, engulfing her.

"I am sorry for trespassing on your territory!" Grith apologized. A flash of light hit her eyes, and the librarian was gone.

"Please keep quiet in the library," Ashley muttered, whacking the side of her head with a hand. "Ow. My ears are ringing."

"Did she burn up?" Grith asked Chris, cocking her head and flicking an ear. "That is a waste of meat." Dragons were large and had to eat a lot, or else they had to make it up in their shimmer stores. She didn't want to waste anything she could still eat.

"I doubt it." Chris frowned. "I think she used a teleportation stone. Hopefully, into the LA River."

Grith's nostrils flared as she smelt blood, strong. She nudged Chris in the side, and he let out a cry of pain, clutching where Grith had touched him.

"You are bleeding," Grith noticed, as a red splotch began to soak through his suit. "Hm. That does not look good. What happened?" She decided against asking him if she could eat him if he died. First, because it was probably rude, and second, because it was a silly question: if he was dead he clearly wouldn't mind being eaten. She wondered if the fight had taken far more energy than she'd thought, or if it was the odd smoke making her hungry.

"Spell backfire," Chris grimaced, pulling his hands away from his side. "I only knew the frequency to shatter the librarian's orb because I was issued a smaller one by VT. I thought I'd be far enough out of range, but it looks like I was wrong."

"Let me look at it," Ashley said, Chris giving her a look of skepticism. "I know healing magic. I might be able to help."

Chris carefully lifted his suit and part of the shirt beneath it, Grith sniffing when she noticed blood dripping from his side. The wound didn't look good — the explosion had ripped away his skin, with shards of blue shrapnel embedded in his flesh.

Ashley peered down to get a closer look, careful not to touch it. "Hold still." Ashley frowned, pulling out a white cloth from her side, drawing a few green runes on it as she placed it over the wound.

Chris grunted.

"This will stop the bleeding and will help with the pain, but I'll need something stronger to actually heal it. The orb released its magic directly into your body."

Ashley got up, peering around the library. The human

turned to Grith, tapping a finger on her cheek as she stared the dragon in her eyes.

Grith tilted her head.

"Dragon saliva has healing properties, and it'll help draw out the magic," Ashley explained. "I can make a cream from it that should do the trick. I've got the base components on me, but I'll need a pot to make it. I saw another exit to the room, so maybe there's something in there. Grith, can you carry Chris? I'm pretty sure he can't walk."

"I suppose," Grith responded, wondering what the best way to do that was. After deciding, she bent her head down, opening her jaws wide to grab him.

Chris let out a yell of alarm, hitting her in the nose before clutching his side again. Blood soaked the bandage. "Seriously? She'll eat me! Wouldn't carrying me on her back be better?"

Grith let out a puff of smoke, flicking her tail. "I will not eat you! I have enough self-control not to do that. I do not think putting you on my back would be a good idea; you would probably fall off. And dragon saliva does have healing properties."

Chris sighed and raised up his arms in surrender. "Fine. Just be careful."

"Very!" Grith huffed, wrapping her jaws around the wizard as carefully as she could, making sure not to puncture him with her fangs. She lifted her head, turning the wizard sideways, his head and legs dangling out. Blood dripped onto her tongue, and she let the forked ends brush against the bandage, lapping a bit of it off.

Chris looked up at one of the dragon's slitted eyes, horrified. "Are you—"

"Healing properties," Grith reminded him with a purr, feeling his body rumble from the force of it. She did admit that it did taste good, and it was extremely odd to be holding prey without planning to eat them. Just one snap, and she'd have a very nice meal. Albeit a very illegal one. Plus, Chris had hurt himself to stop the librarian, and was doing a good job of making it so that Grith didn't have to use the shiftstone. Even if she didn't particularly like him, eating him would have been a rude way to repay that.

Ashley led Grith toward another chamber at one of the spokes of the library, a small passageway with a few rooms leading off from it. After opening a few of the doors, Ashley finally found the one she was looking for.

"A pot!" Ashley announced, pointing to a small pot alongside a collection of more cookware. "I think non-stick will work."

As Ashley pulled ingredients out from her robe, Grith gently set Chris on the floor, giving the blood at his side another lick.

The human looked up with her, though with far less alarm than a few minutes ago.

"That was not so bad, was it?" the dragon trilled.

Chris shook his head with a sigh, and tried to wipe off some of the saliva from his suit, cringing as he moved the wound. "I'm never going to be able to get the smell of smoke and dragon spit out of this suit."

"Nor the blood!" Grith answered before another small bookshelf on the side of the room caught her attention, only a few books placed on it. Near it was a desk with a few biscuits to the side of a book, still open. Perhaps this was the librarian's personal chamber?

"Hey, Grith, can you spit please?" Ashley called, holding the pot out toward the dragon's snout, the green glow from her rune heating it up.

Grith spat a glob into the pot, peering down into it to

see her spittle mixed with other herbs, coming to a boil as Ashley stirred it with a spoon that she'd found.

The dragon turned back to the book on the desk, carefully walking over Chris as she peered over it.

The librarian's scent was thick around it.

Careful not to change the page it was on, Grith picked up the spine with a claw, reading it. "*Teleportation: A Primer.* Chris, you have this one in your lab, do you not?"

Chris only grunted, and Grith continued reading, checking the page that the librarian had left it open to. "Natural teleportation in magical creatures," Grith read, the words written in big letters in the upper corner. Her feathers raised as a few words in an early passage stuck out to her. "'The fae are some of the most adept at natural teleportation, with the ability to teleport short distances at will, along with creating interlocking webs of bubble realms, colloquially known as Faerie Realms, a magical technique that was only discovered by dragons in the nineteenth century.' Hmph. They didn't even give my grandfather credit!"

She thought for a moment. It couldn't just be coincidence. Albiwegan went missing after meeting with the librarian who had a book open to a passage on fae. Grith looked back toward Chris, who was still laying on the ground, clutching his side as Ashley prepared the salve. "Chris, did you recognize the ring that the librarian wore? With the hourglass with the two open ends?"

"The GMI ring?" Chris asked, frowning. "Yeah. The bindrune isn't an hourglass, though. What about it?"

Grith puffed smoke, flicking her tail. "Well, what does it *mean*? What is a GMI?"

"It's a wizard society." Chris frowned. "The Grand Mage Initiative. It's a group of the most respected, powerful, and elite wizards, like my father, and Pa-The Executive, and apparently the librarian. I didn't know they allowed women in, though."

"Ah," Ashley remarked with a grimace. "One of *those* societies. Of course." She shook her head as she walked over to Chris with the pot, putting a dab of golden cream on her fingers. "It's like you wizards are stuck in the fifties."

"Eighteen, or nineteen?" Grith asked, raising an ear.

Chris shrugged and lifted the edge of his suit jacket as Ashley reached for the bandage, dripping blood and dragon spittle onto the floor. "Anyone who's anyone is a part of GMI. Which doesn't include me yet." He winced as Ashley peeled away the bandage, revealing the bloody wound with specks of blue in it. Grith flicked her tongue across her fangs. "This whole thing makes me nervous. If the librarian is part of GMI, she had to have a good reason to attack us. We really shouldn't be here."

Ashley smeared the golden cream over the wound, rubbing it in. "That should soak up the stray magic pretty quickly and start healing it. I'll apply it again later." She grabbed another bandage, writing a few more green runes on it before placing it over the cream, Grith's ears drooping.

Chris glared at Grith as he sat back up. "You could stop glaring hungrily at me, you know. I can see that."

"Sorry," Grith whimpered, tucking her tail. "I do not mean to. Southern Dragons normally do not have to eat that much, but mages usually require a lot more upkeep to maintain the large amounts of shimmer and energy needed in our body to cast spells beyond the basic ones, both from food and hoard size. And though I hunted, I did not sleep very well last night."

"I'm the one who's done all the spellcasting," Chris grumbled, slowly getting to his feet. "Speaking of that, I don't think I have enough essence to cast anything else for a while, so if we run into a crispy librarian, it'll be up to you two. I barely have enough to keep the glamor going."

"Well, she seemed pretty flammable for an 'elite' wizard," Ashley replied. "I'm pretty sure Grith can help with that."

"I think that it would be illegal if I set her on fire," Grith said. "Are we still searching for the fae? I lost the scent."

"Should we give up?" Chris asked hopefully.

Ashley shook her head. "We can keep searching. Albi-wegan wouldn't have teleported away far, so if we wander around the area, maybe Grith can pick their scent up again."

Grith flicked her ears. "I can do that. I am excited; I have not been in downtown LA at night before!"

ELEVEN

G rith was sad to leave the secret library behind, but she hoped that maybe she could make amends with the librarian and maybe come back down here again. She detested the human, but it was Grith who had done wrong. She hadn't meant to intrude on the librarian's hoard, although since she wasn't the one who'd set her on fire, maybe the librarian could be her. Perhaps she needed to give a gift from her own hoard in order to make up? She didn't want to part with any of her mother's books, but it seemed the librarian would appreciate them. She wondered if the librarian could read any Southern or Dragon Pidgin. Probably not. There were a few tomes in human languages around, both modern and ancient, that she might be willing to part with.

Grith turned her head toward an interesting building on the side of the road, taking in a deep sniff as the door opened and a human walked in. Cooked meat made her mouth water, along with the smell of interesting spices that she didn't recognize. Usually, she preferred her food raw and as fresh of a kill as possible, without spices, but they did go well on the frozen meats that she had stored. She curiously poked her head down at the entrance and gave it another sniff, letting out a gasp as the door slammed on her snout.

"Did you find the scent?" Ashley asked as Grith gave her nose a rub.

"Unfortunately, I did not," Grith answered.

Chris let out a long sigh, leaning against the restaurant's windows. "We've been walking for hours and it's getting dark. We should just go home and come back tomorrow."

"My nose does not rely on natural sunlight," the dragon pointed out.

"I think we should keep going." Ashley frowned. "I don't want to give the librarian time to recover. What if she warns the rest of GMI about this?"

"GMI?" Chris scoffed. "Why would they be involved?"

"Just a suspicion?" Ashley suggested, gently pushing Grith to the side as another human tried to walk out the doorway. "Secret wizard cult?"

"It's not a secret, you're just uncultured," Chris grumbled. "And if GMI *is* involved in this, then we should absolutely leave it alone and give up right now! They have a good reason for whatever they do."

Grith poked her head into a large alleyway as the two humans argued. A few bright lights changed colors through a cloth entrance with a few humans standing in line, while some sort of music reached her ears. More interestingly, she spotted a dented trash can with a few scorch marks gracing the nearby wall. They didn't look dragon-made.

"You think they had a good reason, even if they hurt Albiwegan?" Ashley asked, crossing her arms.

"Well, maybe the fae did something bad!" Chris

retorted, throwing his hands up. "Fae do that sometimes, right? Steal names? Make deals to take firstborn children?"

"Alb would never do that! They don't have the power, and if they did, it would be the Council's job to apprehend them," Ashley responded. "Not some weird cult of—"

A puff of Grith's smoke interrupted the two, causing them both to break out in a coughing fit, Chris clutching his side.

Grith's golden eyes stared down at them through it. "I caught the scent!" she exclaimed. "There is some teleportation residue as well."

"Great!" Ashley smiled, brushing away the smoke. "We're back on track!"

"Theirs is not the only scent I recognize!" Grith cheerily responded, swishing her tail as she turned in toward the alleyway. "The librarian came here, too! I think she teleported after them, and there was a chase!"

Chris fiddled his fingers, and fear wafted from him again. He didn't seem particularly thrilled at the prospect of meeting the librarian again. Nor was she; the library had been very rude, and Grith didn't want to get in another fight.

Grith followed the tracks up to the noisy entrance, peering around it and smelling the twin scents inside, along with a bunch of other indistinct humans. The sound of the music grew louder, roaring as bright colored lights hit against her eyes. She tried to go in, only to find the scent of a human under her nose, blocking her path.

A burly man with black glass across his eyes stood directly in front of the dragon, a thin line of felted rope hanging behind him. Grith doubted it would stop a human from crossing it.

"Excuse me, sir," the dragon said, lowering her head to

meet his eyes. "Would you mind moving out of my path? I would not like to step on you."

If the man was looking back at her, Grith couldn't tell, his eyes covered by the shades. "ID?" he asked, crossing his arms.

Grith flicked her ears and cocked her head, confused. "Aidy?"

"He means identification," Chris said, scooching against the entrance beneath the dragon's left wing and holding out a small card with his picture on it.

"Oh. I do not have any cards," Grith glumly murmured. "If you wanted to identify me, you could smell me instead."

"You're good to go," the bouncer replied to Chris, giving Grith a funny look. He let out a laugh as Ashley followed, holding out an ID of her own. "I'm not believing you're twenty-one for a second! That thing's obviously fake."

"I'm literally a bartender," Ashley mumbled, opening her robe and putting the card back, before pulling out a slip of green paper. "Please? We don't want to drink, anyways."

"Speak for yourself," Chris remarked, clutching his head as he looked up at Grith.

The bouncer shook his head. "Sorry, kid, no can do. I like this job; I'm not losing it over twenty bucks."

Ashley scoffed and put the bill back.

Grith didn't have much of an idea of how much human money was worth, but based on her salary on Vertex she didn't think that was much. She opened up the bag at her side and dug her talons into it.

"Will this be enough to make it worth losing?" the dragon asked, holding out three dragon-sized gold coins between her talons. "I could do silver if you would prefer."

The bouncer's eyes opened wide, and he picked one up

from Grith's paw, feeling the weight to it. His nails scratched at the surface, and he stared in disbelief. "Jesus."

"Do you need more?"

The bouncer shook his head, and pulled the other two up, tucking them away in the side of his coat. "No. Hey, is the invitation to smell you still open?"

Grith gave him a purr before puffing smoke into his face, causing the bouncer to turn away and cough.

"Stoners," he muttered, placing a hand on his coat to check that the coins were still there. He pulled the rope to the side. "Well, go right ahead."

Grith stepped through the rope, squinting as the blinding colored lights shone across her iridescent feathers. Blurry humans were moving wildly beneath them, sweat and prey-scent filling the room as loud rumbles burst through the floor, jolting through Grith's body. She stumbled forward, not quite sure where the fae's scent had gone, letting out a whine of pain.

Chris leaned into the wall, hands shaking. "We can't go in there!" he yelled, trying to get Ashley to hear him over the rave. "She'll get touched, and I won't be able to keep up the glamor!"

"They look like they are having enjoyment, but it is too much for me." Grith squinted, flattening her ears against the side of her head. "I am in agreement with Chris."

Ashley grimaced, scratching her head. After a few moments, she drew a small herb with six leaves from her robe, Grith immediately recognizing the smell from the tracking spell that Ashley's mother had done earlier. A green light glimmered from Ashley's hand, and the end of the stem went up in flame.

"Out, now!" Ashley ordered as she threw the herb into

the rave, gesturing both Chris and Grith back toward the entrance.

Grith gave the bouncer another purr as she stumbled beyond him, and Ashley tried to pull one of the dragon's wings further into the alleyway.

"What did you do?" Chris whispered. "It doesn't explode, does it? Oh, please don't say it explodes!"

"Back so soon?" the bouncer asked, frowning. His eyes went wide, and he pinched his nose.

Grith covered her own with her talons as the scent of the burning leaves wafted over towards her.

The music from the rave abruptly cut off, people coughing and retching. Humans walked out in front of her, turning as they left it, muttering grievances to each other about the smell. In a couple minutes, the club seemed like it was almost completely empty but for the sighing bouncer.

"A few very gross potions call for it." Ashley quietly laughed. "Be glad your salve didn't."

Grith let out an unhappy rumble, looking up at Ashley as she held her nose tight. "This does not help. I will definitely not be able to smell the fae now."

"Already got that covered." Ashley grinned, pulling a small clear vial out from her pockets. She uncorked it and blew past Grith's feathers, fluttering against her sides. Ashley whispered a few quiet words to the vial before explaining. "It's a tamed wind. It'll bring the smell out."

"You are very useful!" Grith remarked with a happy flick of her tail. "Both of you know very good magic!"

"Thanks!" Ashley beamed.

Chris just looked more ill than anything, pale as he leaned against the alley wall.

The bouncer squinted as they walked back into the now

empty club. "You three are a weird group, and that's saying something with the people I get in here."

"We are all three normal humans," Grith trilled, lifting a wing as she dipped her head beneath it. With a small poke, she plucked out a long golden feather, rainbow colors forming beneath the lamplight. She held it out to the bouncer, who took it with the utmost confusion. "It is a gift. In case you ever come in need of it!" It was dangerous to give out, but he could make himself a wizard if he desired.

The bouncer stared at the feather for a moment, squinting as he tried to figure out where it had come from. He just shook his head and sighed as the three went in.

Grith trotted into the club, the lights still flashing. No one had bothered to turn them off in their hurry. The awful stench of whatever Ashley had burned lingered like a cloud over the club, but it wasn't enough to keep her from following the trail.

"It appears like all of the humans here were having lots of fun," Grith remarked, swishing her tail. "I am slightly saddened that they all had to leave."

"So, now you experience empathy for us?" Chris snapped, stumbling across the dancefloor. "You're fine with killing and eating humans, but you don't want to interrupt a stupid dance?"

Grith tilted her head. She could smell Chris's anger alongside his sweat, the wizard struggling just to make it across. "Of course I experience empathy. Humans experience empathy for their prey-animals, correct? Just not when you are eating them. And I am not fine with killing humans. That is highly illegal, and . . . mean."

"Illegal and mean?" Chris scoffed. "It's murder!"

"Chris, cut her some slack." Ashley glared. "Before the past couple days, she's literally never spoken to a human before in however many decades she's been alive. Most of what she knows about our species is in the context of us being prey animals that dragons aren't allowed to eat for fear of retaliation. And if you haven't noticed, she's been wandering around LA all day, chatting to strangers, and *hasn't* actually hurt any of them."

"I think that I might have thwacked someone with my tail," Grith unhelpfully added.

Ashley sighed. "I do wish you'd have come to the Key a week or two before going to Vertex Technologies. We have a program that helps magical creatures who've never been around humans before adjust to stuff like this."

"That would have been nice," Grith said, walking into the center of the club as she followed the trail. "I wonder if I could join one of the human dance parties at a future time. It does look like fun, but I do not think I could dance like them." She got up onto her hindlegs, attempting to spread out her wings and wobble around in a dance-like motion, before falling onto her back.

Ashley laughed. "We have parties at the Key sometimes. You could always join there, and you wouldn't need a shift-stone or glamor. Chris can join too, as long as he behaves himself."

"Hey." Chris frowned. "I behave better than both of you."

"I hope I do not accidentally step on him!" Grith warbled. "You will have to be careful, Chris."

The wizard looked unamused at that, stomping after Grith and Ashley as they pushed through the backdoor of the club, Grith lifting her head up to the cool night air.

She gave it a sniff, remarking, "There are scorch marks." She then gestured out into another alleyway with a wing.

She put her snout down to them, wandering around for a few moments.

"So, there was a fight." Ashley frowned. "The librarian used her magic."

"Albiwegan's scent continues this way," Grith said, tucking in her wings as she stepped down the alley, lamp-lights providing a sheen over her feathers, "but I think they were carried. The librarian grabbed them. They were still alive."

"Captured, not killed," Ashley murmured, running after Grith as the dragon stepped out into a larger street, careful to stay on the sidewalk.

Chris struggled to keep up, out-of-breath as they rushed down it.

It was around half an hour before Grith finally saw where the trail was heading, the city becoming quieter around her. A pair of chattering human hatchlings on the side of the road looked at each other, going quiet as she passed, and the dragon walked across an empty road lit only by a flickering lamplight.

A creaking brick building reeking of old age rose a few flights above Grith's head, broken windows across its walls revealing no light inside. Unlike the other places they'd visited, it was in disarray. Even the other buildings nearby seemed to be avoiding it, all of them far closer to each other than they were to the warehouse, as if they were worried it would crumble at any moment and take them down with it.

"Does the trail go in there?" Chris gulped.

Grith gave Chris a toothy grin and eagerly walked up to the building, intent on following the trail to its conclusion. A few paces away from it she let out a yelp, her snout suddenly running into something. She rubbed it with her talons, poofing up flattened feathers, and realized that the smell of magic had joined the scents.

"It's a magical barrier," Chris remarked without even the slightest bit of surprise, knocking on it with his knuckles. "Oh well. Guess we have to go back."

"Really?" Ashley glared. "I know you don't care about Albiwegan or anyone outside of your species except in a sick, fetishy way, but aren't you the least bit curious what's behind?"

Chris shrugged, leaning his back against the barrier. "Nope. I know how to break it, but I can't with the little magic I have left. I wouldn't be willing to break it anyways. It was clearly put here intentionally as a way to keep others out."

Ashley rolled her eyes and drew a green H-shaped rune on the barrier. It faded, and a bang of Ashley's fist just caused her hand to hurt. "I've got nothing."

"Do you think that it is dragon-proofed?" Grith asked Chris.

Chris squinted. "Er, it's a magical barrier. Why would you need to dragon-proof it?"

Grith took a step back and lifted her head, calling flame up to her jaws. She opened them, and orange fire blasted from her maw, a stream of it pouring onto the barrier. After a few seconds, a crack reverberated through the air, Chris falling onto his back as the barrier disappeared out from under him.

"It was not dragon-proofed," Grith remarked. "That was comically easy. I thought I would at least have to change the temperature to blue."

"It was probably just to keep out mundanes." Chris sighed, holding his side as he carefully got back to his feet.

"That's what you said the last time." Ashley frowned.

Chris shrugged, placing his hands in his suit-pockets. "Yeah. Trying to figure out better magical security is expensive, there's so many ways around it. It's kinda a wizard code not to mess with each other's magic or experiments; it's why I didn't tell you about the lock in the meeting room, or how to open it."

"Wait, seriously? You knew the entire time?" Ashley asked, Grith able to get a whiff of her anger. "Wow. You're even more of a jerk than I thought."

"Just following the rules." Chris scoffed. "All rules are there for a reason, whether keeping dragons from eating humans, or making sure we have a productive workplace environment. This one is here to prevent destructive and visible clashes between powerful wizards. Investigation matters like this are normally left to the Council. You're right, I don't care about your fae; I told you that I'm just here to keep an eye on Grith and make sure she doesn't eat any mundanes, or at least doesn't get caught doing it. I think she's smart enough she could have figured out some other way to be hidden without me or my spells. But apparently, even just following you around is putting me at risk, since I had to fight a GMI wizard for the two of you. Do you realize how easily all of us could have died? She wasn't — she isn't weak, just not cunning. She didn't think I'd use her own magic against her."

"It seems then like wizards do not prepare for magical creatures who are not privy to their rules when creating their defenses," Grith said, flicking her tail. "I am thankful for your glamor, however, even if your motives are not particularly glamorous."

"Thanks?" Chris said, uncertain whether to take that as a compliment or not. "And of course we prepare for you all. There aren't enough magical creatures around today for us to bother, and dragons generally stay out of human and wizard business as if your scales would all fall off if you got too close. Well, feathers for you. No one else has magical powers to rival us anyways."

"Excuse me?" Ashley asked, clenching her fists. "What about witches? We're pretty powerful."

Chris laughed, like that was a poor joke. "You're really not. Witches' powers mostly come from the earth and nature, which frankly, isn't doing so good these days. Burning a few twigs has been helpful, but your powers are just parlor tricks to what a powerful wizard can do."

"I healed you!" Ashley squealed.

"And I'm grateful, but I could have done it myself if I wasn't so focused on the glamor and hadn't used so much magic in the battle," Chris retorted. "Anyways, it was Grith's saliva, so really more her than you."

"Asshole!" Ashley accused Chris. "You arrogant—"

"If possible, could we please save the arguing for later?" Grith asked, placing her head between the two. "I think it would be a good idea to go inside before someone realizes that the barrier is missing."

"Right," Ashley muttered, glaring daggers at Chris from behind the dragon's crest. "Let's go."

Grith watched as Ashley stormed off toward the front of the warehouse.

As Chris walked after her, the dragon raised her tail, blocking his path.

"What?" Chris asked, trying to push it out of the way as Grith curled around him, two golden eyes meeting his.

"I wanted to thank you," Grith explained. "You are the first human I have ever truly seen as a dragon-like creature. One that is like us rather than like prey. It is difficult for me to dislike one that I see only as a food source, and my personal distaste for you has made me realize that you have progressed beyond that." She pulled her lips back, long, white fangs glinting in the moonlight. "I do not kill other dragons, but if for some reason I was forced to kill you, nothing would remain of your body but ash. Not a single drop of blood or piece of flesh would be left."

Grith lowered her tail and followed after Ashley, her feathers bristling. She looked back at Chris, the wizard dumbstruck for a moment, before he cautiously joined them.

Ashley crouched down by the twin doors, running her fingers along the wood. "They've been made to look like they're boarded up, but they're not actually attached. I think this place is still in use."

Grith sniffed the bottom of the doors, sensing the scent of the fae, the librarian, along with a few other shimmer-tainted scents. "More than just the librarian came in here. Other wizards."

"There aren't any charms or protections around it," Chris observed.

"Are you telling the truth?" Ashley asked. "Or just lying again?"

"He is not lying," Grith said, sniffing around the edges of the doors. "There are no magical protections. They just thought the barrier was enough, I suppose."

"All right then." Ashley frowned, drawing a rune on the keyhole. With a click, she turned the knob, and the door opened.

Grith squealed when a loud alarm blared through the building, folding her ears against her head. Lights began to flash inside the warehouse.

Ashley glared at Chris.

"I was telling the truth!" Chris shrugged. "No magic."

"Fuck you," Ashley grumbled. "Remind me never to let you into the Key again. Grith, can you please eat him?"

"No," Grith responded, peering into the hallway. "What is it? I do not smell shimmer."

"A mundane alarm," Ashley explained, "not magical."

"We should turn back," Chris suggested once more, leaning against the warehouse wall.

"Grith already got rid of the barrier," Ashley retorted. "We're not going to have another chance to see what's in here after whoever made it figures out it's now missing. I say we keep going."

"Who does the alarm summon?" Grith asked, squinting as the lights flashed in her eyes.

"LAPD. The mundane police," Chris said. "Not wizards."

Grith thought for a moment, tucking in her wings. They'd already come this far. "Then we go forward, and hope we get out before they arrive."

TWELVE

On the inside, the abandoned warehouse didn't seem so abandoned.

White lights flashed in Grith's eyes as the alarm blared, a loud drone in her ringing ears. Blanche tile lined the entrance, the dragon's talons clenching as she tried to keep a hold onto the slick floor.

Ashley and Chris descended behind her, each of their steps quiet and cautious, as if the blaring noise hadn't already alerted everyone in the building.

"It's weirdly empty," Ashley said, her voice barely audible over the alarm. "I thought that there would've been guards, right?"

"Humans have come through here," Grith explained, sniffing the ground, "but they have not for a while. Wizards, I suspect, but none I recognize except for the librarian."

"If we encounter her again, she won't fall for the same trick twice," Chris muttered. "I won't be able to use my magic at all. We'll be doomed."

"I think I have a chance," Ashley remarked. "My magic

isn't designed for combat, but I've got a few ideas, and I'm nowhere near out of essence."

Chris scoffed out a sarcastic laugh.

"You're underestimating witches."

He shook his head. "It's not just that wizards are more powerful and better at combat. The librarian is GMI. They only let the best in there."

"I doubt that she is that powerful if you had defeated her," Grith said, placing a wing over her eyes to shield them.

"I got lucky, and she was distracted by the two of you." Chris grimaced. "She decided that the twelve-foot tall flying reptile-bird was the real threat, and ignored me. If I wanted to join GMI, I'd have to be more valuable. If this whole mess doesn't ruin my chances at it."

"Well, I am sorry that you are not able to join your exclusive wizard club," Grith half-heartedly apologized.

"I mean, I'll probably be fine," Chris continued, his palms sweating. "My family has connections to GMI and the Council. And I haven't actually done anything bad yet, right? Just been an accessory. They'd understand what I did. Oh God, my father is going to be so angry if wind of this gets back to him. I'm so, so fucked."

Grith lifted up her wing as the green glow of magic glinted across her feathers. She looked back, wondering if it was Ashley's, before realizing that it was coming from in front, not behind. The metallic shimmer coated the inside of her nose, the buzz of electricity coursing through her ears.

The passage opened up in front of them into a large circular room, big enough that Grith could have spread her wings wide many times. It only took a moment for her to locate the magic, by sight rather than smell. Green light pulsed from a glinting silver ring three times the dragon's height, as thick as her neck, blue runes rotating around the edges. Her eyes followed four chains from the edge of the ring, vibrating with power. They met at the center, where a pale humanoid hung limply, unmoving. Behind them, a glowing portal flashed on and off, vibrating and becoming cloudy one moment, before changing to a clear blue sky the next.

"Albiwegan!" Ashley shouted, pushing past Grith and running out beneath the chains. She looked up at the fae, their normally white hair grayed as they swung in the chain. "Are they . . .?"

Grith got up on her hind legs, bringing her snout toward the fae. She let out a yelp as green lightning arced from the chains to the side of her neck, a few of her feathers smoldering. She wasn't sure how to distinguish a living fae from a dead one, but careful not to touch the chains, she gave them a sniff.

Albiwegan's eyes opened, lightning crackling as they stared at the dragon's jaws. They shuddered and attempted to turn away, struggling with a whimper.

"It's all right!" Ashley called up. "It's me! Ashley! We're here to help!"

Grith peered beneath the chains, careful not to touch her snout to the oscillating portal. Holding it just close enough that she could feel the magic practically engulf her, she stared into what was beyond it.

An empty blue sky stretched beyond her, not a cloud in sight. Not, not empty — something moving caught her gaze. A large chunk of rock, larger than a dragon, was floating past. Pieces of a crumbling wall flew alongside it, and for a moment, Grith thought that there was a humanoid skull. They made their way across the sky before reaching the edge of Grith's vision and disappearing, leaving the sky once again empty.

"I do not believe that this is Terra," Grith murmured, tilting her head. "It looks . . . lonely."

"Chris, how do we turn it off?" Ashley asked.

Chris was inspecting a large box to the side of the huge ring, with a small pedestal on top of it, loose chains dangling down as they crackled with power, like they were meant to be wrapped around something, or someone. He squinted at a panel full of buttons, dials, and levers, red flashing numbers running across black screens. "I think it's just the lever here, the big one. The other controls target where the portal goes. I've used something similar in my research at Vertex Technologies, but much smaller. Oh."

"Oh?" Grith asked, bending her head over Chris. "Oh."

On the side of the box were two emblazoned letters, a logo. VT.

"What, did you figure out Vertex Technologies made it?" Ashley asked, rolling her eyes. "Unethical and probably illegal experimentation from a company run by an ex-Council member who's also part of a deranged wizard cult? Who could have guessed! Don't look so shocked, just turn it off already."

"It is a better quality plating than the ones they gave us," Grith rumbled. "Almost pure rhodium."

"Maybe we should just leave?" Chris pleaded. "I really don't think we should mess with this. This isn't just some lone wizard's experiment, this is VT. They probably have a good reason to do it; they're powerful and dangerous."

"I am also dangerous," Grith pointed out, placing her tail around the big lever. "Unfortunately, I suspect that I will lose my job for this."

Grith hesitated. She hated working at VT, and they

deserved whatever was coming to them, but if she did this, her income would be gone, and the shimmer in her parents' hoard would dry up. She could lose her more than just her job, but her home, all she had left of her parents. The bubble realm would collapse into nothing, and her memories of growing up there, the leftover scents of them, would al be gone forever.

She could fly away from this and apologize to VT for interfering in their affairs. Everything would be fine, except Albiwegan would still be there. Grith stared at the convulsing fae, trapped in their chains. There were few worse fates Grith could think of than being captured and chained, forced to use their lifeforce for an eternity to power the nefarious machine. She couldn't leave a dragon in this situation, and even if there was a risk of losing her home, she couldn't leave the fae either.

The dragon pulled the lever down, coming to the off position with a clang of metal. The crackling chains stopped crackling, and the smell of magic faded as the runes on the side of the teleporter turned gray, the portal disappearing. The machine was off.

Suddenly, blue light shot up from the entrance of the room, three runes flashing as they exchanged places with each other, and a loud ring shot through Grith's head.

"And that's the magical alarm." Chris sighed. "We're doomed. Dead. In my last moments of life, I would just like to say: this wasn't worth it."

"Hurry!" Ashley yelled, grabbing at the chains. "Can you melt them?"

Grith clicked her tongue, and wrapping her talons around one of them, let loose a column of flame, carefully increasing the temperature until the metal turned orange. She tugged at the chains until the first one snapped.

A jolt of light spread through the flashing runes. Three humans had teleported onto the entrance, and the dragon's fangs bared when she recognized one of them.

The librarian fumed back at her, her spectacles cracked, little left of her hair. "You!" the librarian yelled, pointing to the dragon, her fist clenching around her golden signet ring.

"Wait!" Chris called, stretching his hands to the side. "Please, stop! This is all just a big misunderstanding! The dragon and I are VT employees, we're not—"

"ATTACK!" the librarian squealed, pointing two fingers at Chris, a ball of blue flame shooting out from them.

Chris screamed as he covered his face, turning away as heat approached the three.

With a flash of green light, the ball of flame dissipated.

Chris peered through his fingers to see that a green barrier had formed in front of him, jumping back as another few shots of flame bounced from it, flickering across the surface before fading.

"I told you that you were underestimating me!" Ashley barked as she held out a pitchfork-shaped branch in both hands, green fire bursting through it. "Grith, keep going! I don't think I can hold this for long!"

Grith moved onto the second chain, snapping it as more blasts of blue flame bounced across the barrier, all three wizards shooting at it.

The librarian let out another furious scream, a huge cone extending from her hands.

Ashley winced as the stick cracked.

The dragon gave a look toward the nervous fae, shaking as Grith shot fire on the third chain, tearing it apart. "Almost there," Grith purred, moving to the final one. "It will all be okay."

Ashley let out a yell of pain, holding onto the stick as blue fire pummeled her barrier, rising around her hands. The stick warped, green and blue light mixing, wood splintering away.

Grith shot her flames against the final chain, the links melting, and she pulled it as hard as she could.

The stick snapped with a burst of energy, the barrier falling.

The librarian raised her hands, chanting as the two other wizards joined her. A circle of blue fire spread around the machine, fire rising into the air as it swirled around them.

Ashley jumped back, pulling Chris with her. She looked toward Chris desperately as she fumbled through her robes, while tears fell down Chris's face.

With a snarl, Grith snapped the last chain, Albiwegan falling to the floor. Blue fire rose around them, moving inwards. Her feathers dried from the heat, and Grith spread her wings open, hiding the two humans and the fae within them as the librarian stopped chanting, and the circle of flame contracted.

A flash of white light from beneath her blinded the dragon.

The heat and smoke was gone, replaced with the cool night air, wind brushing Grith's feathers. A different white light hit her from above, while red and blue flashing across her eyelids. Instead of the roar of flame and the buzz of magic, loud sirens blared at the dragon's ears.

"Where the hell did they come from?" someone yelled, a human voice Grith didn't recognize.

The white light moved.

The dragon opened her eyes.

Albiwegan was struggling to get to their feet, shuddering before falling again.

It took Grith a moment to adjust to the sudden darkness, contrasting with the red and blue headlights of cars, strewn across the road outside of the warehouse, humans in black clothing shouting to each other as they formed a line in front of the cars. A helicopter beamed a spotlight down at the four.

"LAPD! Stay where you are; hands in the air!" one ordered them, pointing something Grith couldn't decipher in the lights. "Don't move!"

Smoke reached Grith's nose, the asphalt rumbling beneath her talons. A loud bang cracked through the air, and her head whipped around.

A column of blue flame shot into the air, rising three times the height of the warehouse. Bricks fell, the few windows left shattering as the glow lit up the night like a sun.

Albiwegan's eyes went wide, and they let out a scream of terror, shaking as they ran out from beneath Grith's wing, pushing past Chris and Ashley and sprinting down the road.

"Stop or we'll shoot!" one of the humans frantically yelled, pointing an object at the fae. "Terrorists! Stop!"

"No!" Ashley cried, red and blue lights reflecting in her pupils. She reached into her robe, pulling out a small leaf with a soothing scent from it, green light glowing from her palm as she tried to activate it.

"SHE'S ARMED!" a policeman shouted.

A shot rang out and a gun fired, Ashley screaming and clutching her side as she dropped the leaf, crumpling to the ground.

Grith's nostrils opened, catching blood as Ashley's pooled onto the ground.

More of the humans raised guns, and Chris cried, hiding beneath Grith's wing.

More shots fired.

The dragon's wings stretched open, golden beams of light spreading out from her eyes as a circle of runes formed in the air around her. Her roar split the sky, her feathers glowing as she became a beacon of light.

Chris clutched his head, the last vestiges of his magic torn from him.

A golden ring of light twice Grith's wingspan formed beneath the cluster of bullets as they moved, and they slowed to almost a stop, moving forward at a snails' pace. Shimmer filled the air, and three lines of light formed in the ring, two pointing away from Grith, the third and thinnest to the left of them.

Chris collapsed, falling face-first on the asphalt. Like a broken mirror, the glamor shattered, falling in pieces around the dragon, her roar echoing across the neighborhood.

Screams of terror filled the air, the humans dropping their guns as they ran from the dragon, golden light filling the night as she reared onto her hindlegs.

A tick sounded through the air, and the thinnest hand moved clockwise in the golden circle. Fire welled up in Grith's throat, seeking a place to be let loose, seeking flesh to turn into ash.

Human fear-scent and prey-scent mixed with Ashley's blood. The dragon was hungry, and her shimmer was leaving her, the bullets quivering and continuing to move forward. She wanted to feed.

Prey fled from her, running as fire came from her mouth. One tripped, left behind by the rest of his herd.

Tock. The golden clock moved forward.

Anger welled up in the dragon's belly, her fire heated from it. These humans had hurt Ashley, shot her. They'd tried to hunt her with their bullets, just like they slayed dragons with their steel. The world was unfair, and the dragon wanted those responsible to pay. Humans were the reason witches and dragons alike had to live in hiding. The dragon hated, and she wanted them to hurt.

Tick.

She had to kill them, everyone. It was the only way to keep her world safe. The humans had seen her, they'd seen a dragon and they'd seen her magic. She had to destroy the evidence, and that meant that nothing but cinders could remain of each human. The Council's punishment for killing a human was far less than the punishment of exposing magic. Killing them was the legal thing, the right thing, to do. Rules were there for a reason, and dragons were held to them.

Tock.

The dragon let out a column of flame, asphalt melting as she let it loose from one side of the street to another. Smoke rose in the air. The fallen human stared as Grith drew a line in the street, the flames burning as she created a barrier of fire between her and the policemen.

Tick.

She wrapped her front claws around Ashley and Chris, carrying the two limp humans into the sky, resting between her talons as she took off. The humans on the ground gazed at her as the fire died down, cowering before the line of molten asphalt remaining across the street, the flames not having touched a single one.

Tock.

The second-hand hit midnight, and the clock faded. The bullets continued on their path, but no one was in their way.

Humans are like dragons, Grith decided. Both had the capacity to do good, and the capacity to do evil. Today, a lot had done evil, but she'd seen good as well, from Ashley and even Chris. Just as she thought it was wrong to kill an evil dragon, she decided it was wrong to kill an evil human, whether witch, wizard, or mundane.

With a flick of her wings, the dragon activated her invisibility, disappearing into the night sky of LA, carrying the two humans in her claws.

PART TWO
APPEARANCE

THIRTEEN

Grith's golden eyes stained the blood in her talons orange, her nostrils flaring at the smell. Her wings beat as hard as they could, magic powering her muscles and lifting her into the air. Wind rushed past Grith's snout, feathers flickering as the clothes of the two humans in her claws fluttered, their hair tossing and turning in the wind.

Grith looked down at the two, the city's lights dancing across her eyes. A red stain had spread across Ashley's robes, worsened by the jostling from the flight. She brought the human girl up to her snout and gave the skin a lick, spreading her saliva over the bullet hole. Blood ran down her tongue, and she ignored the urge to bite down, instead pressing her tongue into the wound until she tasted lead. The bullet was still in her, caught by shattered bone.

Grith decided against trying to get it out herself. She didn't think she'd be able to with her tongue, and if she used her claws, she would just make things worse. She gave Ashley a concerned purr, but the human didn't wake. The dragon's saliva hadn't been enough, and Ashley was still losing blood.

Grith turned to her other paw, shaking it and the blonde wizard within it, hair rustling in the wind.

He didn't wake.

She gave him a nudge with her snout and a wet lick across his face, hoping that would be enough to wake him up. It did nothing, and he remained limp in Grith's claws. At least he was stable: after Grith had cast her time-slowing spell, the glamor had caused him to overuse his supply of magic essence in a way comparable to dragon shimmer loss, though instead temporarily draining his life force. Still, he would recover it in time.

She sniffed Ashley's robes. The salve made with her saliva was somewhere in there. Would that be enough? Chris's wound had been bad, and it had worked for that. Grith didn't think she'd be able to get the small bottle open, however, and if she accidentally snagged a talon inside Ashley and tugged too hard . . . she decided she shouldn't attempt to apply it herself. But Chris was unconscious. How long did Ashley have, and was there enough time to heal her? A nervous rumble came up through the dragon's throat.

She took in a breath of the fresh air, trying to calm herself as the noise of the wind rushed past her ears. Not having enough time was a problem she knew how to solve.

Grith moved Chris to one of her hindpaws, dangling him like prey she'd swooped down and caught, lifted into the air. Careful not to squeeze him too tight, she put her forepaw to Ashley. Bright golden streaks worked their way across her feathers as she drew a magic circle around the girl, filling in the edges with the appropriate runes.

The bleeding slowed as a golden glow covered Ashley's skin.

Grith tilted her head, feeling the human's heartbeat become a slow pulse, until finally, almost stopping. She counted the time in her head between two heartbeats. Thirty seconds. Shimmer evaporated from her body, working to slow down the time around the human. The circle helped, but she couldn't hold it for long from her experienced proper time. She was thankful that she hadn't used any magic earlier that day.

A whirring sound caught her attention. Beneath her, the city lights illuminated the spinning blades of a helicopter, a white searchlight searching beneath it. Grith tucked the two humans against her underbelly, soaring up and over it. The light from her magic could be quite inconvenient.

If the helicopter noticed her, Grith couldn't tell. A draft lifted her up toward a cloud, and she dove down toward the mountains to the northeast. Right now, she couldn't worry about if the police had seen her or if they were trying to find her. The dragon had to focus on keeping all three of them alive and safe.

Ashley's heart had sped up to ten beats per minute by the time Grith was over the familiar forest, the entrance to her bubble realm nearby. Her magic was weakening. With another flap of her wings, she dove down, breaking the winds as they blasted her feathers. She held onto the two humans tight enough she didn't accidentally drop them, but not so tight she hurt them.

She didn't roar this time. Grith flicked her wingspurs when the tingle of magic touched her, the gate opening with a flash of light, taking the three into her home. A quarter-moon glistened over the treetops, and the peak she lived on was just as peaceful as any other night.

For a moment, fear bristled her feathers as she landed on the stone platform, the humans in her claws. Her heart sped up, many times Ashley's already. This was the first time she'd ever brought humans into her lair, something her family had warned her many, many times never to do. What if the humans saw her hoard, coveting it?

She flicked her tail as she gently held Ashley in her jaws, leaving Chris to take Ashley down through the tunnels. Her heart pumped faster as Grith felt more and more of her shimmer drained, more blood on the dragon's tongue. There was little chance of either of them stealing from her in the helpless state they were in.

Grith laid Ashley down in her normal sleeping spot, staring as small droplets of blood pooled onto the metal coins beneath her. She clenched her talons, the golden light around Ashley flickering as her heart beat faster. Fatigue ached through Grith's limbs, her wings drooping as her tail fell to the ground.

The dragon bent her head down to the shimmer, scooping up as much as she could in her jaws, gold, silver, and platinum. Heat rose up from her tongue, the taste of metal filling it as it melted. A viscous warmth spread down Grith's neck when she swallowed it, turning to essence and used in her magic. Much to Grith's relief, Ashley's heart slowed once again.

Still swallowing the metal in her jaws, Grith walked back out into the hall, a few specks of shimmer dripping onto the stone floor and hardening. Her limbs ached. That wouldn't last her long, not with attempting to slow the time around Ashley down from a distance. As fast as she could without harming him, she grabbed Chris, taking him back down.

She could barely stand when she dropped him next to Ashley, falling a few feet onto the metal bed. Grith collapsed herself, her wings spreading out over the treasure, the shimmer in them lulling her to sleep.

No. She couldn't; she still had work to do. So, she gobbled up another mouthful of shimmer, then another. Hopefully, this would be enough.

Grith stood up and dropped the spell on Ashley. The smell of blood hit her, crimson pouring from the wound. She had to hurry. She dragged her tail around Chris, golden runes forming wherever her feathers touched. When she'd finished the circle, she extended her wings, the chamber filled with golden light.

The speed of the human's heartbeat increased, pounding like a jackhammer. Grith didn't let up, her wings spread as Ashley's heart raced. Grith didn't bother to count.

Her legs shook at the first bit of motion from Chris, and she dropped the spell.

He stared at her, clutching his head as his heart rate went back to normal. "What did you do to me?" he yelled, twisting his head back and forth as the circle faded. "Where are we?"

Looking beneath his hands at the pile of coins told him the answer to the second question. Grith explained the first.

"I sped the time around you," she quietly said, the dragon swaying back and forth as she felt herself go dizzy. She lost her hold on the coins, shifting beneath her as she fell on her side, barely feeling the uncomfortable position one of her wings had been trapped beneath her in. She took another mouthful of shimmer, dripping between her fangs before she spoke. "Very sped much. Until gained you enough in you to wake."

Chris stared at his hand, flexing his fingers. Grith doubted he had very much magic in him, even with that. Far less than what she'd lost to wake him up.

"Ashley," Grith pleaded, flicking her tongue out and pulling another coin into it. "Salve. Now."

Chris looked over at Ashley, a pool of blood around her from her wound. He nodded, and dug his hands into her robes until he found the golden cream, opening the small bottle to smear it into the bullet hole. His face turned to disgust as he felt the sticky blood coating his fingers, trying not to look down as he spread the salve into it.

"This is a bullet wound." Chris frowned, as though he was about to throw up as he risked a glance. He drew a blue rune in the air, grimacing and shaking just from the small spell, spilling more of the salve onto Ashley's blood-stained skin. "I turned the bullet to water. But how did she get hit by a bullet? Shouldn't it be a burn? There was the librarian, and the other two wizards, and the portal, and . . . oh. Shit."

Chris turned to Grith, eyes wide. His fingers were shaking more, this time from fear rather than exhaustion. Through the molten metals, his eyes caught on the blood running across the dragon's fangs, staining the feathers around her jaw.

"Grith?" Chris gulped. "Did you eat the police?"

Grith tilted her head a little, having regained enough energy to move her wing out from beneath her. "I did not. The blood is Ashley's. I think I have seen enough humans that I would find it difficult to hurt or eat one."

Chris let out an anguished groan, grabbing his hair, pulling out a few blond strands. "No! This was the one time you were *supposed* to eat humans! Or set them on fire, or something! The glamor faded and they saw you; they saw a *dragon*!" He paused. "If this gets out. We're all doomed. Dead. I'm only twenty-five! I'm too young to die!"

"I am deeply sorry," Grith responded, burying her head beneath her wing in shame. Hadn't she done the right thing by not killing the police? She'd thought that Chris of all humans would have been proud. Maybe morality was more complicated than killing or not. Humans were odd. "I will try not to let you die."

Chris let out a deep sigh, smearing a bit more of the salve into Ashley's wound. The bleeding had stopped, and although her breaths were still shallow, they were consistent. "I think she's stable. I don't think there's anything else I can do."

Grith peeked out from under her wing as he fell back, staring up at the ceiling of her hoard room. Her parents had painted it with more stars and constellations than she'd ever seen from their home, with the great stripe of the Celestial Dragon running from end to end.

Chris spread out his arms and muttered, "I feel like I should be more anxious, but I'm not. I'm too tired to be anxious. I can barely stay awake." He frowned as he shifted from side to side, coins moving out from beneath him. "Grith, this isn't a very comfy bed. Haven't you ever slept on a mattress?"

"Shimmer is better," Grith replied with the utmost certainty. She rolled over onto her underbelly, placing her forelegs beneath her and standing back up. "It is how we get enough magic so that our bodies work. The natural magic that wizards get from Terra's aura isn't enough, and we will become sick and die. Covering your underbelly with gold when sleeping will keep a dragon healthy, but more is needed to perform spells. I had to use a lot to save Ashley."

She bent her head back down, coins running across her tongue as she melted them.

"Huh," Chris responded, picking up a golden coin in his hand. He put it between his teeth, biting down. "It's not working for me. I don't sense any more magic."

Grith let out an amused trill. "Magic is needed to melt and digest it, too, and I do not believe humans naturally have that."

"Magic seems to be a very expensive hobby," Chris remarked, placing the coin back into Grith's hoard, the dragon carefully watching that he didn't pocket it.

Grith cocked her head, flicking her tail-feathers across coins as she thought about that. "Dragons need magic to survive in the world, whether shiftstones or bubble realms. So, being a dragon is a very expensive hobby."

She opened her jaws wide, rumbling a yawn, her fangs glimmering in the dim light. Grith took a few steps forward, setting herself down at Chris and Ashley's feet.

Chris stared as she extended a wing over the two, burying her snout in coins.

"Do you think that everything will be all right?" Grith asked. "I am afraid."

"I don't know," Chris answered, turning onto his side. "My father told me that humans often intentionally ignore things that they don't believe in, and it was dark. Maybe the police will all think you were a giant bird, or a mass hallucination."

"Maybe," the dragon murmured, shutting her eyes as she doused the lights with a breath.

The two were quiet for a moment, invisible in the darkness of the cave.

"I think Ashley was right," Chris said. "I don't think I'm

afraid of you anymore. Well, hopefully everything will be fine in the morning."

The feathers on Grith's chest raised up and down. It only took a moment for the exhausted dragon to fall asleep.

Things were not fine.

Grith woke with a sudden start as Ashley screamed, her head perking up and eyes going wide. She puffed fire onto the torch, causing the rest to magically light, the cavern filled with the glow of flame.

"What is it?" Chris grumbled, rubbing his eyes as they adjusted to the light.

Ashley was sitting up, staring at the screen of a phone in her hand.

"Are you still injured?" Grith asked, cocking her head. Ashley certainly seemed lively.

"Look!" Ashley shouted, pointing the phone screen at Grith.

The dragon peered her head over, squinting as Chris moved over to her to watch. Ashley pressed a triangular button, and a video started. Blue and red lights flashed, shaky as whoever was holding the camera moved their hand up and down, a few policemen coming into focus, talking with each other.

"What do you think is going on?" one voice to the right of the camera holder said. "Is that smoke? Is there a fire?"

"If there was a fire, they'd have called the firemen instead of the police," the human holding the camera said, pointing his phone at the warehouse, a wisp of smoke just barely visible. He turned it back, a blur of motion as an officer walked toward them.

"You! Kids! Scram!" the officer shouted, waving a baton in the air. "Turn off that camera!"

The camera shook again, catching a quick glimpse of whoever was next to the camera holder, before the two ducked into an alley.

Suddenly, there was a flash of light in the corner of the screen, and the officer turned away from the kids. The camera peeked out from behind the alley, and a white headlight turned onto the road in front of the warehouse, illuminating four figures.

"Who is that?" Grith asked, cocking her head as she brought an eye closer to the phone. "Oh! It is Chris and Ashley! You are on the screen!"

Chris's hands trembled and he stared in silence, coins clinking beneath his fingers.

"Where the hell did they come from?" one of the officers asked, looking at each other in disbelief.

"L.A.P.D.! Stay where you are, hands in the air!" another shouted, pointing his gun at the four newcomers. "Don't move!"

The camera shook again.

"We should go," the camera holder's friend murmured, pulling on his hand. "He told us to go. What if someone gets hurt?"

"Then I'm making sure it's on camera," the camera holder said, turning back.

"What if *we* get hurt?"

A moment later, a loud noise shook the alley, the camera rattling along with the owner as there were yells. He ducked into the alley, dropping the phone to the ground. It didn't take long before he picked it up, pointing it outside the alley toward a fading blue flame over the warehouse.

"There's an explosion!" he narrated to the camera.

"There might be another!" his friend said, grabbing his hand and trying to pull him away. "Please, we should go."

The camera moved back to the police, more guns raised. One of the figures had darted away, running down the street. "Stop or we'll shoot! Terrorists! Stop!"

Grith stared and Ashley yelled, reaching into her robes, Albiwegan suddenly gone from the screen in a flash of light.

"SHE'S ARMED!"

An instant later, and a gunshot fired, the camera shaking as the holder jumped back.

"Oh my God! He shot her! He shot her!" the camera holder's friend cried, trying to keep her voice quiet.

Ashley let out a scream, and golden light flashed across the street, shadows cast by its intensity.

The camera went shaky, before a moment later, a golden glow blinded it.

"That is me," Grith whispered to the phone as the intensity of the light faded, leaving just the glowing circle on the ground beneath the bullets and two beams shining out from Grith's eyes. Her roar burst from the phone's speakers, caught in static. The camera shook, catching Grith's wings and the sight of her snout.

Even with the blurry camera, the phone had the dragon in full view.

The police screamed, running as Grith opened her jaws, fire filling them. A few seconds later, and it was spreading across the asphalt in a line, orange flame moving toward the camera.

This time, the person holding the camera ran, yelling as he clutched the phone. The video bounced up and down, orange light mixed with gold, before a few moments later it was gone.

"Dragon," he whispered, his breath shaky as he ran

further back into the alley, his friend pulling him back. "Dragon. That was a fucking dragon."

The video stopped, and Ashley pulled her phone away.

Grith stared at it for a moment, before sitting back on her haunches. "Well."

"Can the Council take it down?" Chris asked, his teeth chattering.

"I think they *did* take it down," Ashley replied, reading through the description. "The original one was apparently posted on a messageboard that was taken down by a DDoS attack five minutes after it was posted, but it was too late. There are a few other uploads, but this is the one that became popular. It's titled 'Dragons And Magic Are Real??!??!?!' Right now, it's number one on trending."

"It's fabricated," Chris suggested. "Photoshopped. It wouldn't be that hard to stage something like that."

"A few 'expert' reports claim that it is," Ashley continued, frowning as she dragged her finger across the screen, typing on the phone. "Not much use. There's pictures of the damage that Grith did to the street everywhere. The Council might have been able to clean it up and use some memory spells, but I think it's too late for that with the number of views this video has gotten. Plus, the number two video on trending is a response from the LAPD. They're confirming that the footage is real, and that they're still looking into capturing the animal and the group of terrorists that attacked them and destroyed the warehouse, but there were fortunately zero casualties. They don't use the word dragon, though."

"I did not destroy the warehouse," Grith grumbled, flicking her tail. "And I did not attack them either. If I had, there would not be much left of them to make announcement."

"The humans don't know that," Ashley said, pulling her finger up as her eyes flitted left and right. "But at least reading through the comments, one of the most liked ones is noting that you clearly weren't aiming to kill, and that the police attacked first. Some of the other replies say . . ." Ashley cringed. "Eesh. Nevermind, that's a lot of slurs. Others comments are wondering if it's not just dragons that are real, though, and if it's all magic. The golden circle was pretty visible. Someone here is noticing that Albiwegan teleported on-camera. It looks like the LAPD response is at the top of all the headlines today, though."

Chris buried his face in his hands. "This is awful," he moaned. "I'm clearly visible, right there on camera. Paul is going to notice, and I'm going to be fired!"

"That's what you're worried about?" Ashley asked, lowering her phone with a glance of skepticism. "Your job?"

"You're right, not just my job." Chris gulped. "The Council is going to see that. They already *have* seen that. Do you think I counted as exposing magic? It wasn't my fault, I think that's pretty clear from the video. Are all three of us going to lose our heads for this, or just Grith? I need to ask my father. He has to know what to do."

Grith lowered her head in shame, her wings drooping. "I am very sorry for this. I should have done something different. This was not a good outcome."

Ashley shook her head. "It's not your fault; you did the best you were able to. I'm grateful you saved my life."

Grith wasn't sure, but she thought Ashley sounded hesitant about that. Even she seemed to be wondering if saving her was the right thing to do, or if it would have been better had she died.

"I should go," Ashley said, standing up and putting her

phone away. "I need to check on my parents and the Key. I want to make sure they're alright. Maybe they can help."

"I doubt they can help with this," Chris muttered, standing alongside her. "How many views does the video have? One million? Ten million?"

"Would you like for me to fly you?" Grith asked, perking her head up.

Ashley winced, shaking her head. "I think it's better if you stay away from LA for now, invisibility or not. Maybe just sit tight?"

"As soon as we get out of this bubble realm, I can use a teleportation circle to bring us both to a teleportation node in LA," Chris said, turning to Ashley. "We'll be within walking distance of the Key."

Grith lowered her head again, placing her talons over her snout, and let out a distraught rumble. She'd screwed up, and now the two humans were going to be punished for her mistake. Chris had been right. She shouldn't have been allowed out into the mundane world. Even if she wasn't hurting anyone, she was still a danger.

"It'll be okay," Ashley said, giving Grith a smile. Grith didn't have to read her tone to know that she was lying.

Grith just stared at a few coins as the two humans left her hoard. She let out a puff of smoke. She felt horrible. What could she do? She'd made the wrong decision and ruined all of their lives for it, along with countless other magical creatures. Now that humans knew dragons were real, would they continue hunting them down? Had she condemned her own species to extinction?

A flashing light from outside her hoard room caught Grith's attention. She realized it was from her crystal screen. Pret must be trying to contact her. The reason why was obvious.

Did she really want to face him? She didn't know if she could. She stayed still for a few moments. Maybe he would just give up, and decide that the Council had already beheaded her.

The light didn't stop flashing. With a groan, Grith got to her paws, dragging her tail through coins as she walked toward its source. She might as well talk to him. If she didn't, he would decide to fly over here regardless, and she didn't want to make him do that.

She lumbered over toward the room with the screen, pausing before she walked inside. Holding her wings over her snout and tucking her tail between her hindlegs, she stepped in.

"I'm so sorry!" she cried in Southern, even before she saw her cousin's feathers on the crystal screen. "I'm so, so, so, sorry. Now all the humans know about us, and magic, and I've doomed you and all dragonkind, and it's all my fault, and I'm so very—"

"Grith," Pret interrupted, cocking his head to the side as he ruffled his wings. "It's all right."

Grith peeked out from under a wing, looking at her cousin in shame. He didn't look angry, or even disappointed in her. Somehow, that only seemed to make it worse. He *should* have been angry.

"What happened wasn't your fault," Pret continued, opening up a wing as if to comfort her under it.

"It *was* my fault," Grith whined. "I shouldn't have used my magic, or I shouldn't have rescued Ashley, or I should've set the entire block on fire or something terrible like that! I shouldn't have gone out into the mundane world to begin with!"

Pret clicked his tongue and shook his head, his silver crest swishing back and forth. "Grith, with human cameras everywhere and the internet, something like this would have happened eventually. Probably the next five years. You were just unlucky enough to be in the wrong place at the wrong time, caught up in all this. I'm not just saying this to be nice: really, it wasn't your fault."

Grith paused, letting that sink in. Pret was right; magic would have been caught on camera eventually. That made her feel a little bit better. If she'd accidentally ended the world, at least she could have some solace in knowing that someone else would have done it if she hadn't.

"Right now, I'm more worried for you than anything," Pret continued, giving a nervous glance behind him. "The world will find a way to survive this. But now that this happened, you're in danger from both human and Council law enforcement. The LAPD is looking for you, though I doubt they'll have much luck, and I assume that the Council is debating what to do and if it's worth it to dispatch enforcers."

"Debating?" Grith asked. "I broke the law. Aren't they going to punish me for it?"

"The punishment of death was enough to limit exposure to small incidents that could be kept under control," Pret explained. "But with the cat out of the bag — er, with there being no chance of hiding this — there's not much point in having the law anymore. Any dragon is hard to take down, and a dragon mage from our family will take a lot of enforcers that might be better used elsewhere. Although, there are good optics in punishing you. I have an idea of something that could help, but these communication crystals aren't secure. You still don't have a phone, right? Or a computer?"

"No phone," Grith explained, cocking her head. "Nor a computer."

"All right, all right," Pret responded, swishing his tail as he paced around in a circle. "Would you mind flying out here then?"

Grith flicked her head. She'd been half-hoping that he'd ask her. Pret was the closest dragon in her life, practically the only dragon, and he had a comforting way of optimism about him as if he always knew everything was going to be all right.

Plus, she had something she wanted to ask him, too.

FOURTEEN

Grith watched the road beneath her as she made the flight east to Pret's bubble realm. It seemed the same as it always did, cars and the humans inside them going about whatever their normal business was. Had they seen the news already? Did it matter to them; did it affect their daily routines at all? Or was it just a mere curiosity, something for them to ponder in their time spent hunting meals at the markets or sitting bored inside their offices?

Heat wrapped around the dragon's feathers as the winds pushed her. The golden sun hit down hard on her head, though with her invisibility, the rays went straight through her, glinting off the cars' metal roofs. She left the cars behind as the roads cut off, the land becoming desert, almost devoid of human structures except for the occasional trail or empty road. Rocky outcroppings, bushes, and trees dotted the barren landscape.

Unlike Grith's bubble realm, so close to a large human city, Pret's was far more remote. It made it all the more ironic that Pret had interacted with humans far more than Grith. Maybe the distance made it feel safer for him.

The golden dragon landed by a grove of palm trees, shading her when she removed her invisibility. Was there even much point in keeping it on any more, now that the entire world had seen her? She stepped beneath the fronds, following down a trickling stream until it formed a pool of water, cool air wafting between her feathers.

She peered over it, staring into her own eyes as they glittered back from the surface, her crest wafting from side to side. It was just like Pret to have placed his entrance at a pool of water, forcing any who entered this place to engage in a literal form of self-reflection.

Grith opened her wings, making the correct motions with her wingspurs to open the gate. The scent of magic grew stronger, her feathers raising from the tingle. A flash of silver light suddenly blinded her, and when she could see again, pink mist clung around her snout.

She walked forward instead of flying, waving her wings to waft it away. It thinned, the dry desert sands once again visible beneath her, a flat expanse broken by the occasional grove of palms, and a prominent orange-yellow rock many wingspans high and wide in the center of Pret's bubble realm. Even from this distance, Grith could spot round tunnels dotting the outside, gentle orange lights of flames flickering around their edges.

Like a giant anthill, caverns filled Pret's home, haphazardly placed within the great rock, round dragon-sized tunnels dug between them with neither rhyme nor reason. Grith had always wondered how the rock would be if it had been split in two. For an animal that couldn't fly, the tunnels on the almost sheer sides were almost inaccessible, and the only entrance to the inside were two great, golden doors nestled in one of the cracks. Out of politeness, Grith decided to use these.

She paused at the doors, each of them split into two dragon sized panels, one for each of the four dragon species. A furred stocky dragon of a mammalian shape, somewhere between a bear and a wolf, two long fangs extending from their mouth to beneath their jaw. A wingless serpentine dragon with whiskers, fish scales, a mane, and two horns like antlers protruding from their head. A dragon with leathery wings, thick reptilian scales, and spines running to the tip of their tail. And a dragon like Grith, with a body somewhere between a snake and a bird, feathers ranging in size from the great ones on their wings to down fluff on their underbelly, an attractive crest from their head to the base of their neck.

Grith didn't get close enough to knock her claws on one of the dragons, the two doors bursting wide and hitting the sides of the rock as Pret landed on his front paws before her.

The golden dragon rushed forward with a distressed wail, burying herself beneath one of his silver wings, hiding herself in his feathers. He turned his head with a concerned glance.

"It's horrible!" Grith rumbled, her talons digging into the stone as her tail drooped between her hindlegs. "You saw it, didn't you? Everyone has seen me, they all have. How come their first exposure to magic had to be that? Pret, I was a few moments away from setting them all aflame! Maybe I should have, and this wouldn't have happened, and—"

"Grith, it's okay," Pret said, wrapping his wing around her, holding her against his side. "You did the right thing."

"Do you know that for sure?" Grith asked, lifting her head between his feathers. "Did Ansila's Eye tell you that it would be okay? That we're not all going to die and I haven't destroyed the world that our grandfather worked so hard to create?"

Pret shuffled his wings, and for a moment, Grith noticed a hint of apprehension in his gaze. He raised his wing and stepped back, sitting on his haunches as his eyes glowed silver, an overwhelming sense of magic in the air setting her feathers on edge. Pret placed a talon over his right eye, drawing a silver glyph in front of it.

For a moment, the silver dragon froze, immobile as runes danced around the glyph.

Grith waited, crossing her talons as they tapped against the stone.

The glyph faded, and Pret's ears fell in disappointment. "It's been silent. It hasn't shown me anything in a while. The last thing I saw was a conversation with Albiwegan about you and Holz. I didn't realize . . . you're not angry about that, are you?"

"No," Grith murmured, burying her snout under her claws as she flopped to the ground. "Not angry. Perhaps I'm relieved. If Ansila's Eye suggested that I talk to the fae, and got us into this mess, there was a good reason, right?"

"Probably," Pret replied, shifting his tail.

Probably? That was a far less certain answer than Grith would have liked. When the two of them had been hatchlings, their grandfather had taught his grandchildren time magic as their specialties. Grith had learned time manipulation, and could use it to both speed up or slow time down. Pret had learned a form of seeing, allowing him to use his magic to look a few seconds into either the past or future. Arit . . . it was better not to think about him.

But Ansila's Eye was something else. A power that Pret had been gifted. Or perhaps, a curse that he burdened. For something that allowed him to see into his future or occasionally his past, it was unpredictable. He believed that it was a force for good, but prophecies were rarely understandable until it was too late.

"Regardless, it doesn't want to talk to me," Pret murmured, flicking his eye with a talon. He winced as he knocked it a bit too hard, fortunately with the blunt side. The dragon swept his wing to the side. "Grith, I wanted to show you something."

"Show me?" Grith asked, stepping inside. "This isn't bad again, is it? Last time someone showed me something, it was bad."

Pret peeked around the doors, before the silver dragon shut them. "Mixed?" he answered. "Mixed. Like most things."

Grith followed him into the tunnels. She'd visited them often, but even so, she was never quite sure where each of the rooms was. He seemed to frequently make changes to what was where, moving around hoards and redecorating every so often. This time, he led her up a tunnel so steep she practically had to fly up it, scrambling with her claws over the surface.

The hum of electrical buzzing reached her ears, and she wrinkled her snout at the smell of burning rubber. Whirring fans blasted hot air on her feathers, and she spread her wings out to clear it away, almost knocking one edge into a large rectangular box with odd lights coming from inside.

Pret let out a yelp of surprise, pushing Grith's wing away. "That's fragile!" he squeaked. "And expensive!"

"What is this place?" Grith squinted as Pret leapt onto a large couch-like object covered in black leather, laying his underbelly across it and nestling his hindpaws into two places that looked like they'd been specially made for them.

"The latest in human technology!" Pret replied, giving Grith a toothy grin as he spun around a full 360 degrees on the object he was laying on, swishing his tail. He stretched out his wings and hooked the spurs on their tips into small rubber nibs, using them to tap on a silver plate.

Grith blinked as two large screens lit up from behind him, and a clattering sound came from his talons as he typed on a series of keys glowing colors that made Grith's eyes hurt.

"The keyboard is custom," Pret explained. "Originally, I just found someone to make me a really big one, but it turns out that it's not really ergonomic for talons, and also scratches are pretty easy. This one doesn't just do Latin, but Southern, too, if I want to write something in that! I've got two touchpads for my wingspurs; it takes a bit of getting used to and some weird controls, but it turns out that four usable limbs is a huge advantage in first-person shooters. Don't worry, I don't look into the future; that would be chea—"

"Pret," Grith rumbled, flicking her tail. "I believe you are getting side-tracked."

"Right," Pret replied, turning back to the keyboard and moving around his wings.

Grith stared as a few images popped up on the screen, squinting at the bright light. She read a headline in English as it came into focus, along with a very blurry picture of her.

"Here's one of the major news stations that first broke the story. There were a ton of attempts at debunking, of course, a lot Council-sponsored, but they ended up being not very convincing. Your presence is indisputable. The whole world has been exposed to dragons and magic practically overnight." He scrolled down. "Some comments believe you're a threat. Others think that you were in the right, myself included. Look, this is my comment! The New York Times chose it for the top!"

"Ashley showed me some of the reactions already," Grith replied, glancing to the side as a fan whirred louder. "I already know. I ruined all the work we have done trying to hide ourselves from humans over the past few centuries."

"Maybe, but it wasn't ever sustainable to begin with," Pret explained. "As I explained, there's no way the magical world would have been kept secret for even the next decade. I might be overly optimistic, but I think this is a good thing for the world as a whole, and you shouldn't feel bad that it happened."

"You do?" Grith asked, cocking her head. "I don't see how this can be good."

"It's a chance for harmony!" Pret said, practically stamping his paws up and down in excitement. "Grith, I think that we can build a better world. One where dragons don't have to use bubble realms or shiftstones to hide. One where magical creatures can walk alongside humans, where we don't need a Council."

Grith opened her eyes a little, her cousin's hopefulness rubbing off on her feathers. Had there been a world like that, she never would've had to go to work at Vertex Technologies. She could have worked at any human company; she wouldn't even have needed to pay for the magic for her home. The paradise her mother had wanted for dragons: could it even be possible here?

A box popped up on Pret's screen with a ding, a message from someone named 'pal3brok3nscal3s#6969.'

"'Lol silverdragon#2781 she's your cuz?'" Grith read out loud in English. "Looks like a fkn nerd. Cuntcil is gonna BTFO her u know. F.' Pret? What is a Cuntcil and a BTFO?"

Pret's crest raised in shame, and he dragged the message away and pressed a button saying 'Do Not Disturb.' "Ignore that, she's just a friend." He grimaced, switching to a different tab, another news story. "I've been keeping myself up to date, and just in the last couple hours, a lot has gone on. Magical communities outside the world have started making statements. The first was an open letter published online by a witch's coven in Scotland, detailing a bit of their history, the history of magic, and a hopeful vision for the future.

"The second was an AMA on Reddit, er, an online question and answer session from a pack of werewolves in Seattle that was surprisingly well-received. Even Vertex Technologies made an announcement, but it was pretty much limited to just noting that the warehouse belonged to them, and that they've reached out to the LAPD, who have allowed them back on their property and that they are holding a joint investigation into the events along with the magical government. There have been a couple others, but those were the ones of note."

"Do you really think this will turn out good?" Grith murmured.

Pret changed the screen to an image of a few howling werewolves, holding up a piece of paper together.

"I thought that the Council had their rules for a reason. To protect us."

"I don't know," Pret replied, placing a hindleg on the cavern floor and rotating his chair around to face Grith. "So far, it's just been small players. But human governments are probably going to start holding emergency sessions in the next few days. The Council hasn't made any official statements yet, and appear to be biding their time. The draconic leadership hasn't said anything either, but I doubt the news has even reached them yet. Speaking of that, I think you should make a statement."

"A *what*?" Grith exclaimed, the feathers on her neck ruffling. "A statement? As in, a statement to the public over the cyberwebs?"

"I think it's a good idea! If you explain what happened last night from your own perspective, it might put humans at ease. So far, it's mostly been just wild speculation, and I think you could clarify. Plus, any publicity will keep the Council from acting too harshly."

"That's a horrible idea," Grith murmured, clenching up her talons just at the thought. "I can't. All of my interactions with humans have been barely good at best, and almost biting off body parts at worst. What if I go onto the screen and accidentally refer to humans as prey? I keep doing that. They will think dragons are dangerous and eat humans, which is mostly not true!"

"I could help edit," Pret suggested, extending out a forepaw.

"Oh, no no no," Grith squealed, placing her snout beneath her wing. "Something would go wrong, and I'd say something wrong or take off my clothes or bare my fangs or do something just as terrible that humans don't like! This should be left up to the Council; they are the experts in this sort of thing. What about you? You know lots of humans and have your cybernet device. You would be far better than me."

Pret let out a puff of smoke, lowering his claws. "All right." He sighed, resting his head on its side, horns just barely peeking out from his crest. "I guess, just think about it. Maybe when things have calmed down a little more."

Grith doubted there would be much calming down from here on out. Part of her still expected the world to burst into flame at any moment, or for a Council enforcer brandishing a dragon-sized axe to jump in here and swipe it through her neck.

"If it's all right, can I ask you what exactly happened last night?" Pret asked, cocking his head to the other side of the chair's neck-rest. "I was able to piece together some of it, but I think I'd be able to understand better if you explained it yourself. I saw Ashley and Albiwegan, and I think a wizard?"

Grith thought back to the events of the previous day. So much had happened. She'd explored a whole new world, until it had come crashing down on her wings like sheets of rain. "I talked to Holz, like you suggested. She told me Albi-wegan disappeared, and Ashley, the wizard, and I followed their trail to the warehouse. They were being kept for some sort of Vertex experiment with a portal. I freed them, and we were attacked by wizards, and we were teleported out, and . . . I think you have seen the rest. Along with every single human on the planet."

"A Vertex experiment?" Pret asked, his fangs suddenly bared. His talons clenched around the leather chair, and for a moment, Grith thought he was going to tear it. "I don't like that. I don't know what they're up to, but Grith? Stay safe. Put up extra wards. And if you ever need anything, I'm here."

"I know," Grith answered, purring as she gave him a friendly nuzzle. "Thank you. I think I'm feeling better after this. Less like I accidentally destroyed the world. Maybe even a little bit hopeful."

"I'm glad," Pret purred back, swishing his tail. "Good luck."

Grith turned, walking out toward the edge of a tunnel where there was a hint of natural light. She opened her wings when she reached the sheer rock-face at the end, the cloudy pink boundary of the bubble realm visible in the distance.

Some of Pret's optimism *had* rubbed off on her, fighting a battle with anxiety for her heart. Now, she wasn't sure if she was more afraid or excited for the future.

CHAPTER
FIFTEEN

T he sprawling expanse of LA peered out towards Grith on her flight back, the skyline of downtown poking out from a brown haze, the outlines of fuzzy windows lost within. Cars honked and whirred on the highways beneath the dragon, unaware of her presence above as she headed back toward her home.

A group of humans walked out from a car and into a building, and she wondered what they were doing. Was LA any different today than the day before? The world that day had woken up to see her. Were the humans just looking at the news for the first time shocked and scared, like she was? Or were they hopeful, like Pret?

She tilted her wings as an air current turned her toward the mountains north of the city, wrinkling her snout when the pungent smell of smog touched her nose. Had the humans below been afraid of her when they'd first seen her on their screens? Probably. She wondered if they were right to be.

Watching more humans beneath her, wondering what

they thought, Grith suddenly realized that she'd started to care. Not just caring about how they thought of her, but she was beginning to care about what happened to the mundane humans. She didn't want their world to collapse. She didn't want the humans she'd met to get hurt.

When Grith had made her decision the night before to expose herself and save Ashley, she'd inexorably bound the fates of dragons and humans in this world together. She'd chosen that dragons could no longer live in isolation and secrecy, and chosen that humans could no longer remain ignorant of the magic in their world; with all the benefits and danger that came with that. It was a choice for all of them, a choice that Grith had no right to make. But it was a bit too late to take it back. Her magic didn't allow for time travel.

Then the question was, what was she to do now? Part of her wanted to hide. She'd done enough damage as it was. She'd made a mistake, and she should face justice for it.

But maybe Pret was right. She didn't want all humans to be afraid of her. Even if they were right to be afraid or at least cautious of dragons, who often shared little concern for humans beyond being either forbidden prey or a threat to their species, Grith wanted to believe in Pret's future. No, not believe. Grith wanted to create Pret's future, a future better for both humans and dragons. A symbiotic relationship, where magic could help humans in ways it couldn't before, and where dragons and other magical creatures were able to live freely without fear of their own.

Grith decided that would be the future she would strive for. She'd messed things up, and now, she would work to fix them. She would do what Pret had suggested, even if she was terrified. Make a statement to all of humanity.

She swooped down over her forest, checking for the

familiar landmarks, and spotted the barren rock marking the entrance to her bubble realm. She was almost home. Grith stretched her wings wide as she dove down, feeling the strong tingle of magic rush down her crest to make the motions with her wingspurs to open the gate.

There was a loud crack, and Grith screeched out in pain, her invisibility crumpling when a flash of light hit her in the snout. An almost invisible magical barrier slammed into her, and for a moment, her vision went dark. She thought she heard something break, and certainly felt it. The dragon reached out wildly, uncertain what was going on, her talons scrambling against the hard barrier wrapping around the entrance to her bubble realm.

She opened her eyes, but the world was nothing more than blurs of light and movement. One eye didn't seem to get less blurry. Air whipped up past her, and she realized that the movement was the ground getting closer, trees reaching up. With another cry of pain, Grith extended her wings, the air knocking her to the side as she tried to stay aloft.

Cold covered her feathers, the frigidity dulling the pain. She flapped as one of her wings twisted beneath her, the dragon turning in a tight circle, trees growing closer. As her vision unblurred, she realized that ice had grown across her wing, golden feathers covered in a hard, heavy light blue, the scent of magic drifting up into her nose.

Beneath the falling dragon, there was movement. Grith caught glimpses of humans in green camouflage vests, marked only by a light-blue bracelet around each of their arms. Mist and frost emanated from the hands of one of them as he dove beneath a tree. Another had his hands up against the magical barrier, the two bracelets glowing as it spread up into the air. The Council had sent enforcers to punish her after all.

Survival instincts took over. Grith wouldn't go down without a fight. She opened her jaws, a bright orange light forming in them as smoke rose from her nose.

"Fire!" one of the enforcers screamed out. "Prepare yourselves!"

The humans scattered, yelling and diving beneath the trees for cover, jumping behind tree trunks as they tried to move out of range.

Grith let her flame loose beneath her, though it didn't reach the ground. Instead, she kept it at the lowest temperature she could, aiming at her frozen wing. She winced as the heat licked her feathers, hoping that the fire-resistant oil on them was enough to keep her from lighting herself aflame. The ice melted beneath it, water dripping onto the ground.

The dragon whipped it upright with another jolt of pain, flapping as she tried to rise into the air. Her gaze caught on more of the enforcers drawing runes in the air. Flames burst forth from them, light glinting in Grith's eyes.

She let out a roar as her eyes glowed golden, magic whipping around her wings as she used it on herself. Two magic circles formed at her neck and tail, her heart rate speeding up. The flames slowed, crawling up toward her at a snail's pace. Even with her injuries, she easily dodged them, circling around a bolt of fire as she rose back into the sky, the heat not even touching her.

A high-pitched tone burst through her head, vibrations shaking through her insides. She clutched at her underbelly as they ripped into her, going dizzy and eyes turning dull, her magic fading. For a moment, she was helpless, hardly able to think as pain shot into her, the dragon's wings barely able to move, much less able to keep her aloft.

A ball of fire narrowly missed her wings, only due to her sudden change of direction as she dropped to the ground. Her mind was blank, her wings able to do little but slow her down instinctively as she crashed into the trees.

Branches caught on her feathers, cutting into her skin. An enforcer let out a yell as a half-ton of dragon fell down on him, Grith barely noticing his screams cut short when she landed with a crunch of bones. Dirt, sticks, and blood flew into the air and a cloud of dust rose up, obscuring the dragon's view of the forest.

Her eyes opened after the tone suddenly stopped, the golden glint in them returned. She struggled to put her claws beneath her and get back on her paws, whipping her head around as she saw movement, smelling humans and magic.

Another roar came forth from her jaws, followed by an orange flame. She turned back and forth, spraying it on anything that moved, the fire and heat rising up around her. The flames drowned out yells she could barely comprehend, flashes of light across the humans suggesting that they'd hastily put up magical shields. She shot flame at one, cracks forming in it as fire rained down, the enforcer's face invisible in the smoke and dust.

Grith flicked her wings again, two rotating circles forming across her. Her eyes went to the hazy sky above her, and her injured wings opened wide. She had to escape this.

With the first flap, magic that was unfamiliar but familiar caught her. She let out a screech as the time around her went back to normal, two more golden circles now rotating opposite to the ones she'd made.

Another enforcer with an glowing hourglass in one hand and a magic circle formed over the other, concentrating on her as he nullified her spell.

Grith opened her jaws, fangs stretching down as she prepared another blast of fire. More pain flicked across her neck as she slammed to the ground, her head twisted to the side. She placed her forepaws in front of her, trying to pull herself out from it, only for another magical net to be thrown across her back, her wings and body held tight. She shot fire at an approaching enforcer, but wire wound around her snout, shutting it closed and causing her teeth to dig into her maw, Grith tasting her own blood.

She stared motionlessly as a black-hooded enforcer raised up his hands, a glowing blue axe with a blade as large as a dragon's neck appearing in them. The Council slaying her was to be her fate, she would meet it without fear. Smoke rose up from her nostrils as he approached, Grith using the last of her energy to bare sharp fangs at him, dripping with her own blood.

"Stop! Don't hurt her!" a familiar voice called out. Chris walked forth from the smoke, his hands trembling as he held a silver tuning fork within them, contrasting with a golden signet ring on his fingers. He stared at her with a look she didn't understand, pity, terror, or possibly guilt. She could certainly smell the fear-scent on him. Was he here to rescue her?

"My son is right," said another human with the same ring, as crisply dressed as Chris with hair just as blond, distinct by his lack of enforcer garb. Grith's flames had scorched a red tie around his neck, smoke and embers coming from it. His face told Grith exactly nothing, though she wasn't sure if it was just that she was unsure how to read human emotions, or that he had none that he chose to share. "The Council's orders were to capture it alive. You did that successfully. I can take it from here."

Chris grimaced, keeping his gaze focused on Grith's claws rather than her eyes. "I'm really sorry," he whimpered, rubbing his ring. "I had to tell them where you were. You committed a horrible crime."

Betrayal. Grith bared her fangs again, a deep rumble coming up from her throat.

Chris's heart rate sped up, the fear-scent stronger as Grith's talons clenched up. "I didn't have a choice! The Council has rules for a reason. You had to be brought to justice! I didn't want to do this, but there was no other way. You understand, right? You can forgive me for this, can't you?"

"Chris, it's a dragon." His father sighed, walking up to her until she could have bitten his hands off had her snout been free. He squinted as he crouched, staring at her bared fangs with more curiosity than terror. Grith couldn't smell any fear-scent from him at all. "You can't reason with it."

Grith let out a noise as hands grabbed the sides of her snout. She tried to snap at them, but the binding around her snout let her do little more than get his sleeves wet with her saliva.

He brought his head down until it was on top of her nose, forcing Grith to stare into his blue eyes.

She tried to shut her eyelids as she smelled the magic coming from him, but was unable to pull herself away. Dark clouds formed over his irises, and whispers formed in her in her head. She couldn't turn, couldn't do anything as the clouds grew, the darkness in his eyes expanding until she was lost within it, unable to see anything but the great void surrounding her as she drifted through it, into a peaceful sleep.

Chris's father dropped Grith's snout, scoffing at the unconscious dragon, her golden eyes now black and hazy. With a grimace, he squinted at the enforcer who'd been crushed beneath her, blood staining the dragon's golden down.

"Well?" he demanded, looking around at the enforcers. "Go on. It won't be out forever. Move it."

CHAPTER

SIXTEEN

E verything seemed to hurt when Grith woke back up, the spell on her fading. Her sleep had been cold and dreamless, drifting through a void of darkness, before it had become pierced by pain and the hum of electricity.

She awoke in a remarkably uncomfortable position, thick chains wrapped around each of her legs, stretching them tight so that they dangerously exposed her underbelly, holding her up vertically. Another chain tightened around her wings, belly, and her tail pulled up against her back, shackles chafing and tearing feathers. She'd been cleaned since the battle with the enforcers, the only lingering smell of blood now her own. Good quality rhodium was all around her, her mouth salivating from the shimmer-hunger it caused. Even if much of her magic had been restored over her sleep, she'd used a lot.

She opened a blurry eye, trying to rub at it, though her legs didn't have enough strength to break through the chains. She let out a growl as she tried to twist mid-air, unable to even lash her tail trapped between her wings. Her heart raced, her growls turning to roars of anger as she realized she couldn't even move in the dark room. She was trapped, held captive.

She took a deep breath, her roars calming to rumbles. She had to think and figure out a way to escape. Grith opened her jaws, orange light appearing in them as she prepared to blast flame at the chains, and melt them. Before she was able to expel it, however, the chains vibrated around her. Green lights flashed as Grith suddenly felt her magic drained, shrieking as a coldness seemed to fill her body, ripping away her energy and even her life essence.

Grith stopped trying to make fire, realizing where she was, squinting to make the room come into focus. She hadn't recognized it at first, but she'd been here before. Now, blackened scorch marks covered the walls, the white lights where no longer on. From the corner of her eye, there was a huge teleportation ring behind her, hooked up to a large metal box. The enforcers had brought her back to the warehouse.

"Ah," a voice sounded from the entrance, and a human in a flared suit peeked in. "I thought I'd heard some dragon noises!"

"Bald man," Grith hissed, spitting at Paul as he approached. So far beneath her, he seemed small, even for a human.

He pulled a handkerchief from his suit-pocket, wiping the dragon spittle off from the top of his head. "Well, you're salivating, I see," he remarked, tossing it to the side. "Would you like something to eat? I want you in good shape, and VT has good catering. I'd been hoping to train you a little better for this, but plans often go awry. We've got rhodium and diamonds, of course, as much as you want. I think I'd be able to produce some human flesh, too, if you'd like that instead. Virgins? Anything for you, even if you *have* been a bad girl."

Grith called up her flame again, trying to shoot it down and incinerate him. It faded before it left her jaws, and she let out another roar as green lightning danced between her feathers.

"I'll take that as a no," Paul replied, turning to the chains. "The Lesser Gate is really an ingenious design, and not all our own. Years ago, we found something in an old ruin over near Greece, an ancient technology far larger that this pale imitation. A Greater Gate, we called it, and we spent quite a lot of money on researching it. Sadly, we couldn't figure out how to activate or even move it. There are rumors that dragons have one, too. You wouldn't happen to know anything about that, would you? I'd be interested in seeing it."

Grith glowered in silence.

"So, you don't know?" Paul asked. "That's unfortunate. We based the design on the Greater Gate, but it's been difficult figuring out how to open it. It doesn't just take any sort of magic; it requires either spatial or temporal energies. None of our wizards have been particularly successful, and even fae don't seem to have enough in them to keep it open long enough for our purposes."

"What are you planning to do with me?" Grith snarled, snapping her jaws down at him.

He didn't flinch. It wasn't like she could get anywhere near close enough.

"Are you going to kill me?"

"You're far too valuable for killing, dear," Paul replied, walking beneath the chains, staring up at the dragon as she wriggled. "Besides, I'm the one who saved your life. I'm amazingly lucky that you practically showed up on my doorstep, not only a dragon, but one with your specific form of magic? Normally I require an interview, but you really were a perfect fit for the company. A lot of synergistic energies!"

"The Council?" Grith asked. "You convinced them not to kill me?"

"Of course," he answered. "I'm an ex-Council member myself. For the past twenty years, GMI has been slowly infiltrating their ranks. It was a surprisingly close vote, but I got permission to do whatever I want with you until I'm done, and they'll execute you. You're quite lucky. As a VT employee, you don't just work for me, but I work for *you*. You're my duty, even if animals don't exactly have rights."

"Then I quit." Grith snorted. "I want no part in this. Send me to the Council." She brought forth fire again, smoke streaming from her jaws as the chains pulled her magic into them, like she expected.

"Try not to use too much of your magic yet," Paul replied as he waved his hand, wafting smoke away. "If you do, I'll have to force-feed you, which I doubt will be fun for either of us." He scratched the top of his head. "Do you prefer human meat? You did almost bite off one of your coworker's hands. I've gotten special Council permission to do whatever is necessary to take care of you, and I would like you to be as comfortable as possible."

"Do not feed me humans," Grith growled. "How can you feel that way toward your own species?"

"I'm a wizard," Paul reminded her. "I've progressed beyond human. Mundanes are as much prey to me as they are to dragons." He thought for a moment. "No, prey is too generous. They're more like earthworms, feeding from my garden as their bodies nourish the dirt."

Grith certainly thought that Paul looked a bit like an

earthworm, with no hair and from so far down beneath her. She decided that was probably a bit unfair to earthworms.

"I have to admit, I'm disappointed in you," Paul replied as he finished checking the chains. He stepped over to the metal box, flicking with a few dials. "Dragons are good at hiding, even from wizards. I figured you'd have more restraint. GMI thought we'd have more preparation time."

"Preparation for what?" Grith asked, twisting her tail as she tried to pull it out from the chains.

"Wizards are just as unhappy as dragons are about the current state of affairs," Paul explained, crouching and squinting at a dial, tapping his finger on it. "Both of our races have to hide ourselves from humans out of fear. For years, GMI has been planning for years to put magic back in its rightful place, where wizards no longer have to hide in the shadows. That's the initiative. To create a world where humans serve us, instead of the other way around."

At least to Grith, it certainly didn't look like wizards were serving mundane humans.

"We'd had this in the works for decades." Paul sighed. "In about six months, a large part of the human world was going to fall into disarray, governments completely unable to respond to any threat we posed. We were going to expose ourselves at the opportune time to take power. But you set things into motion a bit too early, and now we're ahead of schedule without the preparations and tests we'd been hoping for."

"Well, I am glad I ruined your plan." Grith snorted, wiggling her wings. How could she get these chains off? Her magic or fire wouldn't work. Would water short-circuit them? She spat on one link, but there was no effect beyond a small flash of green.

"Ruined?" Paul laughed, stepping back from the

machine and looking up at the dragon. "Oh no, far from ruined. Even if the other cities aren't quite ready, taking control of LA will be a good stepping stone. And the Lesser Gate still works."

He turned away from the dragon and stepped out the door, and she writhed again, spitting at the silver box. There was a crackle of green, and for a moment, she'd hoped she'd broken something, but there was nothing beyond that.

When Paul returned, he had a clear diamond in his hands.

Grith squinted as he heaved it up onto the silver box, wrapping more chains around it. She remembered it from Vertex Technologies. A diamond with the space inside warped so much to be a bottomless essence pit.

"I have nowhere near enough magic to fill that," Grith purred. "If I had that much, I would be able to break through these chains like twigs just by flexing a talon. I think you have vastly overestimated me."

"I'm not getting it from you," Paul said as he fastened the chains and changing the positions of a few dials, lights on the panel turning on. He flicked a few switches on and off, looking quite pleased with himself. "Dragons may be the originators of magic on Earth, but the head of GMI knows that you got it from another realm. The end goal of Vertex Technologies has always been to get it from wherever you got it from, and we've just about succeeded, so long as we can keep this portal open for long enough."

Grith blasted fire at him, turning the temperature up as high as she could, expending as much of her magic as possible. Smoke rose into the air, and she let out another roar as more of the chains forced more of her magic from her, drained by the glowing green chains.

"You should be proud of yourself," Paul continued. "This is your contribution to magic. A feat that has never been done before: creating a stable portal to another realm."

He pushed up a familiar lever, dials turning as lights flickered on panels. The green glow on the chains pulsed as it filled Grith's eyes. Her vision became blurry as the chains tightened, crawling around her legs. Her roars became screeches of pain, the dragon's very thoughts becoming blurred and incomprehensible mutterings.

Her head felt woozy, lights around her spinning as the world retreated from her, as if a thin, black film had covered her vision. She felt distant, all of her worries far from her. There was something there, something she hadn't seen before, something that permeated through her. Her vision focused on it, and a claw reached out, touching what was beyond. For a moment, she was connected, an entire world of her own. All of existence was her, and she was all of existence, nothing and everything

Then, it was over. Her head limply flopped against her underbelly, and Grith went still.

Paul barely noticed, his eyes focused on the flashes of green behind Grith, opening wide as the portal stabilized. An empty sky appeared beyond it, and he stepped beneath the dragon, staring out into it. A huge stone tumbled past, while the wizard's eyes followed.

"It's beautiful, isn't it?" Paul asked.

Grith's head lulled, her eyes dulled as green lights flashed across her golden feathers. His voice was far away, like she'd been shoved underwater. His smell was faint, wisps of human drifting away.

"Vertex Technologies' work culminated in this," Paul said. "You could look slightly more impressed."

A few minutes passed, but to Grith, it could have been only seconds or an hour. The dragon was still, her chest slowly rising and falling. Time passed before her, and a sea of her own thoughts consumed her, flickers of memories forming in the blackness. Her parents and her cousins. Her library, stretching out before her, far larger than it ever had been, and she was flying through an endless expanse of shifting tunnels, moving in and out of each other.

The portal flickered out.

Paul frowned. "Your magic drained quicker than I expected," he remarked, before it turned back on, the empty blue sky visible once more. He looked over at the crystal. "Though I suppose that will be enough for now."

Paul grasped a hold of the chains on the crystal, stiffening up as green bolts flickered around his hands. Carefully, he removed them, lifting the object up, taking in a deep breath of victory. His arms trembled where he'd touched the surface, smoke rising from his fingers. "Yes," he murmured, his eyes locked on the crystal. "This will certainly be enough."

Green lines stretched down his arm, twisting up his neck as the magic implanted itself within him. He took a deep breath, glaring at the crystal as if to prove his dominance over it. For a moment, he was still, before he let out a sigh of relief.

"I believe I will be keeping this machine on," he said to the limp dragon, positioning himself beneath her, staring into her dull eyes.

She didn't move. He seemed so far away to her, as if he was a bad dream penetrating the thoughts of her library maze.

"I wouldn't want your magic to accidentally regenerate before I need it. I suspect you'd find a way to escape."

The crystal pulsed as the marks on his arm grew brighter. He opened his other hand, white light spreading from his fingers and forming a disk on the ground. It coalesced into silver, a mirror formed from his magic.

Grith motionlessly stared at it, showing images of the empty sky in the portal behind her.

"I hope you enjoy the view," Paul replied, tucking the crystal into his suit as he left.

CHAPTER
SEVENTEEN

Time passed for Grith as she hung from the chains. Hours felt like an eternity, and beyond the slow pulse of her heart and the filling and emptying of her lungs, she didn't even twitch her claws. Whenever she absorbed essence from Terra's aura, the green chains stole it from her, the portal flickering in and out.

Afterward, Grith was barely able to remember the time she'd spent attached to the Lesser Gate. As her mother had told her, dragons were creatures of flesh and shimmer, of blood and magic, of the earth and the heavens. With her essence stolen from her, her body and mind shut down, and Grith stared with a blank expression at the mirror, unable to process anything that was happening. Even if the world around her had crumbled to dust, the dragon would have been blissfully unaware.

On occasion the portal would activate again, and her blank gaze would land on the pale blue sky. Had she been able to comprehend it, she would have learned that in fact it wasn't empty, just almost so. Rocks and boulders tumbled through the air of various sizes, stones ranging from the size of pebbles to those as large as mountains. Ancient buildings covered the tops of some of the larger ones, some with rubble of a fallen temple built by humans. Had she been paying attention at the right time, she might have even seen the curious snout of a scaled dragon drifting across the sky, wondering what was on the other side of the portal, where it led, why one of his kin was chained up, and how she happened to be a supposedly extinct species of feathered dragon. Unfortunately, he had more urgent matters to attend to, and drifted away into the great expanse.

It was a bit under two-dozen hours before Grith's senses started to return to her, though having no sense of the passage of time in this state, it could have been mere minutes or a hundred years. The chains around her released, and she fell with them, crashing to the ground. The hum of the machine had stopped, the Lesser Gate closed.

"Hey, are you all right?"

Grith didn't comprehend the voice, nor would she have known it.

A fae nervously stepped forward, prodding the dragon's nose with one of their fingers.

She didn't move or even notice.

"I'm here to repay you," Albiwegan said, poking Grith again. "But I can't unless you move. You're not dead, are you? Please don't be dead."

Grith didn't feel the hand on her neck testing for a pulse. She still had one, though it was slow. Her head lulled to the side as the fae tried to push her.

"Oh, you're out of magic," Albiwegan frowned, realizing what the problem was. "That's not good. Ummm, how do dragons get magic again? Metals! You need to eat metals."

They dug around in their pockets for a few moments, the fae's long, white hair curling over the edges of their leather jacket. Finally, they found what they were looking for and pulled out a handful of gold coins, almost the same shade as Grith's feathers.

"Here," they said, holding their hands out, hoping the dragon wouldn't try to snap too vigorously. "Have these."

Grith didn't budge.

Albiwegan sighed, and inched closer to the dragon's snout, placing their hands up against her gums, peeling them open. They grimaced as they grabbed two of her fangs, opening her jaws until there was enough space the fae could slip the coins in.

The coins dropped onto Grith's tongue, and Albiwegan stared and rubbed off the dragon's saliva onto their jacket. Slowly, the coins melted, molten gold dripping back into Grith's throat. Albiwegan paced back and forth, putting their hands on their neck while they impatiently waited.

Then, there was movement. Grith's golden eyes changed from dull to dim, and there was motion in her talons as she brought an uncomfortably twisted paw under her.

"Great!" Albiwegan grinned. "Now that you're awake, we really really need to leave. I think the alarms got broken in the explosion, but I don't trust that a stray wizard won't come in to check on you."

A low rumble sounded from the dragon's throat, her eyes opening wider. Her head raised up, but her neck was tired, so very tired. All of her was tired. Her head tilted down at the movement in front of her, opening her jaws as she saw potential prey move.

Albiwegan let out a yelp as the dragon pushed them over with her head, warm breath across their face. "Easy."

They gulped, staying as still as they could as Grith's fangs pressed up against their skin. "You don't want to eat me. I wouldn't taste good."

Grith didn't quite understand what the humanoid in front of her jaws was saying, the words lost on her ears, but a sniff of the fae's face made her agree with them. They were neither flesh nor metal. Uninterested, she turned away, lumbering toward the huge teleportation ring behind her, each step painful and exhausting.

"That's the wrong way." Albiewgan winced, facepalming. "We need to go the other way."

Grith salivated at the scent of the teleportation ring, walking up until her nose was against it. Placing her talons on the side, the dragon gave it a lick, dragging her tongue up the rhodium plating. When she lifted her metal-coated tongue away, she suddenly felt a bit less fatigued. She'd left a long, black mark had been left where the metal beneath the plating had been exposed.

"Right." Albiwegan sighed as Grith kept licking the side of the teleportation ring. "Metals. Magic. Got it."

After clearing a few square feet of the plating, Grith had enough energy and awareness to comprehend what exactly was going on around her. She looked over at Albiwegan, gnawing on a bit on the corner of the teleportation ring before speaking.

"Oh, hello," she said, confused as to what the fae was doing back here. "I think we need to stop Paul."

Albiwegan laughed, slapping the ground as they stood back up. "One step at a time. Right now, we need to get out of here." They nervously glanced over their shoulder. "I'm not sure how much time I have before someone will realize that I teleported inside."

"That is a good idea," Grith murmured, climbing

around to the other side of the ring and licking away the plating there. "I would make a joke about us having plenty of time, but I am unsure if I am even able to fly or breathe fire with the shimmer I have right now, much less use any sort of temporal magic. I am exhausted. I believe we are in an unfortunate situation."

Albiwegan grimaced, scratching their head. "Yeah, sorry about getting you into this mess."

"You are sorry?" Grith asked, positioning herself so that she faced the fae as she took off more of the plating. She needed as much shimmer as possible, though ruining the Lesser Gate for any future uses was certainly an advantage.

"Yeah," the fae murmured, putting their hands in their pockets. "I'm the one who got captured to begin with, and making you, who I don't even know, rescue me. Then I put everyone in danger by running and caused the whole altercation that apparently literally the entire world knows about now. I think I screwed up."

"Oh," Grith responded, thinking to herself as she lowered her head to the ground. "It is all right. You had been kept imprisoned for a week, and running was a very understandable fight or flight response. I have also had problems with that. I almost bit off a human's hand a while back, and probably should have not almost set the police on fire. Well, I am glad I have someone else to share the blame of screwing up with."

Albiwegan gave her a small smile. "Yeah. To screwing up. And you know what? I'm going to make it up to you. C'mon, let's get out of here."

Grith purred, before realizing a difficulty with the plan. "I cannot fly," she explained, waggling her wings. "I need more shimmer."

"You can still run though, right?" Albiwegan asked,

looking at the dragon's long legs. "If so, I've got an idea. Can I get on your back?"

"If you would like," Grith uncertainly replied, bending her head down as she crouched her forelegs. The fae walked up to her, and the dragon shivered as she felt hands on her neck. A moment later, they swung themself up, placing their feet in front of her wings as she stood back upright.

"Everything is so small from up here!" Albiwegan grinned. "How fast do you think you can go? I'll need you to run when I say so."

Grith thought about it for a moment. "I believe about fifty miles per hour at the fastest, but doing that for any more than very briefly will require me to use my shimmer, which I cannot. It will be far slower if it is for longer periods, particularly with you on my back."

"Hmm." Albiwegan thought out loud. "I can work with that. If there was any day which the normal LA traffic would have been nice, this would have been it, but no such luck. Alright, let's go up, but pause before you leave the warehouse. Do you trust me?"

"Not particularly." Grith snorted. "However, it doesn't seem I have much of a choice. I will follow your plan."

Grith climbed up the slope to the warehouse entrance, occasionally jiggling her wings back and forth. The extra weight on her back of a humanoid was odd. She walked in darkness this time, the alarm lights off as her talons touched cold tile. She much preferred it, even as exhausted as she was.

A thin crack between the doors allowed white-tinted sunlight to shoot in, the dragon squinting. It felt like it had been so long since she'd seen light. The scent of humans and gasoline came in from beyond. She made a motion toward it, before a voice stopped her.

"Stay still!" someone sounded through a megaphone, his voice crackling. "Fae! We know you're in there. Come out, and you'll be peacefully taken into Council custody!"

Albiwegan shifted their weight on Grith's neck until they were practically at a ninety degree angle, peering out through the crack. "There's a line of Council enforcers," they whispered. "Behind them are a bunch of mundane police and cars all around. I think they're prepared for a fight."

"Do you think they are the same ones who captured me?" Grith nervously murmured, her talons scraping against the tile. "I do not think I would be able to get through, especially without magic."

"Doubt it." Albiwegan frowned, squinting as they tried to figure out more of the surroundings outside. "They probably sent an anti-dragon strike team of their top wizards to take you down. From my earlier snooping, I don't even think they know you're down here, just that this is Vertex property they're supposed to guard. Don't think we can fight them regardless."

"Hurry up!" the megaphone yelled with a loud screech of feedback. "Hands in the air! No magic, no weapons!"

"I'm ready!" Albiwegan screamed back. "Coming out!" They grinned and kicked Grith in her side. "Now!"

"Do not kick me." Grith glared before bursting out the doors, the wooden planks on them breaking as they flung out to the side. The dragon took off, her legs flinging beneath her as she ducked her head and broke into a sprint.

The sudden noise and human fear-scent hit her. Yells filled her ears, and her eyes adjusted to the sunlight. Her paws leapt across the concrete beneath them, her wings instinctively fluttering as the wind rushed past her feathers.

"Dragon!" an enforcer screeched, putting his hands up as the rings on his wrists glowed. A line of them clambered for a moment as the dragon barrelled toward them, roaring out a battle-cry. They hastily drew glowing runes into the air, and with it the clicks of guns as mundane police dove for cover. The gap between her and the blockade was narrowing, but not fast enough. Perhaps following Alb's plan had been a mistake.

Gunshots rang in the dragon's ears as blasts of fire and ice burst forth from the runes. Grith rushed head-on to meet them, her fangs bared. Suddenly, a flash of white light shot across her feathers.

There was a moment of confusion as Grith realized that the noise of the cars and guns was now coming from behind her. She peered back as her talons rushed across asphalt, forced to slow to a more sustainable pace as her heart raced. The warehouse, along with the lines of humans, had all been teleported behind her. Or more accurately, Albiwegan had teleported her in front.

"Three!" the fae shouted out, putting their hands in the air in a slightly premature victory pose. "Keep going! Turn to the left!"

Grith abruptly changed her direction, stretching out her wings as she skidded on the asphalt. More bullets and blasts of magic fired as she leapt into another street, bricks cracking as sirens sounded.

The dragon panted as she ran, pale sunlight scattering across her feathers. "Three?" she asked, rushing past parked cars and a red traffic light above her, barely noticing it. Except for the sirens, the city was oddly quiet.

"Three more," Albiwegan explained, wrapping their arms around the dragon's neck as they were bumped up and down, their hair dangling in the wind. "That's how many more times I can teleport with you today with the magic I've got. Not having a real forest *sucks*."

Grith squinted as she rushed down the street. Something seemed odd, and not just the lack of the usual smell of human. She looked up, suddenly realizing that the color of the sky was off.

Curved white crystal covered the sky far above LA, smog trapped at the very top of it while clouds diverted around. Except for the odd tinted sunlight, it was barely visible to the dragon, strange cracks appearing within it along with an odd ethereal glow that reminded her of the Vertex campus.

"Oh, yeah, the crystal shell," Albiwegan explained. "I think a wizard put it up yesterday. It encloses a bunch of the city, and doesn't let anyone in or out."

"Paul," Grith growled, making the connection. "He and GMI have claimed Los Angeles as their territory."

Albiwegan let out a laugh at that, getting a confused head-cock from the dragon. "Sorry, I'm just imagining a bunch of wizards pissing all around LA to claim it."

"Oh, we should prevent that," Grith rumbled. "I would not want wizard scent marks near my home. It would be annoying to have to re-mark it."

Sirens blared louder and she spotted red and blue lights in the reflections of a window. Two police cars were speeding up, taking as much advantage of the empty street as she was. Shots sounded, and Grith let out a yelp as one hit too close for comfort.

The dragon slowed and ran to the left, ducking behind a large van as more bullets hit it. She winced as shattered glass pierced her feathers, before stretching her wings out and rearing on her hindlegs.

Albiwegan yelped as they held on, tightening their legs around Grith's neck, suddenly heating up.

The two police cars swerved as Grith let out a roar, orange light in the back of her throat warning them of imminent firebreath. One rammed into the other, the crash drowning out the dragon's roar. It toppled onto its side, and let loose a puff of flame-less smoke against the car before rushing off down a smaller street as more came up from the side of the road.

Immediately, Grith realized that she'd made a bad turn: a hastily-parked dump truck took up much of the alleyway, more cars piled up behind it in a rush. She opened her wings as she ran, feeling only the smallest bit of lift before realizing she wasn't taking off. The dragon glanced behind her to hear more sirens driving into the alley. It was too late to go back.

"Keep running!" Albiwegan called out as a blast of flame shot over their head, sticking their tongue out at an enforcer leaning out from a police car.

With a growl, Grith sprinted forward, air whisking past her wings as the fae held on tight. Bullets bounced off the back of the truck, while Grith lowered her head, preparing to ram into it.

"Two!" Albiwegan shouted.

With a flash of light, the truck was gone, and Grith was on a wide street, skyscrapers towering over her, sirens in the distance. She kept running forward, flicking her tail in confusion. "I have been here before," she commented as the fae directed her down the street. The normal noises and the smell of food in the air were gone. "But it was far busier, and the cars were moving whereas now they are all still. The shops are all empty." Her ears perked up at an odd whirring in the distance, coming closer.

"Everyone is staying inside today. Wizards took over the city after the shell went up, and the police ordered the population to hunker down until things have settled and it's clear who's in charge."

"Paul succeeded?" Grith asked, horrified. She looked up as the source of the whirring came into view over her, caused by the spinning blades of a helicopter with a number on it. A rumble came up through her throat, shaking Albiwegan.

"It's fine, just a news chopper," the fae said, waving up at the helicopter with a grin. Their grin faded as a black and white helicopter came into view above it. "Nevermind, that one's not fine! Keep running!"

A loud voice echoed from the police helicopter as Grith rushed past a skyscraper, out of view for a moment.

"Dragon!" a booming voice called down. "We are attempting to retain calm and order, and have been working with the magical government. Please surrender at once, and you will be taken in peacefully. Else, we will be forced to open fire!"

"They already did that," Grith grumbled. She let out a roar back up at the helicopter as she rushed, Albiwegan putting their head to one side and covering their ear with a hand. Grith felt their hand grip tighter to her feathers.

"Get to the overpass!" Albiwegan shouted, pointing to an empty bridge.

Shots rang out from above, bullets raining down on the two. Grith let out a yelp, eyes opening as she felt her tail pierced. She gritted her fangs and pushed through the pain, weaving to the side and trying to put a skyscraper between her and the helicopter.

Glass shattered around her as bullets pierced it, Grith wincing as more fell onto her back.

Albiwegan shouted as a shard cut into their leg.

Heart racing, breath heavy, Grith sprinted forward again, diving for the overpass as more shots clattered from above. With a leap, the dragon skid beneath the bridge, crashing into a parked car as she lost her footing. It crumpled as the sound of bullets shook the overpass. Grith peeked out beneath the overpass as the two helicopters circled above her.

She caught her breath for a moment, pain returning. Blood ran down her tail they'd shot her, golden feathers stained red. The dragon gave it a lick, trying to figure out if the bullet was still in it. It wasn't.

She gave a nervous glance to Albiwegan, clinging tight to her backside. Grith nuzzled against the fae's neck in concern when she saw the shard of glass in their leg.

"I'm fine." Albiwegan winced, pulling the shard away, a clear fluid welling up around the wound. "No blood, see?" They nervously peeked up.

The police helicopter had momentarily paused its onslaught.

Grith's heart pounded back and forth in her chest, the dragon still panting. "Where are we going? I do not know how much further I will be able to run."

"The Key," Albiwegan explained, pointing west of the overpass. "We're almost there, and if everything is set up right, we should be safe. Just a little more, okay?"

Sirens sounded again, this time from all around her. She clenched her talons as she got to her paws, seeing red and blue lights as police cars drove toward either side of the overpass. "Just a little further," she murmured, flicking her tail as blood spilt onto the asphalt.

"Time to go!" Albiwegan shouted.

The dragon charged, trying to hold her tail as still as

possible as she felt the wound move. The wind whisked beneath her underbelly, down fluttering in the wind as she let out another roar, threatening to breath flame.

The false threat didn't work this time, the police cars stopping in front of her as humans leaped out. Guns fired at the dragon as wizards prepared spells.

"One!" With a flash of light, they were gone, and Grith was beyond them. The helicopters were in a different position now, turning as they realized where the two had teleported to. Sirens sounded, directed from above as the cars drove towards them.

The skyscrapers were gone as Grith ran down another silent street. Her paws ached, along with the rest of her body. Her tongue lulled out from her mouth, panting. Dragons weren't supposed to run this long.

The lack of the skyscrapers allowed the dragon to get another view of the crystal dome, interrupted by the two helicopters flying beneath it. It reached out almost all the way to the mountains, surrounding the city. She flicked her tail angrily as she realized that her home was on the other side, quickly stopping the flick as pain shot up through it. Almost there.

A sound between a rumble and a groan emanated from the dragon's jaws as two more police cars came into view. She supposed they'd now prepared for the teleportation as well. She charged forward, only to let out a yelp when a magic circle appeared on the street surrounding her, the asphalt beginning to shake.

Grith skidded, trying to slow as a wall of stone shot up, barely avoiding crashing Albiwegan into it as asphalt dust crumbled onto her feathers. The light turned dark, and a similar wall burst up from behind her, rock rising in a cylindrical trap. She flapped her wings, cursing her lack of magic as the police helicopter flew over the top.

"Zero!" Albiwegan shouted as bullets started to fire into the cylinder of stone. With a flash, the they teleported the two to the other side of the police cars, swerving as soon as they realized the two had escaped again.

Grith picked up her speed as she rushed down the street, her heart pulsing. She could feel her vision starting to get blurry as she puffed smoke. Only seeing a familiar street helped her force onwards. "I know where we are!" she purred, stumbling as she ran. "The Key is up there!"

Another magic circle appeared on the ground, Grith yelping as the stone warped and shook. This time, she didn't slow, instead thrusting herself forward as fast as she could. With a leap into the air, the wall of stone burst up beneath her paws, carrying her up with it.

Grith leapt again as the cylinder rose into the air, bullets firing past her as the helicopters moved. She landed on the roof, rushing across it and glancing into the street behind her. The cylinder crumbled to the ground, and a blast of magic shot up from beneath her.

The roof crumbled away, Grith losing her footing and yelp. The dragon stretched her wings with a jump back into the street, wind whisking beneath her feathers.

"I thought you couldn't fly?" Albiwegan screamed out as they saw the asphalt multiple stories beneath them.

"I cannot!" Grith exclaimed as she glided toward the ground, coming in far faster than she'd hoped.

The street crashed up into the two, sirens flashing as the asphalt cracked beneath the dragon. She tumbled over, Albiwegan fortunately flung off her back from the fall so not to be crushed when Grith landed belly-up. Scrapes and cuts lined her back, Grith struggling to have the energy to even get back on her paws.

She managed to just barely twist herself around when sirens blared from both sides, pinching her and Albiwegan between them. She bared her fangs as she heard guns fire, letting out a roar as smoke spilt into the air, her wings spread.

Green light flared up around her, the bullets bouncing from it. Grith blinked as the police continued firing, enforcers joining as blasts of fire spread across a glowing violet dome. She looked towards Albiwegan, wondering if they had caused this, until realizing what had happened.

Protection runes were glowing purple around a doorway behind the fae as they sat up, a key drawn on the door sticking out from the side of their head.

Grith collapsed to the ground, sticking out her tongue as more bullets bounced from the dome. Though the sirens grew louder, the dragon was unafraid. The two had made it to the Key.

EIGHTEEN

"**N**a na, can't get us!" Albiwegan shouted, grimacing as they laid back against the door, sticking their tongue out as more police and enforcers stepped out from the cars. The bullets had stopped, and one of them tried to walk through the violet shield, pushing against it with his shoulders. It didn't budge, however, the entryway of the Key protected. The exhausted dragon tilted her head, showing her fangs, warning him of the fate he would meet if he did manage to break through.

Albiwegan fell back as the door opened.

Grith purred as Ashley stepped through before the human jumped over the fae to Grith.

"You're all right!" Ashley shouted, hugging the dragon around her neck. "I'm so glad! We saw you on the news. We weren't sure what was going on or if you were going to make it."

"We were unsure we were going to make it as well," Grith replied, turning to lick the wound on her tail again. She looked up at the dome, more of the humans outside pounding against it. "You were not exaggerating about the Key being safe."

"It was made for this sort of thing." Ashley smiled, pulling out her vial of salve.

Grith moved her tail over to the human girl as she rubbed some across the bullet-wound. Almost immediately, the pain subsided, though without it the dragon's exhaustion crept in to take its place.

"There are charms and runes all over it, protections built into its very foundation," Ashley continued. "It would take weeks to figure out how to disable them all. They're so complex that Sorcha and even Pret have no idea how they work."

"Or it would take a very powerful wizard," Grith murmured, looking up at the pale crystal shell above the city, the odd light streaming through it hurting her eyes. "I suspect that Paul used the magic he got from me to make it."

"What?" Ashley frowned..

"We should go inside," Grith murmured.

A few more wizards were banging on the walls of the protection sphere, and another had placed his hands on it, causing tremors across its surface. He squinted, as if he'd expected more to happen. The dragon didn't particularly want them to overhear.

Ashley stretched out a hand to Albiwegan, helping them up as the fae dusted off their jacket. "I'm glad you made it back, Alb," she said with a sigh of relief. "We didn't know what happened to you."

"Teleported into the river," Albiwegan explained. "Took a while for me to get back, but I happened to find a dragon on the way!"

Grith peered over the two as she scrunched her wings and walked into the Key. Noises and smells immediately bombarded her. Various magical creatures of all shapes and sizes filled the room, from humanoids that she believed were a few more fae and two vampires, to a snake circling the room that even dwarfed Grith, its tail running out the back door into the outside grove. Sounds in tongues the dragon had never heard before caressed her ears, from whispers that seemed more like electrical vibrations to huge booming in English from a large human-looking person on the left side. She took in scents of all sorts and sized, from animal prey-scent and not-prey-scent to the oddly magical plant-scent of the fae, to the metallic tang of shimmer-scent, stone, smoke, not even listing those scents which the dragon was unsure of in which of the three categories to place.

"It is busy," Grith whispered to Ashley, somewhat intimidated by the crowd.

"Yeah," Ashley explained, "this is the safest place in LA for most of them at the moment. The Council and GMI, I'm not even sure if there's much of a difference anymore, have been trying to round up magical creatures as part of their takeover. You were just the first."

Grith smelled the protection runes around the door again, flashing purple before Ashley shut it behind her. She then ducked her head, curving a tail around her legs as she sat back on her haunches, trying to take up as little room as possible in the crowded Key.

"I wonder if the protections were Pret's idea," she mused.

"They were," a voice said.

Grith peered through the crowd to Ashley's mother, who was slowly moving through it as she pushed Ashley's father's wheelchair, careful not to bump into any of the patrons.

Sorcha gave Grith a wave. "He told us he'd seen a day when we'd need them. Ansila's Eye is what he calls it, right? I've never heard that name before."

Grith tossed her wings up and down. "I am unsure who Ansila is. If Pret knows, he has not told me."

Ashley's father gently looked up at the dragon, wrinkles spreading across his face as he smiled, before it slowly changed to a frown. "We have been trying to contact him, but as of yet, have had no luck. The shield blocks both mundane and magical communications."

"Alb!" a voice shouted.

Grith turned toward Holz, who was pushing aside patrons before practically leaping on Albiwegan with a hug, knocking the fae to the ground again. "You're all right!"

"Ow." Albiwegan winced, hugging Holz back as they struggled to get back to their feet. "Perfectly fine! Just a bit out of it."

Holz twirled and plucked out a few long white hairs from Albiwegan's head, using it to replace the ones in her flower chain that she'd given Grith and Sorcha. She turned to Grith and rushed forward to wrap her arms around the dragon's neck, squeezing it tight. "Thank you for saving them; thank you so much! I don't know how I could ever repay you."

"It is fine," Grith purred, gently pinching her talons around Holz's scarf and pulling her away. It made her feel slightly better about the whole affair. Even if Grith had accidentally exposed herself and magic to the world, at least some good had come out of it.

A crackle of a megaphone suddenly interrupted the

group, and the dragon twisted her head around to the door of the Key.

"Under direct Council orders, the charms around the Key are to be removed immediately!" a voice yelled. "The effective legalities are in place, and a warrant has been obtained from a mundane judge. There are dangerous criminals inside this building which must be apprehended for the public safety!"

"You'll have to make us!" Ashley yelled back, going to open the door. She stopped as her mother placed a hand on her shoulder, shaking her head.

The crowded room became a little quieter at that.

Grith's tail nervously flicked from side to side. What was that Chris had said about magical security? There were plenty of ways around it? And what if Paul decided to use the crystal to force his way through? If he'd been able to use it to create the crystal shell around the entirety of LA, Grith doubted the protections here could stop him.

She hoped that Pret had planned well. And from increased heart-rates and what she thought might have been fear-scent from the more animal of the magical creatures, she wasn't the only one.

"Don't worry," Sorcha calmly spoke, reading the room. "Warrant or not, these barriers will not fall. And if they do, I will fall before anyone can lay a finger on you. Here, you are safe."

A voice talking in the background caught Grith's attention, and she realized that it wasn't from anyone in the room. A television screen had been set up behind the bar, with a local news station playing on it. Grith squinted, realizing that it showed a birds-eye view, and suddenly remembered the news helicopter she'd seen near the police one. Was this what it had been doing?

She felt the oddness of helicopter flight in her wings as it rotated around, the camera moving across the city. An emergency alert warning people to stay inside flashed up in red along the news. A banner reading 'Dangerous predator ridden during police chase . . . can it talk?' ran from left to right, Grith barely having time to read it before it disappeared.

At least at the moment, the only cars moving around LA were police cars and odd, black vans that Grith suspected were Council-related. The city was quiet, and the helicopter camera zoomed in on the windows of a large skyscraper, where humans were walking around inside.

"Thousands of civilians remain trapped, not allowed to return to their homes after the announcement made when the crystal shell went up," a voice on the television announced, Grith reading the subtitles as they came a few seconds later. "So far, there are no reports of casualties, although neither the LAPD nor the Council enforcers, the magical law enforcement, have been communicative. We believe there have been arrests made of those refusing to comply with the orders."

The camera zoomed in on one of the black Council vans as it drove onto the empty highway. She wondered where it was going, when the scene changed, a 'Breaking News' announcement popping up.

A human man in a suit holding a microphone stood on a sidewalk, a huge wall of crystal stretching up behind him. A crowd of a few dozen humans had gathered at it, pounding against the shell as the distorted image of more humans peeked out from the other side. The camera turned, revealing police in black armor with helmets covering their faces forming a wall surrounding them, along with two Council enforcers on the sidelines.

"I'm here at a forming scene at the edge of the shell in Pasadena," the reporter explained. "People have left their houses in order to attempt to break through it."

"What's going on?" a human asked one of the enforcers, walking over toward him. "Please, let us through! Our kids are on the other side!"

The enforcer didn't answer, and the woman took a few steps closer, as if hoping he'd notice her. He raised up a hand, a blue ring dangling from his wrist, and Grith thought that he was trying to tell her to stop until she saw a blue spark form on his fingertips. The dragon's eyes went wide and a rumble came up from her throat as the human kept walking closer, and the enforcer drew a line in the air, the start of a rune.

The human let out a yell as one of the police officers shoved her to the ground, twisting her hands behind her back as another one grabbed her hair to keep her still.

She let out a cry of pain as one of them cuffed her, and the enforcer lowered his hands.

"We've had enough unrest," the enforcer said, turning to another one of the police. "Place everyone here under arrest."

The camera turned back to the reporter as the crowd increased their yelling, and the police stepped forward into it, attempting to circle around as more screams from the other side of the shell were silent.

"It appears they're placing everyone in here under arrest," the reporter explained, nervously looking to the side as he noticed one of the enforcers and a policeman walking toward him. He turned, holding out a badge. "I'm with the local news. I'm allowed t—"

The enforcer raised a hand, drawing a quick rune with

it, and with a crackle of static the television screen turned gray.

Grith stared for a few moments before it changed again, back to the scene from the helicopter. The dragon suddenly swayed forward, her forelegs buckling beneath her as she fell to the ground with a whack.

Ashley let out a yelp, leaping back when Grith's head landed at her side. "Grith, are you all right?" Ashley asked, checking the dragon for any obvious wounds. The one on her tail hadn't fully healed, but had stopped bleeding. "What's wrong?"

"Am almost out of shimmer," she rumbled, shutting her eyes. Unfortunately, her hoard was outside the shell, not that she could fly back to it in this state.

"Out?" Ashley asked unassuredly. "Was that why you weren't flying?"

"Chris betrayed me," she explained, opening an eye to a human above her snout. "He told the Council where my lair is. Had a fight outside it."

"Of *course* he betrayed you." Ashley grimaced, clenching her fists as she glowered at the floor. "Gods, I hate that man more and more every second."

"Paul, my ex-boss, captured me," Grith continued, noticing Sorcha. "He used my shimmer to power the machine that Albiwegan was in. I think he opened a portal to a realm that he absorbed magic from, and used it to create the shield. Ashley, who is the human leader? I believe that Paul is going to try and kill them."

"The US President?" Ashley asked. "Do we really have to save him? Between him and Paul, it's honestly a hard decision. He's up for re-election soon anyways."

"No, the local leader," Grith said, trying to remember

what Paul had said he'd drained her. "He told me he was just going for the human city."

"The mayor of LA," Ashley suggested. "She's new, but better. Do you really think that Paul would *kill* her, and so openly take over the government?"

The dragon raised a talon to the television screen. A recording what Grith had seen earlier was playing, the police protecting the enforcer.

"Nevermind," Ashley muttered. "He's certainly not being subtle about this."

"I believe that being not-subtle is the point," Grith suggested. "He said that GMI infiltrated the Council, so I would not be surprised if they have infiltrated the human governments as well. He wants to send a message that they are in control now. This is his first step."

"So, what can we do?" Ashley questioned. "We need to stop him, right?"

"I can do nothing without at least a little more shimmer," Grith rumbled, struggling to even raise her wings. "It is even difficult to move."

Ashley nodded and turned around, letting out a loud cough to the nervous crowd. "Hey! All of you, it's time to pay for your drinks, alright? We're going to free LA, and Grith here needs as much shiny metals or gemstones as you can spare, please! Anything you have on you would be great!" She turned to her mother. "Mom, can you get what we have? Grith needs magic, as much as possible, as soon as possible."

Grith shut her eyes, her breath slow and tired. She curled her wings around her, resting as she waited. Was this really a good idea, going after Paul and attempting to rescue the mayor? She certainly didn't want him to take over the human city, though Grith wasn't sure if she was the right dragon for the job. She'd probably have to end up fighting with her magic. The last time she'd done that, she'd lost pitifully and had been captured. And the time before that, she'd revealed herself to all of humankind, causing this mess in the first place.

It wasn't that she was afraid of losing. She'd already lost once, and she knew how to fight, with or without magic. Her grandfather had trained both her and her cousins when they'd been hatchlings. While there were few altercations between dragons and humans nowadays, fights between two dragons weren't all that uncommon, and wizards attempting to go after a dragon's hoard weren't unheard of. In her grandfather's day, dragons had to fight to survive. Grith was glad that he'd passed that knowledge onto her.

She had to wonder, though, what was she fighting for? Things could never return to normal; Grith's hatchling years were long-gone. Would she be fighting against Paul, out of revenge? She didn't think so. For her own survival? Though it was true she couldn't escape LA at the moment, this was beyond that. It was true that she recognized the value of human life, still, she wasn't sure she was ready to risk her life for them. Perhaps she was fighting for Pret's vision of a better future for everyone, dragons and humans alike. She liked that idea.

"Here," Ashley said, interrupting Grith's thoughts as clanging metal hit the ground beneath her, the smell of shimmer in her nose. "It's not much, but maybe it's something."

Grith opened her eyes, purring in gratitude. Ashley had placed a small pile of jewelry in front of her, rings, neck-laces, and bracelets. She stuck out her tongue and scooped it into her maw, feeling bits of her energy return as the gemstones and precious metals dissolved. The dragon spat out the stuff that wouldn't dissolve or be useful.

"I do feel slightly better," Grith replied, even knowing it was barely enough to let her fly.

"More shimmer coming through!" Sorcha called as she stumbled through the crowd, carrying a large cloth bag in her hands. With a grin, Sorcha gently set it down and opened it up.

Grith peered inside, digging around with a paw as green crystals fell out next to golden coins. She took a crystal under her tongue, melting as an odd sort of magic she wasn't used to filled her body. The dragon couldn't quite put a claw on it, but it tasted more earthy than metallic, a mix of dirt and something resembling Ashley and Sorcha's scents.

"I'm quite sad to part with these, but I think it should be enough," Sorcha said as Ashley held up one of the green crystals and tossed it at Grith's mouth.

The dragon eagerly caught it, swallowing it down as it dissolved.

"They're replaceable. The gold is Pret's, for when he's stayed overnight, but I doubt he'll mind that you're putting it to good use."

Grith dug into the crystals and gold, taking bites out of it as her magic replenished. Part of her felt like it was a waste — it wasn't as if she wouldn't have regained it by just sleeping on a bed of shimmer for a few nights — but she doubted that she had the time to do that. GMI seemed to move quickly.

Ashley grinned as Grith took in the last crystal, letting loose a puff of smoke. Grith spread her wings wide, getting back on her paws, and flicked her tail back and forth. The bullet wound had almost healed as the dragon raised her head, her crest in the air.

Grith let out a roar, the Key shaking from the force within it. She then turned to the door, her talons sharp and ready, her blood hot from the magical energy once again bursting through her body. The dragon's eyes glowed bright gold, a ring of green surrounding the centers. Even her feathers had seemed to come alight, glittering in the gentle lights of the Key.

Now, she was ready.

NINETEEN

S udden yelling from outside the Key put Grith on alert, her ears perking up as she flexed her talons. She looked over toward Ashley as the yells of humans grew louder, and when the human girl opened the door, Grith got a whiff of far more mixed scents than she'd smelt before. What was going on?

Grith and Ashley walked out beneath the green shield, the police around it distracted. A small group of a few dozen humans had gathered on the other side of a line of cars, stopped only a tail-length away from them. The cops had formed a line between their cars, their hands twitching on their sides as the crowd shouted, Grith hardly able to pick out what they were saying.

"What's going on?" a young human in front yelled, his head turning as a helicopter flew by overhead with a buzz. "Why can't we leave the city, much less our houses!"

"You're working with them!" another human cried, pointing at one of the enforcers up against the back of the protection around the Key. "We saw it on television. Who's in charge of LA now? This is a coup; the US government hasn't said anything!"

An older human with graying hair hidden beneath a black police hat took a step forward, scratching a small mustache on his lip.

"The chief of police?" Ashley whispered. "This is bad."

"The shield has restricted communication," the chief explained, pulling out a megaphone. "So long as it's up, we're acting as we believe is best to keep order by complying with the authorities of the magical world."

"By helping out those who put up the shield!" someone in the back shouted. "Traitors!"

A few of the cops twitched, and moved back to keep the cars between them and the crowd.

"All of you, go home!" the chief shouted with a crackle of the megaphone. "This is an active arrest scene! This is not a civilian matter!"

"Is being unable to contact our families not a civilian matter?" another human retorted.

Grith tuned a few of the words out as a few scents she thought were familiar brushed her nose. She peered over the crowd, before tapping Ashley on the leg with her tail. "Are there familiar humans in the crowd? I cannot tell."

"Let me up," Ashley suggested.

Grith lowered her head, and the human leapt on, straddling around Grith's neck as she raised it back up.

"You're right! There's Dr. Daniels, from the observatory, and that bouncer! What are they doing here?"

The dragon trilled at the two together in the very back of the crowd, conversing to each other about something. She waved a wing and caught their attention, the bouncer laughing and giving her a friendly wave back.

Dr. Daniels got up on his toes, cupping his hands to his

mouth. "Do you have an arrest warrant for Grith?" he shouted at the top of his lungs, the enforcer frowning as he heard the dragon's name. "What crime did she commit?"

"Destruction of public property, reckless endangerment, resisting arrest," the captain shouted back. "She's also a literal dragon! We don't need a warrant, animal control just isn't equipped to take her down."

"And what about the shell?" someone in the front argued back. "That destroyed public property, and it's endangering kids left alone outside! Are you arresting those who put it up? Or are you too worried about finding an excuse for using some of the weaponry our tax dollars pay for?"

Before the police chief managed to respond, the enforcer behind him grabbed the megaphone, the rings on his wrists jingling as he jumped up on a car and made himself visible to the crowd. "That's enough! This is not a mundane affair, and you are not to interfere! Officers, grab your weapons!"

The officers looked at each other, a couple hesitantly pulling guns out of their holsters, unsure what to do. The police chief crossed his arms, giving the enforcer a glare of disdain without saying anything.

"Sir, these are lethal," one of the officers informed the enforcer.

"Yes, that's the point," the enforcer answered, glaring at the crowd as they began to nervously shuffled. "If any of you don't want to get hurt, you are free to turn around and leave at any time. Otherwise, you are interfering with the arrest of a dangerous criminal."

Some of the humans pushed through the crowd, running down the street, not wanting to take part in whatever happened next. Others stayed, refusing to budge while a fear-scent wafted over toward her.

Neither the doctor or the bouncer moved.

"We're being watched on the news," the police captain told the enforcer, putting his hand out in hopes of getting the megaphone back. A buzzing overhead told Grith he was right; a news copter wasn't far from the police one, camera trained on them.

"Good," the enforcer replied, keeping the megaphone away from the chief. "In the new world, open rebellion and aiming criminals will be punished like it should be. Your cities will have none of the weak-heartedness allowing the ruin they have now. I personally promise, with Council authority, that none of you will be punished for anything that happens here. You will be rewarded for doing your jobs, keeping law and order."

A few more of the officers raised their weapons, pointing them at the crowd. Most of the others followed. The one who'd mentioned the weapons being lethal didn't, getting a glare from the enforcer as he placed his gun back into his holster without another word. A few did the same as him, putting their weapons away.

"This is how it's going to go!" the enforcer shouted, raising the megaphone up as it screeched at the crowd. "I am going to give everyone remaining here three seconds. If I don't see every single one of you criminals beginning to leave, I will give the order to fire! If you don't leave, any harm that comes to the rest of the crowd is on you!"

He looked back to the officers as more raised their weapons, a few of their hands trembling as they stared at the humans in the street. More of them started to move back, pushing, the combined racing of their hearts causing Grith's ears to twitch.

"Three!" the enforcer yelled out. "Two! O—"

A jet of blue fire blasted across the top of the police car, engulfing the wizard in the center of the flames. The smell of cooking flesh filled the air only for a moment, before the fire died down, and there was nothing left of him but ash. A wind through the street picked up his remains, blowing them into the air.

The police turned to Grith as the dragon pulled her head back into the safety shield, smoke rising from her nose. She blinked. "Ashley, was it all right of me to kill that human?"

Ashley nodded.

A small cheer came up from the front of the crowd, cut off as some of the cops moved their guns toward the shield, split between the crowd and Grith. None of them wanted to provoke the dragon again, but weren't quite sure what to do without the enforcer's guidance.

"Fire!" the police captain commanded, grabbing his gun as he positioned himself between the crowd and the dragon, making sure they'd catch civilians in the crossfire.

Screams of terror rang through the air as he pulled the trigger, humans in the crowd shoving and diving for cover as he shot.

Grith's eyes opened wide, expecting to smell blood a moment later, but the scent didn't come.

The police chief squinted at his gun, trying to pull the trigger again, but there was nothing but a click.

A green aura glowed from the asphalt, small plants and weeds growing up from between the cracks in the road.

The dragon's tail twitched as a powerful tingle of magic came from behind her, feathers standing on end.

Sorcha's eyes glowed pitch-black as the witch stood in the doorway, vines wrapping around her fingers while they plunged against the cracked sidewalk, pulses of green coming from it, vines crawling up her skin. The gun in the chief's hand rusted, and he let out a yell as it crumbled to ash in his hands.

"I curse you, until the sun has set," Sorcha said with a whisper, though Grith could easily hear the force of her voice fluttering across the dragon's ears, pressure building up in them from the intensity. "Let your weapons become harmless, your nooses unwound, your flames burn as cold as ice. Let you become as powerless as those you wish to harm."

More shouts came from the crowd as guns crumbled away in hands, blown away in the wind. A few of the police attempted to grab at batons or tasers, only for them to disappear before they could even touch them. They looked to each other, stepping back as the humans they'd attempted to kill just a few moments before walked forward, fists clenched.

The chief swung a fist at one of the ones who'd argued with him as the human stepped between the cars. The human grabbed his arm, and with a shout, slammed him into a car-door, kneed beneath his ribcage. More continued forward as the police, now powerless, tried to scramble. Some ran while others raised their fists, brawling with the humans.

Grith watched as one of the police tried to flee by going around the Key's protection sphere.

The dragon took a step forward, before Sorcha put out a hand to stop her, vines wrapped around it as she turned her two black eyes toward Grith.

"Save your power, dragoness," Sorcha warned. "You are still regaining your shimmer, and you will need it in what is yet to come. This is a mundane affair. Allow them to fight."

Grith lowered her head.

Fists flew as the crowd overcame the police. While Sorcha's curse might have rid the cops of weaponry, it appeared that it didn't stop them from using their bodies. With more shouts and grunts, the dragon could smell the blood as it spilled.

Still, it wasn't long before the fight was over, and the police had clearly lost before the larger crowd, fallen to the ground or running as humans wiped red stains from their knuckles.

"I surrender!" the police captain shouted, clutching his side as he lay slumped against a tire. He put his hand over his head as the human standing above him considered what to do.

Sorcha stepped out of the protection charm, small plants bursting through the asphalt with each step. The crowd parted for her as she walked over, squatting next to the chief's side.

He whimpered, turning away.

"Call off the alliance with the wizards," Sorcha demanded, pressing a black fingernail into his skin. "After that, disband the police force. Destroy your weapons and your badges, and place yourselves under house arrest. What consequences there will be for you will be decided after this is over. Those are the conditions of your surrender."

The chief nodded without hesitation, grabbing at a radio, half-expecting it to crumble in his hands. He shakily held it up to his mouth. "New orders. We've surrendered. Tell the wizards we're unable to work with them anymore. Bring down the helicopters. Everyone is to get rid of — to destroy their badges and weapons at once, and return to their homes." He turned to Sorcha with a gulp. "You'll regret this. Not all of us will take this lying down. And you see the shell? The wizards have already won; there's nothing any of us non-magicians can do against them. We've got no choice but to work with them."

Sorcha didn't say another word to him, standing up as she walked back toward the Key.

A few humans in the crowd cheered, but the victory was quiet. Grith knew the police chief was right: this was far from over, and a single battle didn't win a war.

Ashley leapt off from the dragon's back, Grith shaking her wings and wiggling her neck as Ashley ran into the Key. A few moments later she'd brought out a large cauldron, placing it beneath Grith's snout as she emptied ingredients into it, the rune on her hand glowing as she heated them up. "Spit, please?"

Grith spat a glob into it as Ashley mixed it, her mother peering over it with an impressed smile.

"Healing is a good idea, even if this is a bit overkill." Sorcha laughed. "I don't think anyone received fatal wounds."

Ashley shrugged. "Might be useful for later," she replied, scooping out a glob of warm golden cream. With a grin, she brought it out of the protection charm's sphere. "All right, get your healing here! We've got a lot of dragon, so take generous helpings!"

Grith stepped out from the sphere with a little bit of hesitation as a human with blood on her face and a black eye walked up to Ashley with even more, nervously staring at Grith the entire time.

The dragon's nostrils flared at the blood and prey-scent, but she pushed those thoughts away as she lowered her head and layed on the ground, hoping to appear smaller and less intimidating. "It is all right," Grith purred to her. "I will not hurt you."

The human stared at the dragon as the feathers on her snout lifted up in the wind, meeting Grith's golden eyes. Grith wondered if the human was remembering that just a few moments ago, Grith had turned someone into ash. She carefully avoided letting out any smoke from her nostrils.

The human finally let out a chuckle as she took some of the golden cream, smearing it across her eye. "Sorry," she said. "It's difficult to believe I'm talking to a real-life dragon. You're really you're talking to me."

"I had not talked to any humans before the previous week, either," Grith pointed out. She turned toward two familiar scents as they approached, and Dr. Daniels and the bouncer stood by her wing. "Oh, hello! I recall meeting both of you!"

"You're a lot bigger than I last remember seeing you." The bouncer laughed, shaking his head. "I'm Tom, by the way."

"*Grrawwwrrrrrffffff*," Grith growled, noticing him shift back at her fangs. "Um. Grith. I am glad that you both showed up and that you did not get injured. How did you know it was me? I thought I was hidden under a glamor and appeared human." Her eyes went wide as she had the horrid idea that maybe Chris's spell *hadn't* worked, and she had never been hidden to begin with.

"You weren't exactly subtle about it." Dr. Daniels winced.

Tom nodded as he pulled a feather out of his jacket. "You *did* give me this. It wasn't hard to figure it out."

"We both saw the three of you on the news, and pieced things together," Dr. Daniels explained. "I read one of his comments on an article mentioning that he'd seen you the day before and what happened at the club, and we got in contact. After seeing the chase, we both decided to come over and see what we could do. Apparently, we weren't the only ones; this place seems to be resistance central."

"I am very glad for that!" Grith warbled as a few more of the humans waved hello while they got salve from Ashley, unsure to approach further or not.

Grith wasn't quite sure herself how to act. The previous few times she'd been at the center of attention of a group of humans, things had gone far less well. Thinking for a moment, the dragon reached beneath her wing and plucked out a long golden feather, reaching her head up until she matched height with Dr. Daniels. "A gift for you."

"Thank you," he said, blinking in surprise as she dropped it on outstretched hands. "I guess we got a matching set?"

Grith looked over at the crowd of humans, many sitting down in the street. The crowd had placed most of the remaining police in their own handcuffs and put them against the side of the road.

"I would give one to all the humans who helped out, but it would make it very difficult to fly until I got them back," Grith remarked. "I suppose I could give them smaller ones?"

Meanwhile Tom had walked up to the boundary of the barrier around the Key's entrance, inspecting it. With a startle, he stumbled through.

"Magical creatures and those they've personally invited are able to enter, so long as Ashley, Pret, my husband, or I don't keep them out," Sorcha said with a smile, silently appearing out of what seemed like nowhere. "The feather you have guarantees you entry, in case you ever want or need it."

"Huh," Tom remarked, waving his hand through the bubble, before peering in through the door of the Key. He glanced over at Ashley. "You really weren't lying about being a bartender, were you."

"Nope!" Ashley grinned, giving the cauldron a stir for good measure.

Tom's expression darkened, and Grith got a confusion batch of fear-scent from him. He peered in through the doors, eyes wide. "Er, I think you should all look at the news."

"I am I on it again?" Grith asked, crawling behind Ashley, Sorcha, and Dr. Daniels as the three looked in at the screen.

"Shit!" Ashley cursed, getting a glare from her mother.

"Shit indeed," Dr. Daniels murmured.

Grith squinted, a breaking news headline running across it. "Wizards surround city hall," she read. "Mayor taken captive. Oh. This *is* a feces-filled situation."

"Grith, we need to get to city hall, now or never!" Ashley gulped, whipping around. "Er, do you mind if I fly on your back this time? Your claws aren't very comfortable."

"All right," Grith rumbled, lowering her head as Ashley climbed on. She felt the extra weight when she picked it back up, shaking her wings from side to side as she tried to see more of the news. Were they really going to attempt to take on Paul? The dragon was uncertain. Hopefully Albiwegan had been right, and the specially-chosen wizards to capture her were no longer there.

Sorcha looked up at her daughter with a grimace, sighing as she shook her head, like she knew she wouldn't be able to talk Ashley out of this. "If you're certain. But you'll need a distraction if you're hoping to save the mayor. There's no way the two of you can take on so many wizards.

I have something in mind." She peered inside the door, glancing around the Key. "Holz! Would you be able to teleport me to city hall?"

Holz nervously stepped through the doorway, pulling Albiwegan in her hand.

"From here?" The fae gulped. "Maybe. I'm not sure."

"I can boost your magic," Sorcha explained, stretching a hand out towards the two. "It may also involve a little bit of running."

"I've done a lot of riding today, but not much running," Albiwegan mused. "Sure! Why not?"

Sorcha sighed again. "Don't approach until we've cleared the area," she pleaded. "And please, please, just stay safe. If something goes wrong, and you end up in a bad situation . . ."

"The fate of Los Angeles isn't worth my life?" Ashley finished. "Mom, don't worry. I can handle myself. If we need to, we'll get out of there."

Grith looked over toward Tom and Dr. Daniels as Ashley said her 'goodbyes' and 'good lucks' and 'I can handle this, no really' to her father.

"You two should also stay safe," Grith suggested. "The Key will be guarded. I do not know what will happen if we fail, and the wizards stay in control of the human city."

The two nodded in unison.

"Good luck to you, too." Dr. Daniels grimaced, as Ashley tugged on Grith's crest. That was right. They were in a hurry.

The dragon took in a deep breath as she stepped out from the protective dome and into the street, the sun now tinted by the great crystal shell trapping LA beneath it. She raised her wings as wind fluttered beneath her feathers, and Ashley's arms wrapped around the dragon's neck.

With a flap, Grith rushed forward, leaping on top of one of the police cars with a crack of metal. Some of the humans beneath her stared, others scrambling out of the way as the dragon jumped into the air. The wind sliced under her wings while she flapped, taking Grith into the sky.

CHAPTER

TWENTY

Ashley let out a laugh, her arms stretched out wide, wind whisking past them as her robes fluttered. Los Angeles was beneath the two now as they flew east, but an eerie silence filled the air, just a gentle push from the unusual winds. Smog had gathered up under the top of the shell, Grith staying low to avoid the dark clouds above her, the sun now hazy. She didn't spot a single human out on their way.

"You should be careful," Grith nervously rumbled as she swayed, the legs around the dragon's neck shaking from the noise and turbulence. "I do not want you to fall."

"It's fine!" Ashley yelled out into the wind, wrapping her arms back around Grith's neck. "Don't worry, I've ridden a broomstick before. You're just a bit larger."

Grith was unsure she appreciated the comparison. "Why would you ride a broomstick?"

"It was more of a joke gift from my mom than anything." She grinned. "She's got that sort of humor. Look, there's city hall!"

Grith peered where Ashley was pointing, a tall,

rectangular building topped with an angular pyramid-like roof, poking up out of the ground with two wings extending from either side. Trees dotted around it, along with a grassy field and a few more buildings that she thought were more boring and cubical than the city hall. She hoped that the residents had evacuated from all of them.

Robed wizards dotted a large perimeter around the city hall, holding books and the occasional staff or wand. Remembering what Sorcha had said, Grith made sure to keep her distance, tilting her wings to make a wide circle around the city hall instead of going directly toward it, so that she didn't tempt the wizards to attack from afar.

The number of wizards made Grith somewhat hopeful that there were no humans in the nearby buildings. They clearly didn't want any interference for this. It made it far less likely she would set any civilians on fire.

"Over there!" Ashley called, gently patting Grith's neck. She pointed at the green lawn in front of city hall, where a bright light flashed on the side opposite the building.

Three figures appeared from the flash, and Holz teleported Sorcha and Albiwegan into the grass, the latter waving at Grith in the sky.

Grith warbled back, puffing smoke into the sky as a greeting.

"What do you think they are going to do?" Grith asked, noticing that the wizards hadn't yet made any motions toward either of the groups, holding their ground. "Is your mother going to burn that very stinky plant again? I suspect that the wizards have a way to counter that."

"Watch, and don't get too close!" Ashley replied.

Grith did as Ashley suggested, making sure to stay away from both the witch and the tower. Her ears perked up as the tingle of magic crossed them, the green rings in her eyes glowing brighter. She looked around for the source of it, only to realize that the ground beneath the city hall was shining the same color.

Sorcha whispered something, and though the dragon couldn't make out what she was saying, her voice seemed to cause the very air itself to vibrate. Magic permeated Grith's feathers, the smell of dirt, moonlight, and silver. A rotating magic circle laced with runes formed around the city hall, three more interlocking ones turning around the opposite direction in a spiral within.

The sky around them grew dark as an aura flared up through the earth, the dragon trembling even in the sky. But the darkness wasn't the haze; the very sun had disappeared, the ethereal green glow beneath them replacing. Whatever Sorcha was doing, it was like no magic Grith had seen before. She doubted even her grandfather had this type of power within him.

As blood-curdling screams filled the air, Grith realized why Pret had chosen Sorcha to create the Key with him.

Winds howled as black vines as thick as trees crawled up from the circles, grasping onto any wizard unfortunate to be too close. The ground writhed with them as they burst forth from it, wrapping around any limb they could grab. A wizard cried out for help as he tried to fire off a spell, only for two vines to hold his hands in place and drag him down into the earth, piling over him until no trace of him remained.

Flames fired off as the wizards fought back, the vines thrashing and squashing a few before the wizards pushed them back away. Even so, more wizards got caught within, pulled down into the depths and not rising again. She silently thanked Ashley for warning her not to get too close, even if dragonfire probably would have worked well against them.

After a few minutes of horror, the sun returned and the magic circles disappeared, vines snaking as they disappeared back into the ground. Sorcha had fallen to the ground, and was panting heavily while the two fae lifted her.

The remaining wizards shouted as they ran toward the three, who took off into a sprint, the two fae helping Sorcha along. Apparently, they had decided that the witch was a larger threat than the dragon. Grith believed she was in agreement. The area around city hall was quickly cleared, the wizards firing off spells as they chased them.

Suddenly, Grith let out a screech of pain as a loud sound ripped through her body, her eardrums ringing as it tore into her magic.

Ashley let out a scream and the two dropped through the air, the dragon's wings unable to them aloft, her golden eyes going dull.

Grith was barely able to think as the high-pitched tone rattled around her skull, and the ground zoomed up toward her.

A few moments before they crashed, Grith twisted to the side, using what little lift her wings had without magic to glide away. The sound abruptly cut off, and her magic returned, albeit too late. She spread her wings and tried to regain control, only managing to get a little bit of it before the two hit the ground, landing hard on the grass.

Ashley slipped from Grith's neck, wincing as she landed on her back. Slowly, she got back to her feet, looking around to figure out what had happened.

A young human with shaking hands stood a few tail-lengths away from the dragon, fingers clinched tight around a tuning fork.

"I can't let you go any further." Chris gulped, taking a few steps back. "Please, just go. I don't want to fight you."

Grith glared at the human, so small beneath her. Smoke poured from her nostrils. "Step aside, Chris, and I will allow you to survive."

Chris shook his head. "Grith, you don't get it; this isn't a war you can win. You can't beat Paul, and definitely can't beat *GMI*. It runs so much deeper than you think, and they're so powerful. I don't want you to die."

"I warned you," Grith snarled, sticking her head out over Ashley's as fire welled up in her belly, the orange light in her throat turning blue. He'd pretended to be her friend, all to betray her just to save his own hide. Chris had had a choice, and he'd made it. He was a coward, and if he was going to make her fight him, she would give him no mercy.

A moment later, a flame shot forth across the ground.

The smell of burning flesh, however, didn't come. Grith paused, her eyes narrowing as Chris drew a blue pitchfork-shaped rune in the air, a shimmering shield protecting him from the fire.

Grith's talons clenched up in the grass as she bared her fangs. He'd given her over to GMI; it was his fault the human city was in this mess. She opened her wings, golden circles forming at their tips as Chris raised his tuning fork again. She could be faster than him.

"Grith, stop," Ashley said, moving a few steps toward Chris, the air still smokey from the blast of fire. "Save your magic for Paul. I can take care of this prick alone."

"I can help!" Grith huffed, flicking her tail.

Ashley shook her head, glancing up at city hall.

Grith noticed motion from the top floor.

"You can't, you have to hurry. Don't worry, I'll be fine."

Grith shot Chris another glare, making sure he saw her teeth, before running across the grass and taking off into the air.

Chris tried to flick his tuning fork again, before Ashley reached into a pocket and flung a stone at him. Chris yelped as it hit him square in his back, causing him to stumble forward. The blast shot too low, and Grith was gone.

"You shouldn't have done that," Chris said to Ashley, wincing and rubbing his back. "You've killed her, you know."

"She'll be fine, but you should be worrying about yourself. I see you sold out." Ashley frowned, noticing the golden signet ring on Chris's hand. "I can't say I'm very surprised. Did you get anything out of this? Or is this some weird misogynistic power-play to prove you're stronger than Grith or something?"

Chris shook his head. "GMI is the one in control now. I wish you would have joined me. Grith could have willingly helped them, and we'd all have been on the winning side together. Things would be good for us."

"And let them establish some wizard-run authoritarian dictatorship that manages to suck more than the government we've got now? No thanks."

"I'm doing what's right," Chris answered, proudly raising his head. "You of all people should understand. Do you really think mundane humans are fit to take care of themselves? Look at all the strife in LA and around the world. Look how they've destroyed the environment and are constantly at war. There'll be no adorable coexisting world of magic and mundanes; they'll always be afraid of how powerful we are. They'll destroy us and themselves together."

"Please." Ashley scoffed. "You're an idiot if you actually fell for that propaganda. GMI is and has always been part of the problem, not the solution. You know what? I don't actually care what your intentions are, whether you're misguided and noble, or if you just laid your eyes on Grith's hoard and wanted a piece for yourself." She rolled up her sleeves and walked forward, flicking a green rune tattoo up to each of her hands. "I've had enough of you."

Chris scoffed, tilting his head with a look of disdain as he flexed his fingers, blue light shimmering from the tips of each of them. "You're not really going to do this, are you? Anything you have up your sleeve, literally, I can combat."

"Really?" Ashley asked with a click of her tongue, grabbing a plant from her robe in her left hand. It turned to flame as it touched the rune, gray smoke expanding around her.

Chris sighed, shaking his head as he drew a glowing blue glyph in the air. A gentle wind swirled around the unimpressed wizard in a circle, keeping the smoke from even touching him, much less having him breathe it in.

"It's pointless," he continued, looking into the smoke with a glare. "My specialty is sound and light magic. Anything you burn, I can just blow away. There's no reason for you to try and fight me. Just surrender."

Movement came from the corner of his eyes, and he turned a moment too late as Ashley sprinted out of the smoke at him. A fist slammed deep into his gut, Chris's eyes going wide as he stumbled backward.

Chris groaned, and took another couple steps away, raising his hands as his fingers twitched. He began to chant out loud, a glowing circle of runes forming in the air around his body, blue magic welling up in the ground beneath him.

Ashley rushed forward and slammed her fist up into his jaw.

Chris let out a cry of pain as the magic faded, not fast enough to complete it. Blood dripped down his face as he held out a finger, hastily attempting to draw an S-shaped rune in the air.

Ashley grasped his wrist, twisting it away from him and pulling him forward as he finished the rune. Flame burst forth from his palm, missing Ashley by a mile. He tugged on his hand, trying to pull it back, only for a knee to slam up into his gut.

Chris crumpled to the ground, spitting blood from his nosebleed as he tried to look up at Ashley. He tried to force his fingers and do some sort of magic, any sort of magic, before she stomped on his wrist. He let out another cry of pain.

"You're cheating," Chris whined, trying to tug his hand out from under Ashley's shoes. "This is a magic battle and you didn't use magic."

"Wait, did you seriously think I only had just one sort of magic I could use?" Ashley asked, rolling her eyes, raising her right palm to reveal a glowing rune shaped like the slanted top of a building.

Chris's heart raced as he remained still as Ashley closed her palm, glaring down into his eyes. "A-Are you going to kill me? You can't do that! I'm not a bad person, I'm just trying to do what's right!"

"What?" Ashley asked. "No, I'm not going to kill you. You're not worth killing. I'd feel kinda guilty, and then I'd have to go to therapy, and you're definitely not worth the therapy bills. I think I have a better idea."

Ashley kneeled, Chris's blue eyes filled with terror as Ashley's turned pitch-black, magic welling up beneath the two of them. She hadn't ever had a reason to do something like this before, but her mother had taught her.

"I curse you," Ashley hissed, her voice penetrating the air, a wind whipping through the grass. She moved her left palm to Chris's chest, the rune still glowing bright.

His suit-shirt smoldered, and an ear-splitting scream left his mouth as her hand burned into his sternum. He turned from side to side, trying to move out of the way, but Ashley kept her hand steady and unmoving as the words came to her tongue.

"I curse you, until the day you selflessly sacrifice your ambitions for another, so that whenever you use your magic to harm anyone, this rune burns as hot in this chest as the fire you attempted to kill me with."

The black glow left her eyes, and Ashley lifted her hand, her smile gone.

He shuddered and whimpered, looking down at his chest, his breath steady. Ashley had branded the rune black within it, pain pulsing across his skin.

Ashley let him up and right away he turned, crawling across the ground before getting to his feet and sprinting away from the city hall, his hands clutching at his chest.

Once he was gone, Ashley fell back to the ground, staring up at the crystal shell in the sky, barely able to move. The green glow was gone from her hands. She let out a sigh, wondering if that had worked or not. "Asshole," she muttered, hoping she'd never see him again.

TWENTY-ONE

P aul walked across the observation deck of city hall, tapping on a leg with one hand and he clutching the shimmering green crystal in the other. White pillars rose up between glass windows, pointing toward the outside balcony. He tapped a foot as he strode toward the mayor, brown hair falling from the young woman's head as she backed up into the glass.

"Stay back," she warned, reaching into the inside of her suit jacket to pull out a small handgun, shakily pointing it at the approaching wizard. "How did you get in here?"

"I walked in." Paul smiled. "One of your officers held the door open for me." He adjusted his collar as he held up the crystal, the markings leading down it from his arm glowing green as he absorbed magic from it. His wrist twitched, smoke rising from it.

Paul raised his other hand, snapping his fingers together.

The mayor screamed as the glass behind her shattered, spectral white hands reaching through it and clamping around her arms.

The gun fired, whizzing past Paul's side, the wizard barely noticing.

She struggled as they pulled her back to a blue railing at the edge of the observation deck, another ghostly hand peeling the metal back like it was butter.

Paul stepped into the air, flexing his collar again as the wind hit it, pushing up beneath his suit. The hands held the mayor over the edge, leaning her back as she rested within them, her struggles stopped. Her heart pounded as she looked down twenty-seven stories, held only by the spectral hands tightened around her arms. A squeeze around her wrists caused her to drop the gun, falling through the sky.

"LA looks quite beautiful from here!" Paul announced, walking forward until he was within arms reach of the mayor. He peered behind her at downtown Los Angeles, just a few blocks away. Behind that, many buildings of the city sprawled across the land, up until it met the white crystal shell filling the sky.

"I do enjoy a view," Paul continued, looking back into a large, square room behind him, red curtains rolling down behind a podium that was a perfect place to make an announcement. "Do you think this would make a good place for a new office? I suppose I'd have to change the lighting and decor. It's a bit dull for my tastes."

"You'll regret this," she spat. "Even if you kill me, it doesn't make you mayor. That's not how it works."

Paul shook his head. "My ambitions are far higher than just being mayor. I'm going for more of a God-King thing. What about the CEO of America? How does that sound?"

He reached out his left hand, grabbing a hold of the mayor's collar. A whirring caught his attention, and a helicopter came into view around the side of the building, pointing a camera at the two.

"Oh look, we're on the news!" Paul remarked with a crafted grin, pointing at the helicopter and waving the hand with the crystal at the horrified cameramen. "Smile for the camera!" Paul released his grasp and gave the mayor a shove over the edge, the spectral hands letting go as they retreated into the building.

She screamed and fell over the side, dropping out of view a moment later.

Paul continued to wave, and the scream cut off. "That was a bit earlier than I expected," Paul remarked, looking over the edge as wind whisked past his face. Golden feathers rose into the air, meeting him.

Grith's talons had wrapped around the mayor, gently holding the shocked human. The dragon tossed her up into the air again, the mayor letting out another scream as she landed on Grith's neck. Her arms and legs wrapped tight, and she hugged the dragon's neck as hard as she could, hyperventilating and shutting her eyes.

"Ah, Grith, I was wondering when you were going to make it," Paul announced, as the dragon matched his height, flapping her wings to hover a few tail-lengths from the ledge. "At the most irritating time, no less!"

Grith's lips curled back as she bared her fangs, a low rumble in her throat. "I am here to stop you."

"I figured," Paul replied. "Are you going to try and eat me? I don't think I'd taste very good."

"Dragons only eat prey," Grith snarled, her eyes narrowing. "You are my enemy, not my prey. If I killed you, which I very well may do, it would be by burning you until only cinders remain."

Paul frowned. "You don't have very much of a sense of humor."

The crystal in his hands glowed, the lines on his arm getting brighter as they spread further down it, pulling the magic into his body. A snap sounded through the air as his body glimmered, Paul's crisp suit hardening into polished, white armor, shining like a beacon. Two spectral feathered wings expanded from the back of it, as long as his body in either direction, while a pearly sword expanded from his right hand, the green jewel held in its hilt.

"This seems like appropriate garb to slay you in," Paul remarked, swishing the sword back and forth in one hand. "Don't you agree?"

Grith continued flapping. The fear-scent of the mayor on her back was strong, though at least at this point she seemed to have realized that Grith was rescuing her. "Even if you are my enemy, I would prefer not to fight. I believe that the mundane and magical worlds can coexist and help each other, and would like you to agree and work with me."

"I do agree," Paul answered, stretching his ghostly feathered wings and testing them out.

"Oh, well, that is good," Grith remarked, cocking her head. "So, we do not need to fight?"

"I think humans would be much happier under the rule of wizards than they are now, lost and aimless," Paul continued, pointing his sword toward the dragon's snout. "And, in order to achieve that, she needs to die. Do you understand me?"

"That does not seem right to me," Grith responded, using her wings to push her a bit back from the sword. "I do not know very much about humans, but I think that dragons desire freedom, to choose the lives that make us happy, whatever that may be." She tilted her head to the side, letting her get a look at the mayor, who now appeared to be more nauseous than frightened. "Mayor, are humans the same way?"

The mayor weakly nodded.

"I will trust the mayor's judgment," Grith told Paul, flexing her talons. "I will not allow wizards to rule over humans nor dragons. You are not a king."

Paul sighed, stepping up to the edge of the balcony as winds brushed past him. "Unfortunately, I still need to kill her, and you're not the only dragon with temporal powers out there. You have a couple cousins I could use instead, don't you?"

"Do not harm Pret," Grith snarled, puffing smoke.

"This is your last chance," Paul continued, unintimidated by the dragon's threat. "Give me the mayor."

Grith barely had to consider it. "Dragons are not good at taking orders," she responded, opening her jaws as orange light burned in the back of her throat, turning blue when she shot it forward in a cone, covering Paul and the side of the observation deck in flame.

Smoke filled the air as Grith whipped around, the mayor clinging on as the dragon's wings flapped up and down, fleeing away.

"This time, *I* was the one who fired *him*," the dragon purred. "See? I do have a sense of humor."

"This is no time for puns!" the mayor screamed.

A glowing white figure shot out from the cloud of smoke behind them, and Paul flew through the air, sword raised as he followed. "He's coming after us!"

A white glow filled the sword with energy as the wizard soared through the air. Paul lowered the sword, light bursting from its edge, a tingle of magic suddenly running down the dragon's crest. Wind whipped past her ears as an intense wave of power came forth from the sword, a crescent of energy causing the very air to crackle as it shot towards the dragon. The mayor screamed again.

Grith's wings spread wide before it could hit her, golden light surrounding her wingtips as her eyes shined. Two magic circles appeared on her neck and tail, a third around the mayor, their hearts pumping faster. The shockwave slowed down just enough that Grith could tilt her wings and fly around the leading edge, turning until she faced Paul, his movements in slow-motion as he raised the sword back up again.

Grith and the mayor's heart rates slowed back down, the magic circles fading. The shockwave flew past at an extraordinary speed, growing as it slammed into the building. A roar shook through the air as stone and concrete crumbled, a huge gash in its walls as windows cracked, the building split in two and pieces falling.

"Jesus," the mayor whispered as it collapsed to the ground, clutching Grith's feathers tighter as she looked for anyone inside. The news helicopter flew higher, though not too far to capture them on camera.

"You're not going to win this," Paul called, his ghostly wings flapping as he hovered a half-dozen dragon-lengths from Grith. He swung his sword in a figure-eight, testing what it could do, light glinting from its surface. "I've got as much essence as I need. All I need to do is beat you down until you're out again. Even if our battle destroys LA, I will build it up again from the ruins."

"I have all the time I need to stop you!" Grith purred, angling her wings as she flew downward.

"I have been wanting to say that for a while," Grith told the mayor, "but it is not actually true. Even regaining some, my shimmer supply is running low at the moment, and my time manipulation uses much of it."

Paul raised his hand, and a loud snap of his fingers shook through the air. A white sphere of energy spread out from it, crackling.

Grith's feathers stood on end as it approached her, and the dragon whisked her wings up, golden circles surrounding them as the sphere slowed down. The grass beneath her whistled in the wind as she glided across it, the plants unaware of the fate that was coming toward them as the white energy grew.

"Behind city hall!" the mayor suggested. "Oh, I hope nothing inside gets hurt. I have a lot of sensitive papers inside."

"My sincere condolences," Grith warbled, knowing well the importance of papers and books. The lights grew closer as she turned a corner, using the tower as a shield between her and the sphere. It hadn't taken more than a few moments for her to judge the strength of the magic, and she doubted the city hall would be in particularly good shape after it hit.

The sphere hit the ground first, crawling across it in slow motion as the grass under it instantly disintegrated, dust thrown up in its wake as the lawn turned to a brown crisp. The mayor let out a cry when it reached city hall, rumbles shaking through the air and the shockwave pressing into the wall opposite the two. Cracks expanded from around where it first hit, the white stone thrown up like crumpled paper as the glass windows shattered.

Cragged lines appeared around the side of the building as chunks fell off. Though Paul had destroyed the entire front facade, the building had managed to protect the both of them from most of the blast when it shot past her wings, like a current of energy sending her through the air. She regained her flight pattern and balanced out, checking that the mayor was still clutching her neck as a piece of the building fell toward the dragon's back.

She yelped as she dove beneath it, more chunks falling around her. She weaved back and forth as rubble hit her wings, the mayor shouting as pieces dug into her neck. Paul was flying towards them in the falling rubble, his fingers coming together in another snap as he drained magic from the crystal.

A wave of exhaustion burst through the dragon's body as her magic lapsed, time suddenly returning to normal as she narrowly dodged another chunk. The ground rumbled as the sphere of energy expanded into the ground behind her, before dissipating into the air as another nearby building fell. Huge spectral hands appeared in the air, ten times taller than a dragon.

"Hold on tight!" Grith called as Paul's hands grabbed ahold of a chunk of the city hall's remains, flinging it up at the dragon. She let out a roar through the air as she used her magic once more, panting as a clock appeared on the the chunk of stone's surface around a shattered window, ticking toward midnight. She swerved beneath it before her spell ended, and it soared into the sky before landing in the rubble of another fallen building. Apparently, she hadn't needed to worry about accidentally causing any destruction. Paul was doing that all himself.

She twisted away as Paul sent another one toward her, slowing it down with her magic again. Her talons trembled, her wings heavy. Paul had been right about just needing to outlast her, and so far, all she'd done was fly away from him.

Grith let out a yelp as a blast of energy hit the end of her tail, her feathers scorched and blackened by it. She turned again as the air whipped against her injury, twisting her tail mid-air and trying to cool it down.

"Are you okay?" the mayor asked, ducking as Paul sent another blast over her head. "That doesn't look good."

"I am fine," Grith murmured. "I am more surprised that I still have any tail length, based on the size of the attacks earlier." Smoke rose from Paul's hand holding the sword, the green lights puncturing his skin glowing bright beneath it.

Although he has a huge amount of essence, he is unable to use it all at once! Grith realized, remembering how human magic was different than dragon. Paul had to store the energy directly in his body, so he had to keep it inside the crystal until he was ready to use it!

"I am going to fly quickly!" Grith trilled. "I have an idea!"

Hands grasped tighter around her as she raised her wings, pumping them and flying higher into the sky, until Paul was staring up at her instead of the other way around. She would have to be fast for this.

As Paul shot another blast of energy at her from his sword, Grith dove down toward the hovering armored human, tucking in her wings for a moment and using gravity to speed herself up.

The mayor screamed as the wind whipped her hair into the air, feeling Grith drop down.

The dragon's heartbeat sped up as she used her magic once more, Paul's movements slowed.

His sword swung at Grith as she flew toward him, banking away at the last moment.

She touched her talons to the blade, screeching as magic burned away her feathers, and she dropped her magic only for Paul to try and pull it back. Grith's paws felt like they were on fire, but a golden clock appeared around the base of the sword, ticking as fast as the dragon's heartbeat.

Grith let go, her claws shaking as blood dripped from them, and she dove away from the frowning Paul.

"Trying to slow down the power I draw is useless," he said, raising the sword again. "I can just draw more of it."

The green lines on his wrist turned as bright as a spotlight, a glowing ball surrounding him as the crystal shot essence into it far faster than he'd expected. He yelled as energy burst forth from his hand, Grith riding it as she stretched out her wings wide.

White light shot down into the rubble of the town hall beneath her, propelling the shining green Paul upward as it drilled through collapsed floors. Green lightning crackled around the wizard's arm as he waved it back and forth, the beam of light destroying anything it passed through, not that anything nearby was still standing.

"Not slow down, but speed up! Chris was the one who taught me how effective causing someone's magic to backfire was!" Grith purred as the crystal turned brighter, the skin on Paul's arm burning away. "I would like to thank you for assigning me to him!"

Another wave of energy shot through the air, Paul dropping the sword as green smoke rose up from an explosion around him. As it fell, Grith swerved to catch it, only to see a spectral hand reach down and grab it before she could.

She rumbled as Paul flew out through the smoke, only now missing an arm with nothing but a few scorch marks on his armor. The ghostly hand brought the sword back up to him, before attaching where the missing limb was.

"That did not work well as I thought it would," Grith

said, watching as Paul stared down at her, his eyes now bloodshot and furious. "I believe he is angry at me."

The dragon yelped and twisted to the side as he snapped his fingers, an explosion of light to her side almost hitting her wing. Another light blasted in front of her, blinding her for a moment as she tucked beneath it and rolled around. She squinted, trying to figure out where Paul was, only to let out a screech as he hit her claws with a blast, turning away from it as fast as she could.

Grith panted as she spread out her wings, moving away from Paul. A scream sounded from beneath her, and the dragon realized that the load on her back was a lot lighter.

"Mayor!" Grith shouted in alarm as she saw her falling toward the ground. She winced and dropped, using more of her magic to speed herself up, stretching out her talons. Lights flashed as more explosions rocked her from side to side, the mayor a few dragon-lengths from the ground. Grith gritted her fangs, panting as her heart pulsed wildly in her chest, more of her shimmer used up to make her even faster as wind almost tore her feathers from her hide.

She let out a roar as another white flash hit beneath her, barely managing to avoid flying straight into it. The rubble beneath her grew closer as the mayor dropped, Grith's eyes going wide as her nostrils flared. She stretched out the talons on her hindlegs, preparing to swoop down and grab the mayor, the human's prey-scent and fear-scent strong as more lights flashed on either side. The dragon had done similar maneuvers many times before, hunting large birds from above. She panted as she dove down, letting her predatory instincts take over.

Her talons grasped around the mayor's torso, blood around their tips when they tore through the human's suit and into her skin. The dragon's heart pounded, her magic fading away as her eyes dulled from the overuse. She flung the human up into the air as she swooped, the mayor screaming as Grith's jaws went up to meet her, clutching around her.

The mayor whimpered as Grith's fangs poked into her flesh, drops of blood dripping onto the dragon's tongue as she swooped over the rubble and landed on a slab of concrete.

The dragon opened her jaws, letting the mayor fall, shouting. Grith turned away and spat the blood out on the ground, trying to get rid of the taste. The white glow around her faded, and she squinted as she smelled Paul land a few tail-lengths away from the two, laughing at the situation.

"Grith! You're fighting me! This isn't time for a lunch break." He chuckled.

The dragon let loose a blast of flame across the concrete, orange fire curling around him. He waved his sword as she stopped it, Grith's breaths heavy as she struggled to keep herself from collapsing to the ground.

"Even your fire is far weaker than the first time," Paul remarked, smoke wreathing around his armor as he used his spectral hand to point the sword towards the two. "You really exhausted your magic, didn't you?"

Grith didn't bother to respond as she fell, throwing a wing over the mayor to protect the human as a white light glowed across the blade. She shut her eyes as a blast of energy hit her, heat and pain shooting beneath her feathers as it jolted through her body, barely able to even whimper after it had stopped.

The pain kept burning, though it seemed to dull as the dragon opened an eye. Smoke rose from her feathers, many of them blacked around the edges. She tried to raise her head, only to realize that she didn't have the energy to do so.

Footsteps sounded across the concrete as Paul walked toward the dragon, sword raised through the air.

The mayor moved beneath the wing draped over her. At least she was still alive. The blade became visible, a blur of sharp white between Grith and the hazy sky.

With that and the crystal shell, she wouldn't be able to see the sky when she died. She'd wanted to die beneath the stars, but at least her death would be heroic, even if she wasn't quite ready for it. Her life would be over before the dragon had even figured out what she wanted it to be.

"This tends to be the usual fate for those who reveal magic to humans," Paul's voice said, though Grith couldn't see him, only the white blade above her neck. She wasn't even sure she could turn her head. "I think you certainly deserve it."

He brought down the sword, but it didn't hit. There was movement beneath her wings, and there was a shout as she saw Paul fall back, the mayor grasping onto the hilt of the sword as she tried to wrest it from his spectral arm.

The mayor screamed, though the dragon believed it was more of a battle-cry than one of fear. Green light covered her palms as the magic tried to burn them away, the mundane human unprepared for the sudden influx of essence far beyond her normal amount. Still, she refused to let go, trying to pull it from the spectral hand. As smoke rose from her fingers, she managed to push it to the ground, slamming the crystal into the concrete with a crack.

Paul's fingers snapped, and a burst of light shot into her chest.

There was a far louder crack as the mayor's skull slammed back into the concrete, skidding back against into the dragon's body with a thump. She didn't move, and Grith was too tired to attempt to figure out if she was dead or alive. It wasn't as if it mattered at this point. Even if she was dead and the dragon ate her to regain energy, it was a bit too late for it to be of much use.

Paul let out a furious yell and raised his sword, white light streaming forth from the blade as he tried to take energy from the crystal. Green wisps of magic crawled out from a hairline crack in it, growing as the magic freed itself, the crack expanding.

Grith squinted as his white spectral hand changed color, tendrils of green wrapping around it and crawling into the wizard's chest.

His yell became a scream as the crystal shattered, the light streaming from his sword becoming a beacon of green energy blasting into the sky, emblazoning itself on the dragon's eyes. More of the essence shot through his body, bubbling and scorching beneath his skin. A ring of light formed above him, an endless blue sky in the center.

It appeared that Paul's stolen magic wanted to go back to where it had come from.

The wizard'x screeches filled the air as he tried to move away, more tendrils of green magic crawling out the edges of the portal, wrapping around his arms as the power branded him. It joined with the magic already in his body, hoisted itself back into the portal and lifting Paul with it. His feet kicked back and forth in the air to no avail, but the magic tendrils refused to let him go. He tried to grab the edge of the ring, but there was nothing he could do, to keep himself from being sucked into the portal, flung into, body burning from the inside.

When the stolen magic had finally been returned, the

portal collapsed inward, the green beacon fading with not a trace left of the otherworldly essence.

The dragon silently stared as the shell crumbled, Paul's magic disappearing, the haze trapped within released up into the air. Now, Grith could see the sky.

CHAPTER
TWENTY-TWO

More cracks spread around the crystal shell, falling in pieces. They disintegrated within the air, the leftover essence spilling down on Grith like a healing white rain when they hit her feathers. It drizzled down, soothing the dragon's wounds as she closed her eyes.

A familiar smell touched her nose, and Grith heard footsteps as Ashley approached. The scent of blood on her hands was strong.

"Grith!" Ashley cried, placing her hands on the dragon's neck, trying to shake her awake. "Grith, please be all right!"

The dragon's chest raised and lowered. She opened a dull golden eye, a drop of water dripping onto it. "I think I can smell my mother," she murmured.

"No, no!" Ashley sniffled, wiping tears from her eyes, smearing blood across her face. "Please! You can't die on me!"

"Die?" Grith rumbled quietly, too exhausted to cock her head to the side. "I am not dying. I am just tired and injured and almost out of shimmer."

"Oh," Ashley said, relieved and confused. "You're not dying?"

"It was just for a moment," Grith purred, sniffing as she tried to find the comforting scent again to no luck, "but when the portal opened, I thought that I could smell my mother. The scent was old, so perhaps it was just my imagination, but I thought I did as well when Paul used me to open it previously as well." She paused, having some difficulty thinking clearly. "I think the mayor is still breathing. I promise that I will not eat her, even if she dies."

"The mayor!" Ashley shouted. She looked down with a grimace, quickly pulling out a bottle of the golden salve and placing a generous dosage on her hands before laying them on the mayor's head. Blood spilt, mixing with her own and Chris's wherever she rubbed in the salve. "I think she's concussed. I don't have enough magic to try anything else after cursing Chris, but hopefully this will be enough to heal her at least some."

"You cursed Chris?"

Ashley nodded as the mayor made a groggy movement, pouring more of the salve into her hands. "Yeah. I got a little carried away, but he deserved it. Can I put what I've got left on your wounds?"

"Please," Grith murmured, watching Ashley smear the salve on the dragon's tail. Though she was still exhausted, she felt quite better as it coated her wounds and Ashley's hands dug beneath her feathers.

Ashley moved to Grith's injured paw next, soothing the scorched line between her talons where she'd touched Paul's sword. Once she was done there, Ashley used the rest of what she had on the back of the dragon's neck, touching bits of scorched feathers and injuries from where falling rubble or glass had dug into her.

Grith was glad that she'd managed to keep her head.

The mayor slowly rose up, clutching her head as she tried to figure out what had happened, nervously watching the dragon when their eyes met.

A loud rumble involuntarily came up through Grith's throat as Ashley rubbed the scruff of her neck and behind her ears, a low purr.

Ashley laughed, Grith shifting her wings. "I'm glad you're all right."

"This is somewhat demeaning," Grith murmured, "particularly in front of the cameras."

Ashley turned toward the whirr of helicopter blades, wind fluffing up the dragon's feathers. A rope ladder extended from the front of the flying machine and two humans climbed down, landing on the rubble.

One waved around a camera in his hand while the other made a sudden beeline toward the dragon, stopping only when she was a few lengths away.

The reporter turned back towards the cameraman, and he gave her a thumbs up. Grith cocked her head.

"We're live from the scene at city hall!" the reporter shouted as the helicopter moved away. "It appears that Mayor Silva survived the attack. We have reports that ambulances are coming as we speak for her and other bystanders injured, though hospital functionalities at the moment are uncertain."

"Thank you, Shannon." The mayor winced, scratching her head again, her clothes tattered, blood still dripping from a few of the wounds. She sighed and gave the dragon a look that Grith didn't register as neither fear nor anger.

"Can I approach?" the reporter asked, looking towards Grith and taking a few steps forward anyways. "Is it safe?"

"I'm not sure I'd say safe, but I doubt she'll hurt you,"

the mayor answered, leaning back against the dragon's underbelly, the soft down feathers on the back of her neck. "She saved me."

"I will not do humans harm," Grith corroborated, leaving out that there were a number of exceptions to that rule. She decided that it was not normally okay to hurt humans, but there were certain situations in which it was alright for her to do so.

"You can speak!" Shannon announced in glee, kneeling down as she stared at the dragon's fangs, holding the microphone out to them even with the tips colored red from the mayor's blood.

"Multiple human languages and two dragon ones!" Grith answered with a hint of pride.

"Wow." Shannon laughed, turning back at the cameraman and beckoning him forward. "What's your name?"

"Grith," the dragon answered, before nudging Ashley with a wing. "And this is Ashley."

Ashley waved. "Um, hello."

"Amazing!" Shannon said, looking straight into the camera as she leaned towards the microphone, barely intimidated by how close she was to the dragon's jaws.

Grith tried not to breathe on her too much.

"We're witnessing history today! Here is the dragon — I can't believe I'm saying that — the dragon who not only became a worldwide internet sensation, but just now rescued the mayor from . . ." She paused, looking towards Grith for an answer.

"A wizard," Grith replied.

"A wizard!" Shannon repeated with a laugh. "At least before the shell went up, and LA's contact with the outside world was cut off, magical creatures around the world had begun to reveal their existence. But with Grith starting it all, this is sure to stand out!" She tilted her head toward the cameraman, who nodded and shuffled closer to the two, making sure to get a good shot of Shannon squatting down next to Grith's head.

Grith's talons tapped nervously on the ground, her tail flicking as she stared at the camera. Behind it, humans all over the city were watching her speak, and she expected that even more would watch this later. Pret's words echoed in her skull. If there was any time for her to make a speech, it was now. What if she messed up again, and gave humans a terrible first impression of dragons? Second impression?

Ashley gave Grith a comforting rub on the back of her neck, and the dragon took a deep breath. She could do this.

"Er," Grith rumbled. "May I speak?"

"Of course!" Shannon said with glee, leaning so close Grith could practically taste her. "Please! We want to hear what you have to say!"

Grith shifted away a tad, smelling her own fear-scent. "Um. I am very scared right now. More so than when I was fighting Paul. The wizard Paul. That is his name. Or perhaps was?"

Shannon gave her a concerned look.

Grith did not think this was going well so far. "But, *rrr*, I am certain that I am not the only one who is frightened. There are magical creatures and humans all around Terra that I think are as afraid as I am. Just like me, they are scared about what will happen to our once stable worlds, after they have been so suddenly brought together.

"Even though I am afraid, I am also hopeful. I think that this could bring good and opportunity for everyone. Magical creatures might no longer have to live in hiding and be forced to try and be something that they are not.

Humans might have access to magic that has been kept from them and be able to use that to improve their own lives. Although there will be many changes, and I do not know how long the adjustment period will be, I will try my best to help make a better world a reality. A paradise for all of you: for dragons, for humans, and for everyone else. I hope everyone will join me." She flitted her wings. "I think that is all."

"A very hopeful message, straight from the dragon's mouth!" Shannon replied. "Would you mind answering a few questions for me?"

"Um—" Grith murmured, unsure if that was such a good idea.

"Okay, first, I was under the impression that you were the last dragon, since I hadn't seen any others," Shannon said. "But you did say dragons. Are there more out there?"

"T-there are," Grith rumbled. "More. There are more dragons but not that many, and we are spread out."

"All right, so there are more dragons!" the reporter replied. "Next question, why don't you have scales?"

"Shannon, that's enough," the mayor firmly said, standing up. "She's more injured than I am, and there will be plenty of time for interviews later. How about we let her rest?"

"Oh," Shannon replied with a pout, giving Grith another look before standing up. "All right then, let's see what the mayor has to say about this!"

The mayor rolled her eyes as she led the cameras away from Grith, starting up a chat with Shannon about the most recent events.

Grith let out a relieved puff of smoke. "Do you think that I did good?" she asked Ashley, craning her head a little bit. "The reporter did not look afraid of me."

319

Ashley nodded and smiled. "I think you did very well."

There was a flash of white light, and Ashley leapt, tripping over Grith's wings and falling on her back.

The dragon stared as three figures appeared behind her out of thin air.

"Did we miss anything?" Albiwegan asked.

Holz breathed heavily as she leaned on Albiwegan for support, almost collapsing on the ground in exhaustion.

"Quite a lot," Grith answered, Ashley sitting up, a huge grin coming over her as she saw her mother.

"I'm so glad you're okay!" Sorcha beamed, walking around Grith's head to reach out and hug her daughter.

Ashley wrapped her hands back around, a muffled noise coming from her mouth as her mother squeezed her tight. "Was there ever any doubt?" Ashley winced, stepping back when her mother finally let her go.

Holz frowned as she saw Grith, the dragon's eyes dull and her head rested against the cracked concrete. "Hey, Sorcha? I think Grith needs some help. She looks pretty out of it."

Grith's gaze turned to the witch. The dragon hoped that Sorcha wouldn't attempt to hug her as hard as she'd hugged Ashley, but Sorcha only knelt down to Grith's neck, placing her hands a talons-length above it.

"I think I have enough magic left for that." Sorcha smiled, a green glow coming from her hands.

Grith felt some of her exhaustion suddenly alleviated. The dragon head perked up. How much essence did Sorcha have in her if she could still use any after what she did earlier? "Thank you," Grith purred, pulling one of her wings out from under her and slowly getting to her paws, still trembling.

Sorcha shook her head. "Oh no, I should thank you."

"Hey!" Ashley beamed. "I have an idea! How about we all go back to the Key and have that party! I can make drinks *for* Tom!"

"Yes!" Albiwegan feistily agreed, Holz almost falling in surprise. "I was cooped up in those stupid chains for a week! I want to dance!"

Grith flicked her tail. "I . . . think I will pass. I have had enough excitement for the day. Possibly for the year."

The dragon looked up towards the sky, fluffy white clouds moving from one side to the other.

"I would like to go back to my home and rest," the dragon continued, her feathers glittering in the sun. "And maybe just look up at the clouds."

CHAPTER

TWENTY-THREE

The earthy smell of the forest rose up all around Grith, floating into the air as she looked out over her home. The wind whisked past her crest as she stepped out to the edge of the stone, rustling through the leaves. She gazed further out, from the dry grasses surrounding her peak to the vivid green tips of the trees, and then, finally, to the pink mists at the edges of the bubble realm that separated it from the human world surrounding it.

Here, she was at peace.

The sound of talons on stone came up from the entrance behind her, and Grith turned to see Pret. She raised a wing, gently touching it to his silver one, as he stepped up to her side and sat back on his haunches. His head raised and tilted his crest to catch the wind in it. A group of deer grazed in a clearing between the trees.

His tail flicked excitedly, and Grith wondered if he was as interested in hunting them as she was right now.

"I wonder if you really need the mist anymore," Pret

purred. "How long do you think it will be before dragons feel safe living open to humans?"

"I think I like it up," Grith replied. "I prefer my privacy, and I don't particularly want any wanna-be knights going after my treasure."

The location of her bubble realm hadn't been made public, but with traces of the fight she'd had with the enforcers all around the entrance, it wasn't exactly secret any longer. She'd had a dozen humans just in the past few days come up to check the area out, including a couple dressed in armor and waving swords around, demanding a battle from the dragon in hopes of rescuing a princess. She'd ignored them and let them stumble around the hidden entrance, until they'd given up and went home. Grith certainly hadn't kidnapped any princesses, though she had entertained a young human who'd come up here with her older brother looking for the dragon, before giving them both stern warnings about dragon territoriality.

"Oh." Grith realized as she shuddered at the thought of humans pouring into her home to take her hoard. "I lost my job. I still don't have any way to pay for the upkeep of my bubble realm." She buried her snout beneath her talons. This whole thing had started with her trying to work for Vertex Technologies. Even if magic was now exposed to the entire world, she *still* needed the shimmer! She warbled unhappily. How could she get a job now?

"You do understand that you're the most famous magical creature in the world, right?" Pret snorted, flicking his cousin's snout with his tail. "I'm sure you can figure something out. You could probably write an autobiography or even a self-help book, and you'd be piled up with treasure five-times your hoard from the release-day sales alone!"

"What's a self-help book?" Grith asked, batting Pret's silver tail away with her claws.

Pret trilled in laughter, shaking his wings. "You still have a lot more to learn about humans."

Grith snapped at his ears, causing him to yelp as she gently bit the end. "Hmph. I don't think that an autobiography would be very interesting. Humans probably wouldn't be particularly keen about hearing about my hunting or about how I learned magic. Besides, it seems odd for me to write an autobiography when I feel like my life has only just begun." She spread her wings wide, Pret ducking beneath one as she whacked him, intentionally, in the snout. "It's like I'm just out of the eggshell again."

"Maybe it doesn't have to be about you," Pret suggested, tugging at one of his cousin's wingfeathers and getting a loud snarl. "I'm sure humans would be interested in a history of dragons, or something like that."

"I am *far* from qualified to write a history of dragons! Maybe a Post-Revival history of Southern dragons, perhaps, but even then, I'm unsure."

The mention of dragon history caused Grith's mind to drift back to her mother. How true was the legend that she'd told her, Grith wondered. Did dragons really come from another realm, a paradise long-lost? She was less hesitant to believe that than she'd been a week earlier.

After hearing about Grith's and Albiwegan's experiences, Sorcha had hypothesized that the reason her tracking spell couldn't find Albiwegan was because of the Lesser Gate, and that wherever it had opened to was in fact another realm entirely, filled with magic and existing in parallel with Terra. For the purpose of the spell, Albiwegan had been inside the other realm. Grith had wanted to test the Lesser Gate again, but by the time they'd returned to the warehouse, it was gone. Apparently, GMI had managed to get there before they had.

The wind fluttered beneath the dragons' wings, and Grith was silent, contemplating. "It seems like everything managed to work out."

"I wouldn't go so far as to say that," Pret warned as a buzz rang from a satchel at his side. He opened it up, pulling out a small silver tablet before rumbling in concern and placing it back. "This was just the beginning. The world itself is hatching, and what happened here was just the first light on its down-covered snout. Even if you stopped Paul from taking over LA, GMI and other similar groups are still out there, still planning. All around the world, there will be similar fights in many cities and countries. This will test the hearts of humans and magical creatures alike."

Grith looked over at her cousin, a serious expression on his snout, and for a moment, she thought she saw a silver glow in his right eye. "Does that mean I have more work to do?"

"There is always more work to do," Pret answered, "though the load doesn't fall on just your wings."

Grith paused. Pret was right, of course. The Reveal, as it was beginning to be called, might have changed the world overnight, but it was still much the same place as before. Dragons still lived in bubble realms, isolated from humans. A few magical creatures wandered the human world more openly, but many still stayed in hiding. Even LA had almost gone back to a sense of normalcy, except for the wreckage around city hall.

It was still far from Pret's hopeful vision of the future, and Grith was no longer sure if she could in good conscience keep laying idly in her bubble realm, hoping that the world around her wouldn't intrude. If she wanted to make a change, however, she would do it her way.

Grith dug her talons into the bag at her side, rummaging through it until she found what she was looking for. She dangled the shiftstone in front of her snout, now dull, though the name Ashley had written on it was still there.

Pret tilted his head.

Grith let it drop to the ground in front of her and took a step back, pushing her cousin away with a wing as she opened her jaws. Blue flames formed in her throat, and they shot forward a moment later, covering the shiftstone in the glow of fire. Small zaps of sputtering magic bounced across its surface, the stone jolting from side to side like dying prey on its last legs. Grith's flame didn't let up, and finally, energy shot up from the stone like sparklers, crackling through the air as it split apart.

Grith shut her jaws. Smoke rose from a few pieces of the stone, now magic-less rubble. She turned to face her cousin. "It looks like you're judging me."

"I'm not," Pret answered as bits of dust blew away in the wind. "Just curious why you did it."

"I'm not human," Grith replied, tilting her crest through the air as sunlight glinted in her eyes, iridescent rainbow tones spreading across her feathers, "and I never will be, even if they try and make me one."

"Hm," Pret pondered, lowering his snout until it was side-by-side with the remains of the shiftstone, his tail swishing. He puffed air on it, causing the pieces to scatter over the edge of the landing platform. "Well. To not being human?"

Grith lightly flicked him with her tail. "Certainly."

She paused once more. There was something else she

hadn't mentioned to Pret yet, though she wasn't quite sure what he'd think of it if she told him. "My mother," she quietly murmured. "I smelled her through the portal. I thought it might have just been that I was exhausted, but . . . I think it was real."

Pret took a few moments to answer.

Grith suspected what he was thinking. It was almost unbelievable.

"That's surprising," he said, without anything else.

"I don't know what it means. I was hoping that Ansila's Eye had told you something."

"About your mother? Nothing. Would you like me to check?"

Grith clicked her tongue, and Pret placed a talon in front of his right eye as he activated the spell, the silver glyph of an eye appearing in front of it. For something so extraordinary, it seemed so simple. He'd learned it practically overnight, but had told Grith it wasn't something he could teach her. A gift, or a curse, that he burdened.

"Oh," Pret rumbled, the feathers of his crest standing on end.

"Oh?" Grith's eyes went wide. "Do you see her? Is something wrong?"

He tilted his head, unable to focus on Grith as he peered through the glyph. "It's not. Someone else." His tail tucked beneath his legs, his head cowering. "It appears that both of us need to answer to the draconic leadership for what happened," Pret continued, folding his ears back as the glyph disappeared. "Grandfather is coming for a visit."

CHAPTER
TWENTY-FOUR

A dull pain burned across Chris's chest as the elevator floor beneath him shifted upwards. Black mirrors laced with gold were positioned on three sides of the interior walls, and everywhere Chris looked, his reflection stared back at him. His eyes caught those of his father in a mirror, keeping himself an arms-length away from Chris. He didn't return Chris's gaze.

The sharp agony of the burn had mostly faded, but the black mark had been branded across Chris's chest. He hadn't tried to use magic to harm anyone since Ashley had cursed him, not that he'd had any need to. The nurse on his family's estate had warned him of the potency of the magic and that the curse likely worked exactly as intended.

Well, that wouldn't be a problem. Chris just had to not use magic to harm anyone. It didn't seem like he was going to need to fight anyone in the near future anyways; GMI had suffered a huge defeat, and they needed time to figure out their next move.

He fingered his golden signet ring, unsure what to think of it. He'd worked so hard to become a part of GMI, to finally be recognized as a great wizard, only to lose in the most embarrassing way possible to a witch. His father would barely even speak to him, his eyes drawn shamefully to his son's chest even when the mark wasn't visible.

At least Chris took comfort in knowing that this defeat wasn't his alone. All of GMI had lost that day. A failure for not just them, but for wizards and perhaps even the entire human race. Paul was missing, and his survival was dubious at best. GMI had retrieved the Lesser Gate had been retrieved, but it had been partially eaten and would take time to repair. More and more wizards had begun to distance themselves from the group. The optics of the LA incident had been, frankly, not so good for them. At least the Council was still somewhat intact and held some authority and manpower, although it was basically GMI's puppet now with their super-majority.

The elevator stopped with a ding, the arrow pointing to the penthouse level. GMI owned the entire building, including the meeting rooms down below, but this was a personal invitation. His father had mentioned how that could be either a good thing or a bad thing, with the heavy implication that this time it was the latter.

"Hold your tongue," Chris's father warned as the doors opened, and the two stepped out into the penthouse. Large windows lined with black and gold gave the wizards inside a beautiful view of the New York City skyline, Manhattan and Central Park to one side, with Brooklyn and the Atlantic stretching out on the other. This room, one of multiple, reached up two stories, and had been furnished with more mirrors like the elevators in the places where the windows weren't.

Chris felt eyes on him as he and his father approached the center of the room. Luxurious black leather couches had been placed in a semicircle, GMI wizards reclining on each of them. Around two-dozen in total, all discussing matters with each other in hushed voices.

A familiar one placed down a teacup and glared as she saw Chris. He averted his eyes from the librarian that he'd encountered in LA as she adjusted a wig over her burnt scalp.

Chris shuddered violently when violet reptilian eyes briefly met his as he turned, and he found himself staring at a dragon. Curved fish-like scales the color of a slightly opalescent white covered her sinewed body, wrapping around the throne-like chair next to her, set apart from the rest of the wizards. Chris wasn't sure how to judge her at a first glance, Grith being the only dragon he'd seen before. The white dragon was smaller, closer to Chris's own height, and wingless, with two golden antler-like horns at the back of her skull. An ungroomed mane the same color of her horns ran along her spine and chin, while lines of gold ran through the cracks between her scales down from it, like lightning extending beneath her mane. A flash of violet magic suddenly pulsed from two whiskers on her snout and along her scales.

The dragon looked down, evidently not interested enough in Chris to continue looking at him beyond a moment's glance, and Chris noticed that she had a glowing tablet held in one forepaw, and the other tapped on it, with small rubber coverings on each of her claws, a golden GMI signet ring around one talon. Chris wasn't sure if he was more surprised that a there was a dragon in GMI, or that she hadn't been chained up.

His gaze then traveled to the golden throne next to the dragon, the tingle of magic emblazing itself on his eyes. A distinctly humanoid figure sat within, silently watching the crowd of wizards. Chris bowed. His father had mentioned the GMI leader before, known only as the Shadow Lord.

Though Chris could tell that the shape of his body was humanoid, it was entirely covered in what appeared to be cloth, purple wrappings that circled through the air like mist, floating gently as they rotated around four limbs, a head, and torso. He showed not a hint of his skin, just his form, along with two eyes that glowed the same violet as the dragon's magic. Two rings hung from a necklace around the wrappings around his neck, a familiar golden GMI one, along with one Chris didn't recognize: a rusted metal signet ring with an H-shaped rune imprinted on it. The Shadow Lord didn't even notice as Chris entered, his shining orbs focused on the wizards.

"You're late." One of the wizards on the couch glared, tapping a watch on his wrist. "We were just discussing the failure in LA. The two of you wouldn't happen to have any insight to that, would you?"

Chris's father didn't take the bait, and led his son to the only open seats, next to the librarian.

She glared daggers as Chris made sure to sit on the other side of his father than her.

"We have no insight," Chris's father answered. "I was not at the battle at city hall. I have to admit, it's somewhat surprising that so many were scared off by a simple witch."

"Sorcha wasn't the problem," the librarian grumbled. "Had we stuck to the original plan, we would have dealt with her months before the reveal. The *dragon* was the problem. She screwed everything up, along with her *friends*." She glared at Chris as she said the last word.

"I'm not her friend," Chris retorted, crossing his arms and brushing against the mark on his chest. "Maybe you shouldn't have attacked Grith. There was no way you could have won against her had she been able to use her magic. If I hadn't been there, I think you would've ended up as dragon chow."

"Patricia, Chris, that's enough," Chris's father said, putting a hand over his son's mouth. "The situation was unfortunate. It's regrettable you weren't brought into GMI earlier to better understand our plans."

"It was the dragons," the wizard sitting next to Chris muttered in agreement. "They were the problem."

Patricia frowned. "Dragons? There was more than just the golden one?"

"There was a second." The wizard nodded. "A silver one who fought some of our forces outside LA. It attacked the backup we attempted to send in."

"Agreed with that," another wizard concurred. "I was there during the fight. We were completely unprepared; none of our spells were even able to touch him."

The lights in the room flickered, and a hiss of steam sounded through the air. The room immediately fell silent.

The Shadow Lord had sat up, wisps of fabric rotating as a voice echoed through the penthouse. It was a quiet whisper, but backed by force and power. Each of the words were deep and slow as if he had trouble making them form.

"I sense it," his voice said, though Chris wasn't sure where the sound was emanating from. "I have heard . . . enough. Now I am sure."

Each and every one of the wizards focused their full attention on the Shadow Lord as he shifted, no one else willing to speak. Lines of magic flickered through the white dragon's scales, though she was still staring at the screen below her. Chris realized that he was more focused on the dragon than the leader commanding everyone's attention. She suddenly let out a strangely human-like laugh at something she saw on the tablet, interrupting the silence.

"Sorry," she whispered, holding back a snort. "Go on."

There were a few awkward glances around the rooms before the Shadow Lord continued speaking, the lights flickering once more.

"Even beyond the grave, Ansila's influence creeps into this world," the robed wizard whispered. Chris's father trembled at the words. "My ancient foe has hatched anew, and once more, he threatens our plans. For the sake of magic, for the sake of humanity, we must not fail again."

No one knew how to respond, all of the wizards patiently staring at their leader. The room was filled with silence except for the audible heartbeats of the wizards, and the occasional clacking of rubber on the dragon's tablet screen.

Chris's hands shook. He'd planned for this, and if he was going to act, it had to be now. Still, he hesitated, unsure if it would be better just to keep hit head down, but knew he might not get another chance.

Chris stood up. "I know a way to deal with the dragons."

All eyes were on him.

He kept his fingers from trembling, as the violet orbs of the robed wizard turned, like they stared into his soul. Chris was calm and collected. He had to be confident, he had to be better than everyone else. All the other GMI wizards were weak, failures, and if Chris ever wanted to become more than his father, he had to prove himself to them.

"Sit down," his father pleaded, tugging on Chris's hand wide-eyed.

Chris slapped it away, meeting the Shadow Lord's gaze.

"Come forth, boy," the Shadow Lord commanded, his

voice so beckoning Chris wasn't sure he could have resisted even if he'd wanted to. He stretched out an arm, small pieces of cloth rotating around his fingers, hiding them from view. "What do you know?"

Chris then walked across the center of the semicircle. He'd been afraid of GMI's power for so long, but now that he was part of the group, he knew how weak they were. Their power came from having their fingers in everything, but each of the individuals were just cogs in a machine, only doing what their leaders told them. They were just wizards. They were just human.

Well, except for the dragon. Chris's gaze caught on her again, momentarily distracted from the robed wizard. He caught a glimpse of her tablet, where she'd opened up a messaging app and had just sent something. He couldn't help but read it: 'silverdragon81#2187 bitch where u at? that tech bro ur cuz was with showed up here lmfao'.

An angry hissing sound came from the Shadow Lord, more like a machine than an animal, and it pulled Chris's attention back to him. Casually, Chris placed his hand into his suit pocket and pulled out a small slip of paper, showing it to the wizard.

The Shadow Lord's glowing eyes moved down to it. On the notepad, Chris had written down a single three-digit number.

"What is the meaning of this, child?" the Shadow Lord demanded. "Explain."

Chris smiled, keeping his gaze focused on the Shadow Lord's eyes as he quenched his fear. He wouldn't let the GMI leader intimidate him. Just like his father had told him, he needed to act strong, act confident. And he was.

He pulled the tuning fork from his pocket, flicking it with his fingernail, turning a light blue as a quiet tone rang through the air. The mark on his chest heated up, not so much that it truly burned, but just enough that the curse was uncomfortable under his clothes.

The dragon's head turned to him, the light in her eyes flickering, the robed wizard's doing the same a second later.

"I figured out how dragons are able to hold so much magic," Chris explained as the tuning fork turned back from blue to silver. "Humans store their magic as pure essence, pure energy, which has the problem of causing physical harm if there's too much of it in our bodies. It's a hard limit. Dragons do it differently. Certain metals and gemstones, what they call shimmer, have essence within them. In order to hold magic, they store metal in their bodies, specifically high-quality rhodium, and can naturally convert back and forth between shimmer and essence. If you disrupt their shimmer stores, you can stop their magic from working."

The dragon hadn't turned back to her tablet. She was focused on Chris.

He grinned. Now, he had the attention of everyone in the room. He'd looked up to the GMI wizards for so long, but right now, they were all looking up to him.

Chris raised up the piece of paper.

"This is the resonant frequency of rhodium."

ABOUT THE AUTHOR

Rowan Silver has been a reader of dragon books as long as she can remember, and has always wanted to spread the same joy she felt when reading them. Her favorites were those which were seen from the eyes of a dragon, and creating more of those is her goal. In addition to being a writer, she's also a physics student, and loves learning about how the world works. For updates on new books, you can find her and subscribe to her newsletter at www.rowan silver.com.

Made in the USA
Monee, IL
09 September 2022

13690217R00204